Ginkgo's

"I know a little of your background, Inspector," Loring, the State Department official, continued, leafing through his folder. "As a young flyer, you were shot down over China during the Cold War. After bailing out, you landed in a large ginkgo tree. You remained in the mountains for several years with the sage who rescued you and instructed you in the philosophy of the Far East. Afterwards, you served as a health consultant and food and agricultural inspector for various governments and international agencies, schools and hospitals, prisons and courts, teaching natural farming, Tai Ch'i and meditative exercises, and diet and natural health care. In recent years, you have farmed and engaged in home food production, pursued your scientific and spiritual interests, and attended to a steady stream of men, women, and children, as well as endangered birds and animals, who come, or are brought to you, for macrobiotic guidance and protection. You are said to be able to tell everything about a person at a glance and solve the deepest mysteries. When I heard that, I was properly skeptical. However, it would appear you really do have some kind of sixth sense."

"My methods are not nearly so mysterious as they seem," Ginkgo gestured with a spiral flourish of his knobby gingerroot hand. "They are really very simple when you understand the Order of the Universe.

"When you make your mind as empty and spacious as the sky, you can see the underlying rhythm of yin and yang running through all things. Eventually, you can begin to observe without observing and detect without detecting."

Books by the Same Author

The Adamantine Sherlock Holmes
The New Age Dictionary
Dragonbrood—An Epic Poem of Vietnam and America
Out of Thin Air

with Michio Kushi
The Cancer-Prevention Diet
Diet for a Strong Heart
The Book of Macrobiotics
One Peaceful World
The Gospel of Peace

with Aveline Kushi
Aveline Kushi's Complete Guide to Macrobiotic Cooking
Aveline: The Life and Dream of the Woman Behind Macrobiotics Today

with Michio and Aveline Kushi
Macrobiotic Diet
Food Governs Your Destiny

with Gale Jack
Promenade Home: Macrobiotics and Women's Health
Amber Waves of Grain

Inspector Ginkgo Tips His Hat to Sherlock Holmes

By Alex Jack

One Peaceful World Press
Becket, Massachusetts

For Michio and Aveline

© 1994 by Alex Jack

All rights reserved. Printed in the United States of America. No part of this book may be used or reproduced in any manner whatsoever without written permission except in thecase of brief quotations embodied in critical articles or reviews. For information, contact the Publisher.

Published by One Peaceful World Press, Becket, Mass.

For information on mail-order sales, wholesale or retail discounts, distribution, translations, and foreign rights, please contact the publishers:

One Peaceful World Press
Box 10
Becket, Mass. 01223
U.S.A.
(413) 623-2322
Fax (413) 623-8827

First edition: January 1994
10 9 8 7 6 5 4 3 2 1

ISBN 1-882984-01-3

Printed in U.S.A.

"One likes to think that there is some fantastic limbo for the children of imagination, some strange, impossible place where the beaux of Fielding may still make love to the belles of Richardson, where Scott's heroes may still strut, Dickens's delightful Cockneys still raise a laugh, and Thackeray's worldlings continue to carry on their reprehensible careers. Perhaps in some humble corner of such a Valhalla, Sherlock and his Watson may for a time find a place, while some more astute sleuth with some even less astute comrade may fill a stage which they have vacated."

— Sir Arthur Conan Doyle
Preface to the *The Case-Book of Sherlock Holmes,* the final volume of Holmes stories

Characters

Ginkgo	Macrobiotic Detective
Jeff Milton	Ginkgo's Assistant, Journalist
Descartes	Ginkgo's Cat
Dharmapa	Tibetan Spiritual Leader, 'The Head Lama'
Annemarie	Pantomime
Christopher Loring	U.S. State Department Official
Kalavinka	American Student of Tibetan Buddhism
Lance Andrews	Former Olympic Skiier
Tyler Chase	Director of the Snow Lion Meditation Center
Sunyata	Ascetic Student of Tibetan Buddhism
Bardo	Tibetan Monk, Custodian of the Black Hat
Prof. Peter Wilkins	Tibetan Scholar and Translator
Keiji Aso ("Wing")	Boston Museum Curator
Phil Lord	Christian Fundamentalist
Angels of the Lord	Phil Lord's Disciples
James Ryder, Jr.	Curator of the British Hat Museum
Sergei Starov	Russian Art Dealer in London
LDL	Starov's High-Cholesterol Comrade
VLDL	Starov's Very High-Cholesterol Comrade
Chenpo	Tibetan Buddhist Abbot in Scotland
Elsa Klein	Swiss Broadcast Journalist
Ingrid	Klein's Daughter
Rani Ras	Indian Yoga Teacher
Thunderclap	Recalcitrant Yak
Vajra	Regent of the Tibetan Monastery in Sikkim
Norbu	Sweeper at the Monastery in Sikkim
Norbu's Family	Wife & Children at the Monastery
Olé Sigerson	Scandinavian Explorer
Tra Tzil	Central Asian Pilgrim
Potala	Tibetan Freedom Fighter
Jonathan Corn Silk	Hopi Elder
Hawk Maiden	Young Hopi Woman
Avalokiteshvara	Bodhisattva of Compassion
Kombu	Ginkgo's Spotted Owl

RUSSIA

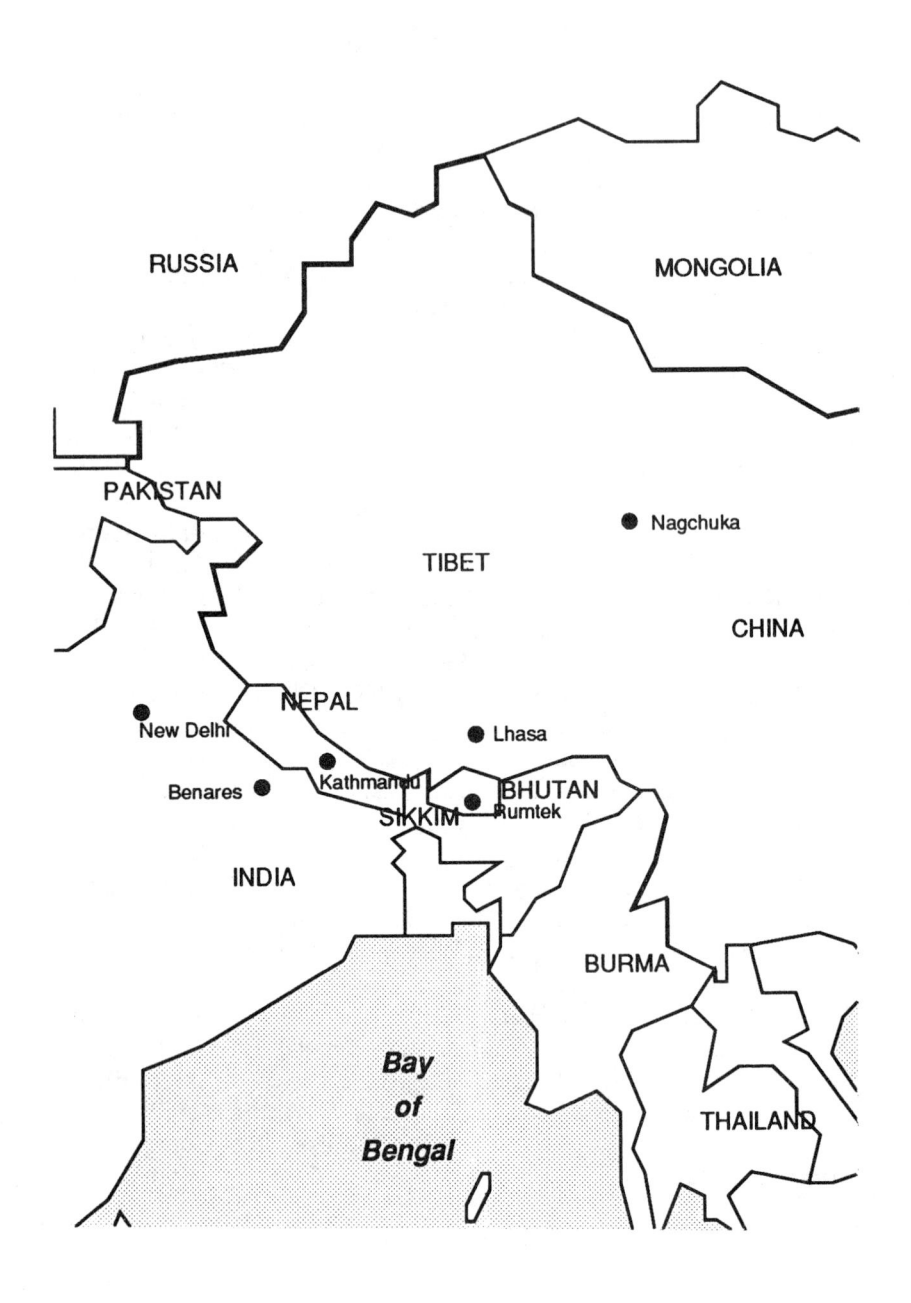

MONGOLIA

PAKISTAN

● Nagchuka

TIBET

CHINA

NEPAL
● New Delhi
● Lhasa
● Benares ● Kathmandu
SIKKIM ● Rumtek BHUTAN

INDIA

BURMA

Bay
of
Bengal

THAILAND

1

BENARES-ON-THE-CHARLES

It began on a bridge overlooking the Charles River. Ginkgo was sitting cross-legged on a stone railing, leaning against a fifty-pound bag of brown rice. His deep-set emerald eyes contemplated the changing shapes of the clouds floating overhead. His knobby ginger root hands held a Chinese flute on which he had been playing an ancient melody. On his knees lay the morning *Boston Globe* opened to the obituary pages. Next to him, from behind the funny pages, I watched the Cambridge girls go by.

"'Music is the harmony of heaven and earth while rites are the measurement of heaven and earth,'" he mused, quoting from memory a sacred text. "'Through harmony all things are made known; through measure all things are properly classified. Music comes from heaven; rites are shaped by earthly designs.'"

"Does that include rock 'n roll?," I observed, as a pretty blonde in tight jeans glided by.

"Today's music is the music of excess, Milton," Ginkgo scowled. "It represents the discharge of excess fat and protein, chemicals and artificial ingredients. How far we have come from ancient times when the earth was governed by an understanding of universal sound and vibration."

"Not so far," I thought to myself. The Beatles, the Rolling Stones, Michael Jackson. These are the real rulers of the modern world. "What do you mean the world was ruled by music?"

"In ancient China, the Emperor had a bamboo pipe that was in perfect harmony with celestial order," Ginkgo explained running his knobby fingers along the stem of his sand-colored flute. "This pipe could give the perfect pitch. All other musical instruments throughout the kingdom could be tuned to it. In this way the whole realm could be brought into harmony with heavenly order."

"The idea of ruling with tone rather than the sword is very appealing," I admitted. "But what was to prevent any pretender to the throne—some Elvis look-a-like from the provinces—from claiming his instrument was the sacred pipe?"

"Only the pipe with the proper length and volume could produce the Yellow Bell, or perfect tone," he went on. "That length and volume were measured by the number of grains of millet or rice which the pipe could hold. That amount of grain became the standard by which all weights and measures were calculated."

Somehow he always managed to bring everything back to whole grains. "Sort of like the platinum rod we use today to measure the meter?" I concluded.

"Exactly, Milton."

"But what happened to the perfect pipe?" I asked thinking of the turmoil and chaos in modern China over the last century. "Did Mao Zedong lose it on the Long March?"

"No one knows for sure," Ginkgo noted holding his own flute upside down and pantomiming pouring some grains into his hollowed out interior. "But by the late Sung Dynasty the holy pipe was lost, and the old measurements, too. Except for a brief revival under the Ming, China has been ruled by foreign powers or ideologies. The world as a whole has been out of alignment with universal harmony ever since."

At length the Inspector put down his slender bamboo flute, and he began to lecture me on the Tao of journalism. Over the last several months my health had improved considerably, and I began writing for *The Phoenix*, a metropolitan weekly. At the time I was researching Harvard's labyrinthine finances, pursuing a lead that the university was secretly investing in the controversial nuclear reactors in Seabrook, New Hampshire.

In Ginkgo's judgment, the obituary page was the most exciting part of the paper. An ace reporter, he instructed, should be grateful for the opportunity to work in "the morgue." Customarily, cub reporters assigned to that department regard it as a circle of limbo even lower than traffic court.

"The press thrives on crime and violent death," my companion asserted, arching a pair of shaggy eyebrows that resembled ravens in flight. "But in our age, almost every death is an unnatural one. As

Seneca said, 'Men do not die, they kill themselves.' The primary way they do this is by not harmonizing with their environment through the daily food they take."

Spreading the newspaper out before him, Ginkgo surveyed the photographs of the newly deceased. From his long study of Oriental medicine and the art of visual diagnosis, he could tell at a glance the kind of diet a person observed and its effect on his or her condition. Jabbing at each picture with the tip of his walking stick, he authoritatively pronounced "heart attack," "stroke," "breast cancer," or "pneumonia," and, skimming the text, I was astonished to discover he was right in every instance.

"There's no nourishment in the press today," he declared, rolling up the paper and thrusting it into my stomach. "Everything is reduced to catchy headlines or news capsules—evidence of a pill-popping and fast food mentality. It seems the only reason we read the paper and listen to the news on TV and radio is to reassure ourselves that the world is in such terrible shape and make us grateful for our own self-induced suffering. The best political reporting today is in the comic strips, the best literature in the sports pages. The rest is trivia. Where is there an account of a brave soul like Gilgamesh who quests for the waters of immortal life?"

A honeybee swirled around Ginkgo's leafy curls, and he hummed the opening refrain of "The Song of Ephemerality":

I Ro Wa
Ni O E Do Chi Ri Nu Ru O
Wa Ga Yo
Ta Re Zo
Tsu Ne Na Ra Mu . . .

"There is nothing so rare as a natural death," he continued, watching the curious insect alight on the handle of his staff. "The reporter who can track down a healthy man or woman who has died peacefully after a full and active life is worthy of a Pulitzer prize. Most of these obits aren't worth two hoots. But if you spent only a few minutes a day reading about the handful of people in the city who lived to be ninety years of age or more, you will learn more about life than Harvard and all its Nobel prize-winning Senecas can teach you. Take my advice, Milton, and become the Woodward and Bernstein of the obituary pages. Dig into the family roots of some of these elderly people. Discover the obstacles they surmounted, recount the adventures they risked. Convey something of their spirit to the world they left behind."

The bee floated up into the air, and Ginkgo watched it disappear against the canvas of billowing clouds overhead.

Beyond the boathouse at the corner of Memorial Drive, the near bank of the river was dotted with people. The bright azure sky and promise of spring had brought out Cantabridgians in droves on this sunny Saturday afternoon. From the bridge we could see tiny figures sitting, reclining, or sleeping on a kaleidoscopic carpet of towels and blankets. Undergraduates pretending to study for their finals, professors pretending to make up examination questions. Truck drivers from Somerville and Everett interspersed between engineers and scientists from MIT, secretaries from Government Center and the Longwood Medical Complex side by side with sociology majors from Radcliffe and Wellesley.

Among the denizens of tenure and timeclock circulated various latter day hippies who had forsaken the mainstream and taken advantage of the fine weather to hawk their wares: silver earrings, leather wallets, sculpted candles, hot pretzels, cold ices, secondhand books and records. The light breeze from the water influenced some of them to move their bodies and stretch in various postures of yoga, Tai Ch'i, Canadian Air Force exercises, kite flying, frisbee tossing, and love making. Others exercised only their imaginations, fantasizing about life in a cabin in Vermont, a Club Med cruise to the Bahamas, or a condominium on Boston's renovated waterfront.

A line of bobbing Hare Krishnas wove through the diverse dreams and desires of this thin ribbon of humanity. The drone of their chant, the thump of their drums, and the tinkle of their bells reverberated through the lofty sycamore trees edging the riverfront. Drivers on the adjacent parkway slowed down and stared in amazement at the gaily-clad Hindu procession before speeding off. Less conspicuous but no less dedicated evangelists moved, singly or in pairs, across the grassy embankment. By now, even I could distinguish from great distances the characteristic dress and mannerisms of Moonies, Scientologists, Nichiren Soshu, antinuke activists, and Greenpeace organizers.

Within a mile radius of Harvard Square some fifty ashrams, dojos, temples, and zendos sprang up. The latest archaeological stratum took its place amid the communes, collectives, study groups, affinity cells, and other political groupings that had sprouted around Cambridge in the late sixties and seventies. The city's physical and mental architecture had assumed an Oriental facade. Colonial, federal, and Victorian Cambridge had become, as Harvard Divinity professor Harvey Cox keenly noted, Benares-on-the-Charles.

For nearly four hundred years, the two facing communities on the Charles had become intertwined with the nation's destiny. From across the country, Boston, the capital of New England, and Cambridge, its enlightened sister city, continued to draw thousands of latter-day Puritans, Minutemen, Abolitionists, and Suffragettes seeking moral, intellectual, and spiritual deliverance. In the cities' liberal political atmosphere and worship of the arts, many pilgrims found a permanent oasis and chose to remain. The nation's highest density of colleges, hospitals, and R&D firms offered well paying employment and social status. A myriad restaurants and boutiques offered rich food and stylish fashion. The coffee houses and film theaters provided scintillating conversation and authentic images. Even the ghettoes and ethnic neighborhoods bestowed endless opportunities for research, service, and reform.

A long crew boat, manned by eight scullers, pulled by. Ginkgo looked up from his contemplation and yelled "Shawmut" to its sinewy occupants, and in unison they called "Shawmut" back. The captain tipped his oar in greeting as the sleek vessel slid under the bridge, and my friend waved his gnarled wooded staff.

Shawmut is the name of a leading Boston bank with branches throughout the area. Its logo features the Neanderthal-looking head of an Indian with a tall feather in his headband, though the only Cro-Magnons I knew of in these parts were the local bankers, baseball owners, and other purveyors of racial and ethnic stereotypes. I figured the greeting had some significance deeper than the current rate of CD's and asked Ginkgo what it meant.

"Shawmut was the native name for the land in these parts," he explained pulling up the hood of his maroon-colored shirt as the wind picked up. "It means Living Waters."

"So you hope to make people aware of the polluted state of the Charles by resurrecting the old name for Mass Bay?"

"Precisely, Milton. Every day millions of people cross the bridges between these two cities. They are vaguely aware that the water is unfit to drink or swim in and won't support fish or marine life. But it hasn't occurred to anyone to connect the condition of the river

14: *Inspector Ginkgo Tips His Hat to Sherlock Holmes*

with their own lifeblood. Just the opposite, of course, is true in traditional cultures. In India, the main artery, the Ganges, is personified as a goddess. Its banks are revered as hallowed ground and just seeing, touching, or drinking the water confers immeasurable good fortune."

"Isn't the Ganges polluted?" I adjusted my patchwork denim cap as a sheepdog with a red bandana around its neck approached walking an attractive young woman on a leash.

"Yes, by modern standards the Ganges is *filthy*," Ginkgo laughed, emphasizing the word. "But the Ganges is teeming with life, and no one ever falls ill from bathing in it. In fact, until modern food was introduced, there was no heart disease, cancer, or other degenerative diseases in India or other traditional societies. Meanwhile, in modern societies, our farms, factories, and hospitals discharge pesticides, oil, chemicals, and nuclear wastes into our rivers, and the experts assure us that there is no connection with rising cancer rates and other illnesses."

Ginkgo picked up the newspaper and carefully tore out the obituary page. The Afghan sniffed my hiking boot and began to lift its leg.

"You must excuse Shiva," the dog's brunette companion apologized, pulling the lead as I recoiled. "He mistook you for a lamp post."

"My young friend is not yet that enlightened," Ginkgo quipped as the woman and her dog scampered off. Folding the obituary page into the shape of a paper boat, he dropped it gently over the side of the bridge and mumbled a prayer for the souls of the dead.

A heavy-set jogger passing by saw Ginkgo drop the paper over the rail. "Hey, buddy, you're littering the environment. There's a trash barrel over there by the boathouse. Why don't you wake up?"

"It's a lot more biodegradable than you are, meathead," I yelled after him. Ginkgo watched in silence as the little paper boat bobbed in the current and disappeared downstream.

Gathering our supplies, we headed into Harvard Square. Like an architect with his compass, Ginkgo wielded his walking stick to measure objects around him, or like a symphony conductor, brandished the sturdy baton to make some dramatic point. In front of Grendel's Den, a hangout for local Neanderthals, he raised it in greeting to a red-faced Irish policeman writing parking tickets. At the intersection of Brattle and Boylston Streets, he shook it menacingly at a Harvard Business School student in a double-breasted suit who cut him off and disappeared diagonally into the subway. Across the street at the Italian fruit stand, he gently tapped the oranges and grapefruits. In Ginkgo's book, tropical and subtropical fruits and vegetables were a no-no, at least in temperate New England. Rushing over to protect his goods, the mustachioed proprietor apologized, "*Bonjourno*, Inspector, I am a waiting a delivery of a nice a broccoli, cabbage, and a turnip greens. Much a vitamin C."

Several buildings down from the Harvard Coop, in front of an ice cream parlor, Ginkgo extended his cudgel and deftly whacked off the top scoop of an ice cream cone which a plump young woman in a pink pants suit held aloft like the torch of Miss Liberty. Her head was turned at the time in order to open the store door for her equally plump companions, and she did not observe the decapitation. With a vacant stare at the burly man with a gruff beard who brushed by her, she buried her dimpled face in the remaining scoop.

Several paces behind, I scurried to keep up with Ginkgo's brisk pace. Bent over under the weight of the fifty-pound rice bag, I could barely stay on my feet. My pauses became more and more frequent as we trudged to Gingko's north Cambridge apartment. Although I was committed to practicing the macrobiotic philosophy and way of life which my mentor embodied, my cravings exceeded my resolve. Sweets, my Achille's heel, continually tripped me up. In the back of my right hiking boot, I had hidden a proscribed carob candy bar. Under the pretext of bending down and tying my laces, I would furtively sneak a hit of simple carbohydrates before staggering on. When the scoop of fudge ripple from the young woman's cone struck me on the forehead, I bolted upright.

"Control your desires, Milton," Ginkgo's voice echoed in my ear, "or next time you will attract something more painful."

As I licked the chocolate jimmies off my face, Ginkgo paused to scrutinize a silver unicorn belt buckle which a street vendor hawked from a folding table on the corner of Church Street. Wrestling the heavy bag of rice to the inside of the busy sidewalk, I pressed my nose to the windowpane of the Kundalini Shoe Emporium, a business run by American members of the local Sikh community. My attention riveted on a young woman in the back of the store. She had long straight chestnut hair tied behind with a tortoise-shell clip, a white leather jacket wrapped around a full gingham blouse, and

16: *Inspector Ginkgo Tips His Hat to Sherlock Holmes*

shapely legs which extended from beneath a tucked up suede skirt.

On the other side of the bench, an attentive salesman helped her lace up a pair of calf-length boots with a tapered toe. A towering specimen, he looked like he played nose tackle for the Pittsburgh Steelers. Adjusting his thick black turban, he scowled in my direction and swung his enormous white *khadi*-clad back between me and his customer. Undeterred, I began to slowly inch my nose along a row of posters and announcements attached to the inside of the front glass.

My eyes wandered across an elegantly handlettered sign describing Sufi dancing at the Episcopal Theological School on Tuesday nights. There followed a typed index card advertising sunrise yoga classes at the nearby Old Cambridge Baptist Church, a professionally engraved invitation for the general public to attend the Vajra Crown Ceremony of a visiting Tibetan lama in ten days at Trinity Church in Boston's Copley Square, and a mimeographed notice of a workshop in Zen Investing at the MIT Student Center on Wednesday afternoon.

Through these Oriental signposts, I finally managed to make eye contact with the momentary object of my desire. I flashed a broad smile and ran my hand through my short curly red hair. I caught her glimpsing at me in a full-length fashion mirror on the back wall as she bent down to try on a black Frye boot with square toe.

After paying for her purchase with a Gold Amex Card, she smartly smoothed out her jacket and fastened the strap. With measured steps and carrying her old shoes in a box under her arm, she marched forward. Swinging the glass door open for her, I unfastened the top bottom of my blue work shirt and dropped my voice. "Sikh and ye shall find."

A touch of color came to her pale countenance, and she pursed her lips. Intoning some bloodcurdling martial arts cry, she kicked me on the inside of my ankle with the pointed toe of her new boots and strode off down the street like Wonder Woman. My eyes followed the contours of her white leather jacket until it disappeared in the void of the Harvard Coop. On its back, stenciled in velvet felt letters, appeared the slogan "Sisters Unite, Take Back the Night."

"Hmm, your kidney and spleen must really need stimulation today," Ginkgo observed, ambling over. With his staff he reached down and massaged the meridians along the inside of my leg and ankle that corresponded with those inner organs.

"A hell of a way to break in a new pair of boots," I responded, wincing in pain. Fortunately, I had another candy bar in that boot which helped to cushion some of the blow. Actually, my ego was hurt more than my ankle. I turned around and gave the finger to the salesman in the doorway who was guffawing and thumping his *khadi*-clad knees.

Ginkgo chuckled and picked up the rice bag. He tossed it effortlessly over his shoulder like one of the overstuffed pillows on display in the front windows of the Gap up the street. I hobbled along as best I could. In the back of the Old Burial Ground next to the Unitarian Church we passed a couple necking amid the tottering tombstones. Across the street, a pair of Good Humor trucks, like guardian angels, stood doubleparked in front of the entrance to Cambridge Common.

To the left of the Revolutionary War memorial in the center of the park where George Washington and his army once bivouacked, several hundred people sat on blankets, newspapers, or the bare ground exercising their First Amendment rights listening to the staccato chords of an electric guitar. A local band performed some familiar rock rhythms. Some fifty dancers—mostly singles, occasional couples, and a smattering of children and dogs—writhed in no particular style to the slightly discordant music. Beyond stretched a ball field where a pickup softball game was in progress. Around the perimeter of the outfield, several people played frisbee. I watched an enthusiastic Airdale race in to the playing area and leap high in the air for the sailing disk while the players held up their game.

Beyond the monument in a clearing of maple trees a pantomime troupe drew another large crowd. Ginkgo and I moved up to the front circle of onlookers as a new skit began. According to a large handlettered sign held up by one of the players, it was entitled "The Education of a Basilisk."

To the accompaniment of a thunderous drum, a large dragon-like creature with a gold crest on his head emerged from behind a tree. Two actors inside manipulated its long cloth body and large paper-maché head. Only the bottoms of their black tights showed. Its fierce eyes bulging and sharp teeth gnashing, the creature proceeded to terrorize the local farmers portrayed by several actors wearing conical straw hats and poking the ground with sticks and hoes. According to legend, the narrator explained, the basilisk's mere look was lethal. One by one, the people of the valley who were unfortunate enough to catch its gaze expired on the spot as if turned to stone. The high-pitched notes of a flute, mingled with the sonorous beat of the drum, vividly evoked the mood of despair and loathing that surrounded an encounter with this beast.

After the scourge returned to its lair, three players decked out as knights assembled to prepare for battle with this formidable adversary. They wore silver football helmets equipped with large cardboard visors, carried wooden swords, and brandished shields reading "Town Council," "Exchequer of the Realm," and "Union of Concerned Alchemists." As the knights preened themselves for combat before a large hand-mirror with a foot-long wooden handle, a young woman in fool's garb and white face wandered into their midst. Short, curly, sandy hair framed a plain oval face. Red and black lines curled around the corner of her mouth and eyes. A black and white jerkin with a jagged fringe collar fit into pantaloons displaying long legs. Her flat red leather shoes ended in a toe with a long spiral. She looked like she had just stepped out of the Tarot deck.

The three knights doubled up in laughter at the arrival of this unsightly maiden. To the strains of light bombastic music, they raucously spun her around among themselves and pushed her out of the circle. She stumbled and fell. Rolling to a halt, she knelt and faced away in total abjection.

Meanwhile, the sleeping beauty had awakened, and the motions of its hideous face indicated that it was time for din-din.

"Terrific ears," mumbled Ginkgo, nudging me in the ribs with his staff.

"Basil's sonar is rather grotesque now that you mention it," I agreed.

"No, the jester's ears, fool," Ginkgo indicated. "Such beautiful ears are extremely rare today. Look at those full lobes, flat against the side of the head. Real Buddha ears."

Ginkgo has a thing with ears. According to traditional Oriental diagnosis, ears mirror a person's whole constitution. Large ears with long detached lobes that rest evenly against the side of the head are the macrobiotic ideal. On street corners, I've seen him abruptly change direction and walk several blocks behind someone he spots with exceptionally fine ears. Nowadays, he claims, because of a change in the modern diet, especially a lack of whole grains and minerals in the mother's way of eating, babies are born with small ears and attached lobes. This, he feels, is a sign of biological degeneration and the impending end of our species. For weeks after he first lectured me on the subject and took me to see the Dumbo-sized ears on Buddha statues in the Museum of Fine Arts, I wore a Boston Celtics basketball cap down over my own rather puny specimens to avoid his wrathful gaze.

One by one the make-believe knights on the Common sallied forth and each time, after locking eyes with the assailant, would fall motionless to the ground. The third contender put on a blindfold to avoid this fate, but the resourceful basilisk curled up and pretended to be a rock. When the hapless champion lay down to rest against it, the creature tapped its shoulder with its scaly tail. When the knight peeked up, the monster lifted its ponderous head, rolled an eye, and zapped the beholder.

The little children in the audience particularly liked the pitiless ends to which the swaggering contenders came. They roared with glee at each demise and hiding behind their parents put their own little hands up to their face to play peekaboo with the lumbering beast. As the blood and gore on the fairy-tale battlefield flowed, the jester slowly stirred to life and began looking intently at the pool of water which her circular hand movements suggested in front of her. Gazing at her own reflection, she felt the various parts of her face, shoulders, hands, and chest. Wiping away her tears, she leapt up to her full height, spread her arms to heaven, and with a broad smile danced joyfully across the lawn. Pirouetting to the tree where the mirror hung, she extricated it, like the sword from the stone, and set forth to the field of battle.

A row of red cabbages had materialized in the field. Bending down she plucked one of the cabbages and in its place put her own long three-pointed fool's cap. She carefully tucked the prongs under so they wouldn't show and slid the mirror underneath, covering up its handle with handfuls of earth. Hearing the basilisk approach, she scurried off. Famished from dwindling numbers of villagers and knights, the lumbering beast proceeded to uproot cabbages for dinner. When it came to the jester's hat, slightly bigger and more colorful than the others, a greedy look came to its bulging eyes. Preparing to devour the tantalizing morsel in its gargantuan jaws, the basilisk exposed the mirror and caught sight of its own horrible re-

20: *Inspector Ginkgo Tips His Hat to Sherlock Holmes*

flection. With a chortle it collapsed in a heap. The cowering villagers reappeared and raised the victorious jester on their shoulders. She dusted off the large cap, merrily put it back on her head, and returned to the castle to the accompaniment of the trilling lute and drum.

The audience applauded loudly and the players, linking hands, bowed several times. One of the male actors took the jester's hat and passed it around for contributions.

A tall professional man standing next to me with an umbrella and briefcase remarked that the skit was an excellent allegory on the dangers of nuclear power. A young woman in jeans and a peajacket disagreed. In her opinion the play was an obvious commentary on the Cambridge housing situation. The basilisk represented Harvard University and the villagers stood for local residents being uprooted from their homes in order to make room for new labs, classrooms, and dormitories.

A middle-aged woman with spectacles attached to a cord around her neck joined the conversation and asserted that the various characters represented Jungian archetypes. The basilisk was what she termed a symbol of the shadow, or the dark aspect of the self.

Entering the fray, Ginkgo dismissed all these interpretations. From a study of the beast's physiognomy, particularly its scaly green and yellow complexion, he announced that the play concerned the plague of cancer sweeping the land. This modern scourge cannot be cured by technology, symbolized by the knights, he asserted. It can only be healed through the mirror of self-reflection and a change of diet to a more plant-quality food, symbolized by the cabbage and other cruciferous vegetables.

When the jester's cap came around, the concerned nuclear scientists deposited two crisp $1 bills. The woman concerned with rent control chipped in a handful of change. The Jungian asked the actors if they accepted Master Card. Ginkgo reached into his orange rucksack and contributed a generous handful of sunflower seeds.

As this foursome continued to bicker, the players gathered up their props and put them in an old blue Dodge pick-up parked along the street. I noticed it had "Loaves and Fishes Mime Troupe" stenciled along a dented side. A voice yelled for "Annemarie," evidently the jester, who was still scrubbing the white makeup from her face, and she collected her gear to join the rest of the players waiting for her in the back of the truck. Discovering that she had too many cabbages to carry in one trip, she tossed one with a cry of "head's up" to the small knot of onlookers. Ginkgo caught it and waved his staff as Annemarie gracefully leapt into the back of the departing truck.

A little priest, dressed all in black, who had been observing everything from a park bench, got up to leave. "You're all wet," he said adjusting his clerical collar. "The play was a Christian parable. Its message was one of simple faith and devotion." He turned on his heel and strolled off.

Ginkgo and I resumed our walk home. At the far end of the park, a young Hare Krishna with upturned eyes and a long topknot approached. I gave him a wide berth, but Ginkgo accepted a long stick of sandalwood incense which he thrust out and gave him some seeds from his pack.

In the next block we passed a hitchhiker sitting astride a wooden railing facing the Harvard Law School across the street. He held a sign labeled "Utopia," and Ginkgo handed him the burning joss stick. The young man smiled, nodded in appreciation, and slowly began waving the incense in blessing before oncoming traffic.

Further ahead we crossed paths with a woman pushing a supermarket cart loaded with canned goods across a weed-filled parking lot. She had tired, heavily mascaraed eyes and a nondescript scarf over her hair curls that looked like a dirty dishtowel.

"Let's stop here and get some greens for dinner," Ginkgo indicated setting the rice bag down in an abandoned shopping cart.

"Here?" I stammered. "The A&P is the last place I'd expect you to go for produce. The vegetables here are all grown with tons of chemicals and pesticides." I began to wonder if during the skit he had inhaled some of the pot that blew in irregular gusts downwind from the band area.

"Not inside, outside, cabbagehead," my friend chided. "Didn't you observe the lamb's-quarters growing in the lot here? We spent several weeks foraging for wild foods last year. Was your education as vain as the basilisk's?"

Pointing with his stick to some knee-high plants several yards from the back entrance of the supermarket, he went over and carefully selected the most tender plants for picking. He made sure to leave others behind for seeding for the next season.

The bleary-eyed woman came over and glowered at us. "Marijuana, I knew it," she fumed. "Why don't you get a job and make something of your life instead of prowling around vacant lots."

"Madam," Ginkgo said raising his arms and assuming the Tai Ch'i posture known as White Crane Spreading Wings, "there is more nutritious food in the parking lots of America's supermarkets than on the shelves inside. If you value your life and that of your children, you will throw your bags of groceries in that disposal over there and get down on your hands and knees and join us."

At this invitation, she uttered some inarticulate cries to the supermarket guard, who fortunately wasn't in sight, and jumped into her Caprice wagon. Then, after locking all four doors electronically, she took some kind of a pill from her purse—probably Valium—and with a lurch shot out into the street. The squeal of her brakes caused us to turn, and we caught sight of a black limousine swerve sharply to avoid her. Inside, to our astonishment, we observed a group of Oriental monks with shaved heads and maroon and yellow robes. The monk in the back seat wore large wraparound sunglasses and sported a Boston Red Sox cap on his head. He remained impassive to the sudden lurch as the monks to either side and in the front compartment reacted in bewilderment and put their hands up in instinctive self-defense. It was hard to see the driver, but he looked like a Caucasian in a dark suit and tie. There was a rainbow-colored decal on the back window of the dark blue Lincoln.

"I'll bet the Hare Krishna honcho in the back seat has sold a lot of incense," I whistled.

"Or Fenway Franks," quipped Ginkgo.

We watched the limo glide down Mass Ave. and pick up the hitchhiker with the "Utopia" sign.

"Now who do you suppose they are and where are they going?" I wondered.

"Buddhists from their robes," Ginkgo said thoughtfully, tugging at his earlobe. "And, no doubt, if you asked them, they would tell you they are on their way to Shambhala—the mythical kingdom of immortal life. Speaking of utopia, Milton, it's almost suppertime."

Around the corner, we turned into Potter Park and walked up to a large green Victorian house that was divided into six apartments, three on each side. Ours was facing the bottom left as you entered.

"Cut this up for dinner and visualize a Buddha in each piece,"

Ginkgo instructed, tossing me the cabbage and lambsquarters as I scampered up the front stairs.

From the kitchen window, I caught sight of my salty companion in the backyard scattering millet and sunflower seeds and playing his flute to the spring crops as twilight descended.

2

WHEN THE IRON BIRD FLIES

G inkgo watched small droplets of sesame oil fall in a wide spiral on the skillet. At the first sizzle he turned down the flame slightly and with a long wooden spoon swept a mound of carrots, onions, and thinly sliced cabbage from a rectangular cutting board into the heavy, black cast-iron pan. Descartes, his cat, snoozed atop the refrigerator in the corner. Its stubby black tail curled over the door in case the fridge was opened while it slept.

I sat behind Ginkgo, perched atop a high wooden stool, hunched over a New England antique pine table, chopping greens. With the tip of a large square-bladed knife, I reached over and flipped the page of the *Boston Phoenix* which lay spread out next to me and scoured the personal section of the classifieds.

"Those lambsquarters ready yet?" Ginkgo called, fishing a strip of wakame seaweed from the miso soup on the back burner and popping it into his grizzled mouth. "When you slice vegetables, I told you to visualize Buddhas, not Charlie's angels"

"I thought everyone had Buddha nature," I smiled capping a purple flair pen which I had been using to circle the ads.

"What have we here?" Ginkgo exclaimed abruptly snatching away the gazette. He wiped his breadloaf hands on his smock and read aloud several of the ads which I had marked.

We met in Harvard Square and spoke of canoeing down the Charles, quiet evenings with wine and moonlight, and early morning walks by the ocean. I've looked for you since. Box 864.

SWF, 26, bright, attractive French professional seeks to meet attractive, SWM 25-35, warm sense of humor, interested in travel, movies, music, tropical fish. Box 926.

One sings, the other doesn't. 2 slightly mad music-loving Fs seek 2 attractive, creative, reasonably together Ms for shared good times. 1. Tall, Gemini, 24, into volleyball, scuba diving, Fellini films. 2. Petite, Aquarius, 31, into videotape, water skiing, Proust. Fortune favors the brave who enclose photos. Box 213.

"Hmm, the Boston Kidney Exchange," Ginkgo mumbled. He bent down and spread the newsprint under the cat's miso bowl.

"I don't understand how you can always reduce everything to a kidney problem, a liver malfunction, or some organic disorder," I replied shoving the chopped up lamb's-quarters into Ginkgo's waiting hand.

"The kidneys rule relations between man and woman," he admonished, dropping the wild vegetables into the skillet on top of the others and adding a few drops of shoyu.

"The kidneys are like an invisible pair of hands in our back which power the pelvic muscles as well as filter the blood and discharge urine and various toxic substances from the body. They govern confidence and will. People who are not strong enough to attract a partner, or who are oversexed and not content with one lover, generally suffer from weak or tight kidneys. They have taken an excess of meat, poultry, salt, dairy food, sugar, alcohol, or drugs."

"Granted, there's something depressing about meeting people in this way," I conceded. "Love and sex are treated as a commodity like cars and used furniture. But it's very difficult to meet someone in Cambridge if you're not Ivy League or have been convalescing."

"If you were truly healthy," Ginkgo chuckled, turning the flame down under the pressure cooker in which the brown rice was cooking, "those of the yin persuasion would beat a pathway to your door. Trust in the infinite Order of the Universe, Milton. It will provide you with everything you need and in the most amazing fashion."

"Look, just give me your picture," I implored, "preferably one that is about twenty years younger and more handsome, and you can have the petite Aquarian all to yourself. I'm sure she'd love to discuss the Absolute with you when you've exhausted Proust. I'll take the Gemini and find something more fulfilling to do."

I ladled some soup and sprinkled some bonito fish flakes into the kitty's bowl on the floor and made a mental note of one of the box numbers which I had circled. Descartes awoke with a start and plopped down on the floor. Except when it was eating, the cat looked every bit as fierce as its master. Its gurgles blurred the pen marks on the newspaper with miso.

"If you are so set on getting a girl in this way," Ginkgo said at last, extending an olive branch, "at least do not appeal to nautical images. Did you notice how all the ads you checked had watery motifs? Canoeing, tropical fish, scuba diving, water skiing, wine, moonlight, walks by the ocean, the cinema, videotapes. These all suggest potential kidney problems. Seeking beautiful women almost inevitably leads to disappointment. They attract many boyfriends, they are too vain to cook, and eventually they become sick and lose their good looks. Far better to find an ugly girl who is devoted and loving. When she has learned proper cooking, she will change her condition. One day she will become very beautiful."

Reaching over, he snatched the pen out of my pocket, and wrote out the following classified: "Wanted: Woman with large ears for mutually fulfilling adventures on the journey to infinity. Only those with detached lobes need reply. Send photo to Box—."

"A picture of the whole face, or just the ears?" I laughed for the first time during our conversation. "I'm afraid such an appeal would attract a lot of kinky replies."

Ginkgo grinned back at me, pulling the long lobe of his own gargantuan ear.

Outside, the weather had changed as it frequently does in New England in early spring. A clap of thunder sounded, and I went into the front room to lower the windows. The wind swept through the trees out front, and a flash of lightning momentarily illuminated the darkened room, throwing the shadow of an ancient Chinese *ting* across the wall. The exquisite bronze vessel, dating to several thousand years B.C., was on indefinite loan to my companion from the Museum of Fine Arts in appreciation for his help in the little matter of the Missing Yarrow Stalk.

Through the drapes I glimpsed the high beams of a car swing into Potter Park. It slowly passed the homes on both sides and pulled up in front of our house. I identified it as a late model Topaz GS, either black or dark blue. As the first torrents of rain fell, a man with an attaché case got out from the right rear side door. He opened a large umbrella and stepped briskly onto the pavement.

A minute later a curt knock sounded outside the door, and I admitted a distinguished middle-aged man attired in an impeccably tailored dark blue pin-stripe suit, white dress shirt, and oval green cuff links. He was lanky, slightly stooped, and though not overweight had a slight paunch. He had a long, narrow face that bulged at the mouth, a dark complexion, high lined forehead, and circles under tired, but expressive blue-grey eyes. His hair was graying around the temples, balding on top, and wavy but neatly trimmed in back and around the sides. I pegged him for a successful lawyer or businessman.

"Inspector Ginkgo," he said handing me his umbrella and light deerskin gloves and addressing himself to my friend, "forgive my intrusion on a night like this, but I have come to see you on a matter of supreme judgment."

Ginkgo had just brought in dinner and set it on a low Japanese-style table in the center of the front room. His eyes lit up at the epithet, and he indicated for our visitor to be seated on a meditation cushion around the table.

"I tried to call ahead of time," our visitor apologized, "but was informed you did not have a telephone." There was a note of urgency in his voice, and he seemed to be in great distress.

"Not doing business with Ms Bell tends to separate the serious visitors from the simply curious," Ginkgo replied stroking his grizzly face and picking up the soup ladle. "Besides, so many people come here for health consultations that I would never get any rest if they kept calling back asking me whether they should use one teaspoon of miso in their soup or two."

"Speaking of miso soup, won't you join us for a little supper, Mr.—," Ginkgo continued.

"Loring. Christopher Loring," our visitor replied with a wan smile.

Ginkgo introduced me as his apprentice vegetable slicer and erstwhile chronicler, while our visitor admired a small bonzai tree on the table.

"I used to play in a tree like that," Loring said looking fondly at the gnarled juniper, "though, of course, the tree was grown up, and

I was the miniature."

The tiny landscape had a temporarily soothing effect on our guest. He knelt down on the cushion before the low table and folded his hands motionless in front of him. Despite the ease of his movements, he was obviously not used to sitting Far Eastern style with legs tucked up underneath him. Ginkgo allowed that our visitor might be more comfortable taking off his jacket and assisted him in laying it on an extra cushion.

"Sitting on the floor is good for the kidneys," Ginkgo said plunking down across from him. "If I am not mistaken, Loring, you have had some back pain recently and are considering surgery for removal of kidney stones. The aduki-kombu-squash dish here will do wonders to reduce the discomfort."

A flush of color came to our visitor's placid face, and he reached up to smooth out the knot of his silk tie. It was suburban lawn green with a wide lapel.

"As a matter of fact," he acknowledged accepting a small cup of soup, a bowl of brown rice cooked with millet, and a plate of stir-fried vegetables, arame seaweed, and the aduki-squash combination, "I have been under medication for some time, and only Tuesday my physician recommended an operation. But he did so only after a battery of diagnostic tests, whereas you have come to the same conclusion without even examining me."

"To the contrary, Loring," Ginkgo interrupted, as he offered our guest a bowl of brown rice, "I have been examining you closely since you entered the room."

Looking away from our visitor to the small adjacent meditation room at a large hanging scroll of Kuan Yin, the Bodhisattva of Mercy, he recounted, "You were born in in the springtime. About six months earlier, your parents moved from New England to the Southwest, probably southern California. However, you often returned east to visit your relatives, especially your maternal grandfather, who lived a long time and whose gracious manners and conversational abilities you are said to have inherited. Your wife is an avid weight watcher. You have a daughter and, if I am not mistaken, a son. The girl is rather unhappy about your line of work, which is serving as a senior government official of some kind. You have come to consult me on a sensitive matter involving a foreign government. Your dog has recently become ill-tempered and you are puzzled why."

Loring remained speechless for a few moments, mopping his brow with a neatly folded handkerchief from his breast pocket. "I arrived here with a dossier on you only to discover that you have a larger one at your disposal on me."

Opening his attaché case, he took out a file on Ginkgo. I leaned over to see if it contained any photos. I still had the slightly mad, music-loving Gemini on my mind. To my delight, there were several.

"I know a little of your background, Inspector," Loring continued, skipping through his folder, "how you were a young flyer during the Cold War and shot down on a surveillance mission over China. After bailing out, you were rescued by a forest dweller who named you after the lofty ginkgo tree in which you landed. You remained in the mountains for several years with the sage, who instructed you in the wisdom of the East. Afterwards, you served as a health consultant and food and agricultural inspector for various governments and international agencies, schools and hospitals, prisons and courts, teaching natural farming, Tai Ch'i and meditative exercises, and diet and natural health care. In recent years, you have farmed and engaged in home food production, pursued your scientific and spiritual interests, and attended to a steady stream of men, women, and children, as well as endangered birds and animals, who come, or are brought, to you for guidance and protection. You are said to be able to tell everything about a person at a glance. When I heard that, I was properly skeptical. However, it would appear you really do have some kind of sixth sense."

"My methods are not nearly so mysterious as they seem," Ginkgo gestured with a spiral flourish of his knobby gingerroot hand. "They are really very simple when you understand the Order of the Universe. When you make your mind as empty and spacious as the sky, you can see the underlying rhythm of yin and yang running through all things. Eventually, you can begin to observe without observing and detect without detecting."

"I'm afraid that's still too abstract for my limited imagination," Loring replied after listening intently. "Can you express it in a more practical way?"

"You obviously know something about fashion," Ginkgo observed, motioning for Loring to pick up his posh suit coat from the adjacent cushion and asking me to don it. "What is the first thing that strikes you about this fit?"

"It's a trifle large in the shoulders," Loring thought for a moment, peering at me through gold-rimmed spectacles that he took out from a case in his hand.

"You needn't be so diplomatic," Ginkgo chuckled. "The truth is it's enormous. But what immediately tells you that?"

"The vertical crease down the back. A good tailor would automatically take it in."

"Precisely," Ginkgo exclaimed triumphantly. "Now let me put it on." He stripped the jacket off me and put it on his own bearlike frame. "What's your first reaction?"

"It's on the tight side," Loring interjected.

"What tells you that?"

"The horizontal creases in the back."

"Excellent," Ginkgo grinned. "There you have it, the whole art and science of visual diagnosis. Imagine, Loring, applying that same system of observation to the human face. What would the presence of vertical and horizontal lines tell you?"

Our visitor closed his eyes as if he were in church and pursed his lips. At last he opened his eyes and with a thin smile said, "Vertical lines would indicate that the subject is losing weight, horizontal lines that he is gaining weight."

"Bravo, Loring," Ginkgo congratulated him thumping him on the shoulderblade. "You have nearly got it. Vertical lines on the face indicate that a person is tight, contractive, overactive—what in the Far East is called an overly yang condition. Horizontal lines indicate that the person is too loose, expanded, underactive—or overly yin. Now the weight we're talking about here is not so much bodily weight, which is secondary. It is the contraction and expansion of the inner organs, which are mirrored in the lines and other features of the face and body. Those are primary. On account of parallel embryological development, changes in our internal condition appear as lines, colorations, spots, and other marks on our face and body. For example, the right eye corresponds to the liver, the left eye to the pancreas. The forehead mirrors the condition of the intestines and so on. If we are in harmony with natural order, we can see internal trouble brewing long before it develops and take appropriate remedial action."

"An English poet described the eyes as spies of the heart," Loring mused, taking off his spectacles and slipping them into their leather case, "but this is the first time I've heard those features spoken of as agents of the liver or pancreas. How disillusioning. I've always thought my furrowed brow indicated a measure of intellect."

"The vertical lines across your forehead and the pouches under your eyes correspond to expanding intestines and kidneys, not brain tissue," Ginkgo explained. "These organs are swollen due to an excess consumption of white flour, sugar, dairy food, and excess fruit and juice. The dark spots in your eyebags further suggest developing kidney stones."

"I guess that explains how you sized up my physical condition, but what about my growing up?" Loring asked. "My parents moved from New York to Los Angeles about six months before I was born in April. How could you possibly know that?"

"The shape and structure of the head reflects the seasons we spend in the womb and the food our mother ate," Ginkgo replied. "The top third of the head develops during the first three months of pregnancy, the middle section during the second three months, and the lower third during the last three months. In general, you have a long, narrow face characteristic of someone born in the spring. The top part is relatively narrow, showing that conception took place in the autumn in a cool environment in which your mother ate more animal food, more well-cooked food, and used more salt than in the spring or summer. The middle and lower parts of your head are slightly wider than would be expected if your mother continued to observe the usual heartier way of eating in a northern environment. It is clear, therefore, that she traveled to a warmer climate and over the winter and spring took more liquids, fruits, and oils that were appropriate for a southern area. Meanwhile, you said you played in a large tree like this small juniper as a child. Trees of this kind are grown ornamentally mainly in southern California."

"And my grandfather, what tells you about him?" Loring said in astonishment. "I idolized him. Everyone always said we were just alike."

"The eyes represent the parents. The left side is the father, the right side the mother. The left and right corners of the eyes reflect the inherited strengths and weaknesses of the grandparents. The inside right eye is the tightest, most compact, most yang corner, indicating the dominant influence of your mother's father."

"And my family? It's true my wife is always dieting and gaining back weight. And my daughter is very critical of her father, much more so than her brother."

"The chain of intuition here was a little more complex," Ginkgo chuckled. "Briefly, from your interest in the bonzai plant here, your preference for the color green, lanky build, gift of gab, and other features and mannerisms, it was obvious you were a Tree person. According to the traditional Far Eastern doctrine of the five transformations, there are five basic types of people—Tree, Fire, Soil, Metal, and Water. A Tree person is very romantic, idealistic, eloquent, and outgoing as well as tall and angular like a tree. Jeff Milton here is also a Tree. A Tree person's partner is often a Fire person, who has a tendency to expand or become chubby. Even if she were a Water person, which is also compatible with a Tree, it was clear that if she ate the same way as you, especially the dairy food, white flour, crackers, and pastries that you clearly take, she would put on excess weight. Moreover, if like most wives, she picked out her husband's tie, she undoubtedly chose your favorite color—green—but the archetype of her form and style—wide."

Loring nervously fingered his broad tie and nodded in the affirmative.

"As for your children," Ginkgo continued, "it was simplicity itself. To make balance for Tree and Fire parents, the universe often sends along a Metal child. Metal people are very independent and strong-willed. Also their energy is naturally counter to Tree people. That your first child was a girl is evident from your generally robust constitution, which I suspected was stronger than your wife's. If the father's sperm is more highly charged than the mother's egg, a girl is born to increase the feminine balance in the family and vice versa. As your condition started to decline, probably inversely with your rise in career and eating away from home more and more, the balance was tipped in favor of the females, and you produced a son."

"And my dog?" Loring inquired. "He's been whining lately and I don't know why. Is he a Metal dog?"

"I have no idea," Ginkgo smiled, reaching over and producing some curly golden hairs from Loring's trousers. "No, as an old farmer, I recognize collie fur when I see it. Your kidney condition suggests you probably get up to go to the bathroom frequently at night. Turning on the lights and arousing a calm, steady creature like this is sure to breed confusion."

"And finally, my purpose in coming here this evening," Loring swallowed. "What makes you think I work for the government and am involved in a case involving a foreign country?"

"It is clear that your eating habits have been very chaotic in the last few years. On the face of it, you attend a lot of banquets."

"Far too many, I'm afraid," our visitor sighed, "and none with such delicious food as this."

"Your physiognomy reveals definite signs of too much caviar, curry, and other exotic fare from around the world," Ginkgo explained peering at our visitor with his own deep-set emerald eyes. "Meanwhile, by nature Tree people are good administrators—they like to branch out and supervise others. Finally, when you indicated that you enjoyed climbing trees as a child, I imagined you delighting in spying on your little playmates below. Putting these three images together, I gathered you were in the intelligence business. Later, when Jeffrey put on your suit coat, I noticed a diplomatic passport in the inside pocket, and that confirmed it."

"You make it all sound ridiculously easy, Inspector. As you have surmised, I am a government official," Loring began his unusual tale. "My official position is Assistant Chief of Protocol for the Department of State. In that capacity I deal with arrangements for ceremonial occasions, including visits by heads of state, diplomatic functions, and other official and unofficial contacts between representatives of our country and foreign nations, as well as with refugees, dissidents, and governments in exile. In this last category falls the object of my journey here. As you may know, His Holiness Karma Dzong has just arrived in this country. He is better known as the Dharmapa, an honorary title meaning King of the Buddha Law. He is the sixteenth in a long line of incarnated lamas who are revered as the oldest spiritual leaders of Tibet."

Loring opened his attaché case and took out a folder containing several 8 x 10 glossy photographs.

"I've seen his face plastered around Harvard Square for weeks," I exclaimed scanning the pictures. "From the yellow and crimson of these robes, I'll bet he was one of the monks we saw this afternoon in a limousine driving up Mass Ave. just around the corner from here. He was in the back seat and had on dark glasses and a Boston Red Sox cap."

"Hmm, same nose," Ginkgo murmured thoughtfully inspecting the pictures.

"The Dharmapa and his party arrived at Logan Airport last night," Loring continued, accepting another helping of brown rice from my companion.

"In Tibetan exile circles and in the Western Buddhist community, his arrival signifies a tremendous event. His lineage is one of the oldest in Tibet, and to most of his countrymen his spiritual authority exceeds even that of the Dalai Lama, who is fifteen years his junior and who studied with him as a pupil. The purpose of the Dharmapa's visit is to perform for the first time in the West the Black Hat Ceremony, the most sacred ritual of Tibetan Buddhism."

"I've heard of Black Belt demonstrations," I joked sprinkling some gomashio, or sesame seed salt, on my rice and vegetables, "but not black hats. Is he going to distribute Mousketeer-like beanies to his disciples?"

"Assuredly not," Loring responded, trying to conceal his irritation at my facetiousness. "In Tibet the various sects are popularly distinguished by the color of their meditation caps. The Dalai Lama's branch is known as the Yellow Hats. Others are called Red Hats, Green Hats, and Orange Hats. But the Black Hat is higher than all of them. It consists of an elaborate crown presented to the Fifth Dharmapa by the Emperor of China in the early fifteenth century."

He took out a fuzzy black-and-white photo taken somewhere in Asia, showing the lama holding the Black Hat on his head with one hand upraised.

"The most renowned hat in Asia. Heard of it many times," Ginkgo said squinting at the likeness.

To me it looked like an Oriental version of Fred Astaire's top hat, inset with gold and turquoise diadems in the front and along the ridges and with a golden spire above. Or better yet, an ornate upside down hexagonal lampshade that you sometimes see in Chinese restaurants. I kept my thoughts to myself.

"Over the centuries, this magnificent crown has been in the possession of each Dharmapa," Loring explained. "On very special religious occasions, it is unveiled and worn by the Dharmapa in an elaborate ceremony. Those who are present consider it the experience of a lifetime."

"Many lifetimes," Ginkgo interrupted raising his shaggy brows. "Legend has it that it brings enlightenment upon sight."

"That must surely be some spectacle," I whistled. "I'd love to see it."

"So would I," Loring said wistfully. "Gentlemen, the Black Hat has just been stolen!"

The impact of this statement caused Ginkgo to drop his chopsticks. It was one of the few times I have ever seen anything interrupt the harmony of his meal. The tale of the missing Black Hat awakened some extraordinary emotion within him, and he proceeded to listen to our visitor with pursed lips and to stroke his grizzly beard. Even Descartes, who had strolled into the room, seemed absorbed and neglected its customary after-dinner clawing of the faded Oriental rug on the floor.

"After arriving at Logan Airport last night and being greeted by his hosts, dignitaries, and officials, the Dharmapa and his entourage drove to the Snow Lion Tibetan Center in Cambridge," Loring recounted. "It is one of approximately twenty centers around the country in which American disciples of Tibetan Buddhism live and practice."

"It's just up the street, about a mile from here," Ginkgo volunteered. "Been there on occasion. There's a good cutting board in the kitchen. Cherry wood, as I recall."

"Where was the hat?" I asked.

"The Black Hat is always kept in a large ceremonial felt box covered with a brocade of silk and watched over vigilantly by a senior monk named Bardo. Owing to the rigors of the flight from London and previous stopovers in Zurich and New Delhi, the Dharmapa retired early in an upstairs bedroom and slept until late this morning. Bardo, whose function it is to care for the hat, occupied the adjoining bedroom.

"After a late breakfast with the Snow Lion staff, the Dharmapa was welcomed to America as the guest of honor this afternoon at a private reception downstairs in the main meditation hall from 2:00 to 4:00 p.m. About one hundred civic, religious, academic, and cultural dignitaries, including the artistic and spiritual elite of Cambridge and Boston, were invited. Some others came from New York, Washington, and as far away as England."

Ginkgo frowned at this last remark because it was obvious he had not been invited.

"I understand, Inspector, that you were to be included in this august gathering," Loring hastened to make up for his indiscretion, "but the staff couldn't telephone you to confirm your attendance."

"I am not in the least distressed to have been left out," Ginkgo replied. "But I probably would be distressed to know who was included. Go on."

36: *Inspector Ginkgo Tips His Hat to Sherlock Holmes*

"During the reception, Bardo remained upstairs with the hat. As part of his spiritual practice he had been copying out the *Great Wisdom Sutra* and was used to long periods of solitude. Actually, the Keeper of the Hat is an exalted office in the Dharmapa's household, requiring years of devotion and patience, and its holder is expected to protect the Black Hat with his life."

"For that a Black Belt would be useful," I quipped.

Loring ignored my interruption. "After the reception, the staff of the Snow Lion and assembled guests saw the Dharmapa off in a limousine for the airport. The Dharmapa will visit disciples in Colorado and Arizona for ten days before returning to Boston for the Black Hat ceremony. That, of course, is the main purpose of his journey here. It has been widely publicized, and the Snow Lion staff expect over a thousand people to attend."

"When was the theft discovered?" Ginkgo asked.

"About 4:30 this afternoon, Tyler Chase, the director of the Snow Lion, went upstairs to confer with Bardo, who had planned to stay in Boston with the hat and continue his sutra copying over the next ten days. It was then that he discovered Bardo lying on the floor in a drowsy, almost unconscious state, with the hatbox open and empty. When the little monk came to, he related that the last thing he remembers is a knock on the door and someone putting a tray on the bedstand. He says he took a sip of the butter tea he customarily drinks in the afternoon and passed out, evidently drugged from something slipped into his cup. Needless to say, the loss of the Black Hat on American soil constitutes a grave embarrassment for our country. It is as if the Pope's tiara were stolen. Inspector Ginkgo, on behalf of the highest circles of our government, I implore you to devote your enormous talents and energies to recovering the hat before the ceremony ten days from now."

Ginkgo didn't respond immediately but turned his meditation cushion toward the scroll of Kuan Yin hanging from the wall and sat cross-legged with his eyes half-closed and hands cupped before his lower abdomen. His cat, Descartes ("I purr, therefore I am"), came and rubbed up against him, but his master was lost in contemplation and didn't respond.

"Loring," Ginkgo said at last, looking up and transfixing our visitor with his penetrating gaze, "I can see how a lost article of apparel falls, in a manner of speaking, under your hat as a protocol official. But the United States has no formal diplomatic relations with the Tibetan government-in-exile. So I don't see why the State Department is so concerned. Since the improvement of relations between America and China, the Tibetan refugee question has proved to be an embarrassment to Washington. For many years, the White House has denied permission for the Dalai Lama to visit this country in fear of alienating Beijing. Now it proposes to aid another high lama, the Dharmapa, in a ceremony that will be deeply embarrassing to the Chinese who occupy Tibet. It would appear the clouded minds who make our foreign policy would have more to gain if the Black Hat ceremony never took place than if it did."

I took the occasion to add suitable derogatory remarks on U.S. foreign policy in light of the Vietnam War and my own experience as a journalist in the Middle East and Central America. I even suggested that the Central Intelligence Agency itself may have snitched the hat or assisted the Chinese in doing so. Our visitor's story just didn't tally.

Loring paled at our probing and stared glumly into his teacup.

"Inspector Ginko and Mr. Milton," he said, addressing me respectfully for the first time, "you are perfectly correct. Shortly before coming here tonight, Merriweather who worked with you at the United Nations, advised me to lay out all my cards on the table because you were sure to uncover the truth."

"Ah, the case of the Ambassador's Little Toe." Ginkgo's eyes lit up and he pulled his earlobe.

"A regional war was averted, several million dollars were saved, and the Secretary of State's head spared," Loring went on, wiping the moisture from his deeply-lined brow. "For your past services to the cause of world peace, Washington holds you in the highest regard. In the language of diplomacy, Gentlemen, let us speak frankly with one another, I have revealed my true title in Washington, but not my true function. As Assistant Chief of Protocol, I am in charge of a legion of waiters, cooks, housemaids, valets, chauffeurs, and other service and delivery workers who staff state functions and embassies around the world. As you can imagine, valuable intelligence is gathered informally at banquets, cocktail parties, receptions, and parades. A clever bellhop is worth two political attachés, and an alert chambermaid is worth a dozen trenchcoat operatives."

"Still playing in the tree house, eh Loring?" Ginkgo chuckled. "Well, proceed. How does the spy business concern the Dharmapa and his illustrious hat?"

"Hidden inside the inner lining of the Black Hat," our visitor continued, as we listened breathlessly, "is some information that could affect the international balance of power."

Taking a sheaf of maps from his attaché case and spreading them before us, Loring pointed to some satellite composite photographs stamped TOP SECRET.

"Earlier this year a pilgrim from Chinese-controlled Central Asia made his way to Sikkim, the tiny Himalayan kingdom on the Indo-Nepalese border where the Dharmapa's monastery-in-exile is located. Except for a few tourists, Tibet has been sealed off from the outside world for the last generation by the Chinese. However, the Tibetans have maintained an underground railway from Lhasa to refugee areas in Nepal, Sikkim, and India, including Dharmsala, the northwest Indian hill station where the Dalai Lama lives and the Tibetan government-in-exile is located. A tiny, but steady stream of lamas, refugees, peasants, and guerrilla fighters continues to trickle in and out of Tibet. Of course, it is an arduous journey, over unchartered mountains, around deep gorges, and by wild animals. Those who survive nature's formidable barriers seldom get past the Chinese border patrols, which are quite merciless."

"Just what kind of information did he smuggle out?" I asked.

"See these markings here," Loring indicated pointing to the aerial maps of the Tibetan, Indian, and Nepalese border. "These are Chinese fortifications in the Himalayas. The PLA—the People's Liberation Army—has constructed dozens of secret bases, tunnels, and supply depots, stretching almost a thousand miles across Tibet. Refugees refer to it as 'The Himalayan Great Wall.' At first, observers associated this military buildup with a potential renewal of hostilities following the Sino-Indian Border War. However, radar dishes cropped up on many Himalayan peaks, and in western Tibet an advanced radar complex was installed in Rudok. The I.I.B.—Indian Intelligence Bureau—confirmed that the facility was designed to track both satellites and missiles as well as monitor incoming flights. Our own analysts at the NRO—National Reconnaissance Office—in Washington saw this as one more indication that the Chinese had decided to move their nuclear operations to Tibet. For over a decade, the Chinese main nuclear facility has been located much farther north in Lop Nor in the vast Xinjiang area of Central Asia. However, Beijing apparently felt it was too susceptible to a Soviet attack.

There were persistent reports that the Chinese were moving a warhead assembly plant, gaseous diffusion plant, and research labs to Nagchuka, a sparsely inhabited part of northern Tibet, over a thousand miles south of Lop Nor. The almost permanent cloud cover during most of the year makes Nagchuka an ideal nuclear testing center and launch site. From above, it is practically invulnerable to spy satellites and planes, and from below, it is isolated from all except a handful of nomads. According to our information, the pilgrim brought out with him a map with the precise location of this new facility as well as a reliable count of ICBMs, IRBMs, and MRBMs deployed there."

"Why would he give it to the Dharmapa? Is the lama involved in espionage?" I asked dubiously.

"Unfortunately, we do not know, since the pilgrim, an old man, reportedly died from exhaustion shortly after arriving in Sikkim. It was amazing that he made it at all, unbelievable that he did so in winter. The traveler was described as a devout believer in Lamaism, and though not himself Tibetan undoubtedly had connections with Tibetan partisans as well as Moslem freedom fighters in Xinjiang. According to our sources in Sikkim, he originally accompanied the Chinese to Tibet from Lop Nor where he was working, possibly as a guide or translator. Over the years the Chinese have integrated very few indigenous peoples in autonomous regions into their military command. However, they have had to make use of native interpreters and menial workers, and some of them could have waited patiently for years to relay this kind of intelligence. As the titular spiritual leader of Buddhists in Xinjiang and as far north as Mongolia, as well as Tibet, it was only natural the information be put in the hands of the Dharmapa. Whoever delivered the map is unimportant. He was probably just an old man who had traversed the dangerous Himalayan terrain in his youth and could be entrusted to carry out the mission."

"And who is your source for this story?" I asked skeptically.

"One of our most trusted operatives, Norbu, a sweeper at the monastery in Sikkim. His family has been associated with us since World War II and the days of the O.S.S. His information is above reproach."

"And the Dharmapa," Ginkgo interjected. "What did he make of the map?"

"As far as we know, the Dharmapa is not aware of its existence, much less its significance. Just before coming to the United States, the Dharmapa and Bardo visited Nepal, and the hat was unattended for several days in the monastery. Only Vajra, the old regent, was present, and he is so feeble anyone could have entered the sanctuary unobserved and slipped the map into the hat's inner lining. According to our source, the pilgrim who brought it expired shortly before the Dharmapa returned from Nepal. Since then, the hat has been under the watchful eye of Bardo."

"And I'll bet its contents were safe from inspection through airport customs," I marveled.

"The hat's as sacred as a diplomatic pouch," Loring replied. "And unlike an ambassador's briefcase, it has its own airline seat when the Dharmapa travels."

"No doubt first-class," I quipped.

"So what do you make of this strange story?" Ginkgo asked Loring. "Who benefits the most from the theft of the hat?"

"It's rather complicated," Loring replied. "There are, as you can imagine, various political factions in the Tibetan Buddhist exile community. Whoever has possession of the map would have a strong bargaining chip with Washington. There is, for example, a militant faction of Tibetans which wants diplomatic recognition of the government-in-exile and direct military support from the West to retake their homeland. There is also a dovish camp that counsels reaching a political accommodation with China in return for the restoration of religious and cultural freedom in Tibet. There is a third camp, headed by the Dalai Lama, which is trying to prevent hostilities from publicly breaking out between these squabbling factions and undermining Tibetan unity."

"So far as we know, the Dharmapa, a lover of paradox and childlike antics, is also in the middle and has no political agenda."

"And what of Bardo?" Ginkgo inquired running his hand through his leafy hair. "Where do his loyalties lie?"

"He is totally otherworldly. He was an orphan and spent his entire life in the monastery before leaving Lhasa with the Dharmapa. He has no family ties or political attachments."

"Hmm, the idyllic scenery of Shangri-la suddenly assumes an ominous cast," Ginkgo muttered gravely after this briefing. "Behind those bright yellow and maroon robes lurk darker hues."

"I can see how Tibet would be a thorn in the romance between Beijing and Washington," I reasoned, "but I fail to see how this intelligence would affect things. The days of the Yellow Peril and falling dominoes in Asia appear to be over."

"Between the United States and China, old passions have thawed and largely melted away," Loring conceded, looking at his gold watch chain, "but as the Inspector here surely realizes, we are dealing with a third force—Russia. Although the Cold War between East and West is over, the Russians still fear the Chinese. They are horrified at the loss of their former empire in Central Asia, including Kazakhstan, the site of their principal nuclear weapons testing center. Should the map fall into the hands of the Russians, the alternative is horrifying to imagine. They could be provoked into launching a preemptive nuclear strike on China, their historic enemy to the East, to destroy its nuclear capability. This event, mind you, is an occurrence some exiled Tibetans—or hot-headed Ukrainians, Lithuanians, Georgians, or citizens of other newly independent former Soviet Republics—would not be adverse to provoking in a calculated gamble to gain or maintain freedom in their own homeland. Even direct Russian strikes on the remote Chinese nuclear facility in Nagchuka would have little impact on the rest of the country. Because of its isolation and high altitude, Tibet could be the sole survivor of the tremendously lethal nuclear fallout that would blanket Asia after a Sino-Russian war."

"A grim prospect," I agreed solemnly, "but such a scenerio would also benefit certain factions in the Pentagon who would like to see the Russians and Chinese destroy each other, would it not?"

"Alas, Mr. Milton," Loring replied, "you have a point. There are extremists in our own government who are nostalgic for the Cold War. They distrust the new democratic regime to disarm and fear a return of Communist rule. They would love to see the two nuclear-equipped armies destroy each other. On this matter, I confess, I learned my lesson following the Iran-Contra Affair. Loyalty to one's country is not necessarily loyalty to the Administration or to the military. My daughter was an exchange student in El Salvador and bitterly opposed my stint at the State Department during that period. Events have subsequently shown the wisdom of her position. Officially, in the matter of the Black Hat, my instructions are to ensure that it doesn't fall into the wrong hands. Unofficially, Inspector Ginkgo, I don't care what you do with the map once you find it."

Ginkgo pondered the lama's photo and asked my opinion.

I was flattered to be consulted and took the opportunity to

42: *Inspector Ginkgo Tips His Hat to Sherlock Holmes*

voice my doubts. My experience as a foreign correspondent left me suspicious of all government officials.

I was also immediately struck with the parallels between this case and the Tibetan interlude of another great detective, Sherlock Holmes. During the past couple of years, I have taken advantage of my convalescence to reread the entire Holmesian canon.

"There's something I'd like to read to both of you which bears indirectly on this case," I said retrieving a bound volume of Holmes's cases from a bookcase by the window. Outside, I caught the soft glow of a cigarette and then the outline of a man leaning against the side of Loring's car.

"Did you know that after Sherlock Holmes's epic encounter with Professor Moriarty in Switzerland in 1891, the great detective journeyed to Tibet? Three years later he returned to London and revealed his secret mission to Dr. Watson, who thought he had died at the bottom of the treacherous Reichenbach Falls."

"No, I'm afraid I haven't read much Holmes," Loring admitted, folding his hands before him in a church steeple. "I can tell you, however, about the exploits of Jeeves, the man-servant in S. J. Perlman's delightful stories."

Thumbing through the book, I read the following paragraph from *The Empty Room*: "I travelled for two years in Tibet, therefore, and amused myself by visiting Lhasa, and spending some days with the head Lama. You may have read of the remarkable explorations of a Norwegian named Olé Sigerson, but I am sure it never occurred to you that you were receiving news of your friend."

"It seems," I ventured, "that Holmes was not just visiting Tibet as an explorer but was spying on behalf of his older brother, Mycroft Holmes, who you may recall functioned in his capacity as adviser at Whitehall, the foreign ministry, 'as the British Government.' Within a few years of Sigerson, or Holmes's, visit, the British invaded Tibet in an effort to counter Russian and Chinese influence."

"I also read the adventures as a child," Ginkgo said in a tone contradictory to mine, "and reread them again many years later one winter snowbound in the Berkshires. I was impressed by Holmes's interest in the Orient, especially in Buddhism. The change in Holmes's character after returning from Tibet is remarkable. He no longer took cocaine, and his cases reveal a good grasp of karma and reincarnation. Give me that book."

Rifling through the large volume, Ginkgo read the following

passage from *The Valley of Fear*: "Everything comes in circles, even Professor Moriarty . . . The old wheel turns, and the same spoke comes up. It's all been done before, and will be again."

"In *The Veiled Lodger*, which took place a few years after returning from the East, Holmes delivers a typical Buddhist soliloquy: 'The ways of Fate are indeed hard to understand. If there is not some compensation hereafter, then the world is a cruel jest . . . The example of patient suffering is in itself the most precious of all lessons to an impatient world.'"

"The Buddhist influence on Holmes was very apparent to Watson," Ginkgo went on scanning the text. "Ha! Here it is. In the same story, the good Doctor goes on to say: '[Holmes] sat upon the floor like some strange Buddha, with crossed legs, the huge books all around him, and one open upon his knees.'"

Both Loring and I smiled at this description because Ginkgo himself sat cross-legged with the maps and photographs spread out around him and one big book open on his lap.

"Holmes's mission to Lhasa may have unwittingly contributed to the British invasion of Tibet in 1903," Ginkgo conceded. "But he probably regretted it deeply. Indeed, his own sudden retirement in that very same year to the Sussex Downs to keep bees and pursue the elixir of life suggests displeasure at His Majesty's Government's forced intervention in Tibet."

During this part of the conversation, I quietly stacked the dishes on the table and took advantage of the opportunity to slide one of Loring's photographs of Ginkgo under a saucer.

"Perhaps Holmes actually studied with the Dharmapa himself," Ginkgo mused closing the large volume before him. "I wonder. The head lama in the narrative is not identified. It would have to be the Dharmapa, the Dalai, or the Panchen Lama. Of course, that Dharmapa would have been the incarnation previous to the one here."

He squinted again at the photograph beside him of a middle-aged monk with square face and merry eyes. "Did Holmes catch a glimpse of the Black Hat and become enlightened?"

"No, in that case, he would probably not have returned to Victorian England at all," he chuckled, answering his own question. "At least not to Baker Street and the dreadful cooking of Mrs. Hudson, his devoted housekeeper."

"Reincarnation is hard to reconcile with my Methodist upbringing," Loring interjected, "but if Holmes's deductive abilities have passed on to anyone, it is you, Inspector. According to what we have just heard, Holmes encountered the Dharmapa of his generation. It is only proper and fitting that you confront yours. And if there is a reborn Professor Moriarty—the Napoleon of Crime, as I believe he was referred to—lurking behind this theft, surely there is no one better to unmask him."

"The way you put it, Loring, I can hardly refuse, can I?" Ginkgo smiled and pulled his long earlobe.

Loring's heavy-lidded eyes lit up, and it appeared an enormous weight had been lifted from his stooping frame. He accepted a fresh round of bancha tea, and we all clinked glasses. Diplomats like to seal bargains with some kind of little ritual, if only a cup of tea.

"The Oval Office will be gratified to learn of your positive response to our request tonight," Loring said taking out a silver timepiece from his vest. "I shall notify Tyler Chase, the director of the Snow Lion Tibetan Center, and Bardo, to expect you for a visit later this evening. Meditation ends at 9 p.m."

"One final question, Loring," Ginkgo asked after handing him some fresh ginger root and explaining how to make a ginger compress for his kidneys, "What does the Dharmapa make of all this?"

"Good heavens," Loring replied assembling his folders, maps, and photographs, including the one of Ginkgo that I had hidden under the saucer, "he does not know of the hat's disappearance. Bardo told Chase the theft was a bad omen and might make it impossible for the Dharmapa to continue the Black Hat ceremony even if it were found. Everyone hopes the hat can be recovered unobtrusively for the ceremony. You see, for the disciples, the ceremony represents the fulfillment of an ancient prophecy about Buddhism coming to the West and the awakening of America's spiritual destiny. They say if the ceremony does not take place, it may be eons before another auspicious occasion arises to introduce the True Law. During this time they believe countless beings deprived of the Buddha's supreme teachings will continue to suffer in the world of delusion."

A gust of cold air suddenly swept through the room, and the Kuan Yin scroll in the meditation alcove swung for a few seconds and almost fell from the wall. Ginkgo's shaggy brows contracted, and he dug his hands further into the long front pocket of his maroon pullover. As my friend remained absorbed in deep thought, I accompanied our visitor to the door and watched him get into the waiting Topaz and disappear into the night.

3

THE SNOW LION MEDITATION CENTER

T he Snow Lion Meditation Center was located on Garden Street about a mile north of our apartment. Ginkgo did not say anything about the case during the walk, but from the amount of water which splashed on me when his staff brushed back overhanging branches, I could tell that he was in a hurry. The rain itself had abated by the time we arrived, and a strong wind sent chills up my stomach meridian. A thin column of smoke curling from atop a large three-storey Victorian residence promised a warm haven from the damp and cold. Heavy curtains suffused light from inside a long row of bay windows, framed by green shutters. Upstairs, at the right side of the house, an orange light glowed through a half-opened window with lace curtains flapping in the breeze.

"Bardo's room," Ginkgo surmised as we turned into the front walkway past a high hedge and followed the stone pathway around to the side entrance. "No doubt still copying the *Great Wisdom Sutra*." He might as well be copying the telephone book for all I knew.

Several cars and a van stood parked in a driveway before a two-car garage which was situated to the right of the house by an enormous oak, whose limbs extended up and over the roof of the tall structure. I noticed a red Mazda 300Z sports coupe with skis in racks slanting from the bumper attachments to the car roof. Its monogrammed Colorado license spelled out the initials LLA. Next to the Mazda was an old rusted-out VW bug with Vermont plates inscribed VAJRA. This Sanskrit word I learned later meant "Diamond" or "Thunderbolt" and referred to the radiant, crystalline quality of the Tibetan Buddhist teachings. I recalled Christopher Loring saying that the Black Hat ritual was formally known as the Vajra Crown Ceremony.

A typed note on the door indicated that meditation was in session and requested visitors to enter quietly without ringing the bell. We entered the unlatched door and left our shoes in the alcove amid at least fifty other pairs which serpentined around 5-gallon spring water bottles, several bags of potatoes, and other storage items. The alcove opened up into a large kitchen where a solitary man with long straight blond hair and thin gold wire frame glasses stood behind a counter filling up a thermos. He was tall, wiry, and between thirty and thirty-five.

"The meditation room is through the door and down the corridor," he indicated without looking up from his task.

"Butter tea?" Ginkgo asked, referring to the staple beverage of Tibet.

"Nettle soup," the young man replied laconically, corking the top of the thermos and setting the saucepan in the sink to drain. He looked up at us for the first time. Behind his thick lenses, I sensed something cold and wild in his contracted, steel-grey eyes.

"Mind if I put over some water?" Ginkgo asked, gesturing to a tea kettle on the stove. He surveyed the pantry and looked up at a large clock on the far wall. It had a Buddha outline drawn around it in bold black strokes so that the clock dial formed the Buddha's stomach.

"Help yourself," the man said. He grabbed a faded parka lying across the back of a child's highchair and zipped it up. "It's all yours."

"Aren't you staying for meditation?" I asked as he descended the steps in the alcove and knelt down to lace up a pair of ranger boots.

"Meditation?" he exclaimed sharply, continuing his nimble finger work. "You call that meditation? That's not even contemplation. It's a co-ed social hour."

Without waiting for my reply, he slipped noiselessly out the side door. A minute later I heard the VW rev up and skid off into the night.

Ginkgo took full advantage of the empty kitchen to examine the fridge, food storage shelves, dishware cabinets, and even the dirty knives and forks in the dishwasher to the side of the sink. My companion has often observed that refrigerators and medicine cabinets are the most important features to investigate in a house where a theft or other crime has been committed. He likes nothing better than to go through garbage for tell-tale signs to a person's favorite snacks and medication.

According to the clock on the wall, meditation had another thirty-five minutes to run. Ginkgo said that he wanted to scout around for awhile and waved me through the swinging door with the admonition to check out the meditators. I left him bending over the soaking pot, licking the remains of the nettle soup from a stubby index finger.

Down the heavily carpeted corridor, past several offices on the left and a dining area on the right, I came to an imposing double door with small glass panes. Through the embroidered curtain I could see rows of straight-backed meditators sitting cross-legged. They sat on firm round red and yellow cushions resting atop thin, square velvet floor mats. I turned the elegant brass door handle and quietly entered the spacious chamber. A high cathedral ceiling extended two floors up. The dark-stained oak beams measured at least sixty feet in length.

The mahogany floor was polished to a high gloss, and I slipped and almost fell when I went over to the side wall to pick up a cushion and mat. I took my seat in a vacant spot several rows up between a rugged man with blond hair and ice-blue eyes wearing a ski sweater and a heavy-set young woman with scruffy jeans and an Aum pendant around her neck. Here and there an eye opened or blinked at my arrival, but most of the group remained oblivious to distractions with eyes half closed, hands cupped in laps or stretched out flat on thighs with palms up and index fingers and thumbs lightly touching. The plump teenager—she couldn't have been much over eighteen—was one of those who took notice and winked at me before screwing tight her eyes and acned face and resuming her contemplation. No doubt a Fire type—just my luck to attract a chubby teenager with a skin problem.

At the front of the impressive meditation hall a large Tibetan wallhanging drew my attention. Mounted on a bright emerald brocade and embroidered with gold and silver filigree, the painting featured the image of a Buddha in the center with multiple heads, arms, and legs radiating on all sides. Geometric patterns on the silk tapestry surrounded this central kaleidoscopic representation. Beneath the wallhanging hung five small photographs with white scarves draped around their frames. I recognized the Dharmapa in the middle picture, which was slightly larger than the others. On the floor stood a wooden altar some ten feet in length and two and a half feet in height and width. An intricate diamond pattern with a circle around it was sculpted on the front. A smaller altar rested atop this foundation on front of which I observed a row of five small incense burners and two white candles in silver holders. A small statue of the Buddha rested atop this altar on a dark maroon cloth. To its side there was a large rattle which I learned subsequently was a Tibetan prayer wheel. It consisted of a metal cylinder engraved with prayers revolving about a long wooden handle. Inside are more prayers and mantras, or mystic inscriptions, printed or written on paper. To the side of the central altar stood a small circular leaf table with a snub-nosed white candle which appeared to have almost burned down to the end. The scent of jasmine incense filtered across the room.

After an eternity of some twenty minutes duration, a gong sounded and liberated me from an endless period of physical and mental fidgeting. Like most Americans, I can sit around all day and not be aware of where the time has gone, but confine me to one spot and I can't sit still for ten minutes. Ginkgo is just the opposite. He can sit in front of a blank wall for hours. Once when he was meditating one morning I asked him a question and when there was no sign of life, I left. That evening, when I returned, he answered my question as if I had been gone only a few minutes.

Evidently some of the others present in the Snow Lion that evening also found meditation sheer torture. For when the chime rang out, an invisible wave of relief swept the room like the end of math class or a long church service. I got the distinct feeling that some of those present performed sitting meditation as a spiritual duty, the moral equivalent of boot camp, before being initiated into the group. My left leg had fallen asleep and felt like ginger ale. As I hobbled over to the side wall with my cushions, my leg buckled and I collided with someone else and ended up entangled in a heap of gold and red cushions. The other casualty, to my surprise, turned out to be an attractive young woman about twenty-five, with clear blue eyes, dimpled cheeks, and a slightly upturned nose. Her flaxen hair fell in swirls about her oval face. Adorned in a long floor-length blue and white cotton dress with a gingham floral pattern, she made me think of a Tibetan Heidi.

The muscular man in the red and white ski sweater came over and extended a hairy arm to the dazed maiden.

"Holy shit!" he exclaimed with a get lost look in my direction. "You took a bad fall."

His reflexes were quick for someone his size. I was amazed at the way he managed to come between us before I could make a move.

"Thanks, Lance, I can manage," she said declining his tanned arm.

Lance flashed his gleaming white teeth and started to say something about taking a spin in his sports car but was suddenly beckoned out of the room by a man in a three-piece suit who was standing in the doorway. He left tossing off some lines from an old Simon and Garfunkle hit :

> *Baby, gotta scoot down the road,*
> *What's my number?*
> *I wonder how your engines feel.*

I was glad to see him go.

"You all right?" my erstwhile companion inquired in a sparkling voice, blinking her long lashes and touching me lightly on the shoulder with long, slender fingers.

"I think I injured by heart chakra," I winced, rubbing my chest. "How about you?"

"OK, I think," she smiled. "My body is pretty supple." She resumed a sitting position and reached across my stretched out legs to inspect my swollen ankle.

I didn't mention that I had bruised it earlier in the day.

"I'm frightfully sorry for running into you like this," she apologized rubbing my ankle with soft circular movements. "Sometimes after a deep meditation, my mind takes awhile to return to sync with my body."

I liked the way she kept referring to her body. I couldn't take my eyes off it. "I know the feeling well," I lied.

"Oh, do you sit? I haven't seen you here before."

"It's my first time," I admitted.

"I guess that makes you a virgin," she blushed. "By the way, my name is Kalavinka."

"Jeff, Jeffrey Milton," I stammered. "Actually I've been meditating since the tenth grade when I used to spend hours watching Kathy Melrose breathe. She sat across from me in geometry and was the measure of perfection."

"What happened?"

"I lost all consciousness of time and space. After Thanksgiving recess, Mr. Sorenson rearranged the seating assignments so that I had an unobstructed view of Sally Bates. She was built like a trapezoid."

"I knew some squares in high school and college," my new acquaintance laughed. "But tell me what brings you here now?"

"Just the opposite problem," I explained. "For some reason the fair sex finds me irresistible and will not leave me alone. Would you believe I had to have my phone disconnected because of all the women who have read my articles in *The Phoenix* and call me up at all hours of the day and night? It's incredible what some of them propose. Finally I just had to have some peace and quiet and find a way to calm my mind."

"Well, you've come to the right place for peace and quiet—and celibacy," she said reaching over and pulling me up. I could tell she didn't believe a word of my story.

We started straightening up the disheveled cushions together.

"Now tell me about yourself," I insisted. "Do you come here often?"

"I've been studying with the Tibetan community in San Francisco for several years," she related. "I moved east a month ago."

"That's a big change. What brought it about?"

"In a word, my parents," she sighed leaning over to puff up a squashed cushion. "You see, Mommy and Daddy are staunch evangelicals and feel that their little girl has lapsed into mortal sin. Even since I was born I have felt separate from their world. They were missionaries in Taiwan, and until age seven I lived there but always found myself attracted to Buddhist playmates outside the mission school. We returned to Dallas, and I had a fairly normal life after that. But after college and working for a year in the environmental movement, I felt a need for a more spiritual community and finally settled on Tibetan Buddhism."

"And your parents couldn't accept it, even though you're grown up?"

"Heavens no," she exclaimed. "They tried to forcibly deprogram me in California. Finally I was forced to leave. I flew out here and took a new name."

"What does Kalavinka mean?"

"It's the name of a legendary Himalayan bird with a wondrous song that appears shortly before the coming of a Buddha."

"You have a most melodious voice," I complimented her.

"Please call me Kali," she said looking up at me with large, liquid eyes. "Kalavinka is so formal."

"I'm awful glad I ran into you, Kali."

"So am I."

As we tidied up the now empty room, the man in the three-piece suit returned. He had short, close-cropped hair, a long serious face, and an aura of impatience. He was the one who had called Lance out of the room.

"Kalavinka," he barked, "you are needed in the kitchen."

Turning to me and extending his hand curtly, he introduced himself, "Tyler Chase, director of the Snow Lion Meditation Center. Inspector Ginkgo is in the study and asked me to retrieve you."

I didn't like his choice of words.

"So you're the head Buddha here?" I replied coolly. "Kalavinka was just filling me in on some of the activities of the center. As a professional journalist, I am full of questions."

"It was my pleasure," she said demurely. I liked the way she pronounced *pleasure*.

Chase backed off at my implied threat to publicize the theft of the Black Hat and turned on his heel.

"Look, Kali," I whispered. "I have to meet some of the monks in the front room. When can I see you again?"

"So you're here on a story after all," she said wistfully. "I don't think Ty would approve of my talking with a reporter."

"It's not what you think," I said. "Can you meet me tomorrow afternoon?"

She hesitated and I turned to see Chase standing in the double doorway. He was tapping his fingers on the glass and straining to suppress a scowl.

"I'll think it over," she said marching quickly out of the room. And then turning back, she smiled, "There's a festival downtown on the Charles Esplanade tomorrow noon, by the bandstand. You never know when a Buddha might appear." I watched her disappear down the corridor, and I followed Chase down the hall.

In the dining room, Ginkgo sat at the far end of a large oval table engaged in an animated conversation with a small monk and a large American. The Tibetan, short, stocky, and with a shaved head, sat to my companion's left. He had small, sad-looking eyes and held his hands clenched at the sides of his dark grey robe. This was evidently Bardo, the hapless custodian of the Black Hat who had been drugged in the upstairs bedroom. The other man I recognized from the Meditation Hall. He wore a tweed sports jacket over his wine-colored turtleneck and was knocking some ashes from a slender black pipe when I entered. He stood up, extended his hand, and introduced himself as Peter Wilkins, professor of comparative religion at Brandeis University and a Tibetan scholar. He sat to Ginkgo's right and served as Bardo's translator.

The three men had been talking about the origins and history of Tibetan Buddhism. There was a line of framed woodcuts on the wall depicting the founders of the religion, and Ginkgo had asked Professor Wilkins to say a few words about each.

"Generally the roots of Buddhism in Tibet are traced back to the eighth century when Padmasambhava, a great teacher from the Orissa region of India, brought it to Tibet."

He pointed to a woodcut of a fierce looking patriarch sitting on a stylized lotus platform and holding a long scepter in his left hand.

"Padmasambhava was a great yogi and magician and is best known as the author of *The Tibetan Book of the Dead*, a manual to attaining enlightenment in the realm between life and death," the professor continued. "The Sanskrit word for such a level is *bardo*, after which our good friend here is named."

Bardo, whose sad-looking eyes remained downcast during most of the conversation, looked up briefly at mention of his name and a glimmer of light crossed his long face.

"Padmasambhava composed *The Tibetan Book of the Dead* in an earlier incarnation, but the time was not ripe yet for the teachings to appear so he hid it in a remote cave to be discovered in a future life. He is believed to have hidden many treasures across Tibet to be found by future disciples as needed to further the Dharma. Some of these are believed to be in caves, others on mountain peaks."

"The Tibetans believe Buddhism in their country long preceded Padmasambhava, don't they?" Ginkgo interrupted.

"All the various lineages go back to celestial Buddhas in incomparably distant eons," the professor replied pointing to a wallhanging depicting a succession of Buddhas suspended in soap bubble-like clouds in one corner.

"Actually the spiritual homeland of Tibetan Buddhism is not Lhasa, the capital, or even India, where the historical Buddha and Padmasambhava came from, but Shambhala, a mythical Central Asian kingdom where the people live a paradisiacal existence and have voluntarily broken all contact with the outside world."

"Some say it's in the Gobi Desert," interjected Lance, who had walked into the room and introduced himself to Ginkgo. "I heard about it while climbing in the Pamirs a few years ago."

With his short curly blond hair, square jaw, and athletic demeanor, Lance Andrews looked like a movie star. Definitely a rival for the attentions of any leading lady like Kalavinka. I figured from his initials and style that it was his red Z out front.

"The Gobi is certainly one location favored by many seekers," Professor Wilkins continued, "but there are others, in the Himalayas, in the Kun Lun Mountains to the north of Tibet, and in the Koko Nor region in East Tibet. Others believe that the city or teaching center remains still operative but is invisible because of advanced technology which jams all radar, weather satellites, and the like. Over the centuries, many explorers have set out in quest of Shambhala, but none is known to have found it or at least returned to tell the tale. Gurdjieff, as you may recall from his autobiography, *Meetings with Remarkable Men*, set out for Shambhala with a caravan of seekers but was forced to abandon the quest after a member of his party died a hideous death. He later found a mysterious brotherhood in the lower Himalayan ranges of Afghanistan that is said to be a school of adepts run by the Shambhala hierarchy."

Turning to Bardo, Ginkgo asked him what Shambhala was and where it was located. The little monk waited patiently as the question was translated.

"Shambhala is where many Bodhisattvas live," he replied eager to explain the teachings.

"What's a Bodhisattva?" I inquired.

"A Bodhisattva," Professor Wilkins explained for my benefit, "is a person who has attained, or resolved to attain, enlightenment but postponed entering nirvana to return to the world to help all other sentient beings attain liberation."

Bardo said something in Tibetan. "Shambhala is where Avalokiteshvara, the Bodhisattva of Mercy, received the celestial Black Hat," Professor Wilkins translated.

"Two hats?" Ginkgo's eyes widened and he held up two fingers in front of the little monk.

Bardo shook his head and held up three fingers. He didn't need to wait for my companion's exclamation to be translated.

"The first hat," Professor Wilkins explained after consulting the little monk, "belonged to Avalokiteshvara, the protector of Shambhala. He is the Bodhisattva of Mercy who incarnates in the Dalai Lama, the Dharmapa, and other high lamas who govern the destiny of Tibet, Mongolia, and Central Asia.

"According to tradition, the second black hat appeared at the enlightenment of the first Dharmapa about a thousand years ago. On attaining the liberating insight, a host of angelic female awareness-beings known as *dakinis* appeared before him, conferring knowledge of the past, present, and future, and bestowing a crown woven from strands of their own hair. All subsequent Dharmapa's were said to wear this Vajra crown over their head, and it was invisible to everyone except the most spiritually developed.

"The third Black Hat—the one that concerns us—dates to the early fifteenth century when the Dharmapa was invited to China by Emperor Tai Mien Chen. Outside the gates of the capital, His Holiness was welcomed by the Emperor and given an elephant to ride. The Dharmapa presented the Son of Heaven a golden Wheel of the Dharma and in return received an auspicious white conch shell. During his stay in the capital, the Emperor offered to unify competing Buddhist sects by force under the Dharmapa's command, but His Holiness demurred, noting that human beings require different teaching methods and all religious expressions partake of one great truth. Reflecting on the wisdom of this reply, the Emperor became a serious student of meditation. One day, while listening to his Tibetan mentor, the Emperor glimpsed the invisible Black Hat over His Holiness's head. He realized that it was a sign of his own spiritual development and progress in meditation. To share this vision with ordinary people, the Emperor had a physical replica of the Black Hat made. He presented it to the Dharmapa. It is this hat that has figured in the ceremony for the last five hundred years and which is said to confer enlightenment upon sight. Historically, the Black Hat has accompanied the dissemination of Buddhist teachings throughout Asia."

"So the presence of the Black Hat in North America precedes the spread of Buddhist teachings to this continent?" Ginkgo drew the obvious conclusion.

"Precisely," the scholar stressed, "and so its disappearance casts a grave spiritual shadow over this part of the globe."

Bardo said something in deep, guttural Tibetan.

"He says that the Vajra Crown ceremony is associated with a famous prophecy of Padmasambhava."

Bardo said something rapidly and gestured to the portrait. Wilkins translated the prediction as follows:

> *When the iron bird flies*
> *and horses run on wheels,*
> *the Tibetan people will be scattered like ants across*
> *   the world*
> *and the Dharma will come to the land of the Red Man.*

"The Tibetans popularly believe that this prophecy refers to Buddhism coming west to the land of airplanes and trains. The land of the Red Man refers to the American Indians. The Tibetan exiles have already been scattered around the world following the Chinese occupation of their country. The Dharmapa, as you know, has just left for Colorado and Arizona. The main purpose of his trip there is not to visit Tibetan Centers, though there are several owing to the mountain regions favored by Tibetan exiles, but to meet native peoples and discuss the prophecy."

Bardo injerjected something else.

"He says that the disappearance of the Black Hat is a bad omen," Wilkins translated. "If it is not found in time for the ceremony here the West may suffer without the liberating teachings of the Dharma until the next world cycle."

"When is that?" I asked.

"Hundreds of thousands of years hence, maybe millions," Wilkins continued. "The Mahayana Buddhists believe that the next Buddha will be Maitreya, whose name means the Loving One. He is currently waiting in the Tushita Heaven as a Bodhisattva and will come to earth in some far distant age."

Bardo spoke up again.

"He says that without the Black Hat the Dharmapa lineage will come to an end. Tibetan Buddhism will disappear from the earth, and America will decline and fall spiritually as India did when Buddhism left its original home."

"Can't the date of the ceremony be postponed until the hat is recovered?" I inquired pointing to a Sierra Club calendar on the wall.

Professor Wilkins conferred with Bardo. "The monk says that the date was selected by the official astrologer of the Tibetan government-in-exile in consultation with His Holiness," the professor replied shaking his head. "It was set at exactly the tenth day following this month's new moon and cannot be changed. The new moon, coinciding with His Holiness's arrival in America, falls tonight."

"What about these teachers?" Ginkgo asked, pointing to some of the woodblock prints on the wall. "These two yogis look exceptionally strong. They are much healthier than any of the Dharmapas. Don't they have any lineages or students?"

Wilkins remained unperturbed by my companion's bluntness and pointed to two portraits. The first showed a yogi with enormous ears, thick eyebrows, and a flat nose. He was garlanded with jewels and flowers.

"This is Tilopa, the first historical recipient of Padmasambhava's teaching. He pounded sesame seeds to earn a living and his name derives from this. *Til* is Sanskrit for sesame. He received his transmission directly from the Celestial Buddha."

"Ha, sesame, I thought so!" Ginkgo exclaimed examining Tilopa's physiognomy closely. "I've seen the same signs of a fertile imagination in some Sufi poets who sang the praises of tahini."

The second portrait showed a cotton-clad yogi in an icy cave with a necklace of skulls around his neck. He had a rounder face than Tilopa but the same enormous ears and concentrated narrowed eyes.

"This second figure is Milarepa, perhaps the greatest meditator and magician in Tibetan history. He lived for many years in total isolation in icy mountain caves subsisting only on nettle soup. He is in a direct line of descent from Tilopa and a predecessor of the Dharmapas."

"Extraordinary yang condition," Ginkgo observed admiringly. "Nettles, eh? Tell me, Chase, there is a young man we encountered in the kitchen earlier this evening making nettle soup. Is this usual fare around here?"

"That would have been Sunyata," Tyler Chase, the director of the Snow Lion, spoke up for the first time. He had a trace of irritation in his high-pitched voice. "He is no longer a member of our community but lives in Vermont in the mountains. He deludes himself that he is another Milarepa and isolates himself from others. He goes off for days at a time to meditate in the woods and lives on roots and berries. When he's in town here, he spends most of his time meditating at night in cemeteries."

"A time-honored yogic practice," Wilkins interrupted lighting his pipe.

"Be that as it may," Chase went on rolling his eyes, "such fanaticism gives Buddhism a bad name. The Cambridge police all know Sunyata by now, but it's bad publicity for Buddhist teachings. The Dharma can be practiced by anyone, especially the average American family. It's not just for monks, nuns, eccentrics, and misfits."

"Do you suspect Sunyata in the theft?" I asked the obvious question.

"He has pilfered food, clothes, and supplies from us," Chase replied disdainfully. "He has no regard for authority."

"Crazy wisdom," interrupted Wilkins trying to be fair. "That's the ideal of the highest teaching. It's a spiritual flouting of convention. Zen masters are proverbial for it. So is the Dharmapa."

"Like wearing the Boston Red Sox cap," Ginkgo mused.

"Exactly," Wilkins agreed tamping his pipe on the edge of the table.

"Sunyata's behavior is neurotic, not enlightened," Chase concluded in an agitated tone. "Still, I don't think he would steal the hat. First of all, he doesn't have the intelligence. Second, he is—for want of a better phrase—under the supervision of a lama in Toronto who is a member of the Dharmapa's school and a sponsor of his trip here. Third, Sunyata did not arrive here until this morning. He was not at the reception yesterday afternoon."

"Is there anyone else you suspect?" I leaned forward and inquired. "Anyone disaffected enough to steal the hat?"

"Not really," Chase responded after a brief hesitation. "There are a few seekers who have not worked out their anger, ignorance, and lust who blame the community for their own ego attachments. But there are no sworn enemies or defectors. Moreover, we have our own security guard which vigilantly watched all entrances and exits to the house after the Dharmapa's arrival. No one not on the invitation list was admitted, nor to my knowledge did anyone else try to enter. We were especially concerned lest journalists, debunkers, and the like turn up." He looked directly at me at this last remark.

"What about the people at the reception? Are there any suspects among them?"

"At least half are regular patrons of our activities," Chase replied condescendingly brushing some lint off his lapel. "They are either sitters or participants in fundraising benefits for the Center or for Tibetan refugees. The other half consisted of civic officials, educators, and artists who might be eligible to serve as benefactors. The reception was a good way to look them over and see whether they might fit into our community."

"Most of the men and women on this list have a personal or professional interest in the Orient," Wilkins added. "I helped draw it up and can vouch for most of them. However, there are several art dealers and collectors I do not know personally. They operate galleries downtown on Newbury Street or here in Cambridge, and we included them because we are always looking for outlets to distribute Tibetan woodcuts, wallhangings, and crafts on behalf of the refugees. My own personal opinion is that one of these art lovers, aware of the uniqueness of the Black Hat, took advantage of the occasion and purloined it. The world of art, as you know, is a cutthroat business, and such an object was probably too much of a temptation for some unscrupulous investor or private collector. It pains me to think I probably had a hand in inviting them to the reception."

Ginkgo suggested that we go upstairs to the scene of the theft, and we adjourned upstairs to a small side bedroom. Simply furnished, the room's furniture consisted of a single cot with a multicolored madras bedspread in an elephant motif, a rollback desk with a lamp with an orange shade, a straight-back chair, an oak bureau with two drawers, and a round wicker chair. The window was open when we arrived, and the ever efficient Chase went over and matter of factly closed it. There was a long scroll upon the desk held down by a worn stone with a stylus and inkwell next to it.

"Bardo, let's recreate exactly what happened," Ginkgo enjoined the little monk, gazing evenly into his eyes. "I want you to work on the scroll, and I will bring you your tea."

Bardo sat down at the desk and unrolled the scroll. He said some prayers while folding his palms together and proceeded to copy out words in large square characters on the parchment from a leather bound book on his right side. It was about the same size as the telephone book after all.

Ginkgo went out of the room and closed the door. A minute later, he knocked and entered with a tea tray. Bardo grunted something but did not look to either side as he continued to work on the page he was transcribing. Ginkgo set it down on the bureau and quietly left the room.

When Bardo came to the end of the page, he folded his palms, bowed, and rolled up the scroll. He got up and went over to the bureau and examined the tea that Ginkgo had left. Ginkgo, who had quietly reentered the room, followed him wordlessly as he set the tray down on the window ledge and sat in a chair in the far corner and proceeded to sip the tea. After a few moments, Bardo lowered his head, and appearing to be drugged, slumped into the chair.

"An excellent performance," Ginkgo exclaimed, rousing the little monk. "Now let's take a look here at the hatbox."

The exquisite box in which the Black Hat was kept measured about two feet to a side and rested on a brocade in a corner of the desk on which Bardo had been copying. The box was silver in color and made of velvety felt with sparkling filigrees of gold and turquoise.

Ginkgo asked if he could look inside, and the monk nodded in the affirmative. Inside was a red plush cushionlike material along the sides and folded up rice paper, evidently used as padding. Except for these packing materials the box, which once contained the world's most unusual hat, was empty. In the wastebasket by the desk were balled up wads of newspaper.

Ginkgo pulled them out and observed that they were from the *Daily Mail* published in London of three days ago. "Where did these come from?"

"He says they were strewn around the room when he awoke," Wilkins said conferring in hushed tones with the monk. "Perhaps the thief used them to wrap the hat in and left the rest here."

Ginkgo muttered for me to smooth out the crumpled up newsprint and put them together in right order. While I did this he examined a small plate he spied under the bed.

"Are these yours?" he asked Bardo.

"No," Bardo's words were translated. "I am on a fast and don't eat solid food. Only tea."

"Then they must be the thief's," Ginkgo observed sniffing the leftover neopolitans, petits fours, and several olive pits. There was also a long-stemmed wine glass under the cot.

"Excellent," Ginkgo exclaimed sniffing the wine, "Dry Sack. Tell me, Chase, what else was served at the reception and who brought the tray up to Bardo?"

"The girls prepared a suitable feast," Chase replied chauvinistically. "There was both vegetarian and nonvegetarian fare. Cold cuts, vegetable cutlets, pastries, dips, crackers, cakes, macaroni salad, mushroom soup, and a bar that dispensed scotch, whiskey, rum, vodka, wine, beer, as well as mineral water and soda pop."

"Kalavinka, one of the women working in the kitchen, prepared the tea," Lance volunteered as Chase fumed and flashed him a dagger look. "However, the kitchen was open to the guests during the reception, and anyone could have spiked Bardo's teapot."

My spirits lifted at Kali's name, and now I had something important to talk to her about. Perhaps she had heard or seen something pertaining to the theft.

Ginkgo did not say anything but went over to the window. Opening it, a gust of cold air blew in and he leaned out. There was a sheer drop twenty-five feet to the ground below. A heavy limb projecting from the oak slanted to the roof. An agile man like Lance could have made his escape through the window.

Ginkgo closed the window only part way, to Chase's consternation, and returned to the center of the room. He took the dried olive pit from the plate of leftovers and to everyone's astonishment popped it into his mouth.

Chase looked alarmed at this unhygienic practice and frowned at the professor who seemed puzzled but not offended by this action. Bardo betrayed no emotion but looked stoically about six inches from his nose.

"And the actual teacup in which Bardo was drugged?" Ginkgo asked, removing the pit and placing it back on the plate.

"It was obviously removed," Chase said. "Over the telephone, Christopher Loring of the State Department ordered us not to disturb anything. I communicated his request to Bardo, but by then the cup was evidently taken downstairs."

"Was it green china, with an upraised curving handle?" Ginkgo asked.

Bardo indicated that he didn't remember.

"No matter," Ginkgo continued. "I've already examined all the

The Snow Lion Meditation Center: 61

cups in the dishwasher downstairs. Three of them had tea residue, but none of them had any evidence of a drug."

"Maybe they were washed before," Lance reflected. "We had so many dishes the women probably did several loads."

"No, the young women assured me that the cups and saucers were saved until the end and this was the last load," Ginkgo continued, shaking his dragonlike head. "No, I'm afraid Bardo's story doesn't hold up. He was not drugged, he was duped. If he had been drugged, his pupils would still be slightly dilated, and the ends of his fingers would probably be red or purple. At the time of the theft, Bardo was not even in the room. He was down the hall in Chase's bedroom looking through a stack of *Playboy* magazines."

A shock wave swept through the room at this pronouncement. Professor Wilkins repeated in Tibetan Ginkgo's conclusions to Bardo. The little monk paled and buried his shaved pate in his hands.

Chase registered both anger and embarrassment, and his face turned a bright scarlet.

"This is outrageous," he flustered. "How dare you impugn the integrity of this servant of the Dharma? His Holiness the Dharmapa would not permit you to make such slanderous accusations."

As Chase stiffened and demanded an apology, tears flowed copiously down Bardo's cheeks. He looked up and rattled off a long speech in Tibetan. He looked up imploringly at Ginkgo and got down on his knees to touch his feet.

"He says you are correct, Inspector," Wilkins translated.

"Get up, Bardo," Ginkgo soothed the little monk. "Now sit down in the chair here and tell us the real story."

This is what the little monk proceeded to relate. As a young boy in Tibet he had been separated from his natural parents at an early age. As was the common practice then, poor peasants often enrolled their children in monasteries in return for an annual payment of money, crop or tax credits, or some kind of spiritual dispensation in the hereafter. Bardo explained that he had dutifully followed his new way of life but could never forget his original parents and playing with his brothers and sisters, the family yak, and various playthings.

Meanwhile, the lamas at the monastery brought him up in the celibate life. For some thirty years of adult life now he had had almost no contact with the opposite sex and had been expected to repress his natural emotions and feelings. However, since traveling to the West with the Dharmapa, visiting New Delhi, Zurich, London, and now Boston, the presence of females had exerted an overpowering fascination. This afternoon, he went to the bathroom down the corridor and on the way back passed Chase's bedroom and happened to see a magazine on his bedstand with a young woman in a provocative pose. Rather than return immediately to his post, he lingered in the bedroom for about ten or fifteen minutes. When he returned, the hat was gone."

"I will lose all of my good karma piled up over the eons and be born in the coldest of the ice hells," Bardo lamented.

Chase blushed at this confession and explained laconically that he kept the magazines in his room to stimulate his tantric visualizations. Wilkins dutifully translated that to Bardo, who looked like he would enjoy Chase's company, however officious, in the nether realms.

"How did you arrive at this conclusion?" the professor asked Ginkgo.

"Once I had eliminated drugging, it appeared that Bardo left the Black Hat unguarded. During meditation this evening, I puttered around upstairs and quickly discovered Chase's extracurricular reading material. One of them had tell-tale evidence of butter tea across the centerfold. It was obvious what had happened."

At least the tea was not spiked, I sighed in relief. For a moment, I admit I had my doubts about Kalavinka.

"So anyone could have just waltzed in here and taken the Black Hat?" Lance concluded.

"Not anyone," Ginkgo replied. "The person we are looking for should be easy enough to locate. He is an Englishman, taller than average, between forty and forty-five, and very dapper. He has a puffy lower lip and a sallow complexion. He smokes expensive tobacco and has an overactive liver. He is devoted to some abstract ideal of art and will sacrifice everything in order to obtain it."

"That's incredible!" Wilkins exclaimed, uncharacteristically showing a trace of emotion. "I remember a Brit of that description. He had a blue pinstripe suit and pocket handkerchief with the monogram S. The reason I remember so vividly is that I got in a conversation with him about Tibetan art. He argued that there was a marked Chinese influence on Tibetan painting and sculpture. I held up for the Indian influence. He asked me where the Dharmapa's personal attendant was staying, and I indicated this bedroom. How stupid of me."

"I fleetingly recall a tall man, very well dressed, with an impeccable British accent, just as you describe," Chase volunteered. "He was not on the original invitation list but accompanied Keiji Aso, one of our staunchest patrons."

"The curator at the Museum of Fine Arts," Ginkgo's eyes lit up. "I know him well."

"You don't think he— ? " Chase reflected.

"Of course not," Ginkgo snapped, "but he can put us on the track of our hat thief. Let me see that invitation list."

"Sergei Starov," Professor Wilkins exclaimed looking over his shoulder. "That was it."

"Sounds Russian, not English, to me," I noted ominously.

"Good, now we're getting somewhere," Ginkgo said. "I will talk with Keiji Aso in the morning. As for Bardo, Chase, and Wilkins here, let this be a lesson to you. Each of you bears some responsibility for what happened here today. Use this opportunity to self-reflect and make progress in the right."

So saying, my companion and I left the three chastened disciples of Tibetan Buddhism.

"How did you identify the thief?" I asked as we turned down Garden Street. "By the remains of food on the plate?"

"With so many items to choose from," he replied, "I figured our friend acted from instinct rather than curiosity. After all, he was after the hat and had no doubt run through the expected scenario in his mind many times. He would take only what he was used to and waste no energy on new items. He took the olives, the continental pastries, and the Dry Sack. In combination with the newspaper, these suggested an Englishman with Mediterranean ties. The yin quality of the food suggested a taller, leaner, more dapper appearance, though oily and sugary confections give the face a sallow complexion and weaken the intestines, causing the lower lip to swell. Most of these deductions were confirmed by chewing on one of the olive pits which he left on his plate. I picked up the distinct taste of fine tobacco, acquired from his own mouth, as well as a number of mental impressions that have yet to be borne out."

"What was the newspaper for?" I inquired noting that all the pages were accounted for.

"On the pretext of going to the bathroom, Starov evidently went upstairs with his food and drink and a shopping bag containing the balled up newspaper," Ginkgo explained. "The *Daily Mail* is quite hefty, and he probably intended to substitute it inside the box. It is about the same weight as the Black Hat. It would greatly help his escape if the theft were not noticed immediately. There would be some ego gratification ten days from now when the London newspaper was taken out during the Vajra Crown Ceremony."

"The kind of signature Professor Moriarty would have delighted in," I gasped.

"Alas, for his malicious intent, Sergei Starov evidently heard Bardo coming down the corridor chanting and didn't have time to conceal his theft. He discretely slipped his plate and cocktail glass under the bed and disposed of the balled up papers in the wastebasket and left hurriedly with the hat in the shopping bag just as Bardo returned."

As we walked home along Garden Street speculating on Starov's identity and employer, a long white Cadillac with Texas plates drew over to the curb beside us. There was a rack on top filled with expensive luggage. In the back seat sat a well dressed middle aged couple. In the front, a black chauffeur leaned out as the front window noiselessly rolled down.

"Top of the evenin', gentlemen," he said deprecatingly, "but we be looking for the Law School dormitory. Could you all point us in that direction?"

"Bates Hall," the lady in the back spoke up fingering a fancy pearl necklace. "That's where my Jimmy is staying."

"Now don't interfere, dear," the man next to her commanded in a smooth patrician voice. "We're here to attend our son's graduation. We'd be much obliged if you could direct us to the Holiday Inn. James said it was near his dorm."

"Sure," I replied, "the Holiday Inn is on Mass Ave. Just hang a right two blocks up, go straight down the main boulevard, take a left and it's on the right—opposite the Chinese restaurant. Big green and yellow sign. You can't miss it."

"Thank you kindly, brethren," the grey-haired man replied. "We'll be there in five minutes, Martha Jean, just hold tight, sugar lump. Harrison, check the roof rack again, would you, boy?"

The chauffeur got out and adjusted the straps holding the luggage in place. "God awful windy tonight, blowing like the devil hisself." He rolled his eyes as if he needed a breath of fresh air or stiff drink to balance the cloistered atmosphere inside.

"I think I'll stroll over to Mt. Auburn Cemetery," Ginkgo mused, "and have a word with Sunyata."

The white Cadillac peeled out. I observed a large "Jesus Saves" sticker across the rear bumper and prayed for the poor devil who had to put up with these parents.

At the corner of Linnean Street, I turned in to Potter Park and Ginkgo, with his head bent down and gripping his staff, plunged into the night.

4

ART IN THE BLOOD IS LIABLE TO TAKE THE STRANGEST FORM

The next morning, we set out bright and early for the Museum of Fine Arts. Ginkgo wanted to talk with his friend Keiji Aso, the assistant curator of Oriental Art, about Starov, the London art dealer who was our prime suspect in the disappearance of the Black Hat. Even in an emergency, Ginkgo declined to take a cab or the MTA trolley line in Cambridge or Boston, preferring instead to walk as was his custom. In the mornings, before the first dietary and way of life consultations of the day, he would hike miles to some favored site such as Walden Pond in Concord, the Decordova Lake in Lincoln, the Deer Park in Newton, or the Beech Park in Brookline. Today the only exception he made was to leave a note on the door, moving his consultations to the afternoon.

The rays of the sun reflected off the water and the skyline as we trekked single file along a footpath on the Boston side of the Charles. Commuter traffic sped downtown on Storrow Drive at a smart clip, and an occasional jogger or bicyclist smiled or waved as he or she passed by. Our Himalayan adventure prompted my companion to discourse along the way some more about Benares-on-the-Charles.

"The Boston riverway fronts on scores of temples," he began the morning's lesson, shaking his cudgel at the buildings and skyscrapers looming ahead. "Only these houses of worship do not contain copper-colored idols of naked torsos and limbs or of monkeys wandering freely among the devout. Instead, the altars are raised to the abstract principles of Science and Medicine. What monkeys there be are securely bound by electrodes and are not allowed to disturb any of the white-smocked initiates in carrying out their sacrifices."

Gesturing with a sweep of his hand from Mt. Auburn Hospital behind us to Mass General Hospital far ahead, he reeled off a list of medical centers, chemical laboratories, and food processing plants that dominated the slowly curving skyline. In the long sleek crew boats gliding along the current, he pointed out that student oarsmen learned to judge their speed and position by watching the approaching contours of the Coca-Cola bottling plant in Alston and the Domino Sugar refining company in Charleston.

"Unlike Benares, there are no burning ghats along the riverbank to cremate the dead and inspire awe in the living," he continued, swinging his arms vigorously as he marched along the footpath. "Instead the business of death and dying is transacted largely in the Prudential Building and the John Hancock Tower, the city's two tallest structures. Here all the hospital forms, coroners' certificates, and insurance policies end up for microfilming before final consignment to the sacred fires.

"Modern medicine and science function as the real religion of the land, make no mistake, Milton," he emphasized, as an ambulance raced by, its siren blaring. "The old religion, Judeo-Christianity, of course, has long fallen into disuse. Like the pagan rites of old, it receives some passing acknowledgment, at most once a week when people visit the ancient altars. But a real seven-day-a-week faith burns within the public breast toward doctors and engineers, lab technicians and biochemists. Those who stand between the individual and his health and safety enjoy the deference and accolades of Brahmins who administer the sacred soma. Anyone who does not have about his person the sign of the Blue Cross, Blue Shield, or other mystic order is treated as an untouchable and is barred from admittance to a temple. Outcasts who refuse to submit to compulsory blood rites such as inoculation are not allowed to leave the country or send their children to school.

"Nine hundred and ninety-nine people out of a thousand do not question these cultic practices and flock to local shrines known as pharmacies. There, the old and arthritic, the young and strung out, the middle aged and tranquilized, bring their offerings and the sacred Vedic-like formula scrawled out by their priest. In return, they receive a vial of pills or tablets which they take several times a day, a sort of magical incantation to propitiate the God of Liver, Spleen, or Bile. Of course, these ministrations, like throwing clarified butter on the sacrificial fire, do little good and have to be constantly renewed. All the while, the rate of degenerative disease steadily climbs. Thanks to the strenuous efforts of the priests, it is unlawful to treat a cancer patient or heart disease sufferer with diet, herbs, meditation, massage, or palm healing. Only purification by fire—in the form of dangerous drugs, toxic chemicals, and deadly radiation—is allowed to root out the pestilence. The old gods are very much living among us, Milton. Untold sacrifices on both sides of Benares-on-the-Charles are consumed each day by the healing flame."

At length, we veered off the river by Boston University, crossed over the Mass Turnpike, marched up Park Drive, cut through the Fens, and walked around to the front entrance of the Museum of Fine Arts on Huntington Avenue. Inside the imposing main rotunda, flanked by Ionic colonnades, we were greeted by Keiji Aso who ushered us into one of the Oriental exhibition halls.

Aso's ebullient manner offset his diminutive stature. Though this was our first meeting, I had heard Ginkgo talk fondly of him on several occasions. Physically, his most prominent feature was the absence of one arm, which naturally served to highlight the other, and earned him the nickname "Wing" by which he was universally known. This sobriquet also tied in with his former calling. During World War II, he served as a Kamikaze pilot but, as destiny would have it, he survived his mission—all except for his pitching arm. In love with the abstract ideal of beauty, as well as major league baseball, he was renowned for pursuing his new vocation as avidly as his old.

"*Konnichiwa*, Ginkgo *sensei*," Wing wished my friend good morning with the deference accorded to an honored teacher.

"*Hiroshiko*, Wing-san," Ginkgo replied politely in the Japanese fashion. "I'm sorry to have disturbed your harmony on such a fine day as this. I know you must be preoccupied with very important matters in the midst of such beautiful surroundings."

"Not at all, Inspector," Wing responded pointing to a case displaying a beautiful cream-colored jade vase with a square base and a delicate handle in the shape of a crane. "As the poets of old noted," he said translating from the calligraphy inscribed on its side,

"'The frog lives in the well all year long, while the crane comes but once a season.' How can I help you?"

After supplying the essential features of the case, Ginkgo asked if Wing met anyone answering to Starov's description at the Snow Lion Meditation Center the afternoon before.

"Naturally, it is my duty to keep abreast of the visiting line-up," Wing grinned, invoking a baseball metaphor and raising his index finger in a triumphant gesture.

"There are not too many Asian art dealers who pass through Boston who do not get in touch with me or one of my associates. Yes, I remember Starov-san very well. He was just as you described him—tall, thin, vain, and with a weakness for Dry Sack."

Wing mimicked Starov's appearance and bearing with brusque movements of his hand. I could not help but think how well he blended in with his environment. The other inhabitants of the room included several deities with either arms and legs missing or with multiple limbs. Wing's one arm served him as well as two or three.

"Starov-san introduced himself as a private art dealer in London. He conversed knowledgeably about Swiss foreign exchange rates but struck me very much as a personal collector," the little Japanese continued. "I noticed the way he looked at the wallhangings and ritual objects on display in the meditation room. He knew their investment value but clearly appreciated their aesthetic quality even more."

"I was afraid of that," Ginkgo sighed. "If it were a question of money, the Black Hat could be ransomed. But if it is to satisfy the sentimental judgment of a private collector, it will be much harder to recover."

"Perhaps this will be of some benefit in your search," Wing said handing my friend a business card from his wallet. The print looked like Zaft italics, wavy and elegant. It read:

> *Sergei Starov Esq.*
> *Dealer in Oriental Antiquities*
> *Regent Park, London*
> *By Appt. Tel. 250-1868*

"Starov-san said to 'give me a ring, old chap' if I ever had any unusual 'one-of-a-kind' pieces to buy or sell," Aso further confided. "I invited him to an unveiling of Persian miniatures we're having here tomorrow, but he excused himself, saying he had a plane to catch in the evening and would be returning home after what he said he hoped to be 'a very successful hunting expedition.'"

"Would Starov have much trouble taking the hat out of the country?" I asked.

"Not unless he wore it," Wing chuckled. "Milton-san, there's a fine line today between acquiring rare art and grand theft. The prices commanded by masterpieces and antiquities are astronomical. Few museums or private investors scruple about the origin of their acquisitions. In many cases, they prefer not to know. There are ingenious ways to establish pedigrees and move goods in an out of countries that would make international drug smugglers and intelligence agencies envious. Unpublicized auctions in Zurich and Berne by a closed circle of dealers are one of the commonest ways to launder questionable paintings and sculptures. You see, Switzerland has no laws restricting the import or export of art or the receipt of stolen goods. As for taking the Black Hat out of the country, all Starov-san would have to do is carry it through customs in a shopping bag. If anyone inquired, he would only have to produce a New Orleans ticket stub and say it was a part of a costume from Madi Gras."

As a tour group of elementary school students entered the hall, Wing led us to his office. Along the way we passed a glass case displaying the ceremonial robes of several former Chinese emperors. Ginkgo paused in front of one cabinet.

"I thought you might be interested, Inspector, in this robe here," Wing pointed admiringly to a magnificent red and gold silk robe embroidered with azure dragons. "This robe belonged to Emperor Tai Ming Chen, who invited the Fifth Dharmapa to China and bestowed upon him the original Black Hat."

"If I didn't know the Museum has one of the finest Chinese collections in the world, I'd think it was a remarkable coincidence," Ginkgo exclaimed marveling at the great butterfly sleeves.

"*Ah so, desuka*, it's truly Tai Ming Chen's," Wing swore. "I confess though I hastily found it in the vault downstairs and had it mounted this morning in honor of your visit after Mr. Christopher Loring called. I didn't think the spirit of the Ming emperor whose robe has been on display for the last decade would mind the sudden transfer in power."

"See the five claws on the dragon," Wing continued for my benefit, fashioning his own wiry fingers into talons. "That's the Imperial Dragon. Only the emperor could wear this insignia. And only the emperor could wear this shade of crimson." He drew a finger across his throat to spell out the consequences.

As we were talking, the group of schoolchildren started giggling and pointing in hushed tones to Ginkgo who seemed entranced with the Emperor's robe. The source of their amusement turned out to be a large painting on an adjoining wall entitled *The Demon Queller Accompanied by a Tiger*. It portrayed a fierce-looking sage with bulging eyes, scraggly beard and mustache, and long ears meditating next to a small tiger under a pine tree. Even I did a double-take, not so much at the resemblance of the demon queller to Ginkgo which was uncanny, but of the tiger to his cat, Descartes, which was positively supernatural. The children's laughter brought Ginkgo out of his reverie and, divining the source of their amusement, pointed to the sage's ear while pulling his own and told the youngsters that the painting was of his great-great-grandfather.

Wing's office was the antithesis of the exhibition rooms we had just left. After seating us in wide-body decorator chairs, our host proudly showed us an autographed photograph of Red Sox baseball great Carl Yastremski and a bat and ball he had used to win a particularly thrilling game. There were several abstract paintings on the wall and a large space-age sculpture in one corner entitled *Vertical Liftoff*. Wing likened this oasis of modernity in the midst of the Oriental collection to a dot in the Yin-Yang symbol.

"Let's check out Starov-san on the ICOA database," he said moving over to a personal computer console on his desk.

"What's ICOA?" I inquired.

"International Council of Museums," he replied as his fingers flew across the keyboard. "They keep a register of dealers, important transactions, stolen art and antiquities."

As a journalist who still pecks with two fingers, I was envious of how fast he could type with only one hand.

"Ah, paydirt!" he exclaimed. "Starov, Sergei Nikolayevich; born Odessa 1937; parents were both active in the Red Orchestra, the Soviet anti-Nazi spy network during World War II. He was educated at the University of Leningrad and did graduate work at Oxford and the Sorbonne. In addition to his scholarships, he worked as a busboy in a Chinese restaurant in London and as apprentice pastry chef at Chez Marzipan in Paris. From 1957 to 1959, he served in the Soviet Army, rising to captain. Afterward, he returned to Leningrad as assistant curator of Oriental art, the Hermitage from 1960-64. He worked as Cultural Attaché, Soviet Embassy in London, 1965-68; private dealer, London, 1969– , specializing in Chinese antiquities, Old Masters, Art Nouveau, and Pop Art. He collects works by Greuze, a famous nineteenth century French painter. In 1970 he acquired the Baron Bruner Collection, a valuable assortment of Chinese pottery and vases, with the help of Sir Anthony Blunt. In 1974 he successfully bid at Southeby's on Andy Worhol's original *Tomato Soup Can* on behalf of a private investor."

"It would seem Starov is an ex-Soviet agent," I exclaimed.

"I'm not sure the Russians let any of their agents retire," Wing grinned displaying a row of bad teeth. "But it seems he left the diplomatic corps and settled in London in the wake of Khrushchev's ouster in 1964. No doubt he had acquired a taste of the good life in the West from his graduate school days and didn't want to be recalled home. Also, it's clear he had some connection with Anthony Blunt, the art critic and notorious Fourth Man in the British spy scandals involving Don Maclean, Guy Burgess, and Kim Philby. Whether Starov is still working for the Kremlin, some breakaway faction of the KGB, or solo, he's what you'd call a tough out."

"Has he ever been in any trouble with the authorities?" I asked.

"Let's check the Interpol register," Wing said, flicking on his modem.

In seconds, a list of recently stolen art works materialized on the monitor. "Nothing here," Wing murmured scrolling through the listings. "Wait, his name is on a list of dealers who bid for a Vernet that came up at Christie's in 1976. He is recorded as the underbidder. The painting was stolen that same day during the luncheon recess."

"Hmm, mealtime thefts," Ginkgo observed with heightened interest.

"That would appear to be his patented swing," Wing agreed. "Of course, Vernets have been disappearing from the market in recent years—partly by acquisition and partly by theft. French realism is not a strong market, so there is some mystery to their loss."

"Could Starov be in the employ of the Chinese, who would seem to have the most stake in not having the Black Hat Ceremony take place?" I asked the little curator.

"Again, *employ* is too strong a word," he replied. "As a private dealer, Starov is undoubtedly in contact with agents and representatives of many governments. For him, it would be strictly a business proposition. If Beijing is behind this caper, it would probably be through the Cheng Pao K'o. That's the Chinese counterespionage service. It includes both native and overseas Chinese as well as a few selected agents of Western background."

"Wing-san, what do you know about the Dharmapas?" Ginkgo said changing the topic.

"The Dharmapas are a very powerful lineage," Wing explained swiveling on his high-back chair and pouring us hot tea from a delicate lime-green teapot resting on an adjacent cabinet. "They were the spiritual and temporal rulers of Tibet for many centuries. They had a civilizing influence on the Great Khans, and Marco Polo speaks in awe of their magical powers in his travelogue."

"So historically they have been aligned with the Mongols as well as the Chinese?" Ginkgo commented, accepting a small cup and setting it down to cool.

"*Aligned* is too strong a word, Inspector," Wing went on waving his outstretched hand in an ambivalent gesture. "As the embodiment of the Tantra and Crazy Wisdom, the Dharmapas are devoted to the spread of the Buddhist teachings. However, compassion and loving-kindness often take forms that are strange by society's standards."

"Can you give an example?" I spoke up. The hot tea was mildly fragrant and momentarily transported me back to the Middle East and some long forgotten journalistic interludes.

"Once after several years with the Mongol chieftain, the Dharmapa wanted to return home to Tibet," Wing related. "However, Kublai Khan had grown so attached to him that he wouldn't let him leave. The Dharmapa left anyway, and so Kublai sent thirty thousand horsemen to abduct him and bring him back to court. When the soldiers surrounded him, the Dharmapa immediately paralyzed them with the Mudra or Gesture of the Two Fingers. However, out of compassion he later allowed them to resume their movements. The soldiers continued to try and capture him, and each time he was bound he would dissolve his physical body. Finally, in anger, the soldiers tried to kill him by poison and by flinging him off a cliff, but each time he eluded them."

"Do you really believe such fanciful legends?" I asked draining my cup.

"I neither believe nor not believe, Milton-san," Wing replied enigmatically. "I do know the Dharmapa was the first Tibetan lama to incarnate by leaving a letter with his attendants forecasting the exact time and place of his rebirth. This has now happened sixteen times since the twelfth century. As in the case of the Dalai Lama and other senior lamas who followed him in this practice, the predictions have been well authenticated."

"What about the previous Dharmapa?" Ginkgo asked sipping his tea for the first time. "Was he living at the end of the nineteenth century?"

"The previous Dharmapa was born in 1871," Wing reported. "At age six he was enthroned and composed a prayer that moved everyone with its depth and maturity. He was deeply versed in the contemplative teachings of all the Tibetan religious sects and made a complete study of medicine. He spent his later life in solitary meditation."

"And where would he have been between 1891 and 1893?" I asked thinking of Sherlock Holmes's incognito visit to Lhasa. "The question has come up whether the Dharmapa might be the Head Lama of Tibet at that time."

"I'm afraid he is not yet on a database," Wing mused, reaching for a dusty reference volume on a shelf over his mahogany desk.

"It says here that in 1885 he was invited to consecrate the newly restored monastery in Li Thang," he said quickly scanning the pages. "The following year, he visited the Khams in East Tibet and studied with Jangon Khongtrul Rinpoche, one of the greatest religious reformers in the history of Tibetan Buddhism. In 1888 he traveled to Lhasa and took up residence part of the time in the Samye Monastery. Samye is a famous monastery outside of the capital. There he enthroned several incarnate lamas. In 1894, he returned to Tsurphu, the head monastery of the Dharmapas in the Tolung Valley northwest of Lhasa. Meanwhile, the Dalai Lama, six years his junior, was not enthroned until 1895, and the Panchen Lama was even younger. In answer to your questions, the Dharmapa was definitely in Lhasa and its immediate vicinity and would have been the Head Lama in Tibet at that time."

"It's hard to think of a twenty-year-old boy as a Head Lama," I reflected.

"Some people are naturally wise from an early age. Others lose what little wits they have by the time they reach their majority," Ginkgo reflected, casting an eye in my direction.

I would have hid in the teapot if I could. In my embarrassment I knocked over my tea cup and only Wing's lightening-like catch saved it from breaking into pieces on the floor.

"Forgive my clumsiness," I apologized. "I imagine these cups are from the Sung Dynasty and irreplaceable. Thanks for saving me some terrible asterisk in the art history books."

"Ching Dynasty, Milton-san," Wing said gently correcting me. "These cups have several centuries' life left in them . . . "

"Even though they are obviously rather clumsy forgeries of an earlier era," Ginkgo completed his train of thought.

I had the distinct feeling of being caught in a verbal joust between two Zen masters. The only china we had in our family was from Woolworth's. To a poor Midwest boy like me, all Chinese dynasties were the same and equally old.

"What can you tell us about the present Dharmapa?" Ginkgo steered the conversation back to the immediate events at hand. "What kind of a person is he?"

"The present Dharmapa first performed the Black Hat Ceremony at age ten," Wing informed us assuming a regal position and pantomiming the act of putting the Vajra Crown on his head.

"Like his immediate predecessor, the Dharmapa is famous for his ability to communicate with animals and birds." Wing's hand and fingers flew into the shape of a fox, hawk, and rabbit, casting childlike silhouettes on the opposite wall.

"In the early 1950s the Dharmapa visited China and clearly saw what lay ahead for his country. In 1958, he left Tibet with a large caravan of monks bearing scriptures, icons, statues, costumes, and other treasures. After settling in Sikkim at the behest of the royal family, he supervised the construction of a large monastery. Since then he has remained completely aloof from exile politics, concentrating on his spiritual duties. The most important of these is recognizing the reincarnations of important lineage holders. Known as *tulkus*, some of them are only a few years old when he empowers them. He is also fond of ritual and dance and is a patron of all the traditional arts and crafts."

"If you like," Wing continued rising from his chair, "I can show you a few Tibetan art pieces on display."

The Himalayan treasures were displayed in a small anteroom at the end of the Chinese galleries off the Upper Rotunda. In addition to the vivid colors—the deep reds, blues, and greens—I was struck by the explicit themes of the works displayed. There was a sculpture of Vajrabhairava, a dog-headed demon with thirty-two arms and six heads, holding a young woman in a most unholy way. There was a wallhanging of a roly-poly deity named Mahakala attired with a necklace of skulls and dancing on a corpse beneath his feet. There was another of Raktayamari, aka the Red Conqueror of the Lord of Darkness, and his consort Prajana in a militant posture astride a red bull. Across the way hung a scroll painting of *The Assault of the Demon Mara on Sakyamuni Buddha* in an rather unsubtle attempt to break his concentration and prevent him from attaining enlightenment.

"I thought traditional Tibet was a really peaceful culture," I exclaimed. "But all these images of sex and violence make Western TV and the media look pale by comparison. Maybe Bardo picked up *Playboy* to purify his mind."

Wing proceeded to explain that in Buddhism a school called the Tantra developed in ancient times which taught that the path to self-realization lay not in avoiding the senses but in mastering them. Instead of ascetic practices, Tantric adepts apply meditative techniques to mastering food, breath, postures, clothing, and—in the most advanced cases—sexual energy. He explained that the Buddha and Bodhisattvas often assumed wrathful forms, like Vajrabhairava or Mahakala, in order to subdue the Lord of Death, symbolized by the corpse, and embraced their *shakti* or feminine aspect, symbolized by *prajana* or wisdom.

"In simple language," Ginkgo observed, "*rakshas*, devils, and demons are beings who think they are free to do anything they want without understanding the Order of the Universe."

"There must be several million of them in this city alone," I concluded.

"There have been many abuses of the Tantra," Wing conceded as some wide-eyed school kids snickered and pointed at the X-rated canvasses. "In India, it is known as the Left-Handed Path and has come into some disrepute among other schools of Buddhism. But in the Himalayas, the Tantra took root and has influenced nearly all teachings."

"Now here is something more heavenly," Ginkgo exclaimed shepherding us over to a small painting of the Goddess Tara, the patroness of Tibet. "She is a real Barley Queen. Just whole grains and vegetables for her, with a little gomashio and maybe an occasional dollop of yak butter in her tea."

The Goddess certainly was beautiful, and her curvaceous physiognomy reminded me of Kalavinka. Next to the painting was an inscription, "I put my faith in the revered Tara who removes all suffering."

"*Sumimasen*, Ginkgo *sensei*," Wing interrupted our reverie glancing at his oversize Mickey Mouse wristwatch. "Excuse me, I have to give a little talk to the schoolchildren in the main hall. I almost forgot. Before you go I'd like to give you a gift from among some new finds which just came in from the Caves of Ten Thousand Buddhas in China. Your help in the Paper Mule Affair led to their discovery."

Smiling broadly, he handed my companion a small packet.

"Seeds of grain and very old ones." Ginkgo's eyes brightened appreciatively as he gently untied the pale violet and white silk scarf in which they were wrapped. It was stained and faded, but appeared to have a dragon motif.

"*Hai, domo*, rice and millet from an urn over a thousand years old," Keiji Aso explained. "There were also several priceless scrolls, jade carvings, and ritual implements. The archaeologists wanted to send them out to a lab for testing. I told them I already knew an expert in the field."

"Strong ki," Ginkgo exclaimed excitedly, weighing the tiny beige grains in his palm.

"*Gomen kudasai*, thank you ten thousand times," Ginkgo bowed deeply and thrust the precious treasure deep inside his orange rucksack. "I'll render my final verdict when I have a chance to taste them."

Wing bade us farewell and scurried down the corridor hailing the eagerly awaiting schoolchildren. On the way out, Ginkgo paused for a moment before a small Chinese sculpture of Avalokiteshvara. The Bodhisattva's meditative posture reminded me of an Oriental version of Rodin's *The Thinker* except for the serene and peaceful expression on its face.

With an imperceptible nod of his head, Ginkgo invoked the aid of the Bodhisattva of Mercy on our quest. Taking our leave of the Oriental rooms, we rode the escalator down to the main floor. Behind us I stared in fascination as the famous lifesize mural of *Washington Crossing the Delaware* brushed past and faded from sight.

5

SONG OF THE FEMALE EARTH BIRD

From the museum, Ginkgo headed off to Newbury Street to pick up some groceries at Erewhon's, and I proceeded to the riverfront hoping that Kalavinka would keep our date.

It turned out to be a gorgeous day. The early morning mist had lifted, and the azure sky was clear and shining. A warm noonday sun bathed the marina, and the billowing sails of small sailboats dotted the blue-green expanse like shimmering streaks of white on an impressionist canvas.

To my delight, Kalavinka was waiting for me on the Esplanade. She had on a simple white blouse, a long rose-printed skirt, and a garland of daisies in her hair. She was helping a little boy untangle a kite that had become stuck in a tree.

"When I was a little girl I used to fly kites too," I heard her say to the youngster as I approached. "My favorite was a turquoise dragon kite. It must have had a tail about ten-feet long."

"I've never seen a dragon kite!" the little boy said, eagerly reaching for the silver kite that Kalavinka had freed. It depicted the helmet of Darth Vadar, the villain of *Star Wars*.

"That's because I grew up in China. That's where kites originated. Did you know that?"

"No," the little boy said thoughtfully. "But I plan to visit there. At the beach, my brother and I always dig a big hole. Mommy and Daddy say that if we dig deep enough we'll get to China. I'd like to come back with a dragon kite."

"Well, you just keep digging," Kalavinka laughed, straightening one of the bent supports of the large diamond-shaped toy. "And one day you will visit not only China but Tibet."

"Where's that?" the boy asked.

"Tibet's the highest part of China. Actually it's the highest country in the world. The wind there is so strong that a kite that goes up sometimes never comes down."

"*Tib-et*," the little boy repeated, emphasizing the first syllable.

"*Ti-bet*," Kalavinka corrected him several times until he pronounced it properly.

The arrival of the boy's mother and older brother, who had been searching for him in the crowd gathering for the midday Charles River Festival, interrupted the geography lesson. Waving farewell, they meandered toward the bandshell to enjoy a picnic lunch.

"Speaking of the wind, would you care to go for a sail?" Kalavinka asked me, as she waved goodbye to the boy who was clutching his kite.

"I'd love to," I replied turning toward the marina. "This is one pleasure I imagine they don't have in land-locked Tibet."

We rented a small boat at the dock and pushed off into the Charles River Basin. In a few minutes we were in the middle of the river, which widens considerably between the Mass Ave. Bridge and the Museum of Science forming a lagoon. There were dozens of other small boats basking in the river, bearing business executives on a lunch break, federal, state, or local employees who worked in Government Center, and young couples like us enjoying each other and the beautiful day. Far down river, I caught sight of a long crew boat pulling under the Mass Avenue Bridge.

"I didn't know you had lived in China," I remarked after we had found a nice spot to drift. "I thought you grew up in Taiwan."

"I did. Taiwan is an integral part of China," Kalavinka replied, putting on some large yellow sunglasses. "My parents were stationed in Suzhou, but after the Revolution the mission was closed down and they fled to Taiwan. The dragon kite is one of the few things I recall from my childhood—maybe because I had to leave it behind."

From my tan knapsack I took out a small bottle of saké and a container of marinated tofu. I produced two small cups and proposed a toast to East West friendship. Kali's luminous eyes widened, and she lightly clinked glasses.

"This is the macrobiotic equivalent to wine and cheese," I explained offering her a small slice of tofu."

"It's so sweet!" she exclaimed brightening a little. "I've never tasted such delicious tofu. Its texture is creamy just like cheese. How do you make it?"

"It's pickled in miso," I explained offering her another slice. "All you do is take a block of tofu, squeeze out the water, and immerse it in a container with a half-inch to an inch of miso all around it. Then refrigerate it for twenty-four hours, take it out, rinse off the miso, and voila, natural tofu cheese."

"Thanks for the recipe," she said returning my smile. "I'll introduce it to the Snow Lion. For a journalist, you seem to know an awful lot about cooking," she said raising the saké cup to her lips slowly.

"Housekeeping is too important to be left entirely to women," I grinned.

"You must be a sheep?" she laughed.

"I beg your pardon," I gagged taking offense at her characterization.

"I'm sorry," she apologized brushing my knee lightly with her hand. "I meant the sheep in the Oriental zodiac. People born in the Year of the Sheep are very domesticated and dependable—though somewhat shaggy around the edges," she added lowering her sunglasses to inspect my locks and wooly V-neck sweater. "What year were you born?"

"Spring of 1960," I said smoothing the back of my hair and sweater. I was pretty sure I didn't want to be a sheep.

"That would make you a Male Iron Mouse," she reflected.

"And what are its characteristics?" I winced at this wimpy-sounding totem. Still it had to be better than being a sheep—or a snake. I think there's one of those on the astrology placemat in the Chinese restaurant I occasionally go to in the Square.

"Very industrious, secretive, partial to tofu cheese, and not given to housework except to impress his lady love," she smiled demurely.

"Bull's eye," I confessed gazing out on the placid waters, "I'm a real Mighty Mouse at heart. And you, what's your sign?"

"A bird naturally," she declared inclining her head and throwing back her shoulders gently. "A Female Earth Bird—a swallow to be exact."

Song of the Female Earth Bird: 81

"Who loves to soar in solitude and follow the promptings of her own independent spirit," I remarked pouring her another cup of sake.

"Exactly," she smiled pouring half of her cup in mine and casting her bright glance around the marina.

In the foreground the crew boat drew closer. I could make out six student rowers and a black man with a bullhorn on the prow. He had on a Crimson sweatshirt. I was glad to see that the Harvard athletic department believed in affirmative action.

"It's a pity the iron mouse and earth bird are so mismatched," Kalavinka sighed as our gaze returned to the immediate environment.

"Fear of the shoals of incompatibility has sunk many a ship in port," I said nonchalantly letting out the sail and turning the small craft 180 degrees.

"I can see that you are a graduate of the Chairman Mao 'Nothing Ventured, Nothing Gained' School of Navigation," she laughed leaning closer to me in the little boat. "So am I."

"Then you believe in the peaceful coexistence of opposites," I returned catching the fragrant scent of the daisies in her hair as the breeze picked up.

"Iron and earth are certainly opposed," she reflected coloring a little, "and the mouse and swallow are both very willful. But perhaps if they put their wills together they can overcome their differences."

"Besides, we're in another time zone," I responded lightly brushing her wrist. It's well known the Oriental zodiac doesn't apply beyond the International Dating Line."

"Now that's something I hadn't considered," she admitted lightly touching my hand. "We'll just have to ask the official astrologer of Tibet."

"You mean there's an official government astrologer?" I said in amazement.

"Of course, he makes up the annual Tibetan calendar."

"How does it work?"

"There is a sixty-year cycle in which the twelve animals of the zodiac rotate along with the five elements. Even years are male, while odd years are female, so that the three qualities that make up each year do not repeat for sixty years. The astrologer's duty is to ascertain auspicious times for state occasions, trips, journeys, weddings, funerals, and other special occasions."

"That's the problem with traditional society," I interjected. "Everything is planned out in advance by the elders, including marriages. I bet there must be a lot of elopements."

"Or abductions," Kalavinka smiled in a careless and lighthearted manner. "Actually the system is more flexible than you might imagine. One of the astrologer's jobs is to fix lucky and unlucky days for the current year. Unlucky days are omitted altogether from the Tibetan calendar, so that some weeks have eight days. People observe an unlucky day as if it didn't exist. A more beneficial day of the month may be doubled in its place."

"That's a dynamite idea," I marveled. "Remind me to include it in my platform someday when I run for Congress."

"I think you'd make a good politician," Kalavinka complimented me. "Now tell me something about yourself and what really brought you to the Snow Lion last night."

Without going into too many details, I told Kali a little about the mystery we were engaged in. The blue sky, the warming saké, and most of all her infectious smile made me feel very mellow. Before long I told her everything about the missing Black Hat except the secret it was said to contain. I confided that Ginkgo and I had been retained to find the hat because of our unique investigative talents.

She seemed to be saddened by the loss of the hat but said she knew something was awry from Tyler Chase's erratic behavior, Bardo's depression, and even Professor Wilkins' uncharacteristic somberness.

I asked her whether she had seen Sergei Starov at the reception, and she said she thought so, but couldn't be sure. When I described his predilection for olives, she remembered a dapper middle-aged man who came into the kitchen with an empty canapé dish.

"But what he wanted even more than olives," she related, "was a stick of yak butter."

"Yak butter?" I said quizzically.

"Yes, the monks use it for their tea. The man said that he had a friend who was a connoisseur of fine foods and he would like to take a little home with him."

"Did you give him any?"

"No, I told him there was just a small amount for the personal use of the monks. But he wouldn't take no for an answer, saying it was very important. Finally I told him to ask the monk in charge and if he consented I'd be happy to give him some from the supply in the refrigerator."

"And did he?"

"I sent him up to see Bardo. Oh dear . . . . " Her eyes moistened with tears.

Leaning over and brushing away her tears with my hand, I assured her that the loss of the Black Hat wasn't her fault.

"The theft was premeditated. All Starov needed was a pretext for going upstairs."

"The curious thing is he never came back," she added, regaining her composure. "I saw him leave the Snow Lion in a big hurry."

"Was he carrying a large shopping bag?"

"Yes, how did you know?" She seemed awed by my deduction.

"Now think, carefully, Kali," I said taking her hand in mine, "do you remember anything distinctive about the bag? Was it heavy or light? Was there possibly something else in it?"

"Why, yes, there were designs of masks on the side, one of comedy and the other of tragedy," she remembered making no effort to withdraw her hand. "The bag was very elegant, blue on white. I was an actress in high school and college so something like that would catch my eye. It had the address of a boutique in the South. Atlanta, no, it was something else."

"New Orleans?" I said.

"That was it. How did you know?"

"Oh dear— " I lamented.

The sky had grown suddenly cloudy, and there was a chill in the air. Down river I could see the crew boat completing its run and turning around. Behind them rose the grey turrets of the Charles Street overpass that is affectionately known to Bostonians as the Salt and Pepper Bridge. I admired the oarsmen's dedication.

"What is your real name?" I asked, hoping to steer the conversation in a more cheerful direction.

"My old name is not important," Kalavinka replied evading my gaze and looking away at the shadows falling on the Boston skyline. "I have tried to let go of the past."

"I was just curious," I said, retreating from what was obviously a sensitive subject. "Kalavinka is a wonderful name, and there is no reason for another."

"Would you sing me a song?" I went on turning the jib and setting a slow diagonal course toward the dock. "My intuition tells me that you can sing as beautifully as the Himalayan bird after whom you are named."

"There's a lovely Tibetan song I learned at a retreat last year," Kalavinka said as her eyes met mine and resumed their glow.

She proceeded to sing the most beautiful song I had ever heard as we drifted lazily toward the center of the lagoon. Her voice was clear and melodious as a nightingale, and I was transposed to those celestial fields where the muses are said to sing and play their harps.

I didn't understand a word of Tibetan, but I sensed that the lyrics were very romantic and she had selected the song especially for me.

"That was lovely," I said looking into her dreamy blue eyes. "Is it a traditional love song?"

"In a way," she smiled brushing back the strands of her auburn hair that had blown about in the wind. "It's a song about a young woman on the Buddha path."

"Can you tell me what it's about?"

"The English goes something like this:

> *I sing a song of the soul's sorrow.*
> *The ephemeral body is like a rainbow in space.*
> *Its beautiful image vanisheth.*
> *When the time for dying is come,*
> *The religion of the gods' protectors is useful.*
> *Riches are like the honey accumulated by the bee.*
> *Although amassed by the bee, others enjoy the use.*
> *If one reflecteth well on the sufferings of the young and old,*
> *And on the sorrows of illness and unrequited love,*
> *The heart trembleth in the breast.*
> *But the passion which teareth faith from the heart*
> *Causeth the memory of it to be lost equally.*
> *I sing a song of certainty.*
> *Mother, keep it carefully in thy heart.*
> *I, young girl, am going to holy religion.*

After explaining the song, she took out a little wooden figurine in the shape of a bird from her cloth shoulder bag. She explained that it was a Kalavinka carved by a monk in Tibet. I held out my hand, and hesitating ever so briefly she placed her own in mine.

"You are as lovely as the Goddess Tara and no doubt as wise," I said boldly closing my hand around the little carving and weighing it appreciatively. "Have you studied the Tantra?"

"So you do know something of Tibetan Buddhism?" she blushed. "Then you probably also know that my vows prohibit me from a relationship with an uninitiated disciple?"

"No male iron mice, no unbaptized disciples. No wonder there are so many monks in Tibet," I quipped. "All the mandala dating services must go broke."

"Seriously, though," I went on as my metaphor brought a smile to her lips, "how does one become a disciple?"

"You must be invested with a sacred thread by an incarnate lama and perform ten thousand grand prostrations to Avalokiteshvara, the Bodhisattva of Compassion."

I sank down into the boat to ponder this obstacle to our relationship as the crew boat moved across our bow. The black coach barked something from the helm. I looked up, and with his upraised oar he appeared as gigantic as a Viking against the blue horizon.

"Jeffrey," Kali said apprehensively. "They're trying to cut us off."

Suddenly the crew boat drew alongside, and I felt the hardened end of the oar in the pit of my *hara*. The black coach pushed me overboard as I struggled, and two of the crew—beefy young men with Harvard sweatshirts and headbands—boarded the sailboat. Binding Kali with her turquoise scarf over her mouth and a rope about her wrists, the pirates rapidly maneuvered both boats to the Cambridge shore and disappeared into a waiting white Cadillac.

Treading water and feeling like a mouse who had just been caught in a steel trap, I clung to a life preserver that the abductors had mercifully left behind. All that remained of my new love was the little wooden carving of the bird and the petals of the white and yellow daisies floating in the placid water.

6

REVENGE OF THE MALE IRON MOUSE

The decaf in the cup was muddy, and I stirred it slowly with a spoon. The waitress returned with some sugar and cream, but I told her no thanks. The coffee shop opened up to a bar, and strains of an old rock hit of the sixties wafted softly through the room. From my table, partially obscured by the dividing wall and the rolling coffee cart, I had a good view of the entrance into the Holiday Inn and the elevator in the lobby without being observed.

Two young women in skimpy swimsuits swept through the corridor on their way to the pool. They were humming the refrain from the jukebox—"Come on baby, do the locomotion with me"—and turning the heads of the local talent. But I was too preoccupied with the task at hand to take much notice. I checked my watch. Ginkgo had gone out to The Great Wall, a Chinese restaurant across the street, and should have been back by now. What if his scheme didn't work? I'd have to switch to Plan B and go in alone.

Three floors up, in Room 345, Kalavinka was being held captive by Phil Lord, a nationally known deprogrammer, her parents, and several ex-disciples of the Tibetan Buddhist community. Lord, a former star fullback at the University of Southern California, a Green Beret, and a successful Afro-American business executive, had undergone a crisis in middle age when his company went bankrupt, his marriage fell apart, and his only child, a son, joined a militant Japanese Buddhist sect. "Seeing the light," Lord had become a born-again Christian, directed his enormous energy, and turned his talents in organization and sales to doing the work, as he was fond of saying, "of Him after whom I was named and have my being."

In just a few years, he had earned a reputation as the most successful and feared deprogrammer in the country. Out of a penthouse in L.A.'s Orange County, he launched a new movement, The Apostles, a network of parents, ex-disciples, and Christian and Jewish fundamentalists dedicated to saving America's children from godless Eastern sects, modern heretical movements, and false messiahs. As a minority group member, he prided himself on his organization's ecumenical ties, and many of his clients were Catholics and Jews, as well as evangelical Protestants. He had even once helped a Muslim belonging to the traditional Sunni sect abduct a wayward family member who had become a Sufi dancer.

Though he had the unofficial backing of many law-enforcement authorities, Lord was opposed by civil libertarians and by many mainstream religious bodies. Outside of the Southwest, the Bible Belt, and other areas where forced conversions were part of the local landscape, Lord scrupulously conducted all of his operations in a public hotel or motel. Usually parents or other family members were present, lest legal charges be filed.

The modus operandi varied little: the subject would be snatched in a meticulously planned operation, military fashion, usually in a remote place, and taken to the motel room, where parents, friends, ex-devotees, and Lord himself—a former prisoner of war interrogator in Vietnam—would spend hours grilling the individual and trying to break his or her attachment to the new way of life. Often, after two or three days of marathon witnessing, Bible reading, tearful pleading, cajoling, promises, and threats of damnation, the person would give in. Lord's own son, LeRoy, was his first successful deprogramee, and with his wife, Grace Ann, also reborn in the faith, the family was now reunited. Critics pointed out that Brother Lord was also making considerably more money than when he ran CFS Incorporated, a chain of fast food restaurants featuring chicken fried steak, but Lord justified his high fees with escalating legal costs. The Saudi prince reportedly paid him $1 million to deprogram his son, an engineering student at Stanford. In one northern state, however, Lord had recently overstepped his bounds and was forced to post bond because of his strong-arm tactics. Smarting from a tarnished media image, his venture into Massachusetts, the cradle of religious liberty, was undoubtedly a personal as well as theological challenge.

As I waited for Ginkgo, I reviewed what had transpired after the events at the marina. It had not taken me long to recognize Lord and piece together the puzzle of Kali's abduction and whereabouts. While swimming to the landing, I recognized the white Cadillac as the car we had seen the night before with Lord playing the part of the chauffeur. The older couple were undoubtedly Kalavinka's parents—the former China missionaries. I recalled her mentioning that they were now living in Dallas. Their destination, the Holiday Inn in North Cambridge, was only about five minutes' walk from our house and fifteen minutes from the Snow Lion.

Still sopping wet, I hitched a ride from Memorial Drive into Harvard Square and reconnoitered the Holiday Inn. It was located on Mass Ave, on the right going north, just up from the Law School. Sure enough, the white Caddy was in the portico of the three-storey motor court. I would have liked to have gone right in, one on one, but I was no match for Lord and his zealots.

Back home at Potter Park, I found Ginkgo with a room full of men, women, children, and animals. From past experience, I knew there was nothing I could do but wait until he had patiently dealt with everyone who had come for advice. In most cases, the people had been vegetarian or macrobiotic for a while and just needed some adjustments. To a young man with anemia, he recommended increased consumption of iron-rich green leafy vegetables. To another with high blood pressure, he advised no animal food, including fish, and regular use of grated daikon and shiitake mushrooms. A heavy-set woman with diabetes wanted to know whether she was improved enough to have desserts yet, and Ginkgo cautioned her to wait for awhile and if she craved a sweet taste to drink the broth from cooking together sweet vegetables such as onions, carrots, cabbage, and hard winter squash. A young couple who were having trouble conceiving were told to cut out all milk, cheese, and other dairy food which was blocking the woman's Fallopian tubes and preventing implantation.

In addition to the usual number of dogs and cats who had come down with arthritis, heart disease, or cancer by eating the hamburgers, ice cream, and other processed left-overs of their owners, there were several creatures from the wild. There was a Northern spotted owl from Washington that had been sent via Air Ambulance. The little bird lived in the old-growth forests and broke its wing when it got entangled in some aluminum cans, the result of encroaching civilization. The owl had no escort and needed physical therapy, as well as dietary counsel, so Ginkgo elected to keep it, and warned his cat, Descartes, who cast a hungry eye in its direction, that the little bird still had one good wing, sharp claws, and could probably fend for itself

While thinking what to name the owl, I glanced again at my watch. It was 10:25 p.m. A gofer from upstairs would be down any minute to fetch the take-out Chinese food from across the street. Earlier Ginkgo had charmed the receptionist in the coffee shop into telling one of Lord's minions who called for sandwiches and soft drinks to be delivered upstairs that the microwave oven was offline and the kitchen was closed for the night. He had her recommend The Great Wall, the trendy Chinese restaurant across the street. Ginkgo noted that the deprogrammers were probably tired of Holiday Inn cooking by now anyway and would be happy for a change. The missionary parents, ensconced in the room adjacent to the one where Kali was being held captive, were probably fond of Chinese food as well.

The soft glow of a red light switched on above the elevator, and a tall young man with a long ragged ponytail and macramé headband came down and strode through the lobby to the front door. I recognized him as one of the oarsmen. The Apostles of the Lord, as the ex-devotees were known, were generally heavy set and not to be messed with. As Ponytail made his exit, Ginkgo strode in from the front door adjoining the pool. He was beaming from ear to gargantuan ear, a sign that his mission had been a success. A wave of relief passed through me. At least we wouldn't have to go in as TV repairmen—Plan B—and pretend to install a new Christian cable broadcast channel. I knew nothing of electricity, at least not the artificial electromagnetic kind.

Ginkgo went over to the hostess and said something in muted tones, which caused her to blush, and then came over to the table and plunked himself down.

"Now it's just a matter of waiting," he grinned, picking up the salt shaker and pouring a healthy dose into my coffee cup.

"What took so long?" I asked.

"Our friends upstairs kept changing their mind about what to order," he replied salting some raw carrot sticks the waitress brought in. "First they were going to share everything. Then the parents wanted a special order of Dim Sum. A few minutes later,

Lord called back and requested sharkfin soup."

"I think he did that only to intimidate Kalavinka," I interrupted grimacing. Coffee with salt is awful.

"Any trouble with the Chinese?" I inquired asking the waitress to bring me another cup when she came by for a refill.

"None," he chuckled. "So many people have complained about MSG in their food that when I explained we wanted three times the usual amount, they were happy to oblige."

As we talked, Ponytail returned carrying two enormous shopping bags filled with the take-out items. Little did he know what lay in store.

"How long do you give the kidnappers?" I asked helping myself to a carrot stick.

"For a healthy person, like me—or you," he responded, hesitating for a second whether to include me in his description, "we would react to the chemicals instantly. But to Lord and some of the beefy crew upstairs, it might take 15 or 20 minutes before any effects are felt."

"Actually, they're not such a bad lot," he went on. "As I have often said, lawbreakers and criminals are just a little too yin or yang. The yang ones have an excess of energy that they use to correct an imbalanced social order through force or violence. The yin ones have weak health and judgment that causes them to cheat or steal. In both cases, proper eating, proper activity, and cultivating a true dream in life will change their behavior."

About ten of eleven, Ginkgo motioned toward the elevator. We agreed that it would be best to strike before 11:00 p.m. when they might turn on the TV and get a jolt of adrenaline from the evening news.

My heart was pounding by the time the clunky lift reached the third floor. I just hoped Kali hadn't eaten very much so she could appreciate the risks we were taking on her behalf.

In the hallway, sprawled in front of the parents' room was a lithe, bearded young man. He was clutching his stomach and panting for breath. The overdose of MSG had begun to do its job.

"A fallen Apostle," Ginkgo observed, bending down and gently stimulating a pressure point on the back of his second toe. The spot was traditionally massaged to overcome the effects of food poisoning. "A pity, the yin are affected first."

We stepped over the prostrate man and proceeded several

rooms to Room 345. "Try the door," Ginkgo indicated with his walking stick.

It was open as he surmised, and we entered nonchalantly. Two more minions were sprawled out—one on the olive carpet and the other on a double bed—and there was the sound of someone coughing in the bathroom. The two young men were both conscious and struggled to rise to their feet as we entered but couldn't make their limbs work. They tried to articulate something, but had trouble forming the words. I gave them a poke, and they fell on their backs, temporarily paralyzed, like upturned beetles.

In the adjoining room, Kali lay atop a queen-size bed. She had on a shapeless beige dress and black tights. Evidently they had made her change as part of stripping her of her identity and self-respect. She had passed out, a small white container of chop suey opened by her side.

Phil Lord was next to her, still conscious, and managed to rise to a sitting position when we entered. His steel grey eyes were flashing, and his face was twisted in a grimace. He had on an expensive charcoal suit, starched white suit, and red silk tie. He was even more powerfully built than I remembered from the marina. From his taut musculature, I could tell that he had maintained his athletic physique over the years. However, like the others sprawled around him with an acute case of the Chinese chills, his nervous system had been reduced to the consistency of jello.

"We are grateful to you for taking such excellent care of our young Buddhist friend here," Ginkgo said checking Kali's eyes and wrist pulse. "Rest assured, Lord, you have not been poisoned, just temporarily incapacitated by MSG. It will pass within the hour. I'll leave a bottle of umeboshi plums for you downstairs with the desk clerk. Take just one apiece. They will act as an antidote and reactivate your nervous system."

"Demons," Lord managed to hiss, grasping Kali's ankle with his right hand in a heroic effort to prevent us from taking her.

"You're lucky I don't throw you in the pool—from three stories up," I said indignantly, wresting his hand from her well shaped leg and scooping her up.

"And don't bother trying to find us, Lord," I added, grabbing Kalavinka's soft blue shoulder bag from atop the dresser. "This whole scene has been videotaped. If you ever lay a hand on Kalavinka again, we'll release the tape to the media, and you'll be back peddling chicken fried steak."

Lord hurled empty curses at us and tried valiantly to summon his fallen legions but to no avail. Everyone remained doubled up in pain and unable to move.

"It's all right, Kali," I whispered, as she came to in my arms. "You're safe. Ginkgo and I are here."

A peaceful smile flitted across her lovely face, and her eyes closed again.

"Don't forget to read your fortune," Ginkgo reminded the deprogrammer, emptying the small sack of fortune cookies in a wide spiral on the bed.

We left, just as we came, stepping over and around bodies in the front room and motel corridor. We took the stairwell instead of the elevator.

The night clerk raised an eyebrow as we passed through the lobby.

"Quite a party in Room 345," Ginkgo winked at him, leaving the umeboshi plums at the front desk. "A little something to sober them up." The night clerk winked back.

By the time we reached the parking lot and the cool night air, Kali's weight—light as she was—proved too great for me. I gladly handed her over to a pair of outstretched arms. I thought they were Ginkgo's. But when I looked up I was dumbfounded to discover they were those of Lance Andrews, the rugged skier we had met the evening before at the Snow Lion Meditation Center. He had on a smart blue polo shirt with gold buttons and tight-fitting gray slacks.

"Holy shit, what are you doing here?" he exclaimed.

"My sentiments exactly," I countered.

"Just jogging in the neighborhood. What does it look like?" he replied to my incredulity.

As luck would have it, Kalavinka missed her rescue and woke up in Lance's reassuring arms, not mine.

7

VISIT TO THE BRITISH HAT MUSEUM

At home, we revived Kalavinka with *ume-sho-ban*, a traditional macrobiotic home remedy consisting of a cup of bancha tea with a sliver of umeboshi plum and a few drops of shoyu or natural soy sauce. I was concerned with her safety and certain that her parents, Lord, and the avenging angels would try again. Though she was over twenty-one, age didn't matter. Her pursuers were determined to save her immortal soul from eternal torment in the fire hell. I encouraged her to press charges or get a court injunction, but she replied that one must have infinite patience to effect lasting change.

"The courts are not the right avenue for me," she explained. "I must convince my family by the light of my example."

As I set out a futon for her in the meditation room, the beams of a car headlight slanted across the front window. Good Lord, they've traced us already, I thought, and they're not just sore about my letting the air out of their tires when we left. But it was not the white Caddy. It was the Topaz, and when I went to the door, Christopher Loring's driver handed me an envelope with a wax seal and Ginkgo's name on it.

"These must be the passports," Ginkgo said when I brought in the parcel.

"Passports?"

"Yes, didn't I tell you, we leave in the morning for London."

I told him that I wouldn't leave without Kalavinka, to which he replied that she would only divert our attention and slow down the search for the Black Hat.

We had a rather heated debate, and in the discussion Kali's knowledge of Chinese and Tibetan came up. Ginkgo conceded that her linguistic skills might offset her weak ears and other constitutional deficiencies and agreed reluctantly that she could come along as a translator.

I went into the meditation room to tell Kalavinka the good news. She was attired in an oversize pastel blue-and-white Japanese robe that I had laid out, and as the color returned to her face she was once again her attractive self. I told her it would be too dangerous to go to the Snow Lion for her things and promised that we would pick up some new clothes in London. She smiled and lightly caressed my hand. I kissed her on the forehead and blew out the candle. That night I slept right outside her door, like one of the wrathful deities that guards the entrance to a Buddhist temple, in case we had unexpected visitors.

But the night was peaceful enough, and the next morning we left Logan Airport for England without a hitch. On the plane, over champagne and homemade snacks, I recounted how I had first met Ginkgo at a peace demonstration at MIT during which he was observing noses as part of his studies in visual diagnosis. Actually, it was not my proboscis that attracted his attention—it was really very average. Rather it was my malaria—a souvenir of my journalistic tour of duty in the Middle East. Amazed at Ginkgo's on-the-spot diagnosis, I took up his offer to recuperate in his home in exchange for some light assistance. As my health improved under his care, I started working part-time for the Clamshell Alliance—an antinuclear group—and writing for local community papers.

"Ginkgo is Holmes and Watson rolled into one," I concluded after relating some of his exploits, "but unlike Holmes and Watson he does his own cooking."

"But isn't Sherlock Holmes fictional?" Kalavinka protested, accepting some chestnut *ohagis*. I had made the small half-pounded sweet rice cakes to take along on our trip.

"Many people think so," I replied refilling her champagne glass and peering across the wing into the darkness. "Sir Arthur Conan Doyle, Watson's literary agent, let the public believe he had concocted the stories in order to protect his subject's privacy."

At Heathrow Airport, we were met by a young man from the Community Health Foundation, the local macrobiotic center, who escorted us to their headquarters in Nottingham. It was nearly evening by the time we arrived, and we were weary from the events of the last two days. After a hearty repast of leek soup, seven-grain casserole, steamed vegetables, laver bread, plum pudding sweetened with barley malt, and grain coffee, I went out with Kalavinka to pick out new clothes while Ginkgo made some telephone calls and retired early.

The next morning over breakfast of miso soup and sourdough bread with apple butter, Ginkgo triumphantly produced a copy of the Dharmapa's British itinerary which he had obtained from the London Tibetan Center. The first evening of his two-day visit to the U.K., following his arrival from Zurich, the Tibetan lama had attended a private reception for members of the center. Ginkgo said he had verified that no dignitaries, civic leaders, or art dealers, including Starov, were present. The next morning the Dharmapa had visited the British Hat Museum in Paddington and then had been driven to Samaye Ling, a Tibetan retreat about three hours' drive north, just over the border in Scotland. The following day the Dharmapa had returned to London and after leading a private meditation session left for Heathrow and the flight to Boston.

We all agreed that the British Hat Museum seemed like the most promising place to start our investigation. The staff of the Tibetan Center could provide us with little enlightenment about this curious place or why the Dharmapa went there, so we hailed a cab to see for ourselves. The big black taxi provided a modicum of warmth against the damp and cold. I hoped to relieve Kalavinka of her lingering chill by snuggling up next to her. But every time the taxi took a curve, she slid toward Ginkgo. I couldn't remember if it was centripetal or centrifugal force, but driving on the left side of the road mandates an entirely different yin-yang game plan for the romantic traveler.

On the way, Ginkgo instructed the driver to stop briefly in front of the hat emporium's more famous namesake, the British Museum. Inside, Ginkgo flashed our diplomatic passports to the startled guards, who waved us through a long waiting line, and we went into the Oriental exhibition room for a moment of *darshan*, or audience, with the world's oldest printed book: a tenth century copy of the *Diamond Sutra*. The *Diamond Sutra* is a Mahayana Buddhist scripture attributed to Avalokiteshvara, the Bodhisattva of Compassion whom the Dharmapa is said to embody. Slipping the passports back into his orange rucksack, Ginkgo chuckled, "These are good for something anyway."

After this diplomatic courtesy call, Ginkgo telephoned Sergei

Starov, the Russian art dealer, and learned from his answering service that he was in Scotland and wasn't expected back until evening. Ginkgo left an enigmatic message that he assured us would bring results: "I have what you want and will meet you tomorrow afternoon at 1 p.m. on the Greenwich excursion boat on the Thames. Come alone." He left the message in the name of Captain Goodwin of the Museum School, Boston.

"Who is Captain Goodwin?" I asked.

"All will be revealed at the proper time," he replied whistling a few bars of *Yankee Doodle*.

Ten minutes later, the taxi deposited us at the British Hat Museum in Paddington. Housed in an ornate Victorian manor house whose grey cupola curiously resembled a bowler—the fashionable men's felt hat of the nineteenth century—the Museum was established in the early 1900s by Cecil Athelstane, a West End impresario, who had acquired historic costumes from the London stage and the private collection of hats amassed by Harold Dumfrey, a seventeenth century Parliamentarian. Inside the vestibule, beneath a faded but debonair portrait, a display case exhibited Lord Harold's trademark, a tall Cavalier hat with a wide brim and cartwheel ruff, that he had worn at the side of Charles I in the Great Civil War.

"It looks like a witch's hat," marveled Kalavinka, admiring the tall crown.

"Aye, and a shocking bad hat 'tis, lassie," exclaimed a lilting voice behind us.

An elderly man, attired in a slightly rumpled blue suit, light grey vest, shiny black shoes, and a threadbare dun skullcap introduced himself as James Ryder, Jr. the director of the Museum.

"The hat of glory in one generation becomes the hat of ridicule in the next," he nodded solemnly, lifting a cane of polished hazel toward the Cavalier's hat.

"Everything changes into its opposite," mused Ginkgo introducing us and signing the big guest register in the lobby.

"Aye, such is life." Ryder momentarily scanned our heads with squinting blue eyes as he led us to the nearby cloakroom.

Ginkgo had the hood of his heavy maroon sweatshirt pulled up. Kalavinka had her turquoise scarf tied back over her fetching auburn locks and the fresh daisies in her hair. I alone stood bareheaded.

"The trick is to keep up with the times and know which hat to wear," Ryder confided handing our wraps to an attendant. "The only thing worse than wearin' the wrong hat is na wearin' a hat 't all." The old man raised a gnarled finger in my direction.

"Are you implying that a man without a hat is less than human?" I protested. "Or woman, for that matter?" I hastily added, sensing Kalavinka's latent feminist sensitivities.

"A bloke withou' a hat is na' yet a real man," the old man chuckled rubbing his dark forehead, "and a lassie withou' a scarf or headpiece is to be pitied. But no harm intended, laddie, to ye or the beasties. Some of our wee friends in the animal world ha' also worn grand headpieces."

Conducting us into the central exhibition room, he limped over to a large floppy hat like the one worn by the old burgher on a box of Quaker Oats. Ryder explained that it belonged to Baron Jeffrey of Wem, the apoplectic dog of James II, and was the ancestor of the modern bowler.

"Hmm, too many pastries," murmured Ginkgo, scrutinizing the likeness of Baron Jeffrey in a small portrait besides the cabinet. "Sugar weakened his circulatory system and caused a stroke. 'Sugarloaf' is truly an appropriate name for this large, floppy hat."

"A hat embodies the spirit of its owner," Ryder went on, pointing to the famous hat worn by Napoleon on his retreat from Moscow and the subject of many paintings. "They show your station in life. From a king's crown to a dunce's cap, everyone has his proper headpiece."

"And I suppose the bigger the hat, the more powerful the wearer?" I drew the obvious conclusion.

"Aye, laddie, in many quarters, that is true. In the Church, the bishop's hat increased in height as the wearer acquired greater wisdom. But there are natural limits to be observed. 'Tis a pity, but England's most famous naval hero, Lord Nelson, died 'cause he exceeded those limits."

Near the second floor balcony overlooking the rotunda, he pointed to the Chelink, the famous diamond-encrusted, feather-plumed hat that had been presented to the British Admiral by the Sultan of Turkey.

"Inside it had its own clockwork that turned the precious stones. In the great battle of Trafalgar, a French marksman observed the diamonds twinkling on an enemy headpiece and drew a bead on the illustrious Admiral. Let that be a lesson to thee, my lad."

Excusing himself to greet some children on a class tour, Ryder hobbled off leaving us to browse on our own. I could see that his eyes lit up when he carefully took each of their little bonnets and caps to the cloakroom.

The museum was a veritable cathedral of hats. The rooms were organized more or less geographically. The large central rotunda extending two stories up was naturally devoted to hats of the British Isles, with adjacent rooms displaying headgear from earlier epochs and far-flung regions of the once glorious British Empire. In addition to Nelson's and Napoleon's famous hats, six other prominent headpieces dangled from the ceiling by invisible guidewires. Their juxtaposition reminded me of mock dogfights between World War I bi-planes in the aviation wing of the Smithsonian Institution.

The fool's cap of Rahere, Henry I's court jester, faced the broad plumed headpiece of the twelfth century monarch. Queen Victoria's dainty lace bonnet remained suspended for all time, still inspiring General Chinese Gordon's fez to ever greater deeds of daring-do. Mahatma Gandhi's soft white homespun cap hung across from Winston Churchill's hard black homburg—a most improbable Damacles Sword to cut the British Empire. Four beanies that once graced the heads of the Beatles knelt in obedience to an elegant green evening hat worn by Queen Elizabeth on her first tour of the Commonwealth.

A quick survey of the thousands of hats that human beings have worn throughout history showed that Ryder was right. The main purpose of hats was not functional—to protect from cold, rain, snow, heat, or other inclement weather—but social and ritualistic. Throughout history and across the cultures, people signified their status in society by their headgear. In the Netherlands, women traditionally wore caps with metal discs indicating their religion. Round discs signified they were Catholics, square ones Protestants. In Italy, the traditional *tovaglia*, made from linen which is starched and folded, comes in many colors. Green indicates the wearer is unmarried, red married, and black widowed. The Uluns, a nomadic tribe of Central Asia, have large felt hats decorated with colored beads indicating the number of stallions, mares, and foals in the family or clan.

My favorite hat of those on display came from Lappland and was known as the Cap of the Four Winds. It had a thick crown stuffed with down or raindeer hair and four bright tassels on top decorated with red, yellow, green, and blue stripes.

"Now that's the kind of hat that would keep you warm in Tibet or Cambridge," I remarked to Kalavinka setting it on her head. Some of the folk and peasant hats hung on pegs and visitors were encouraged to try them on.

"I certainly wouldn't be lost in a crowd wearing this," she laughed adjusting it to a fashionable tilt.

"And do you know what I'd do if you wore it like this with all the four points facing front?" I asked flipping the tassels to the front.

"Well, with all these tassels in my face, I doubt whether you'd attempt anything romantic. You must have something meteorological in mind, such as reading the direction of the wind."

"I'd pull off your mitten," I smiled lightly grabbing her wrist.

"My mitten!" Her eyes widened in surprise.

"Sure, see here. It says that in Lappland wearing the tassels in the front indicates the wearer is single. When a young man takes a fancy to a young woman, he tries to pull off her mitten. If she agrees, it means she lets him have her hand in marriage."

"And if she doesn't agree," Kalavinka blushed, flipping the tassels on the hat to the back, spoken-for position and putting her hands in the pockets of her white cardigan in mock rejection, "she gives her suitor one of these."

From behind her back, she produced a big red fool's cap and put it on my head. The tall stiff hat reminded me of the jester's cap worn by Annemarie, the pantomime on the Cambridge Common. A tag indicated that it was of recent vintage: a dunce's cap bestowed by Chinese Red Guards on their enemies during the Great Cultural Revolution.

"I get the distinct impression I've been naughty and must go stand in the corner," I confessed.

"And while you're there, you could start on ten thousand Grand Prostrations," she teased. "Even in Lappland, the formalities must be observed."

"Very smart, Milton," a deep voice from behind us boomed. Ginkgo had returned from surveying the upstairs of the museum.

"That's what you'll be if you wear this hat," he continued, running his hand up and down the smooth conical crown. "The purpose of the dunce's cap is to make you more intelligent, not to set you apart as foolish. Its tall spiral shape is designed to bring you an extra charge of ki or heaven's force."

"Jeffrey has too much heaven's force as it is," Kalavinka quipped taking the cap off me and putting it back on a its pedestal.

Ginkgo produced a little spiral-bound notebook in which he had been classifying hats into yin and yang categories and fashioning a theory of history based on the size, shape, color, and fabric used in their construction.

"Geographically, we can distinguish three types of hats," he explained as he conducted us through the Latin portico. "In the tropics people usually wear large hats with wide brims made of palm leaves, straw, feathers, or other very light material. The sombrero here is a good example. These hats are more yin—large, soft, expanded. In the cold and polar regions, people wear sturdy hats made of fur, skin, or other strong animal material. The Mongolian felt fur hat is typical. These hats are more yang—small, hard, compacted. In the temperate regions of the world, people generally wear hats made of cloth, linen, or some other plant material. These hats are more balanced."

Motioning for us to follow him, we entered the American Room, a small antechamber that served to remind us of our country's former colonial status.

"As the United States grew more contracted and beef from the West reached the American table, hats became more horizontal and less vertical," Ginkgo said pointing to the change in fashion at the end of the nineteenth century. "Note the difference between Abraham Lincoln's tall stovepipe hat and Teddy Roosevelt's Rough Rider hat with a broad brim."

Despite the room's small size, it contained an impressive array of hats from the nation's chief executives. I shuddered at the thought of what would have happened if Washington had worn a Chelink crossing the Delaware.

"Women's plumage too changed," he added, noting a row of ladies' hats adorned with egret feathers that were fashionable in the 1880s. "The Audubon society and the modern environmental movement started to protect the egret which was being killed by the thousands. Naturally—or should I say unnaturally—the source of the desire on the part of modern American woman to dress up as a feathered bird was the ingestion of too much eggs and poultry."

"During the next stage of development, " Ginkgo continued his tour guide lecture, "when the country grew more expansive in the early twentieth century—from the introduction of more sugar, soft drinks, ice cream, and other relaxing substances—hats became taller, lighter, and more expanded again. Hence the popularity of the top hat in the '20's and '30's." To illustrate his point, he pointed to the silk hat worn by Franklin D. Roosevelt at his first inauguration.

"And what phase are we in today—waning or waxing?" Kalavinka asked admiring some of the flapper hats of the '20's.

"Modern society has become so contracted," Ginkgo chuckled, "that hats have almost gone out of style. Not wearing any hat—or clothes, for that matter—is very yang, though there are exceptions." I could feel his penetrating gaze.

"A capital theory, Inspector," interjected Ryder, who had just reappeared after bidding farewell to the schoolchildren. "But in my 'umble experience, hats have declined owing to a general decrease in nobility. Democracy—a decline in monarchy, empire, and law and order in general—that's what killed the hat. Observe this space here between Mr. Eisenhower and Mr. Nixon. During his campaign in 1960, President John Fitzgerald Kennedy, appeared without a hat. The world has not been the same since."

"Now that's a novel conspiracy theory," I observed trying to suppress my incredulity. "JFK sealed his fate when he appeared bareheaded before the gods."

"In many parts of the world, laddie, it has been a crime for men to go without a hat or for women to go about with their heads uncovered," Ryder returned, shaking his white head at the apparent ignorance of the younger generation. "Hats are the bedrock of the social order."

With a sign in her radiant look for me to deal tenderly with him, Kalavinka took the old curator's arm and gently led him over to a bench. To my annoyance, I found myself the odd one out as Ginkgo assumed the seat on her right side, and I was left to bring up a small folding chair.

Ryder's prattle that the hat makes the man—or woman—struck me as very much like Polonius's moralizing advice to Hamlet. If he were not so decrepit, I would have been tempted to thrust him aside. Ginkgo seemed to read my thoughts and sent me an Elder Hamlet ghost-like glance to cool my ardor, while my comely Ophelia gave the old man a daisy from the garland in her hair.

"I agree, Mr. Ryder, that the wearing of hats is connected with power," Ginkgo ventured with an air of deep sagacity, "but of a spiritual rather than a material kind. The earliest hat in both East and West, according to one of the exhibits, was a small skullcap."

"That would be the *potasus* or *pileus*," the wizened museum director explained raising his cane toward the Greco-Roman Room. "It was popular in the ancient Hellenistic world, among the Celts, in Arabia, and many cultures. It was the emblem of freed men."

"Aha," exclaimed Ginkgo tugging at his earlobe as he does when he is challenged. "Free men, Mr. Ryder, not freed men! The original hat, a small skullcap, was worn over the crown *chakra* at the top of the head."

"Crown checker?" He leaned toward Ginkgo cupping his ear.

Kalavinka lightly touched the top of Ryder's head to indicate what Ginkgo was referring to. *Chakra* is the Sanskrit word for one of seven energy centers that are believed to be aligned in the spiritual channel between the top of the head and the intestines and reporductive region.

"The crown chakra is traditionally the seat of universal consciousness," Ginkgo went on holding his palm level over Ryder's head for a few moments. "In traditional cultures, when a man reached maturity—adulthood—he was given a small cap to put over the crown chakra."

"Like the Jewish yarmulke," I spoke up as Kalavinka flashed me an admiring glance.

"Exactly," Ginkgo nodded his head. "Such a hat lightly stimulates the crown chakra and serves as an everpresent reminder of the wearer's spiritual goal. Such a cap is the sign of a free man—a man who understands the Order of the Universe—not just a yeoman who has graduated from economic or political servitude."

"The only trouble with your theory, Inspector," Ryder replied, shaking his head, "is that for thousands of years before the *pileus*, human beings wore animal skulls, skins, and hides on their heads. These predate skullcaps and all other cloth hats."

"From time immemorial, the American Indians wore buffalo heads and feather headdresses," I chimed in knowledgeably, catching the old curator's approving eye.

"Aye, laddie, headpieces originated with the ancestral hunt. Way back when the world was covered with ice, our kinfolk put on antlers, skins, and hides to absorb the vital force of the animal. Later, when the earth warmed up again and farming started, people switched to wearing wreathes, floral crowns, and cloth hats."

I could see that Ginkgo was about to launch into one of his favorite topics—the Golden Age, a paradisiacal era of natural agriculture that he believed preceded hunting and the ice age.

"What about the little skullcap on your head?" I asked Ryder, diverting the conversation and sparing us a recitation of Homer, Ovid, and the other ancient poets Ginkgo was fond of quoting in favor of his theory.

The small dun-colored hat the old curator wore over his thinning white hair appeared to contradict his social Darwinism. "I cannot help but notice that you aren't wearing a buffalo's head or raven's beak."

"You ha' divined me secret, laddie," Ryder acknowledged with an echo of mischief in his raspy voice. "This is me favorite hat, a small monk's cap from the Middle Ages. But do na' misunderstand me. The same principle holds true for cloth hats as for animal skulls. The soul remains. And the soul is na' always with the big and tallest but with the weeist."

"The soul?" Kalavinka asked in her quiet way.

"Ay, lassie, the vital principle," he replied reaching over and squeezing her hand. "I discovered it over a half century ago. I was an ambitious young man and had just started working here as a clerk. It was the time of the Great War and I had a ken to join the Navy and be another Drake or Nelson. But the Navy would na' have me. They said I was na' big or strong enough. Naturally it was a grand let down. By the by, I was promoted to apprentice restorer. One day, Mr. Athelstane, the founder and director of the Museum, said that an American movie director had paid a pretty penny for the exact design and measurements of Napoleon's hat. They wanted to make a duplicate for a film. He authorized me to wear it in order to make notes for the movie director. I wore it for the better part of three days. Of course, this raised me spirits tremendously. I felt I was the luckiest lad in all Brittanica. The experience did wonders for me confidence. But it was totally different than I expected. I thought I would be filled with courage and bravery. But all it gave me was nightmares.

"Well, that was me introduction to the soul of hats," Ryder continued folding his thin hands to his chest and sniffing the daisy Kalavinka gave him. "From that time on, with Mr. Athelstane's permission, of course, I tried on the helmets of Crusaders and Saracens, the war bonnets of Indian chiefs and African warriors, the headgear of

Samurai and Aztecs. They too produced bloody nightmares and feelings. Then in the course of things, I met and settled down with a sweet young lassie. She had the most beautiful Scottish bonnet a lad ever laid eyes on. My dreams of glory on the high seas and desert sands faded to the practicalities of domestic life.

"But I was hooked on hats. Some made me feel smart, others dumb; some brave, others cowardly; some peaceful, others violent. As the years wore on, I went from apprentice restorer to master felt-maker and eventually to Museum director. But I could na' resist wearing the hats of the grand ones. At one time or another, Bess—God rest her soul—and I tried on the hats of all the leading lights of society—Pitt, Disraeli, Queen Victoria, Lloyd George, Churchill, Hoover, Roosevelt. We relived the glorious achievements of the Empire, but also the terrible divisions and conflicts, the sadness and pain, the pity and regrets.

"Finally, in our middle years, Bess and I discovered the ordinary hats of everyday life—not new hats, mind you, but hats that ha' actually been lived in. A Viennese baker's cap, a Highlander's tam o'shanter, an Indonesian rug weaver's hat, a Sioux headband with only one feather. These hats were modest, but their souls were more stable and happy. The last twenty years of our life together was truly golden on account of these hats. For many years, my favorite hat was the *laripipe*."

"That would be one of the long, funny-looking fools caps," I recalled from one of the exhibits I had passed.

"In the sweet by and by, they used to carry their bob in the end of the laripipe," Ryder explained, brandishing his cane. "That's the source of our Old English phrase, 'Give someone a good larruping.'"

"What else has been kept in hats beside money," Ginkgo interjected, his curiosity aroused by this literary tale. "Was it customary at other times for people to store or hide things in their hats?"

"Aye, especially in the Victorian era," the stooped curator replied. "Edward Fitzgerald, the poet who translated the *Rubaiyat*, kept his pipe, tobacco, and boots in his top hat. Dr. Strong, the schoolmaster in *David Copperfield* kept word slips for his dictionary in his headpiece. According to Sherlock Holmes, Dr. Watson traveled about with his stethoscope in his topper. In your country, Abraham Lincoln stored papers in his stovepipe hat, which according to his law partner served as 'his desk and memorandum book.'"

"What about in recent times?" Ginkgo went on.

"Alas, your New York City police officers are the last of a dying breed," Ryder replied. "There is a small plastic pocket inside the department's dark blue, eight-pointed regular issue. On a trip to the States several years ago, I conducted an informal survey and found that your coppers keep a variety of personal momentoes, photographs of their wee 'uns, religious artifacts, good-luck charms, lottery tickets, and cricket cards in their hats but very little quid."

"Baseball cards, not cricket," I gently corrected him. "I guess court jesters like Rahere who hid their farthings in their laripipes weren't so foolish after all," I concluded.

"And a pretty penny he amassed," Ryder asserted admiringly. "Did you know that Rahere founded St. Bart's?"

"I'll be darned," I responded picking up on the nickname of the great London hospital. "St. Bartholemew's is famous as the site where Sherlock Holmes and Dr. Watson first met."

"Aye, Rahere founded it in the twelfth century," the ancient museum director explained, caressing the petals of the little yellow flower. "On a pilgrimage to Rome, he contracted malaria and vowed to build a hospital if he were healed of his affliction. In a dream, the Apostle Bartholemew appeared to him and indicated the site at Smithfield where the hospital was to be built. Upon Rahere's return to London, he raised money from wealthy merchants and churchmen. So in addition to sovereigns, his laripipe was full of mirth and laughter. In those days, sickness was believed to be the result of a melancholy humor. In addition to prayer, tom foolery was considered an excellent antidote for sickness. Rahere called it 'cure by myscheff.'"

"Sounds like Norman Cousins," I interjected a modern parallel. "He healed himself of a fatal illness by looking at old Marx Brother movies and other zany material."

"Aye, through pranks and pitfalls, merry clothes and a merry hat, Rahere restored the spirit of many an Englishman, beginning with the king. I loved wearing his old laripipe, but after Bess passed away, I grew lonely and despondent. Old Rahere's hat no longer cheered me up. I eventually returned to the church and took a ken to ecclesiastical hats. Of course, by now I had learned to stay away from the mitres and tiaras. Many of the ordinary monks' caps also gave me headaches and nightmares, but this one lifted me into a realm of grace tha' words canna' describe."

"No doubt, a saint's hat veiling the inner light," mused Kalavinka with the same sweet consideration. "A greater treasure than a monarch's crown."

"And this, Ryder, brings us to the object of our visit today," Ginkgo declared leaning forward in his cushion, keenly attentive. "The hat we are interested in not only gives the wearer tremendous ki, or soul as you would say. It is so strong that anyone who sees it is uplifted and transported into a realm of universal consciousness."

"Aye, the Black Hat of Tibet," Ryder said bringing his cane down hard on the floor. "Now there's a shocking good hat."

"The Black Hat," Ginkgo nodded looking evenly into the old man's misty eyes. "We understand the Dharmapa came to see you here last week. Please tell us how about that visit."

"The Black Hat is the most renowned hat in the Far East," Ryder began as a cloud momentarily passed over his weathered face. "The Museum's Board of Directors—distinguished scholars, producers, artists, designers—were concerned with what would happen to it after the Dharmapa attained his heavenly reward. Tibetan Buddhism is on the wane, and he may be the last of his line. The Board hoped that he would leave his hat to the Museum for permanent display and edification of future generations. It needs a stable place safe from revolutions, changes of government, sectarianism, and natural disasters. In the past, the Tibetan Center in London has helped us secure other rare hats from Central Asia. Through their good offices, we arranged for the Dharmapa to come here. We asked him to bring his hat so we could broach this proposition and measure and photograph it for future display."

Ginkgo dug his hands deeper into the large pocket on the front of his maroon pullover. He was clearly agitated about something.

"You have led a most adventurous life, Mr. Ryder" Ginkgo said at last. "I salute your discoveries. I believe you have fashioned a more dynamic theory of world history than Arnold Toynbee, Marshall McLuhan, or any other modern student of culture and civilization. But I believe there is something you have left out about your meeting with the Dharmapa. Your intentions were not entirely custodial. You planned to take the Black Hat and deliver it to Sergei Starov, the Russian art dealer who was posing as the Museum photographer."

The old man paled. "Borrow, Inspector, not take," he replied dropping his voice to a whisper. "Starov assured me he would na' leave the premises. He said he needed only five or ten minutes alone with the hat in the darkroom. Then he would return it to its box, and no one would be the wiser."

"No one but me," Ginkgo chuckled taking the old man's crippled hand and massaging its tawny skin. "What did he offer you?"

"I'm ashamed to say so, but he offered me enough quid to retire to Montecristi. That's a little village on the Pacific Coast in Ecuador. They make the world's best panamas—smooth as silk, fine as linen. Turn them upside down and they hold water just like a Stetson. The damp and chill here are na' good for me arthritis. All me savings have been eaten up by Bessie's past medical bills, and me salary goes into pain medications."

"That's written clearly enough across your face and limbs," Ginkgo noted.

"With just a few thousand quid," Ryder went on, "I could retire to Montecristi and supplement me pension as a guide for tourists looking for elegant boaters. It was a terrible temptation. I was of two minds about the venture from the start.

"The morning of the Tibetan's visit finally arrived. At the last minute, I called Starov and told him I could na' go through with it. He was furious and came over and threatened me, but I didn't give in."

"His signature on the guest book in the lobby was scrawled with full force," Ginkgo observed.

"So that's how you knew about him?" Ryder marveled.

"Yes, he signed in just before the Dharmapa."

"So what happened?" I asked hanging in suspense. "Did the Head Lama bring the Vajra Crown?"

"His Holiness arrived with a hat," Ryder resumed addressing me, "but 'twas na' the Black Hat. He turned up wearing a fore-and-aft—a Sherlock Holmes cap. He must have plunked down a few bob for it at a local souvenir shop."

"The Dharmapa has a marvelous sense of humor," Kalavinka said patting the old man's arm. "In Boston, he wore a White Sox baseball cap."

"Red Sox," I corrected her.

"Aye, lassie, I was completely taken aback. His Holiness explained that the Black Hat could na' be shown except during special ceremonies. As for preserving it in a museum, he said, and I remember his words exactly, 'The sacred hat has a way of reaching its proper successor.'

"After giving His Holiness a tour of the Museum, I asked him which hat he most fancied. He smiled and said the small one I had on. I offered to let him try it, and he put it on for a few moments and lapsed into a deep meditation. Then he thanked me, returned it, and advised me to go to Regent Park."

"Regent Park?" Kalavinka asked.

"Aye, lassie, the great botanical and zoological gardens about a mile from here."

"But why Regent Park?"

"Aye, why indeed? I told His Holiness that I was a wee bit lame, and the damp, cold weather, especially at this time of year, was na' good for me arthritis. I told him it was hard getting around without Bessie at my side. But he just smiled and said I must go to Regent Park, and as long as I had the monk's cap on I would never lack for companionship."

"And did you?"

"Na' yet, lassie." Ryder drew his coat around him, indicating that it was too cold to venture out.

"You are to be commended, Ryder, for resisting temptation and standing up to Starov," Ginkgo said much affected by the old man's story. "Remorse runs in the family, and your father would be proud of your decision."

"So you know about me personal background as well?" Ryder slapped his knee. "You ha' been sleuthing upstairs in the Sherlock Holmes' Room, don't deny it."

"You made it rather easy by leaving a bookmark in Dr. Watson's collected works on the shelf open to *The Adventure of the Blue Carbuncle*," Ginkgo explained clearing up the little mystery. "That's the story in which James Ryder Sr., your late father, played a leading role."

The name Ryder suddenly took on new meaning as the true identity and past of the old curator unfolded. As I later explained to Kalavinka, in *The Adventure of the Blue Carbuncle*, Sherlock Holmes was confronted with one of the most baffling puzzles of his career. The adventure began on Christmas morning when Peterson, a London policeman, arrived at 221B Baker Street and brought Holmes a rather seedy and disreputable hard felt hat and a good fat goose ready for holiday roasting.

The bobby explained that he had come upon some roughs attacking a stranger on the Tottenham Court Road early that morning. The policeman rushed up to defend the man from his assailants who had knocked off his hat. But the man, in evident shock, ran off, leaving his hat and Christmas goose behind. Inside the hat were the initials H.B., and on the goose's leg was a small card, "For Mrs. Henry Baker." As there were thousands of Bakers in London, returning the battered billycock to its owner presented Holmes with an intellectual problem. As for the goose, Holmes turned it over to Constable Peterson and his wife to "fulfill its ultimate destiny."

Over the next several days, Holmes ingeniously deduced the occupation, age, character, and habits of the hat's owner through microscopic examination of dust, stains, and other markings on the hat. Meanwhile, Peterson rushed back to Holmes' Baker Street flat and produced a scintillating blue stone that his wife had found in the crop of the goose. Holmes immediately identified it as the Blue Carbuncle, a precious gem found on the banks of the Amoy River in Southern China that had recently been stolen from the Countess of Morcar.

The Countess had been staying at the Hotel Cosmopolitan, and a local plumber was accused of taking the carbuncle from her jewel case. The plumber denied taking the stone, and the jewel had not been recovered. After finally locating Henry Baker through placing a classified in the newspapers, Holmes traced the goose back to a Mrs. Oakshott, who lived on the Brixton Road and fattened fowls for market. Then after further investigation, he confronted her brother, James Ryder, the head attendant at the Hotel Cosmopolitan, and forced him to confess that he had stolen the jewel. Ryder's confederate, Catherine Cusack, was the Countess's maid. She had let him in and out of the Countess's room. After the theft, Ryder tried to dispose of the carbuncle by force feeding it to a goose at his sister's house. However, when he later opened the goose that he asked his sister to set aside for him, he discovered that it was the wrong goose. The goose that swallowed the Blue Carbuncle was sold to Henry Baker.

Stricken with remorse, Ryder pleaded with Holmes for mercy. Sherlock Holmes thought for a long while, then opened the door leading out to Baker Street and, as it was Christmas time, let him go. "I suppose that I am commuting a felony," he explained to Dr. Watson, "but it is just possible that I am saving a soul. This fellow will not go wrong again. He is too terribly frightened. Send him to jail now, and you make him a jailbird for life. Besides, it is the season of forgiveness. Chance has put in our way a most singular and whimsical problem, and its solution is its own reward. If you will have the goodness to touch the bell, Doctor, we will begin another investigation, in which also a bird will be the chief feature."

"After Mr. Holmes pardoned my father," Ryder picked up the narrative, "he vowed to devote his life to helping others. He joined a missionary society and prepared for foreign service. But na' long after, Miss Cusack, the Countess's maid, discovered she was in a motherly way, and they married. My sister, Nellie, was born, and several years later I came along. Eventually, my parents received a call to minister in China, in Shansi Province, and left Nellie and me in the care of relatives. But alas, they died in a big uprising."

"That would have been the Boxer Rebellion," Kalavinka explained softly to me. "My parents were also missionaries in China, and as a child I heard many stories of that terrible event."

"So you grew up with your aunt and uncle, the Oakshotts?" I concluded.

"Aye, and a houseful of geese," Ryder smiled broadly.

"That would explain your liking for fowl," Ginkgo noted lightly massaging the old man's tightened shoulders.

"Aye, you could say that I grew up on roast goose, just like the one that swallowed the Blue Carbuncle," Ryder said.

"How did you get started at the Hat Museum?" I asked out of curiosity.

"One day, still a wee lad, I went to Baker Street to see Mr. Holmes and Dr. Watson. I wanted to tell them what became of me parents and of their final sacrifice. I told him how they had saved a whole village that was under siege. Mr. Holmes invited me in and listened thoughtfully to my story. He puffed on his pipe and said that he had done the right thing to let father go.

"Then I screwed up my courage and asked the great detective if I could become a Baker Street Irregular like Wiggins and some of the boys Father had told me about and whom I had read of in Dr. Watson's adventures.

"'The Irregulars have long since disbanded,' Mr. Holmes said wistfully. '"A shame, too, for they were my eyes and ears in the great city of London. Nothing could transpire without one of them quickly bearing the intelligence to Baker Street. But then so much has changed. Crime is on the wane, the official force is using fingerprints and other new-fangled methods, and small boys like yourself are more interested in earning a shilling by polishing the wheel-spokes of a new motorcar than patrolling the Thames.

"'I regret I have no work for such a fine boy as yourself,' Mr. Holmes continued, "'but I believe I know someone who does.' He paused for a moment and then went over to the hatrack by the fireplace.

"'Dr. Watson has abandoned me once again for the fairer sex, and shan't be needing this anymore.' He handed me Dr. Watson's old black bowler, gently brushing away a layer of dust which had accumulated despite the good housekeeping of Mrs. Hudson, their landlady.

"'Under the influence of the Prince of Wales, this regal headpiece has gone out of fashion,' Holmes went on referring to the recent ascension to the throne by Edward VI. "The good doctor now sports a fedora."

"'And what am I to do with his old topper?' said I.

"'Take this hat and go to the Covent Garden Theatre,' Holmes instructed me. 'Look up a Mr. Athelstane. He is an expert costumer. Indeed, he designed some of the operatic gowns worn by *the woman.*'"

"Of course, by the woman, he was referring to Irene Adler, the great contralto who outwitted Holmes in *A Scandal in Bohemia* and remained the love of his life," I explained for Kalavinka's benefit.

"Aye, laddie," Ryder picked up the narrative again. "Mr. Holmes dashed off a note and handed it to me. 'Athelstane is setting up a new Hat Emporium in the West End and has repeatedly solicited me for my old deerstalker.' He pointed to the famous ear-flapped cap by his Inverness coat on the rack by the mantle.

"'But I'm afraid I can't satisfy him, at least while there's some life remaining in this old frame and a divided world to unify,' Mr. Holmes continued resolutely. "Athelstane will be content with Watson's bowler here, and doubtless offer you a position as a small reward.'

"So that, Inspector, is how I made Mr. Athelstane's acquaintance and got started as an errand boy at the Hat Museum."

"What happened to Holmes' deerstalker?" I inquired. "Did you ever obtain it?"

"Nay, laddie," Ryder replied with a forlorn expression. "It followed Mr. Holmes to his retirement on the Sussex Downs. Mr.

112: *Inspector Ginkgo Tips His Hat to Sherlock Holmes*

Athelstane made many subsequent requests. They were politely answered with gifts of honey and royal jelly from the great detective's beehives, but alas no hat. A pity, of course, because it's even more famous than Napoleon's great hat. Every schoolboy, university don, and coal miner from here to Newcastle asks for it."

Ryder offered to show us around the Museum's Sherlock Holmes's Room, and we adjourned upstairs to a recreation of the great detective's sitting room at 221B Baker Street. It was like walking into the pages of a Conan Doyle adventure. Above the fireplace, on the mantle were replicas of the famous curved pipe and the Persian slipper where Holmes kept his tobacco. A bearskin hearthrug extended to the coal skuttle, and the sideboard containing index books and a gazetteer such as those Holmes once kept. To the side, looking out of the bay window was a deal-topped chemical table with an assortment of bunsen burners, retorts, a microscope, lens, and spirit lamp. On a small dining table was laid out a model of a sumptuous dinner from the larder of the good Mrs. Hudson, featuring—what else—roast goose!

The hatrack by the basket chair had a variety of hats that figured in Holmes' most famous cases and which Ryder had collected over the years. These included Henry Baker's hat that launched *The Adventure of the Blue Carbuncle*, Hugo Baskerville's large three-cornered hat, a silk top hat once worn by Colonel Moran at the Cavendish Club (and inside of which, as Ryder showed us, he used to conceal extra cards), and the tam-o'shanter worn by Joseph Harrison in *The Naval Treaty*.

There was also an elegant deerstalker. "Now whose hat is this?" I asked in surprise. "I thought you said Holmes kept his traveling cap."

"An understudy, as they say in the theatre," Ryder apologized holding up his cane. "Mr. Athelstene himself made it because of popular demand. "But as you can see from the plaque on the wall here, we are mindful to tell people it's na' the genuine article."

"What about Professor Moriarty?" I asked further. "Did he have a hat? Or was he one of the forsaken ones who went to limbo bareheaded?"

"Aye, and a formidable topper it was," Ryder recalled. "A real magician's hat, mind you. But its whereabouts constitutes a mystery. Like its owner, it probably remains at the bottom of the Reichenbach Falls after his final struggle with Sherlock Holmes."

In the sideboard, Kalavinka spotted a bright pink bonnet. Hobbling over to the cabinet, Ryder unlocked it and indicated that she could try it on.

"A perfect fit," she exclaimed, admiring herself in the reflecting lens of the microscope and adjusting the wide brim.

"Most sexy," I agreed. "The way you have it tilted down sharply to the right reminds me of Marlene Deitrich."

"Do I strike you as a sultry entertainer?" she replied. Then turning to Ryder with a sparkling smile, she added, "Whose hat is it, anyway?"

"A great actress's to be sure," he beamed. "Why it's Miss Adler's, of course. After marrying the King of Bohemia and retiring from the opera, she gave it to Mr. Athelstane in appreciation for designing many of her costumes."

While we sat around the table chatting and drinking tea brought in by an attendant, Ginkgo performed some palm healing on Ryder's hands. Holding his own broad right hand over Ryder's gnarled fingers and holding his left hand up to heaven, Ginkgo concentrated deeply, sending ki or natural electromagnetic energy to the arthritic joints and dispersing stagnation.

"How do you feel?" he asked the old curator after about ten minutes' treatment.

"Why, it's amazing," Ryder exclaimed picking up a teacup and balancing it in the palm of his hand, "there's a little movement in these middle two fingers for the first time in years. I say, Inspector, next to Mr. Holmes, you have the keenest mind and kindest heart of anyone I ever had the honor of meeting."

"That's one of the nicest compliments I've received," Ginkgo smiled deeply moved by the old man's words. "You have widened our own horizons immensely, James Ryder, and we are grateful to you for your help. Just one final word of caution. For better health and to reduce your arthritis, avoid savory geese and other animal food like this." Ginkgo pointed to the plastic goose and trimmings on the table.

Unzippering his rucksack, Ginkgo took out a packet of brown rice, some aduki beans, some miso in a little package, and a couple sticks of dried wakame seaweed. "If you eat nourishing foods like this, as well as plenty of fresh vegetables, your arthritis will gradually diminish. You can adjust to any climate and won't need to go to the tropics for relief."

Ginkgo took out a card with the name and address of the Community Health Foundation and pressed it into the old man's hand.

As we turned to leave, Ryder thumped his cane on the floor and called us back. Rummaging through a wastebasket under the dining table, he took out a faded deerstalker.

"I almost forgot," he said, brushing off some of the dust which had accumulated. "This is the Sherlock Holmes cap His Holiness was wearing when he visited last week. He left it behind, and we didn't have any use for it because of Mr. Athelstane's elegant reproduction here. I'm sorry it's so dusty, but it's a shame to discard anything, especially a hat. I'd like for you to have it, Inspector. Maybe it will come in handy in your quest."

Ginkgo accepted the checkered cloth cap with murmurs of thanks and absent-mindedly thrust it into his rucksack. I could see that his mind was focused on the next item of business: the meeting with Sergei Starov, the Russian art dealer and master thief.

In the vestibule, I helped Kalavinka tie the turquoise scarf over her head and pulled up the collar of my raincoat to hide my own bareheadedness. Ryder hobbled up to see us off and said that he was suddenly feeling so good after the palm healing that he would take that walk to Regent Park after all. Bidding farewell to our genial host and guide, we left the wondrous palace of hats and plunged into the thick London haze.

8

DOWN THE RIVER THAMES

The ancient spires of London gently rose and fell as the small steamship proceeded down the Thames. Though not as bold and brash as other international capitals, London had a timeless grace and charm as centuries of history and literature swept before us. Leaning against the rail, Kalavinka gazed intently at the far towers of Big Ben. She had struck up conversation with two little girls on deck, and they were eagerly pointing out to her famous landmarks on the Southwark side of the river including the spot where Jonathan Small threw the Agra Treasure overboard while being pursued by Holmes and Watson. The sun had come out, and Kali loosened the soft turquoise scarf around her head, letting her beautiful long auburn hair blow in the warm breeze.

On the other side of the deck, Ginkgo looked out toward the skyline of the City. As a tourist guide began to recite the rollcall of prominent heads that had been chopped off in the approaching Tower of London, nearly all the passengers who had been on the other side of the boat, including Kalavinka's two small acquaintances, rushed over so as not to miss any of the gruesome details. The English, young and old, have a passion for the sensational which has not diminished with time.

The grim toll in this chamber of horrors, we were surprised to learn, included Lord Harold Dumfrey, the Parliamentarian and hat fancier, who had prematurely tried to add the crown of Charles I to his collection when he crossed over to the Roundheads. According to legend, he denied his apostasy and insisted on wearing his own broad plumed Cavalier's hat to the block. Despite my own English ancestry, I found something alien in the British love of pomp and circumstance. Like most of my fellow countrymen, I am at heart a democrat and thumb my nose at the faintest odor of monarchy. As the ancient tower receded in the distance, I paid silent tribute to William Penn and other Quakers who refused to doff their hats to king or commoner and escaped the Lord High Executioner's axe by fleeing to America where the choice of wearing or not wearing a hat was an inalienable right.

Sergei Starov, the art dealer, had not shown up for the meeting—or at least not yet identified himself. Ginkgo appeared unperturbed. There were several dozen people on board the vessel, including a number of businessmen with valises. Anyone of them could be the debonair Russian-born thief. I imagined that he was checking Ginkgo out before he made his approach lest Scotland Yard or Interpol agents be close by. Prior to boarding, Ginkgo, Kalavinka, and I had split up and were now in different parts of the boat. Ginkgo assured us that Starov would not come alone, despite the message he had left with his answering service, and we should be prepared for action. Under his arm, Ginkgo carried a large oval hatbox that he had asked Kalavinka to obtain from Harrod's. Made of heavy bookbinder's stock, the hatbox was printed with an Old English pattern in navy and cream and trimmed in burgundy. Traditional drawstrings held the covers tight and simplified carrying. A bright blue ribbon and silver bow had been tied around the distinctive container for further elegance and protection.

The excursion boat picked up speed and moved into mid-river as London receded from view. I sauntered toward the stern and an isolated area between two lifeboats. By my watch, it would be another forty minutes until we reached Greenwich, a valuable bloc of time to do my Grand Prostrations. Ever since Kalavinka explained that she could only go out with me if I became an initiate into Tibetan Buddhism and performed ten thousand Grand Prostrations, my single-minded goal in life was to find a lama and be invested with the sacred thread.

When I heard that the Dharmapa had visited the Samaye-Ling Monastery in Scotland during his stay in Britain and that there was a resident lama there, I conceived of a way to realize my dream. After our visit to the British Hat Museum, I convinced Ginkgo that we should investigate the Scottish connection. The Head Lama undoubtedly took the Black Hat and Bardo, its hapless custodian, with him on his overnight journey, and it was possible that the hat had been taken there. Ginkgo himself was skeptical of my plan but preoccupied with the meeting with Starov. He spent the better part of the afternoon and evening on the phone to Wing, the curator at the Museum of Fine Arts in Boston, and to other art dealers and collectors in Berne, Zurich, and Liechtenstein. I invited Kalavinka to accompany me, but she decided to remain behind with Ginkgo and help translate. They hardly seemed to notice when I left.

The first part of my Scottish sojourn was uneventful. At the monastery everyone agreed that nothing out of the ordinary occurred during the Dharmapa's visit. He spent most of his time leading meditation and meeting with refugees and advanced students. Chenpo, the monastery's abbot, a shy young monk who could not have been much older than I was, recalled that Bardo kept watch over the big hatbox the entire time and received no visitors in his room. Acting on impulse, I asked him what the Dharmapa was wearing when he arrived. He grinned and said that he had on his usual robes and a Guy Fawkes' cap, and this light-hearted entrance set the tone for the visit as a whole, which would long be remembered for its warmth and humor.

I told Chenpo about the Dharmapa's visit to the British Hat Museum in a Sherlock Holmes hat and wearing the Red Sox cap in Boston. The abbot laughed and said the Dharmapa was a master of the Vajrayana teachings, or Crazy Wisdom. He also mentioned that the Lama expressed concern about fox-hunting in the British Isles and the next morning went out by himself to the heaths, to meet "our bushy-tailed brothers and sisters." The abbot reminded me that Buddha preached to all sentient beings, and that the Dharmapa was famed for being able to converse with birds and animals.

I had introduced myself as a journalist writing a feature story tracing the Dharmapa's visit to the West. Gradually, I brought up my own journalistic forays in the East, and my interest in things Oriental seemed to win his sympathy. To my inquiry whether I could become initiated into Tibetan Buddhism, the Abbot explained that it required only three months' preliminary meditation and enthusiastically welcomed me to stay in one of the meditation retreats on the heath. I said there must be some mistake, since I had been told only the Grand Prostrations were required. He replied that some lamas who had come to the West had waived the residency requirement because most Westerners were unable to stay in one place that long. Noting that Samaye-Ling was a traditional monastery, Chenpo pointed out that some concessions had already been made to modern times by allowing candidates to prostrate themselves lengthwise when making a circuit around the monastery rather than widthwise as was customary. He revealed that several years' studying physics at Cambridge had contributed to his own adjustment to modern civilization.

I had heard of people taking up residence in Nevada for ninety days to get divorced. But this was the first time I had encountered a similar ordeal in order to get involved. As I felt my hopes dissolving, I instinctively reached for my passport and showed the Abbot my transit visa. It showed I had to leave the country within twenty-four hours. Couldn't he make an exception? Chenpo thought for a moment and then said that since I had come so far, distance in this case could be substituted for time. Thank you, Padmasambhava or Albert Einstein, wherever you are! Within an hour, he invested me with the sacred thread and showed me how to do Grand Prostrations.

As I was leaving, the Abbot wished me a safe journey and asked me to send him a copy of my article in the *Daily Mail*. When I reminded him that I wrote for the *Phoenix*, not the *Mail*, he apologized and said he had confused me with "the other journalist." The other journalist? He then revealed that another writer had visited the monastery only the day before on a similar assignment and had asked many questions about the Black Hat, the hatbox, and the Dharmapa's itinerary.

I asked whether or not the visitor was tall, dignified, and a chain smoker. The Abbot confirmed that he was and produced a business card for S. Starov, with the address of Le Chapeau du Chef, ("The Chef's Hat,") a fashionable French restaurant in the West End. The lama further related that Starov had arrived with a big camera and lighting equipment and spent considerable time alone in the rooms which the Dharmapa and Bardo had occupied in order to take photographs for his story.

Thus my visit to Scotland proved doubly rewarding. In addition to making headway in securing Kalavinka's affections, I discovered that the London art dealer had been here just before I had. It evidently meant that the Black Hat which he had taken in Boston did not contain the secret map detailing Chinese nuclear sites in Central Asia as he had expected. He must have come to Scotland to find out whether the map had been hidden in the monastery, accidentally fallen out, or otherwise been left behind.

I thanked the Abbot for his valuable help, noting that Starov and I were colleagues. I told him I would be seeing Starov the next day and would be sure to remind him to send a copy of his article and pictures. Bidding farewell to this serene outpost and its colorful prayer flags dotting the heath, I caught the last train back to London and arrived at Charing Cross Station by 10 the next morning. As I expected, Ginkgo was elated at my report and said it confirmed his intuition that Starov's attempt at the Snow Lion Meditation Center had been unsuccessful.

Kalavinka too seemed impressed with my sleuthing. When she caught sight of the sacred thread beneath my shirt, she complimented me on my perseverance. "I'm pleased you have become a stream-winner," she said lightly touching the thread against my chest and referring to a traditional title for a wannabe Bodhisattva.

"I pray that you extinguish the flame of ignorance, anger, and desire," she added blushing, "and speedily reach your goal."

Now in this secluded part of the London-to-Greenwich excursion boat, I continued with my Grand Prostrations. I recited the fourfold refuge, visualizing the refuge tree with Padmasambhava in the center, and a host of Buddhas, Bodhisattvas, *dakinis, arhats,* and *dharmapalas*. The Abbot told me to imagine them in any form I liked. That was easy. Even the ones with multiple arms and legs assumed Kalavinka's perfection of form. I was well on my way toward completing the ten thousand, having completed 1,232 obeisances on the night train back from Scotland. I quickly mastered the technique and got it down to about one prostration every 15 seconds. That translated to about four a minute and, allowing for a five- or ten-minute break, some two hundred an hour.

The warmth of the mid-afternoon sun on my cheeks as I lifted my head felt good, and soon I was into my routine. But whispers and giggles drew me out of my concentration, and to my surprise I found I had attracted a small audience of children, including the two little girls who had been chatting with Kalavinka. I told them I was doing yoga, an explanation that had sufficed with the conductor and the few late-night passengers on the train from Glasgow.

One of the little girls asked if she could join. Soon I had a half dozen youngsters, including some boys who had been dueling with water pistols, bowing to the sun and prostrating themselves on the deck. Kalavinka came over and rested her hand over a life preserver affixed to the railing. "I see that you are already spreading the *dharma*, or Buddha Law," she exclaimed, her cornflower blue eyes meeting mine for an instant. "Someday, Jeffrey, you will be a great teacher."

As we smiled at each other, our attention was drawn to the starboard bow where Ginkgo, the large hatbox resting on a bulkhead beside him, was approached by a tall, slender man in a beige suit. Kalavinka and I sauntered forward with several children in tow to take up observation posts as well as overhear their exchange.

Ginkgo had exchanged his maroon pullover for a tan corduroy suit and bright red tie with a monogrammed G. The last several days he had been fashioning a spurious identity as Captain Goodwin, a former explorer and lecturer at the Museum School in Boston who had been dismissed for some irregularities in disposing of Oriental antiquities. With the help of Wing at the Museum of Fine Arts in Boston and Wing's contacts in the international art world, he had laid a paper trail in the computerized databases that Starov was sure to consult upon receiving his blunt invitation to today's meeting.

"Rather like a Dufy seascape," Starov opened the conversation with an expansive gesture to the horizon, alluding to the work of a contemporary French artist noted for placid harbors and waterways bathed in a warm glow of pastel color.

"Except for the hint of a squall from the northeast as in a Turner landscape," Ginkgo replied, referring to a British realist whose bucolic renditions of sleepy nineteenth century village life were noted for ominous skies and other portents of disaster.

On the leeward side, behind Ginkgo, to the northeast, about ten yards away, two heavy-set men approached and took up lookout positions. Turned up raincoats could not conceal their high cholesterol profiles and mind set.

"As I believe they say in your country, Captain Goodwin, life is an endlessly entertaining procession of the good, bad, and ugly." Starov contemptuously turned his back on the two uglies.

The dapper Russian-born art dealer spoke English flawlessly with a pronounced British accent. Producing a gold cigarette case from his jacket, he offered Ginkgo a smoke.

"Without the uncarved block, there would be no Buddha," Ginkgo contemplated, invoking a celebrated Zen aphorism and

Down the River Thames: 121

leaning over to accept a light.

"A sentiment that often comes to mind whenever I use this," Starov said balancing the gold cigarette case in his palm and returning it to his suit pocket. "In its previous incarnation it was an exquisite miniature Dancing Shiva in a Madrasi temple."

"But obviously it became, in a manner of speaking, too hot to handle," Ginkgo commiserated exhaling a thin spiral of smoke, "and had to be transmuted."

"A regrettable hazard of our profession, Captain, but in the next round, it may return as a glorious wedding band . . . "

" . . . to unite two former enemies," Ginkgo concluded the thought.

"The VCR is more likely to do that," Starov laughed, exposing a row of gold-capped teeth and casually turning his attention to the hatbox on the bulkhead. "But that is something the *papakhas*—big hats—in my native homeland don't understand."

"Bureaucracies are the same everywhere," Ginkgo agreed with a dismissive gesture of his hand. "Whether in Russia, America, or far off Tibet, they crush the true and the beautiful for their own petty nationalistic ends."

"So you have the Black Hat! What makes you think I would be interested in it?" Starov's eyes flashed a glance at the two fatty acids who started to inch forward but slunk back at a curt gesture of his long, languid hand.

"Your foray into the Dharmapa's quarters in Cambridge attracted considerable attention," Ginkgo replied evenly, "whereas mine did not."

"As a Boston archaeologist, you undoubtedly had contacts at the Tibetan Center which allowed you access to the monk's room before the reception," Starov reasoned, eyeing the patterned hatbox narrowly. "That would explain why the original hatbox was empty when I opened it."

"If I knew of your interest in the Vajra Crown, that unpleasantness could have been avoided," Ginkgo continued interposing himself between the large oval container and the advancing Russian art dealer. "Only later did word of your rather clumsy attempt reach me. Fortunately, the authorities have not been alerted. As far as everyone is concerned, the Black Hat is still in its original Tibetan container."

"Alas, there is still a trace of my Russian upbringing that twenty years in the West has not completely erased," the tall, dapper art dealer conceded ruing his clumsiness.

While listening to this exchange, I glanced over at LDL and VLDL—Low Density Lipoprotein and Very Low Density Lipoprotein—my nicknames for Starov's meaty retainers. The major difference between them was that VLDL was a head shorter, a foot thicker, and several stones denser. They gave me a menacing glance between mouthfuls of a submarine sandwich they had taken out of their attaché cases. I wondered if they knew about Kalavinka and my relationship to Ginkgo.

"But in the manner of tracks, Captain," Starov went on, contracting his thin, high arched eyebrows, "yours have not been entirely invisible. I know all about your visit to the Mad Hatter."

"A basket case, old Ryder," Ginkgo replied, picking up on the nickname of the museum curator. "But he made me an excellent offer. He is very interested in the hat."

"Interested is hardly the word, Captain," Starov corrected him dryly. "Ryder has been fixated on the Black Hat for fifty years."

"I know all about his parents' Chinese sojourn," Ginkgo observed, his softly focused gaze lighting on a seagull swooping overhead. "But you must enlighten me about his missionary interest in this particular specimen."

"It's more personal than professional," the art dealer related in a contemptuous tone. "The story begins at the end of the nineteenth century when his parents first came to China. They were attached to a Christian mission, but their real interest was searching out precious gems in the region of the Amoy River. The dream of finding another Blue Carbuncle proved irresistible. After repeated failures, their quest took them to the services of a local geomancer. After taking all their money, the old magician whetted their interest in treasures of the spirit. Filled with fanciful stories of magic and the occult, the Ryders left for distant Tibet. Their goal was to meet the Head Lama and be the first Westerners to see the Black Hat and become enlightened. But the Ryders were never heard from again. Back in England, their children concocted the pious fiction that they had perished in the Boxer Rebellion. Afterward, their son nursed a burning desire to obtain—and destroy—the hat that had lured away his father and mother and caused them to abandon their family."

"It's hard to believe such a kindly old man could nurse such lifelong vengeance," Ginkgo replied running his hand through his leafy curls.

"Beneath the aura of an elf in Santa's workshop is the cunning of a Mad Hatter," Starov returned with some emotion. "Instead of inspecting the hat for future exhibition, Ryder planned to incinerate it in the fireplace in the Sherlock Holmes' Room. In this way, he would fulfil his sacred vow to avenge his mother and father's death and prevent untold suffering to other children around the world whose parents deserted them for the siren song of Tibetan magic. Naturally I heard of his bizarre plan and endeavored to thwart it. Fortunately for all of us, the Dharmapa arrived without the Black Hat."

Kalavinka and I were as astounded by these revelations concerning the Museum director as was Ginkgo.

"His Holiness turned up with a Sherlock Holmes cap—a clear signal that he had deduced the old curator's intention," Ginkgo chuckled after listening to this curious tale.

"I have no desire to see the Black Hat prematurely go the way of all hats," Ginkgo went on, running his hand suggestively over the elegant hatbox behind him. "Of course, beside Ryder, there are other interested parties, present company not excluded. Anyone who would go to such lengths to obtain the hat in London, Scotland, and Cambridge should not be left out of the bidding."

"What are you asking?" Starov said indifferently, taking out another cigarette and tapping it against the gold case. "Whatever the Admiral offers, I will double."

As Ginkgo later explained, he was referring to a senior U.S. Naval commander who had one of the world's largest private collection of hats. He had begun as a cabin boy collecting hats at native ports of call. Now as one of the country's top commissioned officers, he had access to the highest diplomatic and military circles around the globe. His hobby was well known, and he would often receive distinguished hats as gifts from foreign governments and embassies anxious to do business with Uncle Sam.

"Small potatoes," Ginkgo replied laconically. "Even with the Pentagon's generous procurement policy, the Admiral is in no position to add this bonny bonnet to his collection. But the Architect is a different story. For him money is no object."

The Architect was the nickname of a Hong Kong developer who had made billions in the New Territories. He had lavished much of his wealth on a collection of Oriental headpieces that he had begun as a rickshaw boy at the turn of the century with hats left behind by his customers.

"True enough," Starov conceded as his eyes roved over the deck, "but in exchange for such a work of art surely only another equally unique and priceless object could suffice. What else is on your shopping list?"

"The *Conestabile Madonna*," Ginkgo answered promptly, referring to a famous circular painting by Raphael of Mary and the baby Jesus holding a small book in his hands. It hung in the Hermitage in St. Petersburg.

"The prize jewel of Russia's national art collection!" Starov exclaimed momentarily lapsing into Russian.

"And naturally if anyone could obtain it, Starov, it would be you as a former curator of the Hermitage," Ginkgo replied coolly. "What do you say to an even exchange? Willy 'the Wall,' the noted fence in Berlin, could make the arrangements."

"You overestimate my abilities, Captain," Starov indicated tersely. "There are some things in Russia even the General Secretary cannot arrange. I'm sorry, Goodwin, but you must be reasonable. If it's religious art you want, I can get you Raphael's *Virgin and Child with St. Joseph* or icons that have not been on the market for ten centuries. If millinery is on your mind, I can arrange for Rembrandt's *The Condemnation of Hanan* with three superlative turbans, or for the true fetishist there's Matisse's *Woman with a Hat*."

"Suppose, for a moment, that I decide to deal with you, Starov," Ginkgo said winding the hatbox's fancy blue ribbon around his finger. "What assurances can you give me that you'll not destroy the Black Hat like Ryder?"

"My intentions are wholly aesthetic," the suave art dealer replied. "My client is a private collector. Like you and me, he is a realist. He knows that Tibetan Buddhism is a vanishing religion. This is probably the last of the Dharmapas. My client will take infinitely better care of the Black Hat than the squabbling lamas and hippie converts who will inherit it in the interregnum after the Dharmapa passes away."

"And who might this selfless conservationist be?" Ginkgo inquired.

"Naturally if I told you my client's name, he would no longer be my client," Starov answered imperiously. "But I can tell you this. He is neither artistic nor religiously inclined. He has no interest in

Oriental art or Buddhism. His hobby is simply collecting black hats. He's a movie buff and over the years obtained the silk hat Fred Astaire sported in *Top Hat*, Charlie Chaplin's little black derby, the black Stetson that adorned Hopalong Cassidy in the Westerns, the black hat worn by the Wicked Witch of the West in the *Wizard of Oz*, and Michael Jackson's black fedora. The Tibetan Black Hat is the chief void in his collection. He simply must have it and came to me."

"A pity that he will be disappointed," Ginkgo concluded picking up the large parcel. "For your sake, I hope that he doesn't collect heads as well."

"Unfortunately for you, Captain Goodwin," Starov replied gesturing toward his two spearcarriers, "there are two gentlemen here who do. You have thirty seconds to reconsider, accept my counteroffer of another masterpiece or priceless icons, and return home a wealthy man."

As LDL and VLDL dropped the waxpaper from their meatball sandwiches over the side and put on their black leather gloves, Kalavinka and I exchanged worried glances. These were no hippie deprogrammers as we had bested in the Holiday Inn in Cambridge. From their meatcleaver hands to their swollen noses from too much vodka, they had the physiognomy of "wet agents" found in KGB thrillers and James Bond movies.

Ginkgo remained unmoved. "It's the *Conestabile Madonna* or nothing," he said evenly.

I wondered what my companion was trying to prove. The hatbox he had procured from Harrod's was empty. He had achieved his goal, confirming that Starov did not have the hat or map. What did he stand to gain by provoking them except a broken skull? I would have settled for the Rembrandt and a couple of icons.

At Starov's signal, the two lipoproteins made their move. One lunged for Ginkgo and the other went for the hatbox. But their quarry was faster and with his hands raised in the Tai Ch'i posture "Step Back to Drive the Monkey Away," he yielded as they came forward.

Regaining their footing on the slippery deck, they made a headlong charge at Ginkgo, whose back was turned to fend off Starov. The art dealer had his hands on the big oval container and was clawing at the blue ribbon.

"The chain, Milton," Ginkgo yelled in my direction. Shaking off my dazed immobility, I rushed over and unhooked a small metal chain that served as a guardrail to a service off ramp.

With the deftness of a ballet dancer, Ginkgo turned just as LDL and VLDL hit him. Keeping his *hara* or intestinal energy center straight, sinking down, and pivoting on one foot, the collision propelled them toward the gap in the railing like two billiard balls cushioning into a side pocket. I could hear surprised oaths in Russian as they hit the water.

I started to reconnect the chain but thought better of it as Starov pulled a revolver and motioned me away.

"You have performed me a double service, Captain," Starov said taking the hatbox from Ginkgo. "I have been trying to detach myself from those two cherubs for a long time. Their aesthetic sensitivity is limited to the hue of hemoglobin."

"Don't be so sure, *Tovarisch*," a voice behind him proclaimed. Tovarisch was the Russian word for "Comrade."

It was Kalavinka. She had come up from the other side and stuck a water-pistol in Starov's back. She had obtained it from one of the children playing on deck.

"I'll take that," she said coolly, reaching around and taking Starov's gun.

As Ginkgo relieved him of the hatbox, we became aware of commotion in the forward part of the vessel. Several crew members had observed our altercation and were approaching.

"The choice is now yours, my friend," Ginkgo mused unhooking the chain and nodding toward the chilly waters. "Be apprehended and face deportation back to Russia or join your friends for an invigorating dip in the Thames. I understand they have an opening for a curator in the new gallery in the Lubyanka. You have 10 seconds to decide." The Lubyanka was the notorious headquarters and prison of the former KGB in Moscow.

"I admire your proficiency in the Tai Ch'i art of Pushing Hands, Captain," Starov declared. "It was not listed in your vita. But rest assured this canvass is not completed. We shall meet again." He went over the side with his head up like a French aristocrat to the block.

As the boat steamed forward, Kalavinka tossed a life preserver toward the three dark heads bobbing in the distant waters.

"They are still sentient beings after all," she smiled turning toward Ginkgo and me. "And it is the duty of a Bodhisattva to save all creatures."

"Unless we find the Bodhisattva's hat," Ginkgo noted gravely, "that great goal may remain unrealized."

Attention now focused on Zurich, the Dharmapa's stop previous to London. We didn't need the famous clockworks at Greenwich to tell us that just six days remained until the Black Hat Ceremony.

9

REVELATIONS IN SWITZERLAND

We arrived in Zurich the next morning. The flight from Heathrow was uneventful. Ginkgo dozed and Kalavinka curled up in her seat, with the big hatbox between them, while I did Grand Prostrations in the rear compartment. The flight was half empty, and my obeisances attracted little attention except for a British dowager. Emerging from the lavatory, she admonished me to show more self-control and if that didn't work try knocking louder next time.

Our first stop was a condominium on Albistrasse to see Elsa Klein, a German broadcast journalist celebrated for her brazen questions and expensive tastes. Her television specials were popular throughout Europe. She had a beguiling manner that caused her subjects to open up and reveal their innermost secrets. As one former prime minister lamented, "I told her more than I told my priest at confession."

On his brief stopover in Zurich before flying on to London and Boston, the Tibetan lama had visited Ms. Klein at a downtown television studio. The main purpose of the Dharmapa's visit had been to meet with Tibetan refugees. Several thousand had settled in Swiss mountains and villages, and this snow-peaked land was sometimes known as Little Tibet.

"Deliveries are at the rear," the doorman at the Helvetica Arms sniffed when we arrived. I was carrying the big hatbox, and his comments seemed directed at me.

"This is not a delivery," Ginkgo retorted striding into the chandeliered lobby. "We are here to see Elsa Klein."

"I regret that Madame Klein is unavailable," the tall doorman replied blocking our path. "She is engaged through next Christmas. If you would like to leave your card, I'll inform her secretary that you called."

"Give her this instead," Ginkgo said, handing the doorman a picture of the Black Hat that Christopher Loring of the U.S. State Department had furnished us at the start of our journey. "She'll see us at once."

A few minutes later, the doorman returned from Ms. Klein's tenth floor suite and reported that her next appointment had been suddenly cancelled and we could go right up.

"Merry Christmas," I laughed. The doorman's mouth was still agape as we swept past into the elevator.

Upstairs, a middle-aged lady in haircurls and bathrobe met us at the door.

"Would you tell Ms. Klein that Inspector Ginkgo is here," I instructed the maid.

"I am Elsa Klein," the woman replied in excellent English, smoothing a trace of blue-green makeup on her swollen eyelids and temples. "Pardon my appearance. I was up half the night at a discotheque with the Princess of Monaco and the Oil Minister of Oman."

The vestibule opened to a spacious front room with a panoramic view of the Swiss capital. In the distance, we could see the Italian Alps.

"It's the cook's day off," she went on, motioning for us to sit down. "The chauffeur has disappeared again with the Ferrari, and my secretary is carrying on an affair with a delivery man in the sauna downstairs, so I am quite alone."

"I'm Inspector Ginkgo, and these are my associates, Jeff Milton and Kalavinka," my companion explained as we took our seats on a plush white davenport. Everywhere there were flowers and hanging vines, potted palms and tropical shrubs.

"We are here on behalf of the U.S. Department of State. As you may know, the Black Hat is missing, and its disappearance puts Washington in a diplomatic quandary."

I was surprised at Ginkgo's bluntness. It was the first time he had mentioned to anyone that the hat had vanished.

"Would you care for some fresh coffee and pastry?" Ms. Klein gestured to a large box of chocolate eclairs, turtles, and mousses on the table. "The Chancellor of Austria sent them around in hopes that I would edit out a small remark from this evening's Klein Report that he now very much regrets making. I am undecided whether to accept his bribe."

"We've just eaten, thank you," Kalavinka replied diplomatically for all of us. "But don't let us keep you from your breakfast."

"I heard something the other day from the Chinese ambassador about the hat being lost or misplaced," Ms. Klein acknowledged, turning to Ginkgo and fluttering her long eyelashes.

"Religion and politics make strange bedmates as it is," she continued adjusting a vase of orchids on the table. "Add fashion to the cauldron, and it's not surprising that something boiled over. But how does any of this concern me?"

Her fingers hesitantly reached for an eclair. She was clearly torn between helping herself to another pastry or waiting until we left. I had a feeling appetite would triumph over good manners.

"You interviewed the Dharmapa several days ago on his visit to Zurich," Ginkgo replied as she reached for the sweets.

His penetrating gaze caused her to reconsider, and she hastily closed the pastry box and folded her hands in her lap. I noticed her lavender nails, long and immaculately polished except for a chip and discoloration on the right thumbnail.

"Tell us about that meeting," Ginkgo asked, sniffing at a delicate long-stemmed white orchid in the vase in front of him. "Was the lama apprehensive? Was he wary about his journey or the safety of the Black Hat? Do you have any idea who might have wanted to steal the hat, or who had the opportunity? As far as we know, it may have been taken here in Switzerland."

"I hope you don't think *I* took the hat?" Ms. Klein declared in amazement. "It's really not my style."

As we talked, her hands strayed to the framed photograph of a small girl that stood on the marble coffee table. The child had a delicate constitution and pale look.

"Is that your daughter?" Kalavinka asked in a pleasant tone.

"Yes, her name's Ingrid."

"She has your smile."

"Thank you, she is a very special little girl."

"Does she go to school here?"

"No, not at the present time," Ms. Klein stammered. "She's visiting relatives in Leipzig. The climate there is milder and more to her liking."

"You were telling us about the lama's visit," Ginkgo reminded her, counting the number of leaves spiraling around the stem of the orchid. "What did you interview him about?"

"We discussed the usual things—the survival of Tibetan culture and customs, relations with China, the growing popularity of meditation in the West. You're welcome to a videotape of the interview. I'm sure they have one down at the studio."

"What about the Black Hat?" Ginkgo prodded. "Didn't you quiz the Dharmapa about his famous headpiece?"

"As a matter of fact," Ms. Klein added averting Ginkgo's concentrated gaze, "I did ask him to bring it to the studio so we could get some visuals. I planned to tease him about its color. Black just doesn't attract people in the West. I was going to suggest that he dye it fuchsia or teal green."

"And did he bring it?" Ginkgo asked twirling the orchid in his hand.

"The Dharmapa was much more chic than I expected," she replied shutting her swollen eyes and recalling the visit. "He arrived wearing a Tyrolean peasant's hat—you know, the cocky little mountain cap with a feather. When I asked him where the Sacred Hat was, he just smiled and said it was in Shambhala—the Land of Perfect Peace. He said that if I wanted to see the Black Hat I would have to journey there myself."

"You didn't ask him about any secrets?" Ginkgo continued, lifting the big hatbox to his knee and playing with the bright blue ribbon.

"Secrets?" Ms. Klein exclaimed glancing nervously around the room. "What secrets would the Dharmapa's hat possibly contain?"

Suddenly it became clear to all of us that she knew of the map believed to be hidden in the hat.

"I wasn't referring to the hat as such," Ginkgo said slowly turning the patterned oval container in front of him. "I was thinking of the lama's personal life. Maybe he harbors fantasies of being a political leader or a rock star."

"Well, His Holiness did reveal that as a youngster he was fascinated with motor cars. Two vintage automobiles were brought over the Himalayas in the '30s—an Austin and an MG. They were disassembled and carried by Sherpas and then reassembled in Lhasa. He said that they caused a sensation. He learned how to drive them and loved to race around the countryside. Farmers, soldiers, and yaks were all amazed. They thought the cars were some strange animal. Eventually they ran out of gas and were put in a museum."

"Hmm, just as in Erewhon," Ginkgo mused reflectively. *Erewhon*, the utopian novel by Samuel Butler was one of his favorite books. In addition to making ownership of machines or mechanical devices a criminal offense, the Erewhonians held that sickness was a crime, and those found guilty were put in jail for violating natural order. In contrast, thieves, swindlers, and others who had committed dishonest or immoral acts were sent to the hospital and given proper foods to change their attitude and behavior—a policy similar to the way in which Ginkgo dealt with crime.

"The Dharmapa sounds remarkably human after all," Kalavinka smiled.

"He reminded me very much of the Pope," Ms. Klein said, "friendly, outgoing—and mischievous."

"Do you think he might have taken his own hat?" Ginkgo's question startled me. I must admit I hadn't considered the possibility until now.

"Naturally that would be the first question I'd ask him today," Ms. Klein vowed. "If he's as enlightened as they say, he should have known that someone was after his hat and would have taken measures to safeguard it for his own protection."

"Now the classical place to hide such a hat would be under another hat," Ginkgo surmised. "Are you sure, Elsa, you didn't look under the Tyrolean hat when he arrived?"

The arrival of a casually dressed young man with a gold chain around his neck and an armful of clothes from the dry cleaners interrupted her reply. He tossed some car keys on a glass end table.

"Don't forget, Cherie, you have to be at the station in 20 minutes," Elsa reminded him in German.

"Hans, my current chauffeur," Miss Klein said demurely switching back into English as he disappeared into the bedroom.

"I'm sorry, Inspector Clouseau—I mean Ginkgo—I'd love to banter with you for awhile more, but I have to get dressed," she said rising and signaling an end to our conversation. "The head of UNICEF and an international choir from twenty-five nations is expecting me at the studio. I can't keep the children of the world waiting, can I?"

"You've kept your daughter waiting long enough," Ginkgo said sniffing the orchid and placing it slowly across the top of the hatbox. "I don't suppose the UNICEF choir will mind if you're a few minutes late."

Both Kalavinka and I were shocked at Ginkgo's harsh words. Ms. Klein froze in the hallway, between the microwave and the jacuzzi.

"Ingrid," she lamented, tears streaming from her eyes. "Oh God, how much do you know?"

"Only what I can see from her picture," Ginkgo said softly taking her hand and leading her back to the sofa.

"Your daughter's extremely sick. I'd say from her pallid complexion she has leukemia." He held the picture up to the light.

"She has ALL," Ms. Klein confirmed, "childhood leukemia."

"The doctors here have given up on her?"

"They've done all that they could."

"Except for a former East German specialist?"

"Yes, there is an experimental clinic in Leipzig that is controlled by elements of the Stasi, the former East German secret police. They have developed a new drug which is keeping her alive. I lied to you. Ingrid's not visiting relatives. She's at the clinic there, and I'm too busy with my career to be very much of a mother to her."

I had thought that the Stasi had disbanded when Germany reunified. But apparently as in the KGB, special units of the feared East German intelligence agency continued to operate or had gone freelance, offering their services to the highest bidder.

"And the price for her treatment is your cooperation in certain espionage matters?" Ginkgo went on.

"I've been forced into supplying certain intelligence," Elsa confessed sinking into the large divan. "I despise such blackmail, but have no choice. My daughter's life is at stake."

"Maybe not," Ginkgo replied as she dried her eyes with a small white handkerchief Kalavinka handed her. "But we'll get to that in a moment. Tell us now honestly, Elsa, what did the former Stasi agents ask you to do when the Dharmapa came?"

"They told me that the Black Hat contained some secret papers vital to international security," she faltered sinking back into the oversize white cushions. "They asked me to find a way to be alone with the hat for a few minutes and substitute a duplicate."

"A fake hat!" I whistled.

"Yes, a clever imitation made by Stasi craftsmen."

"How were you going to substitute it?"

"I made arrangements to interview him at the studio. During the filming, I planned to substitute the fake hat for the real one."

"And what did the agents in Leipzig tell you the papers contained?" Ginkgo commanded.

"They said the papers contained information on Tibetan guerrilla operations on the Chinese and Indian borders."

"You doubted them?"

"That was pretty low-level intelligence to involve Stasi operatives, even in hard times," Elsa said quite subdued. "Naturally I was curious to what the papers really contained. My friend the Chinese ambassador disclosed that the papers contained information on an ultra-secret project of the American CIA in the Himalayas."

"The CIA!" I whistled through my teeth. "Now we are getting somewhere. What kind of project was it?"

"Ironically, its codename was OPERATION H.A.T.," she explained. "The initials stand for High Altitude Testing program and referred to a small portable nuclear-powered tracking device that the Americans set up in the Himalayas in the mid-'60's to monitor Soviet and Chinese atomic tests in Central Asia."

"How was it installed?" I asked. I couldn't imagine how it was set up without the knowledge of governments in the region.

"The CIA hired expert mountain climbers and skiers to assemble the small SNAP generator from parts carried in their backpacks—rather like the old Austin and MG carried over the mountains to Lhasa. They assembled it on the slopes near Nanda Devi, one of the tallest peaks, on India's northeast frontier with China. But an avalanche later buried the spy station under tons of snow, threatening to contaminate the headwaters of the Ganges River with Plutonium-238 and poison tens of millions of people. The U.S. and India, which was covertly involved in the logistics of the project from the start, frantically tried to recover the lost generator. But because of snow drifts and ice floes, the spy station could now be anywhere along a several hundred-mile stretch of almost inaccessible terrain."

"Did the Chinese Ambassador cite any source for this report?" I asked incredulously.

"He said a pilgrim from Central Asia brought information to the Dharmapa's monastery in Sikkim with the exact location of the

SNAP generator. He said that before the old man passed away, he left an account of this information in the lining of the Black Hat. The actual source for the report was said to be a Sherpa employed at the monastery who had long been a trusted informant for Beijing."

At least that much tallies with the report we received, I thought to myself.

"The Chinese Ambassador surmised that the Dharmapa or someone in his party was bringing the papers to the United States to bargain for political concessions."

"Recovering the nuclear reactor would be a bright feather in the cap of the Russians or Chinese," I quipped. "Imagine what the people of India would do to any Government shown to be involved in an enterprise that could result in poisoning the sacred Ganges?"

"Or the Pakistanis, if they got hold of it," Elsa interjected. "Kashmir, the Punjab, and northern India are already a powder keg. It wouldn't take much to destabilize the entire region."

"You've been an invaluable help, Elsa," Ginkgo acknowledged, leaning over and tapping her affectionately on the shoulder.

"And my daughter?" Ms. Klein asked expectantly.

"Your daughter can recover," Ginkgo assured her, "but you will need to change her way of life. Her past way of eating has been extremely imbalanced. She has taken too much ice cream, soft drinks, and Swiss chocolate. Also too much canned and microwaved food. That and not enough whole grains, fresh vegetables, and home-cooked food in general. When was the last time you cooked a meal for her?"

"We've always had the best Swiss chefs," Elsa replied tremulously.

"And the foods they prepared were so delicious, rich, and creamy," murmured Ginkgo. "But such fare creates big difficulties, don't you think?"

"But what can I do?" Ms. Klein implored welling up with tears. "I never learned how to cook."

"Is your daughter free to travel?"

"Yes, her movements have not been restricted. In fact, she is due to come back to Zurich for a holiday in a few days."

"Good. Then my advice is to take her to America and stay for a while at the Kushi Institute in western Massachusetts."

"Is that another clinic?"

"It's a school, not a clinic. They teach macrobiotics. There you will learn proper cooking and universal principles of balance and harmony which you can then use to end your daughter's suffering—and your own. I don't know what your surgeon told you, but having a hysterectomy is no security against ovarian cancer."

"Good Lord, how on earth did you learn that?" Ms. Klein marveled as a flush appeared on her full, white cheeks. "No one, not even Hans knows I had a hysterectomy. He thought I was spending the weekend with the Princess on the Riviera."

"Milton here knows my methods," Ginkgo explained with a wave of his knobby gingerroot hand. "They are based on careful observation of the features of the face and body. The small vertical line above your lips corresponds with the contraction of the reproductive organs. This is a common sign among middle aged women who have had a hysterectomy. The chip on your right thumb suggests that your right ovary in particular is troubled."

"I'm scheduled to visit Boston in a few days for the Black Hat Ceremony," Ms. Klein disclosed. "You may say I'm on follow-up assignment for the Leipzig connection. I think I'll use the occasion to take Ingrid to the Kushi Institute as you recommend."

"You have no more reason to fear those who are blackmailing you," Ginkgo observed taking a copy of educator Michio Kushi's *The Cancer-Prevention Diet* out of his rucksack and leaving it on the coffee table. "Go to your daughter and live in health and peace."

"One further thing, Elsa," Ginkgo said as we prepared to leave. "Could you give us the duplicate Black Hat?"

"If it will aid you in your search," she said with her most winning "on air" tone.

She got up and went to a magnificent Klee print on the far wall. Behind it was a wall safe—the first I had ever seen outside the movies. She opened it with quick, deft movements and took out an object wrapped in tissue paper. As Ginkgo slipped it into the hatbox he was carrying, Kalavinka and I caught a glimpse of a majestic black crown embossed with gold and turquoise and white diadems.

We left the famed German interviewer considerably more humble than when we arrived. Although we had not come any closer to finding the hat, we had learned that the papers or map it contained might be more of a threat to Washington than Moscow or Beijing. It was disheartening to realize that our own State Department was deliberately misleading us and using us to cover its own radioactive tracks.

10

APPOINTMENT AT THE REICHENBACH

Before arriving in Switzerland, the Dharmapa had visited New Delhi, and we all agreed that proceeding to the Indian capital was the next logical step on our quest. At the airport, howeve, we learned that the next plane to Delhi was not until late that evening. That gave us nearly twelve hours to kill. I proposed that we visit the Reichenbach Falls, the site where Sherlock Holmes and Professor Moriarty had their famous death grapple. Ginkgo was at first hesitant to go off on what he called "a sightseeing expedition," but then had the inspiration to call Washington's bluff and telephone Christopher Loring, the State Department official.

"I told Loring that we had recovered the Black Hat," Ginkgo reported, returning from the phone booth in the Lufthansa terminal. "I told him that it contained a sealed letter hidden in its lining addressed to the Dalai Lama."

"The hat is a duplicate," I objected, "and there was no letter. What do you hope to gain by this deception?"

"Obviously Ginkgo means to verify Elsa Klein's story," Kalavinka replied retying the large bow ribbon on top of the hatbox.

"Very good, Kali," Ginkgo chuckled, picking up the oval container by its drawstring cords and twirling it like a globe. "If the real reason Washington wants the map in the hat is to conceal its nuclear hanky-panky in the Himalayas, the CIA will make an attempt on the bogus hat in our possession."

"How did Loring react?" I asked.

"Of course, he instructed me to immediately turn the Black Hat and its contents over to the U.S. Embassy in Berne," Ginkgo related. "But I told him that we felt a spiritual obligation to take the letter directly to the Dalai Lama in India. Naturally, he objected, and naturally I reminded him of our original bargain. I took the case only upon the condition that I would prevent the letter or map from falling into unfriendly hands. Loring understands that the Dalai Lama can be counted on not to reveal the existence of Chinese nuclear sites in Tibet and risk a missile attack or terrorist action on his homeland. But he would be apt to disclose the existence and location of a lost atomic spy station in the Himalayas."

"Very clever," I whistled realizing that now every American, as well as ex-Soviet, agent—not to mention assorted Germans, Pakistanis, and Chinese spooks—between here and India would be after us. "How did you leave it?"

"Loring offered to charter a plane for us to fly to Berne and discuss it with American officials there. I told him I would meditate about it."

Within an hour, a private jet was put at our disposal, but once we were aloft, instead of the Swiss capital Ginkgo commanded the pilot to set down in Interlacken, the alpine ski resort. From there we rented a car for the leisurely drive to the Reichenbach Falls.

Ginkgo graciously retired to the back seat to snooze, while Kali and I rode up front. Soon he was fast asleep with his massive head propped up against his orange rucksack. This ubiquitous container served as my companion's suitcase, briefcase, refrigerator, and laboratory all in one. A veritable apothecary shop, it held countless samples of rocks, seeds, leaves, dried fruits and vegetables, seaweed, pressed flowers, and other biological specimens, such as the Chinese grain that Wing gave him at the Museum of Fine Arts. From inside its various compartments, I have also seem him take out his flute; the *Book of Songs*, the *I Ching*, the *Gospel of Thomas*, and other classics; a change of underwear and socks; and rice balls, miso, shoyu, mochi, and other foodstuffs. I could never fathom why Ginkgo insisted on carting all of this stuff around. And it was a mystery to me how he always passed through customs without being inspected. With his unshaven appearance and baggy clothes, he must have been high on the authority's profile of known terrorists, smugglers, and penniless artists. But he was always waved through as if he were invisible.

Behind the wheel of the light blue Renault, I passed the time with Kalavinka by lyricizing about Sherlock Holmes's Central European exploits. I speculated on Holmes's possible affair with Irene Adler in Montenegro, the disappearance of Lady Frances Carfax in Lausanne, and the fate of Lowenstein of Prague, whose elixir of life derived from a Himalayan monkey which figured in *The Adventure of the Creeping Man*.

"What else did Sherlock Holmes do in retirement besides raise bees?" Kalavinka asked slipping into her white cardigan as we proceeded through the mountains.

"According to Watson, he wrote a monograph on the segregation of the queen and began work on his magnum opus *The Whole Art of Detection*," I replied.

"When did he pass away?" she asked turning around and spreading a blanket over Ginkgo who had fallen asleep in the back seat. "I imagine a lot of people pilgrimage to his grave."

"No one knows when Holmes died," I confessed pulling out and passing a lorry filled with hay. "After he retired following *His Last Bow* in 1914, he was not heard from again. He was about sixty, so he must have lived another ten or twenty years."

"You don't suppose he kept some of Lowenstein's elixir of life?" Kalavinka smiled prettifying herself in the mirror on her window visor. "After all, he was a master chemist."

"Some of Sherlock Holmes's more fanatic fans," I replied, "console themselves with the thought that in retirement he lived on royal jelly, a byproduct of the hives that is renowned for longevity. But it's stretching credulity to think that a man born in 1854 could still be alive."

"It's said that beekeepers have the longest life span of any profession." A deep voice issued from the back seat.

Ginkgo who had been napping since we set off in the little Renault suddenly opened an eye as the conversation turned to Holmes's health and vitality.

"But their longevity has more to do with the bees' stimulation of the beekeepers' meridians than with ingesting honey, wax, or royal jelly," our dragon-like companion continued taking a big yawn and clearing the sleep from his eyes.

"Unless Holmes radically changed his way of life, it is doubtful he lived to see the Second World War as portrayed in the the rather fanciful Basil Rathbone movies in which he is shown combatting the Nazis."

"From what I gather," Kalavinka said sliding in my direction as we took a sharp curve, "Holmes was the typical bachelor. I imagine he was so busy saving the world that he didn't pay much attention to his grooming or take time for his meals."

"In the way of diet, Holmes was a typical Victorian," Ginkgo declared leaning forward in his seat. "In the stories, he is described eating large amounts of ham and eggs, meat and poultry, and other animal quality fare prepared by Mrs. Hudson, his landlady. He and Watson also enjoyed dining out at London's most fashionable restaurants. The strong yang animal food Holmes and Watson took was balanced with strong yin in the form of boiled, mashed, or baked potatoes, plenty of sweets and savories, and brandy, Scotch and soda, or wine after dinner."

"Holmes was representative of his times," I conceded passing a bus loaded with children on a skiing holiday. "But not everyone in Victorian England was a Sherlock Holmes. What foods or combinations of foods gave rise to his unique deductive abilities?"

"Surely even a silly goose like you can intuit that after our visit to the British Hat Museum a couple days ago," Ginkgo exclaimed.

"Roast goose," declared Kalavinka emphatically as I drew a blank.

"Bravo, Kalavinka," Ginkgo declared reaching over the seat and patting her on the head. "Throughout the Canon we find that Holmes was especially fond of poultry, including roast goose, paté de foi gras, and curried chicken. You will recall that at the end of *The Blue Carbuncle*, he proposed to Watson that they begin another 'investigation in which also a bird will be the chief feature.'

"But as much as he liked the domesticated variety, Holmes's penetrating intellect was shaped in particular by wild game. You may recall, Milton, that one of Holmes's favorite dishes was a brace of woodcock. He also enjoyed grouse or partridge. It's not for nothing that Sherlock Holmes's trademark is the deerstalker, the traditional hunting cap of the English countryside. Wild game are much stronger, more alert, and more intelligent than their domesticated cousins. The wild fowl Holmes preferred turned him into the elemental hunter, stalking his quarry in the guise of criminals and spies."

The air considerably thinned as the little car climbed the winding mountain road. I rolled up the window and flicked on the heat. In the rear view mirror, I noticed that the same Citroen had been following us now for several miles. The thought crossed my mind that we were being followed.

"What of Professor Moriarty?" I asked pulling off at a scenic spot and allowing the Citroen to pass. "He was Holmes's intellectual equal. What gave rise to his warped intellect?"

"Moriarty is an interesting study in visual diagnosis," Ginkgo replied waving to several small children in the back of the big French car. "From Watson's description and Sidney Paget's likenesses in the *Strand* magazine, we find that he too ate a lot of animal food, especially eggs, which account for his insight into the binomial theorem, the dynamics of the asteroid, and other mathematical and scientific talents. Eggs are one of the natural foods of snakes and gave rise to the peculiarly 'reptilian manner' in which he oscillated his head. However, by themselves, eggs did not produce Moriarty's genius. The other factor was a touch of lemon. This small citrus fruit gives tremendous sharpness. He was probably habituated to tea with lemon—an American influence."

"It's a shame that Holmes—and Moriarty—did not discover the inner world of meditation," Kalavinka noted returning the visor to the upright position. "They would never have tried to destroy each other."

"After his sojourn to Tibet, Holmes stopped taking drugs and his view of life became broader and more compassionate," Ginkgo explained to her as he had to Loring on the evening he first accepted the case. "His attraction to bees and honey indicates a more yin, possibly semi-vegetarian, orientation. Probably after his journey East and exposure to Buddhism, he cut back on red-meat and poultry. Certainly his quest for the chase diminished. In this regard, he prefigured the hippies and spiritual seekers of recent times. However, unfortunately like most nineteenth century romantics and bohemians, Holmes did not discover or appreciate the staff of life—whole cereal grains. In this respect, he was the archetypal modern man—*homo analyticus*. Holmes and Watson embodied the spirit of modern science and medicine. They represented the modern view that every effect has a physical cause, and every disease has a single cure. How symbolic that their first meeting should have been in the chemistry lab of a hospital—St. Bart's, that venerable institution founded by Rahere, the fool to Henry I. How mirror like that Holmes and Watson's most memorable enemies should also be men of science like Professor Moriarty and Jack Stapleton, the entymologist who created the fiendish hound of the Baskervilles through improper diet and behavior modification.

"In the last analysis," Ginkgo continued, "Holmes could analyse everything except himself. The order of the universe is infinitely amusing. How wonderful that his very address—221B Baker Street—should take its name from the age-old district of London bakers and breadmakers. The true source of human health and happiness lies in the grainmakers' art. Yet in several decades living there with his lens and microscope, Holmes never detected the origin and meaning of his address and the treasure which it symbolized."

From Meiringen, we followed the winding mountain road to the top and parked the Renault in a visitors' area. A half dozen other cars were parked there including the Citroen and a red Fiat with a "Jesus Saves" bumpersticker. Most of the vehicles had ski racks on the rear or top. There was still considerable snow and ice on the ground at this altitude, and the temperature was noticeably cooler than in Interlacken or Zurich. Ginkgo pulled the hood of his maroon jacket up and stopped to admire some wild grasses that were peeking up through the snow. I was surprised to see that he had taken the gaily decorated hatbox out of the car.

"Keep an eye on this," Ginkgo said to Kalavinka, gesturing toward the hatbox which he had placed on the ground beside him. I'm going to take a stroll into that clearing to look for some dinkel."

Dinkel, or spelt wheat, still grew on Swiss mountain farms and meadows and was traditionally one of the best grains for sourdough bread production. Clearly the Reichenbach Falls was a low priority on my companion's agenda.

"Why don't we leave the hatbox in the car?" I said, annoyed at the thought of it coming between Kali and me on our hike to the Falls.

"You never know who might walk off with it," Ginkgo replied whistling a few bars of *Yankee Doodle*. I couldn't tell if he was referring to the hat or the car.

"I'd be happy to put it under my wing," Kalavinka said, picking up the pretty parcel.

"It strikes me as unnecessarily provocative," I pouted, warming my hands with my breath.

"See how light it is," Kalavinka said with a finger to her lips indicating for me to be silent. "All I need is something to balance my

Appointment at the Reichenbach: 143

other hand."

Just when I was despairing at losing an opportunity to advance my cause, she linked her other arm with mine.

"And as for you, Sherlock, take this to keep you warm." Ginkgo fished the deerstalker out of his pack and placed it firmly on my head. I had completely forgotten about it since Ryder gave it to him at the Hat Museum in London. It was faded and rumpled from being lodged in Ginkgo's gear.

"Give Kalavinka a proper tour. I'll meet you back at the car in an hour," Ginkgo said disappearing into the tall grass.

I felt slightly ridiculous putting on the faded light brown checkered cap. It reminded me of wearing a baseball cap backwards like a catcher and forwards like a pitcher at the same time.

"Oh, don't you look dashing, Jeffrey?" Kalavinka complimented me, reaching over and adjusting the angle. "We must get your picture at the Falls."

With the funny-looking cap on my head and the pretty girl on my arm, I soon forgot all about the frigid weather and possible pursuers. The fragrance of Kalavinka's hair blowing in the wind and her sparkling laughter transported me into that season where it is eternally spring.

Arm in arm, we followed markers along the path that had been put up to guide visitors to the steeper elevations and the site of Holmes's and Professor Moriarty's fatal encounter. A mother and father with two small children passed us on their way back. The kids both had on Sherlock Holmes's caps and pointed and giggled in French when they spied mine. I recognized them as the family in the Citroen.

About ten minutes later we were overtaken by a party of Italian monks. They were accompanied by an enormous St. Bernard which bounded up and tried to give me a slurpy kiss. It was all I could do to prevent it from knocking me over. One of the monks, a tall, thin man with a small brown cap and long rosary, apologized in broken English for the dog's misbehavior. He explained that they were Franciscans while the dog was a Dominican.

Somehow the theological distinction passed over my head, but Kalavinka smiled good-humoredly and said it was a good thing the dog wasn't a Jesuit or it would have pinned me to the ground until I had converted.

"We are great fans of Signore Holmes," the tall monk continued as his two small rotund companions beamed in agreement. "We admire how he outwitted Signore Moriarty at Victoria Station by disguising himself as a venerable Italian priest in black hat and cossack and catching the Continental Express. And after his fight to the death with Herr Professor, he went to Fiorenza as every Italiano knows."

"Nice doggie," I said shooing the St. Bernard away from the hatbox.

It had the end of the long blue ribbon in its jowls. If we weren't careful, it would soon have the duplicate Black Hat in its grasp. Thinking quickly, Kalavinka diverted its attention by taking a carob-covered rice cake from her cloth shoulder bag and tossing it into the brambles and ferns that fringed the chasm.

As we turned around to watch the dog bound into the underbrush, a solitary jogger in a blue ski jacket and red cap with goggles came into view. He was about a quarter mile behind us, swinging his arms briskly.

The three monks exchanged worried looks and disappeared into the thicket to retrieve their energetic charge.

"Where's my treat?" I said extending a hand as they disappeared from sight.

"No snacks for you, I'm afraid," Kalavinka replied pivoting on her heel until her shoulder bag was just out of my reach. "You must keep a clear mind on these trails or we're liable to have an accident."

"Just a bite," I entreated reaching around her waist and lunging for it. "All we've had for the last twenty-four hours is rice balls, Takuwan pickles, and nori strips."

"Promise you won't let Ginkgo know I gave you this," she said sternly before splitting another carob cake and handing me half. "Remember, he says too much yin for men leads to accidents."

"Cross my heart and hope to die," I pledged devouring the heavenly tasting morsel.

By the time we reached the summit, the lower sky had turned a deep grey and black. The sun which had been so bright had disappeared behind a mass of billowing clouds. The chasm had widened considerably during our ascent. As we rounded the bend of the curving trail, the Falls came fully into view. Its torrent, swollen by melting ice and snow, plummeted several hundred feet into the gorge below. The spray sent up from the dark rocks below was as thick in some places as the smoke from a steam engine. Though the path skirting the Falls widened at this point, I was surprised that a guard rail had not been put up. One false step or slip on the ice and the unwary traveler could slide over the precipice and join the late lamented author of *The Dynamics of the Asteroid* in the abyss below. Above, ice-covered boulders rose up several dozen feet to where the treeline ended.

A rock jutted onto the narrow path. I recognized it as the spot where Holmes rested his alpenstock cane and waited for Moriarty after Watson received a spurious message to return to Meiringen and attend to a dying Englishwoman. Kalavinka set the hatbox down by a small plaque that had been erected by a Holmesian society to commemorate the site. She took out her Instamatic and motioned for me to stand in the slanting light. As I adjusted my lapels and cap, I suddenly realized why the Dharmapa had asked James Ryder at the British Hat Museum to go to Regent Park.

"Kali, I've got it!" I yelled moving out of position.

"Got what?" She lowered her camera and threw the trailing end of the bright blue and white muffler over her shoulder.

"Why the Dharmapa asked Ryder to go to Regent Park."

"What made you think of Ryder all of a sudden?" she asked putting her hands on her hips. "Does strolling with a girl on your arm always turn your thoughts to business?"

"The monks' skullcaps," I explained. "They were the same as Ryder's. They were Franciscans."

Her usually expressive face turned blank at this theological turn of phrase.

"Don't you see?" I explained. "The old curator must have been wearing St. Francis of Assisi's original skullcap. By his own logic, hats retain the spirit of their owner. St. Francis was celebrated for being able to talk to the animals. Wearing St. Francis's hat would enable him to communicate with the animals. The Dharmapa also is said to be able to converse with all creatures. He intuitively understood the cap's significance, and that's why he encouraged Ryder to go to Regent Park. Regent Park is the site of the London Zoo. For a lonely old man, the companionship of birds and animals would help make up for the loss of his wife."

"Why that's marvelous, Jeffrey," Kalavinka declared coming over and kissing me on the cheek. "I do believe you've solved it!"

She especially seemed to like the monogamous ending. Basking in her admiration, I felt incredibly light-headed and intuitive. Despite Ginkgo's admonitions, I told myself that I must really be eating well.

As we stood there embracing, I had another sudden insight.

"Watch out, Kali." A split second before the rumble of the avalanche registered in my conscious mind, I pushed her in a decidedly nonmonagamous fashion.

As she fell backwards into a snowdrift, an avalanche of rock and ice crashed down beside us. Tons of debris hurtled into the gorge, producing a shower of crystal and ice and a tremendous echo that reverberated from mountain to mountain. The force of the avalanche hurled me toward the edge of the cliff, and my last thought before losing consciousness was that this was divine-earthly retribution for having eaten the carob-covered rice cake.

When I came to a few moments later, I saw someone in a blue and white ski jacket, red ski cap, and goggles on his forehead leaning over Kalavinka. He was stroking her hair and vigorously rubbing her hands with his own to bring back the circulation. I recognized him as the stranger we had seen in the distance while talking to the monks.

"Kali, are you all right?" I pulled myself up and staggered over to where she was being revived.

"Yes, thanks to Lance," she replied in a barely audible whisper. She appeared to have bumped her head and not remembered my pushing her out of the way.

"Lance?"

"At your service," the samaritan grinned, revealing a mouth of gleaming white teeth.

"Lance Andrews? What are you doing here?" I said in amazement, recognizing the disgustingly handsome skier whom I thought we had seen the last of at the Holiday Inn in Cambridge.

"I'm entered in the finals of the Euro Cup in Interlacken," he explained tightening the shoelaces to his designer hiking boots. "I had a free afternoon and came out here to take in the solitude. But it seems I can't escape the company of beautiful women, especially those in danger."

Kalavinka got up with Lance's help and blushed. Inside, I turned red with anger. Lance's presence could not be just coincidental. And now for the second time, for him to take the credit after I had rescued Kalavinka was too much.

"And you, Sport, what are you doing here?" Lance turned to me condescendingly, brushing snow off Kalavinka's collar and sleeves. "The last I heard was that you had gone to London with that stout fellow. What's his name?"

"Ginkgo," a deep voice above us interrupted.

We all looked up in astonishment and saw Ginkgo pressed against a ledge in the rock face above calmly weighing a handful of dinkel. In the confusion of the moment, I had completely forgotten about the leader of our expedition.

I recognized the ledge where he was resting as the spot where Holmes had left his silver cigarette case and a note, hastily scribbled at Professor Moriarty's convenience, for Dr. Watson describing his final moments. It was only after returning from Tibet two years later that Holmes revealed to the good doctor in *The Empty Room* that he did not fall into the abyss below, but managed to get the best of Moriarty and pull himself up to the ledge after the professor tumbled into the gorge.

"Ginkgo, are we glad to see you," I exclaimed.

"Likewise, I'm sure, old carob bean," he chuckled glancing at the outer edge of my ear, which had evidently reddened from something extremely yin in the last half hour. "It appears we were being followed."

"You mean the avalanche was no accident?" Lance's eyes widened in amazement.

"I found these up on the ridge."

Ginkgo held out a handful of rumpled up wax paper, the remains of a pepperoni pizza, and the ends of several filter cigarettes.

"Starov and his atherosclerotic apparatchiks," I exclaimed. "They must have been lying in wait for us."

"And one of them left this behind," Ginkgo said producing a small brown skullcap.

"The monks!" I exclaimed. I knew somewhere I'd seen before the tall, thin figure and the two short, saturated ones with the bulging veins in their necks.

"They left in a snowmobile that was parked on the far ridge," Ginkgo went on lowering his orange rucksack to me. "They fled quickly when they saw that their effort had failed."

Ginkgo's pack weighed a ton. It must be filled with stones, I thought to myself.

"Holy shit! " Lance exclaimed. "Who is Starov and what does

pizza have to do with anything?"

"Milton will fill in the details," Ginkgo replied sliding down to the pathway. "Meanwhile, time is of the essence, and we have a flight to catch to India."

"Now what have we here?" he continued taking Kalavinka's left arm. "That's a pretty deep cut."

Kali herself had not noticed the gash until now. Some rocks from the avalanche must have struck her, or she fell harder than anyone thought. Blood was dripping from the laceration onto the pathway.

"Do you have a handkerchief?" Ginkgo asked her.

"It's in my travel bag back in the car," she replied.

Lance and I indicated we hadn't any either. As we both started to peel off our shirts to bind up her wound, Ginkgo shook his head. Rummaging through his rucksack, he took out something delicately wrapped in cloth. It turned out to be the packet of grain bound in silk from the Museum of Fine Arts.

"But where to put the rice and millet?" he mused untying the corners of the faded silk covering?

"In here," I said thrusting forward the deerstalker. "Put it in the hat."

Ginkgo poured the tiny grains as I held the faded Sherlock Holmes' cap. They fell in a wide spiral just up to the brim.

"That ought to do it," Ginkgo said to Kalavinka, dressing her wound with the ancient silk scarf.

Untying the ear flaps of the deerstalker, he folded them up and over the rice and millet in the hat, retied the bow, and gently placed the cloth hat and its precious contents back in his orange carry-all. Taking out a deep-red umeboshi plum from a jar in another part of his pack, he plopped it in Kalavinka's mouth. "This will help alkalinize your blood system and promote clotting."

She offered no resistance, and within seconds a touch of color returned to her pallid countenance.

"Now where is the box containing the *Black Hat*," Ginkgo muttered to himself with strong emphasis, surveying our immediate surroundings. By his inflection, both Kalavinka and I realized he wanted Lance to think the hat in the box was genuine.

"Good grief," Kalavinka declared surveying the ledge around her. "It must have gone over the cliff."

As we searched, there came a great howl up ahead. Momentarily, I flashed on the hound of the Baskervilles. But it turned out to be the St. Bernard, its orange coat covered with snow and trailing a bright blue ribbon in its mouth.

"Noble friend," Ginkgo declared dropping to his knees and rubbing the big dog's big jowls. "Show us where the big hatbox is buried. It has a very valuable letter which we must deliver to a holy man in India."

The dog bounded with us up the path to a snowbank, and after a few minutes digging we uncovered the big oval box, battered and bruised, but still in one piece.

"The monks have taught you well," Ginkgo said massaging the enthusiastic St. Bernard behind the ears. The big dog showed its appreciation by putting its front paws on his shoulders and licking his face. Kalavinka produced the last of the carob-covered rice cakes from her shoulder bag and gave it to Big Brown Eyes as a reward.

With the dog in the lead, we hastened back to the parking area. As the shadows lengthened and a cold wind struck, the voice of a ghostly mathematician and astronomer seemed to follow us from the abyss, echoing from ridge to ridge. I fancied I heard it gleefully counting the days until the time ran out for the merciful spirit of Tibetan Buddhism to be empowered in the West:

Only five days left until the Black Hat Ceremony.

11

THE JEWEL IN THE LOTUS

After returning to Zurich from the Reichenbach, we caught the evening flight to Delhi. Lance gallantly volunteered to drop out of the ski meet in Interlacken and provide his muscular strength to our party on the continuation of our travels. I assured him that such a sacrifice would be as unnecessary for our welfare as it would be unsportsmanlike to the contestants he would leave behind. But to my chagrin, Kalavinka warmed up to his invitation, and to my surprise, Ginkgo readily nodded his assent, noting that Lance's protection might come in handy on the next leg of our journey.

On the ride back to Zurich, Ginkgo kept up the fiction that the big hatbox we had rescued at the Falls housed the real Black Hat containing a letter addressed to the Dalai Lama. Kalavinka and I didn't say anything, but it was obvious Ginkgo expected Starov, the art dealer who might or might not be working for the KGB or some spin-off, the CIA, and possibly the Chinese or Pakistanis—whom we had not yet heard from—to make another attempt on our cargo, if not on our lives.

At the Tibetan Center in New Delhi, we learned that the Dalai Lama was teaching in Bodhgaya, the site of Buddha's enlightenment. To reach Bodhgaya, we had to pass through Benares, India's holiest city, and take a train. Before returning to the airport and catching a local flight to Benares, we decided to visit Rani Ras, a Hindu yoga teacher whom the Dharmapa had visited during his brief sojourn in the Indian capital. On our way out of the Tibetan Center, Lance inquired whether there was a resident lama who could initiate him into Tibetan Buddhism. To my alarm, there was a lama present, and Lance elected to remain behind and catch up with us later.

"Holy shit, am I in luck!" he exclaimed.

I'll never forget how seductively Lance winked at Kalavinka and flashed me his most carnivorous grin, as he bowed his head and followed the tottering monk into the meditation room like a choir boy.

The ride by horse-drawn cart to Old Delhi alone with Kalavinka and Ginkgo revived my romantic aspirations.

"Your arm looks pretty good," Ginkgo said poking the bruise above Kali's left elbow.

"Yes, thanks to the male dragon," she replied.

"How did you know Ginkgo was born in a dragon year?" I asked. "Practicing a little Tibetan astrology on the side?"

"I wasn't aware of his sign," she explained, "though now that you mention it, he is rather formidable in appearance and manner. I was referring to the dragon on the scarf."

She handed Ginkgo the old silk scarf that he had used to bind up her wound. Though caked with blood, we could make out the outline of a frolicking dragon embroidered in its ancient folds.

"What makes you think it's a male dragon?" I asked in mock consternation.

"The claws, of course," she replied counting off five talons. "Male dragons have an odd number, females an even number."

"For a Female Earth Bird, you are awfully observant of small details," I teased. "Too bad you missed your real rescue back at the Falls."

Examining the scarf and putting it back in his pack, Ginkgo proceeded to nap. I took advantage of the opportunity to fill in Kalavinka about some of the subcontinent's colorful history. Since South Asian civilization was not one of my strong suits, I concentrated on the Victorian Era and mused on Watson's wound in the Afghan campaign, the Agra Treasure that figured in *The Sign of Four*, the snake that appeared in *The Adventure of the Speckled Band*, and other Indian themes in the Sherlockian canon.

Kali poked fun at my history lesson, singing a few lines from a rock hit:

> *Don't know much about history.*
> *Don't know much about biology.*

152: *Inspector Ginkgo Tips His Hat to Sherlock Holmes*

> *Don't know much about science books,*
> *About the French I took.*
> *But I know I love you,*
> *And I know that if you loved me, too,*
> *What a wonderful world it would be.*

The carriage let us off at a small rundown ashram near the Red Fort. Passing through a lush garden filled with bougainvillea and jasmine, we came to a weatherbeaten sign on the door proclaiming in English and Hindi, "Welcome to Brahma Bhavan." The mud-brick interior, faded pink in color, was devoid of furnishings except for a scraggly madras curtain framing a window to one side, a large square platform in the back, and a creaky ceiling fan overhead. The platform supported a red silk divan on which reclined a plump middle-aged woman propped up by meditation cushions and pillows. She held a large bamboo fan in her right hand. Spying us, she dismissed some young devotees who were sitting at her feet and bade us to sit down.

"You have had some training in hatha yoga, isn't it?" she observed after Ginkgo introduced us and eased himself into a half-lotus position on the woven straw floor mat.

"I'm a mere beginner," he declared bringing his palms together and touching her swollen feet in the Indian style.

"I'm a little stiff from traveling," I apologized, assuming a spot to Ginkgo's right and trying unsuccessfully to twist my foot onto my thigh.

Kalavinka sat behind us with her legs demurely to the side. "I am here to learn the wisdom of the East," she said simply.

"May the gods smile upon you," Rani Ras blessed us with a benevolent wave of her fan. "Your karma has brought you to Mother India, and your good deeds in past lives have brought you to Mata Ras." She seemed to be short of breath and reached for a glass of water.

"What does *Mata* mean?" I inquired.

"*Mata* is Sanskrit for 'mother.' Please call me Mataji. Everyone does."

From her once fashionable dress, cultivated manners, and slight British accent, I deduced that she was the granddaughter of Daulat Ras, the admirable young Indian scholar from Oxford who figured in Dr. Watson's story, *The Adventure of the Three Students*.

The Jewel in the Lotus: 153

"I am quite sure there is no relation," she laughed. "Ras is as common a name as Smith or Brown."

"Please excuse my young colleague," Ginkgo chided. "He is obsessed with the literary fantasies of the West." He reached over and snatched the deerstalker I had been carrying and put it back in his knapsack.

"Everyone is welcome in Brahma Bhavan." Rani smiled, barking something in Hindi to a pupil in a back room behind a bamboo door hanging of a large swan.

"Mataji, what does Brahma Bhavan, the name of your ashram, mean?" Kalavinka asked straightening the legs of her tight-fitting jeans.

"Brahma is the Supreme God," Rani replied smoothing the folds in her cavernous white sari. "*Bhavan* is the Hindi word for lodge or rest house. Brahma Bhavan is the 'Refuge of Brahma,' where seekers come to receive the highest spiritual teachings."

"In America, we've heard a lot about Krishna and Shiva," I noted, "but not much about the other gods. Who is this Brahma dude?"

"There are three principal gods in Hinduism—Brahma, Vishnu, and Shiva," she explained pausing to take another sip of water from the large brass pitcher at her side. "Brahma is the creator, Vishnu is the sustainer, and Shiva the Lord of the Dance is the destroyer. After creating the world, Brahma retires into blissful meditation. He leaves the actual running of the universe to his assistants, Vishnu and Shiva. Then when the universe ends, everything is destroyed until—how do you say it?—Brahma dude awakens and creates a new universe."

"What is your special teaching?" Ginkgo inquired lifting his other leg into a full lotus.

"Here at Brahma Bhavan, we teach Raja Yoga, the science of pure mind," she replied laying a chubby finger on her gold nose ring. "We don't teach postures, serpent energy, or worship. Most of our students have spent many years studying hatha yoga, bhakti yoga, kundalini yoga, or tantric yoga before coming here." Was I being suspicious, or did she cast a disapproving eye on Kalavinka and me when she mentioned the *tantra*?

A young man with long hair, sandals, and love beads brought in a pot of tea and a tray of Indian sweets which Rani proceeded to pass around. The devotee was dressed all in white and had a Brooklyn accent. From his upturned eyes, I figured if he were typical of the students here, there was a fortune to be made in deprogramming.

"I wonder if Phil Lord offers finder's fees," I leaned over and quipped to Kalavinka.

"Jeffrey, abduction and deprogramming are no laughing matters," she replied sharply, jabbing me in the back with her finger. She had sharp nails.

"I was only kidding," I moved to reassure her.

"Materialism in your country has reached a dead-end," Rani declared casting a heavy lidded eye in my direction. "It is only natural that young people should seek a higher spiritual truth."

"It's not always easy for those of us conditioned by material values to choose a guru," I replied squirming to keep my legs from falling asleep.

"In India, the lotus is an ancient symbol of purity," she went on, suppressing a slight cough. "It grows in the pond sending up a beautiful blossom that is uncontaminated by the mud below. Raj yogis in the East focus on this image to rise above the imperfections of the material world."

"Blossom and root are one," Ginkgo noted enigmatically. "Don't you think, Mataji, that the lotus root, which grows in the mud and muck, is the most nutritious part of the plant?"

"In ancient Greece, as I recall," Rani countered, "lotus-eaters became famous as dwellers in false paradise. In India, we prefer to contemplate the symbolism of the flower rather than take its life."

"Actually, the lotus in Asian art and religion does not refer to a flower at all," Ginkgo continued, rising from the lotus posture. "The lotus refers to the ancient symbol of the infinite spirallic universe. Our solar system, our galaxy, our unfolding history upon this earth—all appear in the form of a lotus."

With some seeds from his pack, he sketched an outline on the floor of the solar system, showing how the sun formed the center, the planets formed the bud, and the comets formed the petals of the lotus.

"Viewed as a dynamic whole," he explained weighing the rest of the seeds in his palm, "the solar system forms a truly beautiful flower."

"The Tibetan national mantra is *Om mani padme hum*," Kalavinka offered, entranced with Ginkgo's simple drawing of the Earth, Venus, Mars, and other planets circumscribed by comets from the periphery of the solar system. "It is usually translated as 'The Jewel in the Lotus.' If the lotus refers to the universe as a whole, what is the jewel?"

"The jewel is the mind or consciousness that apprehends this universal order," Ginkgo explained with a broad smile. "Of course, the human form is also spirallic, and the twelve meridians make a stylized lotus blossom. The ancient meaning of the mantra *Om mani padme hum* is 'I salute the understanding of the Order of the Infinite Universe.' This means learning how to change yin into yang and yang into yin. It is not rising above the impurities of the world. It is remembering our common origin and destiny. It is transforming difficulties into blessings, war into peace, sickness into health. One who lives his life according to principles of balance and harmony and distributes this knowledge to others is a Bodhisattva, or person developing toward universal consciousness."

Rani was clearly vexed by this lecture and seemed on the verge of getting up and erasing Ginkgo's *mandala*.

"My companions and I came to India to find a true teacher," I cut in before she had a chance to rebut his theory or show us to the door. "Recently, we visited the Tibetan Center and were impressed with the teaching of the Dharmapa. But we also heard great things about Brahma Bhavan. Now we have to make a decision whether to take refuge here or journey on to the Tibetan monastery in Bodh Gaya."

"The Dharmapa is an old student of mine," Rani said mollified by my flattery and popping a large round brown sweetmeat into her mouth. "Just last week he came to Brahma Bhavan for a consultation."

"It is unusual for a high Buddhist lama to seek the advice of a Hindu yogini, isn't it?" I asked using the Indian vernacular.

"Not at all," Rani chuckled fanning herself rapidly. "You see, here in India, the Buddha is considered an *avatar* of Vishnu. Other incarnations of Vishnu include Rama and Krishna. Thus it is only natural for a priest of Vishnu to come to a teacher of Brahma for spiritual guidance and instruction."

"We heard that the lama has a sacred hat which he reveals to initiates in a special ceremony." Ginkgo steered the conversation toward the purpose of our visit. "It is said to confer enlightenment on sight."

"Don't be fooled," Mata Ras scoffed, closing her fan and striking it hard on the platform. "Nothing truly spiritual can come out of a hat. The Tibetans are very good at magic and deceiving people with symbols and rituals. But if you want to attain true liberation, you must leave all physical props behind."

Rani's indignation appealed to common sense. I realized that there was not a single religious carving or statue to be seen in her ashram. Anyone who abhorred graven images couldn't be all that bad. Maybe I was premature in my judgment about her yinned-out disciples. I gave up the thought of becoming a New Age bounty hunter.

"Did the Dharmapa heed your advice?" I asked reaching for a sweetmeat until stopped by Ginkgo's penetrating gaze.

"Does a child mind its mother?" Rani laughed rearranging the folds in her sari to mask the spreading perspiration stains under her arm. "I scolded the lama for taking the Black Hat to the West. But as usual I don't suppose it did any good."

"During *satsang*, or spiritual discourse, the Dharmapa indicated that this was his first visit to India and the West," Kalavinka reported accepting a plump *gulab jamin* from the tray of sweets. "Have you two met before?"

She picked up on the obvious discrepancy in Rani's account faster than I did. I liked the way she lied about our attendance at the Tibetan Center. Cool and convincing.

"The Dharmapa and I have met many times in past lives," Rani explained clutching the silk fan to her sagging bosom like a grieved mother. "But each time it is the same. He willfully disobeys. What am I to do with such a mischievous child?"

"Perhaps you shouldn't try so hard to take away his toys," Ginkgo said pointedly.

Rani's face reddened at Ginkgo's veiled allusion to making an attempt on the Black Hat, and she moved to cover the lower part of her heavy face with the fan.

"Why not follow Brahma's example and let things take their natural course?" he continued, gesturing with an open palm.

"My small self wishes it could," Rani sighed, momentarily setting down the fan and countersigning a credit card voucher which another devotee brought in for her attention. "But it is my *dharma* to support this ashram and spread the teachings of Brahma."

"The rising cost of *maya*," Ginkgo quipped staring at the American Express card register.

"My advice, children," Rani said shrewdly sizing up Ginkgo's last remarks on the Hindu concept that all is illusory, "is to go to Bodh Gaya and master the *tantra*."

"But I thought Raj Yoga is the highest teaching?" Kalavinka exclaimed innocently. Like me, she evidently couldn't tell if Rani was trying to get rid of us or using reverse psychology to entice us to stay.

"*Jai* Brahma!" Rani acknowledged, disposing of the last sweetmeat on the plate. "Sooner or later you will return to Mataji. Whether you do so in this lifetime or some other is up to Brahma. You will be excusing me, young friends, but Mataji must attend to her students. *Namasté.*"

"Mataji," Ginkgo said bringing his palms together and bowing. "There is just one tiny favor. What does Brahma recommend to cure bronchitis?"

Rani Ras paled and reached for another glass of water, but the pitcher was empty.

"Bronchitis?" she rasped.

"Yes, my daughter suffers from chronic bronchitis and diabetes," Ginkgo continued tapping the middle of his forehead as if stimulating his Third Eye. "For many years, she has sought a cure in vain. She has prayed to God for help, meditated long hours, fasted for days without end. But nothing has worked. She used to be a wonderful dancer. But her sicknesses have progressively crippled her, and now she can hardly get around. She would like to undergo kidney dialysis, but that is very expensive and painful. It is so sad. The affliction has tried her sorely. She has even sunk to betraying the confidence of her loving father in order to obtain money for her treatment."

"Lord Brahma!" Rani exclaimed, bowing low and reaching out to touch Ginkgo's feet. "I have been waiting for thee for so long. Thou who canst see into thy poor disciple's aching heart, please forgive my transgressions."

"You are forgiven, my daughter," Ginkgo said paternally, wiping away her profuse tears with a hankerchief. "Shiva and Parvati can attest to your devotion."

She looked over at us in disbelief. I nodded sternly like the God of Destruction, and Kalavinka linked her arm in mine and smiled back radiantly like Shiva's comely consort.

"In order to be fully healed," Ginkgo instructed arching his shaggy eyebrows, "you must tell us exactly what happened with the Dharmapa. Why did you invite him here? Why did you try to take the Black Hat?"

"I'll start at the beginning," Rani said dabbing her eyes with the hankie. "I used to be a classical dancer in the Bharat Natya tradition. I gave many performances and had many pupils. Once I was invited to dance at Shantiniketan, the school founded by Tagore outside of Calcutta. There I met a wonderful young man named Ananda who was a brilliant artist. We married and started this ashram. But over the years, our health declined. My husband suffered from high blood pressure and a nervous disposition that caused him to give up painting. I had a serious weight problem and had to give up dancing when I lost my coordination and balance. After Ananda had a stroke and passed away several years ago, the whole weight of administering the ashram fell to me. Unfortunately, my condition has continued to deteriorate, and I can hardly stand up any more or teach.

"I've been to the best doctors in the capital. They recommended kidney dialysis two or three times a week. But as you can see, I am but a poor widow. Even if I qualified for treatment, I don't have a motor vehicle to get to hospital which is located in New Delhi near Lodi Gardens. Without funds, treatment was impossible.

"Then one day, a young millionaire from America providentially turned up. He offered me a princely sum in exchange for inviting the Dharmapa to the ashram and allowing him a few minutes alone with the Black Hat. I thought he was sent by you."

"Could you describe this young man for us?" I inquired, jamming my leg unto my thigh at last. If I were to be Lord Shiva for the afternoon, I had better learn to play the part.

"He was about the same height as you, my Lord," Rani replied squinting at me, "but stockier and—pardon my saying so, Lord of the Ferocious Countenance—better looking. Also his hair was lighter—in fact, blond."

Ginkgo, Kalavinka, and I simultaneously thought of Lance and exchanged knowing glances. Although I regretted the comparison with her visitor's deplorable good looks, I could get used to being treated as a celestial being.

"What was his motive in gaining access to the hat?" Ginkgo asked thoughtfully.

"It was very commendable, Beloved Father," Rani replied snapping her fingers at a disciple who poked his head in the door and pointed to the empty pitcher. "He told me that he had been a student of the Dharmapa's in Sikkim for many years. But he said he had questioned the need for idols and relics and had been expelled by senior monks from the monastery. He said that he had been forbidden to attend the Black Hat Ceremony, and thus his only recourse was to be alone for a few minutes with the Black Hat by himself.

"Naturally, I tried to talk him out of this plan and get him to see that the hat was as much a superstitious icon as the statues and incense to which he objected. But he was determined and planted the seed in my mind of setting up a Western-style yoga operation with one of the international hotels here. In this way, he convinced me I could attract hard currency to finance my dialysis as well as keep the ashram afloat."

"You should know that Lord Brahma never expects anyone to violate her conscience," Ginkgo gently reproved her. "But go on with your story."

"One of my former dance pupils is a high official in the Ministry of Culture. Through her I made arrangements for the Dharmapa to visit Brahma Bhavan and requested that he bring the Black Hat with him. I let it be known that I was too sick to travel to Sikkim for the ceremony and would like a private audience.

"The scheme failed, however, when the Tibetan arrived without the hat. Instead he came wearing a simple white Gandhi cap. I expressed my disappointment and explained that I could no longer travel. He said not to worry and that soon Lord Brahma and his attendants would arrive and ease my suffering."

"The Dharmapa is a true prophet," Ginkgo declared tugging at his long earlobe. "We will show you how to regain your health, and one day you will be well enough to dance again."

Rani broke down sobbing at the thought of dancing again, and I noticed a tear roll down Parvati's face.

"What must I do?" Rani implored wiping her teary eyes.

"Your woes result from neglecting the teachings of the forest sages," Ginkgo explained. "Do you recall in the Upanishads where it is sung:

> *I am the food, I am the food, I am the food;*
> *I am the eater, I am the eater, I am the eater;*

> *I am the link between, I am the link between, I am the link between.*
> *I am the first among the visible and the invisible.*
> *I existed before the gods. I am the navel of immortality.*
> *Who gives me, protects me. I am food;*
> *Who refuses to give me, I eat as food.*
> *I am the world and I eat this world.*
> *Who knows this, knows.*

Rani nodded and intoned the verses in Sanskrit. "Food is the secret of eternal life, my daughter," Ginkgo continued. "In this *Kali Yuga*, or dark age, people all around the world have forgotten the ways of their ancestors and the wise ones who have come before. Here in India, white rice has replaced brown rice, dairy food is eaten in large quantity though it is contrary to the climate and environment, and spices, sweets, and cold beverages have become a way of life. By returning to the true way of eating of Raja yogis in the past, you will recover your health and vitality. Lotus root is especially beneficial for your condition. It helps to open the lungs and enable you to breathe more freely."

As Parvati and I watched spellbound, Ginkgo gently massaged her swollen feet and initiated her into ancient dietary practice.

12

TO DIE IN BENARES

Three thousand, one hundred, eighty-five; three thousand one hundred, eight-four; three thousand, one hundred, eighty-three . . . Each time I pressed my nose to the Ganges's embankment, I counted off another Grand Prostration. As I raised my head, the golden light reflected from the windows and rooftops of the temples and palaces edging the river caused me to squint. As the morning wore on, the number of bathers in the river had diminished like sands in an hourglass. At daybreak, the local citizenry—merchants, priests, vendors, rickshaw drivers, students, beggars—came to the *ghats*, or long terraced stone steps leading down to the river, to do their morning ablutions before beginning the day's rounds. Most of the men were clad in soft white *khadi*, the women in red, blue, green, or white saris. Many of the children wore nothing at all.

After bowing to the sun and breathing deeply, the Brahmins would cup their hands, turn, and sprinkle water in the four directions. Householders used the occasion to bathe and wash their garments. Supplicants set adrift small prayer boats consisting of banyan leaves filled with marigold petals, rice flecked with vermillion, and clarified butter. Beyond the shoreline, men with smooth poles steered long curved boats filled with tourists up and down the riverfront which extended about five miles from the Malaviya Bridge in Rajghat to the north to the Hindu University in the south. Now as midday approached, it was mostly pilgrims, holy men, and visitors from afar who joyfully waded into the swiftly-flowing current, which was said to cleanse all sins and—at death—promised direct admittance into Lord Shiva's heaven. I couldn't help but thinking that all of these people—plus millions of more from Kashmir to Calcutta—could die agonizing deaths from radiation sickness if plutonium from the lost nuclear reactor contaminated the headwaters of the river.

Raising myself to my knees, I looked up and caught sight of a monkey scurrying across the lattice-work fence in an Islamic-style mansion on the bluff. It was making screeching noises and paused to reach up for a mango hanging from a tree. Below, a funeral procession wound its way slowly down the terraced steps. Several men wearing only tucked up loin cloths bore the litter on their shoulders toward a thin column of smoke further up the river. The steady drone of their chanting, *"Ram, Ram, Ram, Satya Ram,"* grew more urgent the closer they came to the Burning Ghat. The corpse, wrapped in white from head to toe, reminded me of a mummy. But unlike the ancient Egyptians, who sought to preserve their remains for all times, the Hindus believed in cremating the dead as quickly as possible.

Rocking back on my heels and balancing myself with my fingers at my sides, I became conscious of the sound of a bell behind me and to my right. I turned to glimpse a large sway-backed cow making its way in my direction. It had some vegetable stalks in its mouth, no doubt alms from some poor undernourished soul who worshipped these public nuisances in hope of a better rebirth.

Speaking of holy cows, I glanced over at Lance Andrews, the Olympic skier, who was performing Grand Prostrations beside me. It seemed like he was gaining on me, and I sank to the pavement as quickly as I could. Between us sat Kalavinka, perched cross-legged on a crate, her lovely auburn hair falling over her shoulders, now offering encouragement to the one and then to the other. She had on a loose-fitting white top and faded jeans and was weighing some small object in the closed palm of her hand. Further up the riverbank, Ginkgo reclined in the shade of a mushroom-shaped stone canopy, the oval hatbox on his knee, listening to a storyteller discourse on the adventures of Hanuman, the Monkey King.

As Lance and I competed for Kalavinka's favors, the sun over Benares—a dazzling ball of red—approached its zenith. By midday the sandy expanse of stone steps leading down to the Ganges was hot to the touch. Lance stripped to his waist, and I did likewise. Kalavinka loosened the top button of her short-sleeve white blouse and kicked off her leather sandals. She raised one hand over her eyes to shield herself from the glare of the sun. Her Scots bonnet had been lost in the avalanche and presumably now rested at the bottom of the Reichenbach Falls.

The sound of a gong summoned many of the faithful along the riverbank to the nearby Golden Temple for afternoon worship, and the knots of listeners further up the *ghats* dispersed. Ginkgo strolled along the long stone steps to where we were doing Grand Prostrations. Some unresolved questions still lingered in my mind following our encounter with Rani Ras.

"I can see how you diagnosed Rani's condition yesterday," I reasoned as he approached within earshot. "Her shortness of breath and coughing indicated chronic lung problems such as bronchitis. And she was sedentary, overweight, loved sugar, constantly drank water, and generally fit the profile of a diabetic. Specifically, the ridge above her nose was dark and swollen, corresponding with pancreatic malfunctioning and problems with insulin production. But how did you know she was a dancer?"

"As you also probably noted, like many Indian women she was wearing a nose ring," he replied plunking down next to a large upright stone streaked with saffron powder. "Classical dancers particularly favor this type of jewelry. When I arrived and touched her feet, I observed that she had the perfect arches characteristic of this profession. Her reference to Shiva as Lord of the Dance further suggested her devotion to this art."

"You make it all seem so simple," Kalavinka marveled squinting at him. "I can see why you strike some people as a reincarnation of Sherlock Holmes."

"It's alimentary, my dear Kali," Ginkgo chuckled in a mock English accent. He took the deerstalker out of his knapsack and put it on her head to protect her from the sun's glare. Earlier he had carefully replaced the rice and millet in the silk dragon scarf. "As the *Bhagavad Gita* teaches, 'All beings are made from food.'"

"Speaking of food, how much longer until lunch?" Lance asked as he fell to the pavement. "Purifying yourself like this, you work up quite an appetite. You don't suppose they have a McDonald's here?" Even Kalavinka winced at his bad taste.

During the last hour, Lance had spurted ahead and was doing about two prostrations for every one of mine. My endurance had flagged, and I calculated that by the time we left for the train station he would have assumed the lead.

"It is said that the Ganges has flowed since the beginning of creation and will protect the people until the end of time," Ginkgo mused ignoring Lance's question and gazing at the lengthening shadows on the water. "Every year when the northern snows on Mt. Kailas melt and the monsoon rains begin, the great river overflows her banks. What a pity if this river were ever to become contaminated."

"Holy shit! It couldn't get much filthier than this," Lance retorted gesturing at an open sewerpipe that drained into the river. "It's a wonder the whole population doesn't come down with tuberculosis or smallpox."

"I was thinking about nuclear pollution," Ginkgo said pointedly.

"Now that India is a nuclear power, I guess there is some threat of an atomic accident," Lance conceded waving away a beggar who approached him with a piteous stump. "But I can't believe they would be foolish enough to build a nuclear reactor near the Ganges."

Kalavinka and I exchanged puzzled glances. It seemed our erstwhile guardian protested too much.

"Let's hope not, my friend," Ginkgo said offering the beggar the last rice ball from his pack. "From the sun, I'd say we have another hour until we have to leave for the station and the train for Bodhgaya departs. I'll go forage some lunch."

He set the impressive oval hatbox on Kalavinka's lap, tapped her on the head, and set off up the wide steps toward the marketplace.

"So what's really in this big container?" Lance asked nonchalantly, flexing his rippling muscles and wiping off the sweat from his bronzed torso.

"As Ginkgo told you last night," I replied putting my shirt on as quickly as possible, "it's the sacred hat of a high Tibetan lama. It contains a letter which has to be delivered to the Dalai Lama, and he's in Bodhgaya."

"The three of you take turns carrying it around like the crown jewels," Lance observed jogging in place. "Why don't you just Fed Ex it?"

"It's irreplaceable and has to be delivered in person." I was beginning to get annoyed with his persistent questioning—and body odor. He probably used an aerosol deodorant that depleted the ozone layer.

To Die in Benares: 165

"I take it that then your trip will be finished, and you can relax?" He turned his back to me and faced Kalavinka who still held out her enclosed palm meditatively.

"When we reach Bodhgaya, the seat of Buddha's enlightenment," she replied lowering her hand to her side, "our mission will be accomplished."

"I know of a nice ski resort in Nepal," Lance continued tightening the black leather belt to his designer slacks. "It has a wonderful view of Mount Everest. What do you say, we—the two of us—take a little trek in the Himalayas? There are many sacred pillars and hidden valleys to explore. We could have a great time."

"I thought you said you've never been to India before?" I cut in before Kalavinka could answer. I could just imagine what kind of good time he had in mind. Sacred pillars, indeed!

"That's right, Sherlock," he replied curtly dusting off a grey Stetson that he had acquired in the Duty Free shop at the airport. "This is my first time to India. I've been to Nepal before for the qualifying heats of the Asian Cup giant slalom. My flight came through Rangoon. I tied for first—owing to jet lag."

"The mountains are too cold and inaccessible at this time of the year," I countered stepping in front of him and facing Kalavinka. "Why don't we—the two of us—go to South India. There are miles and miles of remote sandy beaches to roam."

"I'm sure we—the two of you—will be very happy traveling together, whether you go north or south," Kalavinka replied coyly. "As for me, I'm not sure what direction I'll take after our journey is over."

She opened her hand and revealed a small wooden bird. It was the carving of the Kalavinka which she had first shown me on the sailboat in Boston on the Charles River and which I had returned to her after her rescue at the Holiday Inn.

"Like my namesake, I have to follow my own intuition."

"But since it's a Himalayan bird," Lance declared buttoning his loud Madras shirt, "it's fated that you will end up in the Abode of Snows—with a strong protector of the *dharma* at your side."

"But before this turn in the wheel comes to pass," I countered without skipping a beat, "the bird must wait patiently in the tropics and complete its passage through the three earlier recognized stages of life. From what I've seen, you are an accomplished student and wanderer. You only lack a suitable partner to become a householder in preparation for final liberation."

As Lance and I jockeyed for her attention, my eye caught the sight of another funeral procession winding its way along the riverfront. The pallbearers appeared stockier than most Indians. From their profiles, they obviously ate a lot of animal food. Probably Muslims or some lower caste Hindus whose hereditary profession was butchering animals. They had three dark vertical chalk marks on their forehead, but I didn't know enough about Indian religion to know to which sect they belonged.

"I appreciate your flocking instincts," Kalavinka responded at length. "But by nature, the Kalavinka is a solitary creature. From time to time, she may nest with a kindred species, but it is her destiny to renounce all worldly ties and be free." She held the little bird out to the River of Illusions and then returned it to her shoulder bag.

Her allusion to nesting sent a burst of adrenaline through Lance and me, and we resumed our prostrations at a furious clip.

One thousand, nine-hundred, and twelve; one thousand, nine-hundred, and eleven; one thousand, nine-hundred, and ten. As I lifted my nose from the ground, the funeral procession veered and headed directly toward us. That's strange, I thought. The Burning Ghat is straight ahead. Why are they turning up here? Also, it registered that the corpse was not swathed in red or white cloth like the others I had seen. The dead man lay with his hands crossed over the length of his long body. He had a white turban on his head, and a long trident lay across his chest. The trident is associated with Shiva, and many *sadhus* in Benares carry one. I concluded he must be a holy man or a smallpox victim, two of the types of corpses that are disposed of directly in the river without cremation. I resumed my prostrations.

Fortunately, Kalavinka had also been observing the funeral bearers and had keener reflexes than I. "Red alert!" she exclaimed jumping up. "It's the Russian art dealer and his henchmen."

I looked up just in time to see Sergei Starov leap from the funeral cortege and lunge for the hatbox with the upraised trident. With just a turban and loincloth on, he looked more formidable than I remembered him in London when he was wearing an expensive suit. Kalavinka adroitly yanked the large patterned container away with not a second to spare. With the other hand on her head to steady the deerstalker flapping in the breeze, she started running barefoot toward the marketplace. Lance and I kicked up some sand to forestall the advance of the pallbearers, whose short, squat profiles proved to be none other than LDL and VLDL, the two Type A terrorists. The other two seemed to be local Indians who had unwittingly been hired for the occasion. They seemed as shocked at the revival of the corpse as we were and went scurrying in the other direction.

We scrambled up the paved steps into one of the crooked lanes that led down to the river. Its narrow corridors contained tiny shrines, candles and incense lit by passing pilgrims, and decorative patterns of shells, flowers, and mythical animals made with colored powders. At its end, the lane opened to the busy central marketplace. We sprinted past rows of expensive Benarsi sari shops, stalls selling bronzeware and religious artifacts, and rows of money changers, food sellers, shoe shiners, and other sidewalk vendors, the Russians close behind. Turning toward the main thoroughfare, we came upon a line of unattended bicycle rickshaws. The drivers were evidently taking a tea break or in temple.

"Hurry," I shouted opening the side door and ushering Kalavinka into the seat and climbing in after her.

"OK, Mr. All-American, show us your stuff," I commanded Lance in my most authoritative voice. "Put the Olympic medal to the lotus petal."

Without hesitation, he took the handlebars, pushed off, and clamored aboard the driver's seat just as Starov and his high-cholesterol comrades arrived.

The dapper British art dealer commandeered another rickshaw and held out a fistful of rupees to a heavy-set man crossing the street. The swarthy bystander quizzically pointed a finger at his chest and at an authoritative nod from the steely-eyed foreigner mounted the driver's seat and took off after us.

The other two Russians, red in the face and short of breath, arrived momentarily and hijacked another vehicle. The race was on.

Through the narrow streets of India's holiest city, we flew, the three cyclo-rickshaws pursuing each other like ancient chariots of war in the Hindu epics. Riding in the back seat with my arm around Kalavinka was one of the highlights of the whole adventure. Barking orders to Lance, who transported us like a beast of burden, added to the excitement. I couldn't help but compare us to Shiva, Parvati, and their son, the elephant-headed Ganesh. Also, the drawn up hood of the rickshaw's cabin was not unlike the old two-wheeled covered carriages of Victorian London. Images of Holmes and Watson dashing through the English capital in a hansom with the game afoot flooded my mind.

In all fairness, I must confess that Lance earned the gold in this competition. As a cyclist, he was superb, keeping his head low, slipstreaming behind other vehicles on the downhill, and expertly weaving around old women with water jugs on their head and dodging small children darting into the street. Unfortunately, his large cowboy hat provided our pursuers with a convenient landmark amid the scores of other cyclo-rickshaws.

The chase ended at the northwestern boundary of the city, in Rajghat where the main trunk road turned onto the high Malaviya suspension bridge spanning the river. A team of elephants in harness, pulling logs for construction, was crossing the bridge, and traffic had come to a near standstill. We abandoned the rickshaw and ran along the sidewalk, but the art dealer's firm shout to halt, and upraised revolver, froze us in our tracks.

"All paths lead to Benares," he said calmly closing the distance between us.

"'You see how the birds fly into my snare of their own accord,'" he smirked, quoting Catharine the Great on securing the famous art collection formed by Sir Robert Walpole for the Hermitage. His puzzled driver remained behind.

I placed myself in front of Kalavinka who held the big hatbox, and Lance stepped in front of me.

"We're not afraid to die," Lance said bravely with his hands on his hips like John Wayne.

"Besides, we'll go directly to Shiva's heaven," I heard myself adding.

"Don't be foolish," Starov said as the two atherosclerotic apparatchiks arrived and handed him a dress shirt. "As we say in Leningrad, 'The only heaven is a warm supper and a loo that works.' Besides, this bridge is outside the city limits. If you die here, all you will get is the reward of being eaten by our feathery friends below."

I looked down at the base of the steep embankment and was startled to see a vulture on nearly every rock.

"I don't know about you, Sherlock," Lance said sheepishly standing aside. "But I'm not bulletproof."

I can't say I would miss the former Olympic skier if he were to end up as a breakfast of champions. Even Kalavinka registered surprise at how quickly Lance capitulated.

"Just as I surmised, Tex, you're a drugstore cowboy," Starov sized up Lance, "all hat and no cattle."

As I stood my ground, shielding Kali, the Russians turned their attention toward me. I sought to stop them in their tracks with the Mudra of the Two Fingers. But I was not as skillful as the Third Dharmapa who froze the advancing warriors of Kubla Khan who were determined to take him by force back to Mongolia. I'm afraid my *mudra* meant the same in the Russian vernacular as it did in the American and only served to egg them on. With a sneer on his beet-red face, VLDL shoved me aside like a piece of wilted lettuce and sent me sprawling to the pavement. Fortunately, an elephant had left his calling card on the spot, somewhat cushioning the blow.

"It's too bad your ringleader, Ginkgo, alias Captain Goodwin, the prophet of phrenology and pseudoscience, the chief inspector of soil and agricultural produce, isn't here," Starov mused contemptuously, snatching the hatbox from Kali's defenseless grip. "As a faux detective and art critic, he would appreciate the aesthetics of this encounter on the high boundary between the sacred and profane."

"Oh, but he is," a familiar voice boomed. I turned in astonishment to see Starov's rickshaw driver with upraised trident. It was Ginkgo! I hadn't recognized him attired in a loose-fitting Indian style shirt and baggy pants and wearing a long brown scarf twisted around his head.

My companion was whistling *Yankee Doodle* in triumph. Now I realized why. Captain Goodwin was a character in the song.

Father and I went down to camp along with Captain Goodwin,
And there we saw the men and boys as thick as hasty puddin'.

"I'll take that," Ginkgo gestured with the pointed end of the trident to the hatbox as Kalavinka disarmed Starov of his revolver, and the two candidates for coronaries stood aside. "As chief inspector of natural agriculture, it's my responsibility to rebalance the soil in which pests, predators, and parasites flourish."

"*Marchpane!*" Starov exclaimed momentarily lapsing into Russian. "We can still cut a deal," he continued, backing away clutching the container. "In return for the hat, I can arrange for you a priceless collection of art spanning the history of food. From the Hermitage, there is Valazquez's *Repast*, showing two youths at a

170: Inspector Ginkgo Tips His Hat to Sherlock Holmes

breakfast of bread, mussels, wine, and pomegranates with an old man holding a root in his hand; Lucas Cranach the Elder's *Madonna of the Apple Tree*; Cezanne's *Still Life* with a central dish of fruit; and Gaugin's *Where Are You Going?* with a Tahitian girl with breadfruit. As a bonus, I'll even throw in *The Old Woman Frying Eggs* that disappeared from the National Gallery in Edinburgh last month."

"Not even for *L'Angelus* would I barter with you," Ginkgo replied, referring to François Millet's famous fifteenth century painting in the Louvre of a farmer and his wife praying in a field of ripening grain.

"I can see I mistook you for a sensible man. Unfortunately, my client has run out of patience," Starov said evidentally referring euphemistically to the renegade KGB faction or whomever he worked for. "Either my client gets the hat or no one does."

Before we could stop him, he leaned over the railing of the high suspension bridge and flung the hatbox into the swirling river below.

Then with a sharp command in Russian, he instructed the two lipoproteins to hurry back to the Varanasi end of the bridge and the near shore. He ordered them to find a footpath down the steep embankment where they could recover the hatbox from the swiftly moving current.

To prevent LDL and VLDL's escape, Lance snatched the revolver from Kalavinka and commanded the two waddling henchmen to stop.

"I don't think Ginkgo will let you stand in our way, Tex," Starov said confidently taking his gold cigarette case from his shirt pocket.

"Since we met in London, I've carefully researched your portfolio," the art dealer continued. "The hue of blood isn't a customary color on your palette."

Lowering the pistol after a gesture with the trident from Ginkgo, Lance dropped the utility bag which he had been carrying on a long strap on his shoulder and suddenly scaled the high railing along the side of the bridge. Before we could stop him, he dove into the rapids below.

Even I confess to invoking a silent prayer on Lance's behalf. I had to admire his courage and prowess, however reckless. I only hoped that if he survived he would break an arm or leg and be unable to continue with his Grand Prostrations.

Following Lance's daring leap, Starov muttered an oath in Russian and loped off to catch up with his saturated sidekicks and prevent the American athlete from recovering the hatbox first.

Om namah Shiva,
Om namah Shiva,
Om namah Shiva

Ginkgo leaned over the rail and recited the *mantra* of the guardian deity of Benares in a deep voice.

For what seemed like an eternity, the brackish gray waters remained still. Then far below, we saw a light-colored head surface and with deep strokes start swimming toward the hatbox which was already a good hundred yards further away and floating downstream at a fast clip.

"Not a bad exchange," Ginkgo said picking up the golden cigarette case that Starov had let fall on the pavement. "A valuable jewelry box for a poor German imitation of the Black Hat."

Beckoning to a group of dusty pilgrims coming into the city, he handed them the little gold box that had once been a Dancing Shiva in a South Indian temple and instructed them to take it as an offering to the Golden Temple. The pilgrims eyed us as if we were gods.

I picked up Lance's small athletic bag which he had dropped by the bridge. It contained his red ski cap and designer goggles, toiletries (including three different deodorants, a stick, a roll-on, and an aerosol spray), several clean shirts, and a pack of condoms. "Quite the Eagle Scout, always prepared for any emergency," I thought to myself, flinging the latter over the railing into the swirling river. "He won't be needing these any more."

"Our task in Benares is accomplished," Ginkgo said ushering us back to one of the abandoned rickshaws. "The plane to Sikkim leaves within the hour."

"Sikkim?" I exclaimed.

"Of course, there is no need to see the Dalai Lama in Bodhgaya," he smiled opening the rickshaw door for Kalavinka. "The real trail leads back to the Dharmapa's home monastery in Sikkim."

With Brahma and Parvati in the back compartment and the Lord of the Fearsome Countenance at the handlebars, the little rickshaw sped down the trunk road to the Benares airport.

Only four days to go until the Black Hat Ceremony.

13

THE SAGA OF TALL IRON SHEEP

From Benares, Ginkgo, Kalavinka, and I took a single-engined Fokker prop plane to Sikkim, the small postage stamp-sized kingdom in the Himalayas between India and Nepal. From Gangtok, the capital, we journeyed by land rover and yak-back through lush valleys, over tall mountains, and around steep gorges to the Dharmapa's monastery. The contrasts in the different environments and climates through which we passed were striking. In the subtropical zones, we traversed dense jungle and donned conical straw hats to shield us from prickly vines and the intense heat. In the temperate regions, the way took us over beautiful rainbow-colored hills and down carefully terraced dales where hearty farmers with ruddy cheeks and ready smiles gathered newly scythed stacks of spring barley. In the high mountains, the terrain became more rugged and precarious, and we often had to dismount and lead our pack animals single-file over deep gorges and rocky trails. As we steadily gained altitude, we exchanged our lighter apparel for parkas, heavy mittens, and fur hats to protect us from gusty winds and biting cold.

The higher we climbed, the more refined the atmosphere grew. Breathing the pure mountain air filled me with a sense of deep peace. Ginkgo also found the trek exhilerating and kept us entertained pointing out delicate wildflowers and grasses and singing ballads and folk tunes in a variety of tongues, including a traditional Tibetan planting tune he learned from our Sherpa guide. Kalavinka seemed strangely remote and uncommunicative during the trek,

The Saga of Tall Iron Sheep: 173

a mood I attributed to the harrowing experience of being chased and threatened at gunpoint in Benares.

I sensed she was preoccupied with Lance. But I couldn't tell whether she was upset that he had let her down when he submitted to Starov at the bridge, or whether she was worried about his fate at the hands of the pursuing retainers. When LDL and VLDL got through with him, he would be reduced to a side of onion rings. On the other hand, if he survived, he would probably claim a thousand bonus prostrations as a frequent flier—or diver.

"I'm sure it was disillusioning to discover how fickle Lance was in the thick of battle," I tried to comfort her, watching a thin line of smoke curl from a thatched house in the distance. "But sometimes it's better to suffer disappointment earlier rather than later on."

"Especially when it concerns matters of the heart," she responded as the color returned to her pale countenance. Framed by the soft lining of the parka, her oval face never looked more lovely. If all went well, I would complete the few hundred remaining prostrations at the Dharmapa's monastery, and she would be all mine.

"By the way, I didn't thank you for saving our lives," I commended her, nodding to a passing party of Sikkimese carrying baskets of firewood strapped to their backs with a cloth sash tied around their foreheads. "If you hadn't realized that the body on the litter with a trident was Starov, I might now be a piece of Swiss cheese. That was a neat bit of detective work. How did you recognize him?"

"Elementary, my dear Jeffrey," she recounted as we rounded a gigantic boulder and came upon a steep chasm. "The first thing I noticed was that the corpse and the pallbearers had three vertical lines across their forehead. Then I saw the trident lying across the naked body like a medieval knight born aloft with a great lance—or sword."

At this Freudian slip, she blushed, and I could tell that my rival's chivalrous name, ice-blue eyes, and rugged physique continued to exert a powerful fascination over her feminine imagination.

"Silent alarms went off in my mind," she continued as the path curved and a majestic view of even higher crescent-shaped peaks opened up in the distance beyond. "Something was wrong. I realized that vertical lines are the symbol of Vaishnavas, not Shaivites. But the trident is carried by followers of Shiva, not Vishnu. You can tell worshipers of Shiva by the horizontal stripes across their forehead. Obviously, the approaching funeral cortege was a sham. Someone unfamiliar with Hinduism had smeared the wrong charcoal markings on the corpse's forehead or placed the wrong implement in his hands. It would be like dressing up as Holmes and Watson and giving Watson the deerstalker and Holmes the medicine bag."

"Bravo, Kalavinka," Ginkgo congratulated her, handing her a pink rhododendron. He had been behind us and evidently overhead the conversation.

"Your discovery is another marvelous natural example of yin and yang in the world around us," he continued as we came to a netted rattan bridge spanning the deep gorge. A small wooden sign in Hindi identified the rapids below as "The River of Sorrow."

"The symbolism goes back to Vedic times, when the Indian people had a clear understanding of universal order. The Sanskrit terms for yang and yin are *rajas* and *tamas*. The more *rajasic*, or yang, people identified themselves with horizontal lines, the more *tamasic*, or yin, people with vertical lines. Then later further distinctions were made between big yang and small yang, big yin and small yin. In this way the fourfold social order began. But over the centuries as their diet declined, the people lost the simple commonsense understanding of complementarity, and the modern caste system began. Knowledge of energy and vibration declined, and rigid, fixed categories developed, culminating in untouchability and other superstitious practices."

The narrow bridge swayed in the wind, and it was all Kalavinka and I could do to maintain a grip on the fraying rattan railing and not go over the side. Ginkgo's discussion of vertical and horizontal only compounded my sense of vertigo, and I couldn't take my eyes off the turbulent waters cascading over the sharp rocks below.

"It appears that the animals of the Himalayas also lost it in antiquity," I said nodding to Thunderclap. The big shaggy yak that Ginkgo had been leading stopped halfway across the bridge and wouldn't budge in either direction.

"Noble creature," Ginkgo soothed rubbing the fierce-looking beast behind the head. I recognized that he applied pressure on the same points of the animal's occipital lobes that he had often used to calm me down. At the other end of the high swaying structure, our Sherpa guide sat on his haunches with his hands clasped around his knees grinning at our predicament.

From his knapsack Ginkgo took out a jar of barley malt and held it in front of the stubborn animal. "Our woolly friend here is too yang and afraid of heights. He's foraged way too much leftover animal food from the Sherpas. Such a pity because he really has a very tender disposition."

"That's enough," Ginkgo murmured, wrestling away the glass jar before the yak swallowed it whole. "If you eat too much, you'll become too relaxed and go to sleep. With the wind picking up, this is no place to take a nap."

The yak's small hardened eyes dilated, and a dreamy expression replaced the steely glare of just a few minutes previously. With a smack of its gargantuan lips, the great beast lurched forward, and we continued without further interruption toward our destination. The Sherpa scratched his head in wonder. It was evidently the first time Thunderclap had crossed the River of Sorrow.

Less than an hour's trek from the bridge, we entered a sunny vale. Sweet scents of jasmine, marigold, and azaela filled the air, and a pair of white birds flew up from a turquoise pool with mutual coos of delight. By the terraced fields of ripening grain, several young girls with pretty soft dark green gowns and little boys with traditional striped shirts smiled and turned small Tibetan prayer wheels as we passed by.

The fields ended at a cluster of small white-stucco houses where a robust young man stood holding a broom over his shoulder like a soldier at attention. He had on the waterproof wool girdle worn by Tibetan nomads and a wide leather belt adorned with tiny stones and metal disks.

"Welcome to Pleasant Valley," the slightly ridiculous looking figure saluted us in passable English. "I am called Norbu and serve as the head sweeper at the monastery. On behalf of His Holiness the Dharmapa and His Excellency, Vajra, the venerable regent, I have the honor of meeting and showing you to your quarters. Please accept these humble gifts and refreshment."

At a snap of his fingers, the children we had passed in the fields reappeared carrying gaily wrapped presents. From one of the sheds, a small boy emerged with an enormous pushcart containing decanters of homemade millet beer, a pot of brick tea, and bowls of a thick soup containing slender noodles and slivers of cabbage and tomato. There was also a selection of cigarette packs from around the world and a box of choice Cuban cigars.

"We are delighted to be in this happy valley," Ginkgo replied on behalf of our group. "My friends call me Ginkgo, and these are my associates Jeffrey Milton and Kalavinka. We are here on a pilgrimage. We too have brought a few gifts for our gracious hosts."

From the yak's saddlebag, he took out the red ski cap and goggles that Lance had left behind at the bridge in Benares. Norbu put the fancy polyester hat over his mane of dark hair, pulled down the goggles, and whooped around with arms stretched out like an airplane. Obviously, he had never seen a plane before except from a photograph and mistook Lance's fashionable skiwear for a pilot's headgear.

"Someday I will fly over the snow mountains and wear these," he said proudly. "May the Buddha bless you, Honorable Chingko." *Chingko* was the Tibetan word for mountain barley, and Norbu persisted in calling my companion by this name.

For the children, Ginkgo produced a large handful of yinnie treats which he distributed to the glee of the eager little hands that engulfed him.

"Aren't they adorable?" Kalavinka smiled making sure that each child got his or her fair share of rice syrup candies. "You are blessed, Norbu, to live in a valley with such beautiful children."

"Alas, I am not a monk, Mademoiselle," Norbu replied looking down and vigorously attacking the path with the long curved broom in front of him. "My wife and I do our duty as best we can to spread the faith."

"These are all yours?" Kalavinka inquired in astonishment.

"Plus two small ones at home," Norbu beamed raising a cloud of dust in front of him, "and one on the way."

"Planned parenthood obviously hasn't reached here yet," I quipped in an aside to her.

"I'm afraid that it has but in the reverse way," she replied accepting a cup of fragrant tea from one of the little girls. "Before the Chinese came, it was the Tibetan custom to have large families in order to support the monasteries. Many poor women were expected to have a baby each year and died in childbirth. Others were abandoned by their husbands in favor of a more fertile match."

I was surprised at her strong convictions and quickly changed the topic.

After we had finished exchanging pleasantries and had a bite to eat, Norbu led us to the nearby monastery. Located in a cedar grove on a hill, the imposing building had a spectacular view of the mountains in all directions. White, pink, and yellow rhododendrums surrounded the main building, which was festooned with long prayer banners, and we entered by passing between twin sculptures of turquoise-maned snow lions holding eight-spoked wheels of the *dharma*. The colorful three-story structure was unlike any other shrine or temple in Asia. The lower storey was built in the Indian style, the middle storey in Chinese fashion, and the upper storey in the Tibetan manner. Norbu explained that the Dharmapa designed it himself in order to synthesize the three main cultures and civilizations of the region. Squiring us under the blue eaves and curving slate roof, the engaging little sweeper slyly noted that the Tibetan architectural features on top were symbolic of the highest teachings.

The inside of the spacious monastery was as richly decorated and furnished as the outside. Fleeing Tibet several years before the Chinese invasion on the basis of a prophetic dream, the Dharmapa and his retinue had the luxury to assemble a large caravan, and most of the monastery's original treasures accompanied him into exile. These included priceless statues, wallhangings, relics, icons, books, costumes, mirrors, and other ritual implements.

After showing us to our rooms, Norbu left us to wash up and rest. After a light supper of parched barley, vegetable dumplings, and butter tea, we were summoned to the main sanctuary to pay our respects to Vajra. The old regent had tutored the Head Lama as a boy and joined him on his flight to safety. Seated on a prayer cushion and reciting the sacred mantra of Tibet, "*Om Mani Padme Hum*," the wrinkled venerable looked about four hundred years old. Kalavinka served as interpreter.

As I adjusted to the candlelight in the dim sanctuary, I became aware of the vivid paintings and statues encircling the slightly raised platform where the main altar was located. The wallhangings depicted the full panoply of gods, goddesses, Buddhas, Bodhisattvas, *arhats*, *rakshas*, and *dakinis* in the Tibetan pantheon. There was an unfinished sculpture of a *raksha* or demon in one alcove that reached nearly to the ceiling of the high sanctuary. I later learned this effigy was being carved entirely in butter for the forthcoming spring festival.

"Welcome to the land beyond the River of Sorrow, Chingko," Vajra said putting down his prayer wheel and accepting the traditional white silk scarf that is presented to high lamas during an audience. "How is the weather in Benares at this time of year?"

"Invigorating, *Rimpoché*," Ginkgo replied using the polite title of Precious One given to senior lamas. "The snows in the north will soon melt, swelling the Ganges and revitalizing life throughout north India."

"The Ganga has protected the people from the beginning of time," the lama nodded thoughtfully, lighting a small candle. "It is a fount of purity and wisdom."

"May it ever remain so," Ginkgo agreed reverently.

"What brings you to our small out-of-the-way community?" Vajra said cupping his weathered hands on the lap of his vermillion robe.

"The imperishable dream of a healthy, happy, and peaceful life for all beings," Ginkgo replied meeting the regent's serene gaze.

"Well said, Chinkgo," Vajra exclaimed picking up and tinkling a small bell at his side. "I have met many Westerners over the years, but few have enunciated the *dharma* as clearly as you. How can I be of service?"

"We are deeply interested in our fellow countrymen who have trod the Bodhisattva path before," Ginkgo replied drawing himself into the half-lotus position. "What can you tell us about the friends from the West who came to Tibet many winters ago?"

The old regent proceeded to regale us with stories of past travelers and adventurers. He was not very good at recalling names, but from his vivid recollections we pieced together that he had met Alexandra David-Neel, the intrepid Frenchwoman who had journeyed by herself over the Himalayas in search of the mysterious and occult; G. I. Gurdjieff, the indomitable seeker from Central Asia who had visited Lhasa in his youth, became a great esoteric master, and confidentially appointed each of his closest disciples as his successor; and L. N. Tolstoy, grandson of the great Russian novelist, who had led a small team of Allied intelligence agents through Tibet in the 1940's in an effort to contain Japanese influence.

"What about Englishmen?" Ginkgo asked, gazing at a display case behind the altar filled with slippers and shoes. "I was under the impression that some adventurous souls came to Tibet from London at the end of the nineteenth century, in what would have been the Wood Horse Year in the Tibetan calendar."

"That would have been during the time of the previous Dharmapa," Vajra said gently rubbing his crown *chakra*. "I was but a green shoot myself, barely out of seminary."

It was a relief to learn the lama was not four hundred years old. The movie *Lost Horizon* and other tales of explorers finding the secret of physical immortality and living forever repulsed me. Still, I calculated he was well over a century old and in full possession of his wits, no small minor miracle in an age when many people in their fifties and sixties accept the Golden Parachute and bail out from sentient life.

"There were the Travelers," Vajra continued reaching back into the corridors of his mind. "Husband and wife, very noble indeed. They arrived in Tibet from the East shortly after the British invasion and were appalled at the needless suffering and loss of life caused by their fellow countrymen."

We encouraged him for more details, and the old regent proceeded to recount a memorable tale. "One day, a young Tibetan patriot set fire to a British encampment, and the soldiers demanded that the people of the local village hand him over. When they didn't, they threatened to burn down the whole village.

"The Travelers, who had been passing through on their way to Lhasa to visit the Dharmapa, heard about the village's plight. That night, they went to the British camp to intervene on the people's behalf, arguing that it was not British *dharma* to punish a whole community for the offenses of one of its members. The captain replied that Britannica's scales of justice did not extend to Tibet and the people had to be taught a lesson. The couple pleaded and finally convinced the officer to relent by offering them Mrs. Traveler's jewelry, which had financed their trip to Tibet and was said to be priceless. However, the British officer did not keep his end of the bargain and the next day surrounded the local temple where the visitors were praying for deliverance. The Travelers managed to delay the soldiers while the villagers escaped through a back gate. When they defied the captain's instructions to come out, the temple was set ablaze. The villagers venerated the heroic couple ever after as Bodhisattvas, and their courage and self-sacrifice are remembered today."

"Are you sure their name was Traveler?" I spoke up. Something in the story sounded vaguely familiar.

Kalavinka translated my question, and leaning toward her the old lama nodded in the affirmative. "The boy who had set the fire later came to Lhasa and studied at the monastery. He was quite sure of the name."

"In Tibetan, what does *traveler* mean?" I persisted. "Maybe there was a mistranslation from the English."

Kalavinka conferred with the lama for a few minutes, smoothing her lovely blue and white dress. "Tibet is a land of great distances," he explained, lighting a long stick of sandalwood incense and putting it in a little golden holder shaped like the sacred syllable Aum. "In our language, a traveler signifies someone riding on the back of a horse, yak, or other animal. Someone on foot is a walker or pilgrim."

"Aha!" I exclaimed triumphantly. "A traveler is a rider. Mr. and Mrs. Traveler are none other than Mr. and Mrs. James Ryder of Sherlockian fame. The old curator of the British Hat Museum was correct about his parents. They saved a village from foreign massacre, only we thought he was referring to the Boxer Rebellion in China in 1898, not the British invasion of Tibet in 1903!"

It was a relief to know that he was telling the truth and that Starov had made up out of whole cloth the tale about his vengeful designs on the Black Hat.

"Well done, Milton," Ginkgo said, thumping his knee. "You really must be eating well."

Kalavinka too seemed impressed and hastily filled in the Regent about our discovery.

"Ask Vajra," Ginkgo continued, shifting into a full lotus, "if he remembers another Englishman who came a few years earlier and studied with the Head Lama."

"No," he replied emphatically, lighting another butter lamp, "but there was a Scandinavian. He wore the same kind of hat your young friend here has on."

"Of course, Holmes was disguised as Olé Sigerson, the Norwegian explorer!" I declared to my companions. "In Tibet, he was never known as an Englishman."

"Sigerson was a very gifted man," Vajra recalled fondly, folding his wrinkled hands into a steeple. "After exploring Tibet for nearly two years, he visited Lhasa and spent some days with the Head Lama. In fact, I owe my promotion as Regent to him."

"You must tell us about it," I said eagerly leaning forward on my round cushion and playing with the earflaps of the faded deerstalker in my lap.

"There was considerable intrigue in Lhasa at the time," the old Regent began. "The State Oracle at Drepung prophesied that the Dharmapa's life was in danger. In a trance, he revealed that the Regent was behind the plot, but there was no evidence to support it. Even in our remote land, the vision of the highest seer would not be enough to depose someone, especially the most powerful official in the capital. Until the Dharmapa reached his majority, the Regent ruled the country with an iron hand and built up a personal empire extending from Cham to Nagchuka. His young Holiness, who was only a teenager at the time, appeared more and more drained of energy. Speculation increased that the Regent had resorted to sorcery in order to retain his power.

"The Scandinavian explorer arrived at court and requested private instruction in Buddhism from the young lama, whose brilliant mind was not otherwise affected by these developments. The two would meet in the meditation hall for two hours every morning. In the course of his travels, the explorer had acquired a good working knowledge of Tibetan, which served him well in his studies. Inevitably, rumors of the cause of his young tutor's alarming decline reached his ears. Teacher and pupil soon became fast friends and shared meals, concerts, and long walks together incognito through the local bazaars.

"One day, the European remarked that the Dharmapa's vitality and spirits visibly increased in the meditation hall. His young Holiness replied that this undoubtedly resulted from the sanctity of the large chamber and the power of the teachings. The European wasn't convinced and asked permission from the Dharmapa to inspect his wardrobe and personal effects. The senior monks and attendants braced at this proposal and worried that the newcomer might be part of the plot or—worse—a foreign spy or journalist. But I spoke up on his behalf. You see, I was just a newly ordained monk from the provinces and had a small room in the remotest part of the monastery opposite the visitor's. I noticed that he had the most curious habit. While sitting cross-legged on a cushion, he would light a long curved pipe and lose himself in thought for hours on end. Though odd, his method of meditation struck me as genuine, and I vouched for his sincerity. The venerables relented, and the European was allowed access to the Dharmapa's personal quarters. The explorer emerged rubbing his hands together gleefully and retired to his room, where he meditated in his singular fashion. I noticed that he went through three pipefuls of tobacco.

"The next day a great banquet took place in honor of Milarepa, one of the founders of our faith, and all the dignitaries and senior officials, including the powerful Regent, were present. The Dharmapa, looking drawn and pale, introduced guests and visitors, including the Scandinavian.

"The tall explorer then proceeded to shock the assembled crowd by announcing that he had evidence that the Regent had plotted to kill the young lama. The angry official rose and ordered the monastery guards to arrest the rash speaker, but the Dharmapa intervened and said that he must be allowed to present his case. The guards temporarily sheathed their swords, and everybody waited anxiously to see what this tall foreigner with the odd-looking hat could come up with which had escaped the best minds in Lhasa.

"'Your Holiness,' he began pointing to the floor, 'would you be so kind as to remove your shoes.'"

"'My shoes?'" the perplexed young master repeated.

"'I realize it is a rather unusual request,' he continued pacing up and down behind the head banquet table, 'but I am persuaded the honorable footwear hold the key to this entire affair.'

"Everyone in the room, myself included, now knew for certain that the foreigner was crazy. In our country, a man sometimes will have too much barley beer and act disrespectfully to his seniors and be forgiven the next day. But this was no occasion for silliness. A Tibetan would have been banished to the frozen wastes of Nagchuka for a lesser offense.

"Though I felt his request was improper, I realized my own fate now hung on his. Without thinking, I rose and said, 'Allow me the privilege, Your Holiness, of removing your shoes.'

"The bemused Dharmapa allowed me to take off his small green slippers, and I in turn presented them to the Scandinavian.

"'Let us now examine the sacred shoes,'" he said holding them up to the light for all to see. 'On the outside, they appear to be perfectly normal, but on the inside—well, see for yourself.'

"Picking up one of the ceremonial dinner knives, he proceeded to pry off the heel of one of the Head Lama's slippers. Concealed inside, to the astonishment of those present, was a slender piece of paper containing a magical inscription with the Dharmapa's name, birthdate, and ordained date and time of death—that very day and within that very hour.

"All eyes turned to the Regent, who denied all knowledge of the hidden curse. But the European proceeded to call a number of witnesses from the multitude in the back of the sanctuary. These included a personal servant of the Dharmapa who had been duped to lend the Regent his master's shoes for an evening; a cobbler who testified he had been hired by the Regent's manservant to fashion the hollowed-out heel; and an astrologer who unwittingly supplied the Regent with information on the most propitious time for the demise of someone born at the same time and place as the young lama.

"The Dharmapa asked the Scandinavian how he had discovered this treachery.

"'It was evident,' he replied taking a deep breath, 'that His Holiness enjoyed his usual vitality when in the meditation hall but not upon other occasions. Aside from the blessings of the chamber, the only physical difference was that His Holiness did not have his shoes on. As in most parts of the East, it is customary to leave one's shoes or slippers outside when entering a temple or shrine. From this observation, it was a simple matter to deduce that the mystic incantation was rendered powerless whenever His Holiness took off his footwear.'

"The Dharmapa then asked him how he had located the witnesses. The lanky explorer chuckled and said, 'I have engaged the services of some youngsters I met in the marketplace. In return for a few coppers, I had them make discreet inquiries in the cobblers' district until they found a shoemaker who had been visited by the aide to the Regent. From there, it was an easy matter to piece together the rest of the plot. With the help of the urchins, the attendant and astrologer were ferreted out in the same way.'

"Needless to say, the Regent was forced to resign and sent into exile in Nagchuka. In gratitude for the small part that I played in the affair, the senior monks and cabinet selected me as his successor, and I have served by the Dharmapa's side as Regent ever since. The multitudes acclaimed the foreigner as an embodiment of Manjusri, the Bodhisattva of Wisdom, but he denied any special attainment, noting that he was just a poor student of human reason.

"'Personally,' the Scandinavian confessed to me later at my investiture, 'I do not believe in the power of magical spells and the occult arts. But I know enough of human psychology to know that people who do believe in their efficacy are susceptible to their influence. Their misplaced belief gives them a kind of illusory power over their lives. I trust that as Regent, you will cure His Holiness, who is otherwise the paragon of learning, of this lingering superstition.'

"A few days later, Tall Iron Sheep (as we affectionately came to call him after his unusual height and the year of his birth) announced that he had to return to his homeland. The Dharmapa bid him a fond farewell, earnestly thanking him for saving his life, admonishing him to moderate his pipe-smoking, give up dabbling in drugs, and continue his studies of Buddhism. He also playfully challenged him to turn his great powers of deduction to spiritual ends and discover Shambhala, the source of happiness."

"So ends the Case of the Enchanted Shoes," Ginkgo mused when Vajra had concluded his account. "A marvelous tale. The Baker Street Irregulars lived on in Tibet."

"Live on," the spry old Regent corrected him, rearranging the twinkling lamps in front of him. "Norbu, the resourceful sweeper here at the monastery, is the grandson of the chief lad in the Lhasa marketplace whom the Scandinavian recruited. He supplements his meager income here and supports his large family by providing the great powers large doses of Tibetan refugee gossip, leaks authorized by the Tibetan government-in-exile, and snippets of genuine intelligence. His eleven children are the eyes and ears of the Valley, and anything you say or do quickly finds its way to those who trade in secrets for a living."

"Thanks for warning us," I spoke up, "but as principal adviser to His Holiness, why do you put up with such insubordination?"

"A lama's work is not easy," the old man laughed lighting another stick of incense. "There are many things in this world of impermanence that he must overlook. If you try to control people, they resent it. In my long life, I've found it's best to let things take their natural course."

"That is, in your long life since becoming a monk," Ginkgo corrected him good-humoredly. "For you were the little boy who set the British army encampment on fire, weren't you?"

"Indeed," Vajra smiled setting down his red lighter, "neither the Scandinavian nor the Dharmapa ever deduced that. How did you know?"

"Your countenance brightens whenever you light a butterlamp, candle, or stick of incense," Ginkgo explained, "and you still do so frequently. Of course, in your youth, this can be traced to eating spicier and oilier food than is normal in Tibet. I suspect your mother was from South India and continued to cook in that style.

"My mother was from Cape Cormoran," Vajra confirmed, referring to the city on the tip of the subcontinent. "She came to Tibet on a religious pilgrimage, married a local farmer, and raised a family."

"Also if I am correct, it would appear you were born in the Year of the Male Fire Snake," Ginkgo went on studying the lama's physiognomy. "Fire people are attracted to activity, entertainment, and celebration of all kinds, especially anything having to do with fire or light."

The old lama indicated that he had been born in the year Ginkgo surmised.

"You have been very generous with your time and memories, *Rimpoché*," Ginkgo said drawing the conversation to a gentle close. "We are grateful for this talk with you this evening. I hope we can meet again in the morning."

"I've enjoyed it immensely, Chinkgo," he replied putting out the long row of candles with a silver candle snuffer. "Tonight's conversation has brought back many fond memories. I'll always remember how after our mysterious Scandinavian visitor left, His young Holiness turned to me and said, 'Vajra, do you think we really were visited by the Bodhisattva of Wisdom?'"

14

DEVIL WITH A BLUE DRESS ON

The next morning, we learned from Norbu some details about the pilgrim from Central Asia who was believed to have brought the map that was hidden in the Black Hat.

"Tra Tsil arrived last winter," he recounted over a breakfast of brick tea and barley gruel. "He was exceedingly thin and gaunt, but with clear-cut features. Everyone was amazed because the Valley is sealed off at that time of the year. Usually we have no visitors. At first, we thought he must have come from the south. But he indicated that he had crossed the Himalayas."

"Do you know whether his route took him from the northeast or northwest?" Ginkgo asked gazing from the veranda to the white conical peaks in the distance. He was evidently trying to determine whether the secret parchment involved the reported Chinese nuclear testing site in Nagchuka to the northeast or the portable American reactor said to have been lost at the headwaters of the Ganges to the northwest.

"It was difficult to say for sure, Chingko," the elusive Sherpa replied. "Although he appeared in his late fifties or early sixties and had a strong, sinewy body, Tra Tsil was totally exhausted from his arduous trek and was taken to the infirmary to rest and recuperate. I was so busy sweeping in order to keep barley on the table for my little ones that I didn't pay too much attention to the visitor."

Norbu rose from the low table and picked up his broom, as if getting back to work. Ginkgo, Kalavinka, and I all realized that information from him wouldn't come cheap. On the other hand, there was some hesitancy in his voice which suggested he didn't quite know what to make of us or our real reasons for being here. He had already capitalized on this story to intelligence agents from the three superpowers, so it must have been a mystery to him whom we represented and what we wanted to hear.

"We certainly wouldn't want to detain you from your appointed rounds," Ginkgo replied in the expected fashion. "Perhaps if we made a donation to the monastery and the Sweepers' Benevolent Association, you could be persuaded to help us."

"Tra Tsil's pilgrimage definitely began somewhere in Central Asia," Norbu said resuming his seat and stuffing a large wad of bills from Ginkgo suggestively in the band of his new red ski cap. "It was hard to tell his true nationality. He spoke a smattering of several tongues. Though not Han Chinese or Tibetan, he might have been Turkish, Mongolian, or Uighur. For most of the time he was here, he was confined to bed and said little or nothing. As for his own background, he mentioned only that he was a seal-maker and that was the origin of his name, *Tra Tsil*, which means wax. Bhakti, my valiant wife and mother of my children, helps in the infirmary and caught snatches of his delirious ramblings. In his more lucid moments, Tra Tsil described passing through the fierce sandstorms and forlorn expanses of the Takla Makan Desert, over the treacherous Tarim River, through the mighty Kunlan Mountains, around the wilderness of swampy marches, frozen glaciers, and quicksand bogs of the vast Chang Taug Plateau, and then along the rim of the high Himalayas to Nepal and Sikkim."

"That takes in just about everything," Ginkgo chuckled. "Of course, when you're traveling in Central Asia, you necessarily do so in arcs or spirals, not in straight lines."

"Chinkgo has been to Central Asia before, isn't it?" Norbu asked in wonder.

"Yes, when I was your age and that of Milton and Kalavinka, I traveled across the Middle Kingdom to the Kunlun Mountains," Ginkgo replied. "In recent decades, the Kunluns have been sealed off by the Russians and Chinese. There is a special place there called the Peach Blossom Pagoda where I spent the sweetest days of my youth. In Benares, I heard that a pilgrim from Central Asia had come overland to the monastery here. I was curious whether he might have visited that lovely pagoda or heard some news of its present existence."

Ginkgo took a worn piece of red jade from his pocket. "I found this on the banks of the Tarim River. According to legend, Buddha's tears fell on the spot and created its smoothness."

I recognized this part of Ginkgo's tale as true. He had shown me the stone on several occasions and told of visiting a special pagoda during his Chinese sojourn many years before.

"So you really are spiritual seekers?" Norbu said in amazement, examining the stone and returning it to Ginkgo. "I must admit that I thought you might be spies or journalists."

"Heaven forbid," I protested, somewhat taken aback that he had classified members of my profession even lower than trench-coat operatives.

No further information pertaining to the purpose of Tra Tsil's journey was forthcoming at this meeting, and I noted that Ginkgo was careful not to bring up the subject of the Black Hat. As far as Norbu knew, the pilgrim had not met with the Dharmapa and died peacefully within a week after his arrival. Following Tibetan custom, his body was left in the valley to be picked clean by vultures.

Norbu volunteered to show us the open-air burial site, and Ginkgo excused himself saying he wanted to join the old regent for morning chanting and would catch up with us later. After walking for about an hour through the bright meadows and fields, the path veered off through woods to a rocky promontory where those who died in the valley were laid to final rest. A vertical pile of stones marked the spot, and Kalavinka pointed out Sanskrit and Tibetan mantras painted in red and black on their sides. There was a solitary pine tree to one side and a variety of delicate wildflowers underfoot. There were no bones or any other obvious sign of death as I feared.

After exchanging information with us on funeral customs in Tibet and the United States, Norbu noted the time on his big digital watch and said that he had to return to the monastery and clean one of the guest rooms. After breakfast, a radio message had come in from Gangtok of a trekker who was arriving in mid-afternoon and would be staying the night. Kalavinka and I decided to stay and wait for Ginkgo.

From my flight bag, I took out a small Sony Walkman which Norbu's children had lent me (at an extortionist rate of 10 rupees a day) and some cassette tapes. Soon the rhythmic back beat of Buddy Holly and the Crickets was blaring across this bucolic grove, and Kalavinka and I were dancing to *That'll Be the Day, Peggy Sue, Maybe Baby*, and other rock 'n roll classics. Kali was a fantastic partner, and

Devil with a Blue Dress On: 189

I regretted that I didn't bring along some slower tunes that would have enabled us to embrace.

Maybe Baby, I'll have you.
Maybe Baby, you'll be true.
Maybe Baby, I'll have you someday.

    Still, we both enjoyed the music immensely, and one of my fondest memories will always be twisting the afternoon away in that peaceful grove and the crescent-shaped peaks in the distance. Finally, we collapsed in a heap together on the grassy carpet. Only the promptings of conscience (less than three hundred Grand Prostrations to go) and Kali's faint protest to wait until nightfall prevented us from consummating our passion.

    Returning to our senses, we found some wild honey in a cleft of the rocky promontory and, at its grassy base, some wild strawberries. From a nearby pond, we gathered some large lotus leaves to use as plates. Kalavinka spread a large blue and white Tibetan shawl on the ground, and we settled down for a picnic.

    "This is a very peaceful place," I commented setting a lotus leaf before her, "not at all like I imagined. There are no half-eaten corpses, no bones, not even any vultures."

    "Except for the little column of stones," Kalavinka agreed giving me a handful of strawberries which she had gathered in her skirt, "you'd never know any human beings had wandered into this paradise."

    "When you come to think of it," I continued putting a dollop of wild honey on each plate with a twig, "this is the most biodegradable way to die."

    "Yes, the Tibetan way is more natural," my companion concurred removing a tortoiseshell clasp and allowing her long auburn hair fall to over her shoulders. "It's reassuring to know that your remains will go to nourishing the food chain and fertilizing the fields."

    She pressed her palms together, I followed suit, and we observed a moment of silent blessing before beginning our repast.

    The fruits we had gathered from the wilds were the most delicious I had ever tasted. "Don't tell Ginkgo what we've been eating," I urged. "He would wag his finger and say, 'Milton, you're setting yourself up for a big fall.'"

"Yes, he really has a bee in his bonnet about honey," she acknowledged savouring the sweetened fruit. "Surely there is more to life than chewing and good intestines."

"As we shall soon discover when I have completed the last of my prostrations," I declared running my palm across her blue and white cotton shawl, taking her slender hand in mine.

The lyrics of a rock song reverberated through my mind:

Devil with a blue dress,
Devil with a blue dress,
Devil with a blue dress on.

"Now, Jeffrey, don't let yourself be deflected from your goal," she said lightly touching my cheek. "You never know what can happen between now and then if you aren't careful."

Frankly, at her touch I forgot all about the Black Hat and our reasons for being in Asia. The one thing I knew for sure was that Lance was out of the picture. Unless I broke my leg, I would finish the last of the Grand Prostrations before sunset, and the Male Iron Mouse and the Earth Fire Bird would be free to chant the *Kama Sutra* together until sunrise.

As we started to entwine again, Ginkgo turned up. He announced his presence by whistling the rock lyrics,

Just dropped in
To see what condition
My condition is in

and set his knapsack down with a thud, and surveyed the scattered lotus leaves.

"Hmm, what have we here?" he exclaimed running his thick finger through the sticky remains and licking it while we hastily buttoned up our clothes.

"Milton, this is much too yin for you," he chuckled. "You're setting yourself up for a big fall."

Kalavinka and I roared with laughter.

"Don't feel left out," Kalavinka said handing him the last handful of strawberries from her skirt pocket. "We saved some for an old honeybear like you."

"I'm just yang enough to survive a treat like this," he laughed devouring the berries and the last residue of honey.

"What did you learn from Vajra?" I inquired as he settled back on his elbows, took off his sandals, and stretched out.

"The mystery of the Bodhisattva's vanishing hat is all but solved," he announced triumphantly. "Vajra disclosed that he had a dream before the Dharmapa left that the hat would be imperiled on its journey to the West. As Regent, senior lama of the order, and tutor to His Holiness, he took it upon himself to remove it from its customary resting place in the ceremonial box."

"You mean it's been in the monastery all this time?" I exclaimed.

"Yes, it's been safe in the meditation hall."

"And the map?"

"That he has no knowledge of. However, tonight he said he would unlock the cabinet behind the altar where the hat is kept and let us take a look."

"And the Black Hat Ceremony?" I asked. "Was he going to notify the Dharmapa?"

"He already has," Ginkgo explained with a giant yawn. "Vajra had a wire sent from Gangtok to Arizona where the Dharmapa is visiting the Hopi Indians and explained that the Black Hat is still in Sikkim."

"A lot of people will be disappointed," I whistled.

"Yes, but he felt it was too dangerous to proceed with the Ceremony at this time," Ginkgo explained for our benefit. "The old regent said that he had the authority and responsibility to do whatever was necessary to uphold the Dharma."

"What about the prophecy?" Kalavinka inquired. "Can the Ceremony be rescheduled for another time?"

"From an astrological point of view," Ginkgo replied, "Vajra indicated that the autumn would be more auspicious, and he said he would recommend that the Dharmapa return to the West at that time and enable the prophecy to be fulfilled."

"So all that remains," I concluded, "is to inspect the Black Hat tonight and recover the map."

"That should wrap it up," Ginkgo said yawning and stretching out fully in the midafternoon sun. "I don't know about you two cubs, but this old honeybear needs his nap."

Within a few minutes, he appeared sound asleep. While Kalavinka cleared up the picnic things, I decided to finish off my prostrations and soon found my nose pressed to the ground. The soft grassy clearing was vastly superior to the hot paved banks of the Ganges, and soon I slipped into my routine, like a rocket counting down to launch. Two hundred twenty-four, two hundred twenty-three, two hundred twenty-two, two hundred twenty-one . . .

The tension and mounting excitement of reaching the goal seemed to affect Kalavinka, and she came over and lightly ran her lips across my perspiring brow.

"It's turning chilly," she said moving out of the lengthening shadows into the sunlight to tie back her hair again. "If you don't mind, I think I'll slip away . . . "

". . . into something more comfortable," I completed the thought.

Kalavinka's caress and coy words set my heart aflutter, and I think I broke the world's record for most GPPHs—Grand Prostrations per hour. As she disappeared into the forest, I could still see her in my mind's eye as I bowed to the sun and all sentient beings and focused on the image of my tutelary *dakini*.

When I finally finished my exertions, I collapsed on the ground and looked up at the vast blue sky. Infinite peace surrounded me, and I felt like I had climbed Mount Everest or landed on the moon. Little did I know that my efforts would prove to be all in vain.

Ginkgo finally roused me from my reverie, and we set off for the monastery as darkness fell. On the way, he asked me didn't I think it strange that there were no bones at the open air burial site. I related what Norbu had told us about the birds and animals carrying the remains away.

"Yak chips," he replied testily. "If wild animals are anything like Descartes, they would leave something on their plate. Unlike humans, animals know when to stop and don't eat to excess."

I thought it a poor example. Descartes, his cat, had a ravenous appetite and polished off not only its own plate but anything else in the kitchen that wasn't securely bolted down or locked up.

Noticing my heavy breathing, Ginkgo asked me if I had completed my "austerities." I said that I had to which he replied that it was fitting I should do so in a graveyard. I said that death was the furthest thing from my mind this evening, to which he returned that the "death of illusion was the beginning of the Bodhisattva path." "To go beyond the wheel of suffering one must first experience it fully."

Devil with a Blue Dress On: 193

He seemed to be hinting at something heavy on the horizon, but I dismissed it as so many Oriental platitudes. I never dreamed of the heartbreaking disillusionment I would soon experience.

Back at the monastery, we discovered that the Black Hat had been taken from the meditation hall and that Kalavinka had fled. According to Norbu, she left in the company of an American climber whom we quickly identified as Lance.

I was disconsolate and insisted that she must have been kidnapped by Lance or taken against her will. I couldn't believe that she would leave of her own accord or desert me on the eve of our *tantric* honeymoon.

"Kalavinka and Lance have been secret agents all along," Ginkgo explained to me in the meditation hall. Shards of broken glass from the cabinet behind the altar littered the floor. Their sight lacerated my heart.

"Kalavinka contrived her own deprogramming in Cambridge," Ginkgo went on, "with confederates impersonating her parents to establish her bona fides with us."

"What about Phil Lord?" I asked.

"The deprogrammer was real," Ginkgo averred, carefully picking up the broken glass. "His involvement added an aura of authenticity to the abduction. By engaging his services, she and her cohorts counted on us to rescue her and take her along."

I thought back to our first meeting and now realized it wasn't just coincidence that Kalavinka and I bumped into each other at the Snow Lion Tibetan Center or that the white Cadillac bearing Lord and Kalavinka's "parents" stopped and asked directions for the Holiday Inn. I recalled too that it had been her idea to meet and go sailing at the Charles River Basin where she was abducted. We had been set up.

"Who is she working for?" I said in bewilderment.

"She is really a member of a California student political group with ties to the Cheng Pao K'o, China's counterespionage service," Ginkgo explained gently closing the door to the cabinet. "Beijing, of course, had also been tipped off to the existence of the map by the enterprising Norbu."

"And Lance?"

"Lance is a covert American operative," Ginkgo explained evenly without any trace of anger or betrayal. "He was one of the original members of the mountaineering expedition that installed the nuclear-powered spy station in the Himalayas. He has been shadowing Kalavinka."

"How did you discover all this?" I stammered in disbelief.

Ginkgo disclosed the existence of his own team of helpers, including Wing, the museum curator in Boston who has a worldwide network of sources in the art world. In Switzerland, Ginkgo said he realized that only Loring, the U.S. State Department official, could have tipped Lance off on their spur of the moment trip to the Reichenbach. Acting on Ginkgo's suspicions, Wing turned up a significant gap in Lance's athletic career, pointing to his participation in the Himalayan expedition. As Elsa Klein revealed and Wing's Indian sources confirmed, the top-secret mission was led by Olympic skiers recruited by the CIA for their mountaineering expertise and patriotism. A clandestine training camp was set up at Camp Hale in Colorado, a former high-altitude combat training station used during World War II. I recalled Lance's Colorado background and love of climbing. The shoe—or rather hat—clearly fit.

According to Ginkgo, Wing also turned up anomalies in Kalavinka's background pointing to her true sympathies. Her real name was Laurel Fieldstone. She was born in New York, not China. Her parents were Quaker schoolteachers, not missionaries. She had studied Chinese and Tibetan at the University of California in Berkeley where she majored in acting and where she became involved with a pro-Chinese faction of the protest movement.

Fleeting comments she had made on the practical wisdom of Mao Zedong, on the need for a Chinese-style revolution in India, and on the excesses of the old Tibetan regime flooded my mind. Why didn't I pick up on her true sympathies sooner?

"I didn't sense her true allegiance right away either," Ginkgo explained in sympathy. "Something, however, about the way she put on Irene Adler's hat in London at the museum bothered me."

"I guess that was just too much of a coincidence," I sighed.

"The hat itself didn't betray her," Ginkgo continued. "It was the way she wore it. I became so absorbed in classifying hats according to yin and yang, I forgot the way a person wears a hat is as important a clue to their condition as the kind of hat they wear."

"She pulled it down sharply to the right," I recalled. "Remember, I remarked that she looked like Marlene Deitrich."

"Wearing a hat pulled down in the front or to the right is more yang," Ginkgo explained. "Wearing it on the back of the head or to the left is more yin. Look at photographs of movie stars, society ladies, and other fashionable women some time and you will see what I mean. The angle Kalavinka wore it at—with the brim tilted at a forty-five degree angle to the right—was extremely yang. This was the sign of a very active woman—exactly the opposite of the aura of innocence she had been cultivating up until then. Before the mirror, our consummate actress friend for a moment let her true personality shine."

"All is lost," I concluded sadly, thinking not only of my own sorrow but also for the first time of the theft of the Black Hat and what its loss might entail for the environment and planet as a whole.

"How many times have I taught you not to hold onto appearances?" Ginkgo grinned broadly. "The hat Lance and Kalavinka took is the German duplicate."

"But that was lost in the Ganges!" I exclaimed.

"So it appeared," Ginkgo said mischievously. "Actually I anticipated just such a turn of events, and unknown to you, Kalavinka, or Lance, I removed it before we arrived in Benares. It was wedged into my knapsack all the while, though I thought for a moment we might lose it when old Thunderclap sat down on the swaying bridge. This morning at the monastery, I put it in the cabinet behind the altar and then made up the story about Vajra's dream."

"I wondered why Kalavinka left the forest clearing so suddenly," I admitted. "She obviously fell for your ruse. And the trekker Norbu mentioned coming this afternoon was undoubtedly Lance. She immediately sensed that and hastened to find a way to return to the monastery before he arrived and locate the headpiece first."

"Exactly, Milton," Ginkgo beamed thumping me on the chest. "And inside the German-made look-a-like I have inserted a wry message that will take American and Chinese intelligence several days to decipher. No doubt our honeymooners are now half way to Gangtok, gingerly not letting one another out of their sight, and arguing how to split the hat and its contents."

"So what's next?" I asked forming the trace of a smile at Ginkgo's humorous marital imagery. "Do we return to Boston?"

"That's easier said than done," Ginkgo said as his expression turned more pensive. "Norbu reports that Kalavinka and Lance severed the far end of the the bridge over the River of Sorrow from its moorings to prevent us from following them. They also cut the lines to the monastery's radio link to Gangtok, so we are effectively cut off from the outside world."

"Oh, what a woman!" I exclaimed quoting Sherlock Holmes when he had been outwitted by Irene Adler.

"Couldn't we ford the river somewhere else," I suggested, "and make it back to the Sikkim capital by morning?"

"Possibly," Ginkgo replied, "but even so we'd never get to Arizona by tomorrow afternoon."

"Arizona? What's happening tomorrow afternoon?"

"Didn't I tell you, just before the radio transmitter was cut, an urgent message from Wing came in that the Dharmapa has decided to hold a special Black Hat Ceremony for the Hopi Indians tomorrow. Bardo and the other members of his entourage are flying out there from Boston to take part in the ceremonies. If the Black Hat isn't found in time to be used in the desert festivities, the Dharmapa will undoubtedly cancel the performance in Boston and the prophecy will fail."

"What can be done?" I cried in bewilderment, momentarily forgetting my own sorrows. "It looks like we've been checkmated."

"A sage doesn't regret the past, worry about the future, or cling to the present. The Order of the Universe will show us a way," Ginkgo said simply, taking out his Chinese flute and lapsing into a plaintive tune.

Leaving him pondering our latest and most decisive setback, I returned crestfallen to my little room. Deep feelings of anger and rejection vied with admiration and pride toward the recent object of my affections. I couldn't tell if I felt more deceived or outwitted by Kalavinka.

The only solace I could take in my tearful state was coming upon a small Tibetan carving that had been left behind on my bedroll. Resting inside the crown of the Sherlock Holmes hat which she had also placed there neatly, it was in the shape of the legendary Himalayan bird with a wondrous song that is said to appear shortly before the coming of a Buddha.

15

A DAY OUT OF TIME

I could not imagine how we could get back to India within twenty-four hours, much less to Arizona for the Dharmapa's meeting with the Hopis. But we did—thanks to Vajra, the old Regent, and Norbu, that resilient Sherpa and his large family. It came about in this way.

Later that evening, the old lama encountered Ginkgo in the meditation hall piping on his Chinese flute. My companion had an odd assortment of jars, cups, funnels, and beakers in front of him, as well as the old silk scarf containing the rice that had been found in the Caves of the Ten Thousand Buddhas. Some of the beakers appeared to be of antique vintage, and I surmised that they may have been used by Sherlock Holmes—alias Olé Sigerson—in experiments during his free time.

Rumor had already reached Vajra about the flight of the two Americans and the cutting of the bridge and radio lines. It was not difficult for him to piece together what had happened. Ginkgo apologized for disturbing the harmony of the monastery and explained the true nature of our mission.

"For a long time, I had been apprehensive about the wisdom of His Holiness journeying to the West to perform the Vajra Crown ceremony," Vajra admitted looking up from a small hand-held Pac-Man game he had been playing—a gift from Norbu's children. "The political situation regarding Tibet has become very volatile in recent years. I warned the Dharmapa not to undertake a journey of this magnitude until passions had subsided."

"Did your anxiety have anything to do with the pilgrim who turned up several weeks ago after crossing the Himalayas in winter?" Ginkgo inquired setting down his flute.

"On the contrary," Vajra replied turning toward me and eyeing me narrowly. "Over the years, I have become pretty adept at telling genuine pilgrims from spies and journalists. Tra Tsil was a pious devotee and had a calming effect on everyone at the monastery."

"I thought he was confined to his bed," Ginkgo observed with a hint of surprise.

"He was—up until the last day," Vajra replied concentrating on Pinky, Blinky, Inky, and Clyde, the little monsters scurrying around the electronic maze. "It was his dying wish to see the Dharmapa. Unfortunately, His Holiness was on a visit to Nepal and was not expected back until evening. The pilgrim asked if he could wait for him in the meditation hall."

"You mean he came here?" I exclaimed.

"Norbu and his family brought him to the sanctuary," the Regent went on, adjusting the folds of the maroon robe over his thin shoulder. "He was well enough to sit cross-legged on a cushion and chant the *Heart Sutra*. However, when they returned from supper, he had passed away to the Honorable Fields."

Ginkgo and I exchanged knowing glances. From Vajra's testimony, it was clear the pilgrim had access to the cabinet where the Black Hat was stored and could have left the map in its lining unobserved. His request to see the Dharmapa before he died tended to support this supposition.

"So he never saw the Dharmapa?" I concluded.

"No, His Holiness was delayed and didn't return from Nepal until the next day," Vajra recounted, winning another round from the voracious toy midgets. "However, the story of the visitor's last request and death in the meditation hall deeply moved him. Later that day His Holiness walked to the burial site to pay his last respects."

"Did he make any other comment about the pilgrim?" Ginkgo asked thoughtfully.

"Something unusual occurred at the burial site," Vajra related as we listened intently. "After returning from Nepal, the Dharmapa explained that he had decided to take my advice and postpone his journey to the West. There was some rancor among different Tibetan factions at the conference in Nepal. Naturally, I was relieved at his decision. But after returning from the grove where the good pilgrim's bones were left, His Holiness again reversed himself and expressed confidence that the West was ready for the teachings."

"A sudden change of heart," Ginkgo murmured accepting the lama's offer of the little battery-operated game. "Do you know what happened?"

"I asked His Holiness what led him to change his mind again," the lama nodded suppressing a smile at Ginkgo's lack of electronic game-playing skill. "He said that the pilgrim's heroic trek across Central Asia in the winter to visit him, only to pass away before seeing the Vajra Crown, made him realize how important it was to bring the teachings to other countries."

"And that was all?" I followed up.

"That was all he said," Vajra smiled, leaning over and showing Ginkgo how to tilt the puzzle so that the 'power pellets' changed the monsters' color to blue and turned the chasers into the chased. "But a few days later, when Norbu's children went to the burial site with fresh flowers and incense, they discovered no trace of the body."

"We too noticed the absence of any remains," Ginkgo noted holding the little toy intently with both hands.

"It caused quite a sensation," Vajra related. "The people of the valley who flocked there reported experiencing the lingering presence of celestial music in the air. A tale started among the pilgrims that Tra Tsil was a Bodhisattva in disguise who had appeared to inspire the Dharmapa to visit the West and fulfill the ancient prophecy."

"What did you make of these miraculous reports, *Rimpoché*?"

"Experience has taught me that everyone is a Bodhisattva in disguise," the old regent chuckled. "But some Bodhisattvas are more enlightened than others. Norbu's children led me out to the grove to see for myself. I too felt uplifted by heavenly music and returned to the monastery feeling deeply peaceful. That night I slept more soundly than I had since the Frenchwoman walked on my back many years ago."

That must have been some shiatsu, I thought, at his reference to Alexandra David-Neal, the intrepid French adventuress. The breeze from outside was noticeably chillier, and I took the deerstalker from my travel bag.

"In order for Padmasambhava's ancient prophecy to be fulfilled, we have to find a way to return to America," Ginkgo said evenly to the old lama, losing another yin-yang contest to Pac-Man and laying down the toy. "Can you help us?"

"Chinkgo," Vajra responded picking up a prayer wheel and revolving it with his bony hand, "on the surface, you and your young friend here appear as dry hulls—spies and journalists—but underneath you have the hearts of mountain barley. The sound of your flute is as pure as the celestial music I heard in the grove. I will assist you in any way I can to uphold the *dharma*."

"We have to be in the Four Corners region of the American Southwest by tomorrow afternoon," Ginkgo continued picking up a handful of grain from the rice and millet in the silk scarf and letting it fall gently through his fingers. It was clear that he was visibly touched by the regent's kind words. "The Dharmapa has decided to hold a special Vajra Crown Ceremony for the American Indians."

"Even if we found a way out of here and returned to India," I reasoned, untying the large earflaps of the Sherlock Holmes hat and securing them under my chin, "it would take another day or two to fly back to the States."

"There is a meditation that projects you across vast distances," Vajra disclosed after pondering our dilemma for awhile. "The fourth Dharmapa once used it to appear in Beijing at the Chinese court when he was actually conducting a festival in Lhasa."

"How long does it take to learn?" I inquired looking at my watch. The thought of beaming ourselves to the Hopi Mesa like Captain Kirk and Commander Spock would help make up a little for the loss of Kalavinka.

"An average of three lifetimes," the regent responded thoughtfully.

Although disappointed at the length of time this advanced meditation took to master, my left brain calculated that if I practiced diligently I could be reborn as a member of the original crew of the Starship *Enterprise* in the twenty-third century!

"We don't need an extra lifetime, only an extra day," Ginkgo mused softly. "There must be a way."

"I know where we can get an extra day!" I exclaimed holding the deerstalker to my head as a gentle gust of wind entered the room.

"Surely it's not by subtracting one day for crossing the international date line," Ginkgo rejoined.

He explained the reference to Jules Verne's famous novel, *Around the World in Eighty Days*, to the venerable Regent. To our surprise, the old lama noted that he had seen the movie version on video and inquired after Shirley MacLaine who played the female lead.

"Actually, we don't gain a day, we lose one," I went on breathlessly at my sudden insight. "I remember Kalavinka telling me that in Tibet there is an Official Astrologer who has the power to declare certain days inauspicious. These days are then simply omitted from the calendar."

"This is so," Vajra acknowledged. "He is presently traveling with the Dharmapa in your country. The astrologer's duty is to ascertain auspicious times for state occasions, trips, journeys, weddings, funerals, and other special occasions. Unlucky days are not counted. They are indicated by a black circle on the calendar and simply passed over."

"So the ten days we have in between the theft of the Black Hat and the Ceremony could be extended to eleven days by declaring one day unfortunate," Ginkgo concluded with a broad smile.

"Such is our custom," Vajra confirmed.

"And if we could get the astrologer to declare tomorrow a bad day, that would push the old schedule back an extra day and allow us time to get back?" Ginkgo looked positively glowing.

"I hate to bring up the practical details," I interrupted as our beautiful plan, like a Chinese kite, fell back to earth. "But we can't get in touch with the astrologer. All of our communications have been cut off."

"Leave that to me," Vajra smiled. "We lamas know how to communicate over long distances without telephones or telegraphs."

"That could give us just enough time to find a way out of here and return to India," I observed.

Outside, the waxing moon was already high in the sky. The thought of crossing the River of Sorrow at night in a coracle and retracing our steps was not reassuring.

"Whenever something practical needs to be done," the lama winked, lighting a small candle and handing it to me, "people here turn to Norbu. He is more knowledgeable in the ways of the world than any of the lamas."

"I don't know if we can afford his rates," I quipped.

"There is one final request, *Rimpoché*," Ginkgo said, gesturing to the cabinet behind the altar. "Could we borrow the white conch shell that the Dharmapa received from the Chinese Emperor five hundred years ago?"

"If it will help you in your quest," the venerable replied with a slight bow.

"I will return it with the Dharmapa or Bardo," Ginkgo pledged as the old lama reverently took the large cream-colored shell from its display case and handed it to my companion.

I couldn't imagine what Ginkgo had in mind.

We thanked Vajra for his invaluable aide and went off to locate Norbu. The little Tibetan was in the kitchen sweeping up after dinner.

"No problem," he assured us after listening to our appeal. "Be in the lower field in an hour."

I couldn't imagine what rabbit the resourceful Sherpa would pull out of his hat, especially at this time of night. But I noticed that he was in extremely good spirits, having sold back to Lance his own red ski cap and goggles, at an enormous profit.

"Holy shit! I had one just like this but lost it in Benares," he quoted the handsome American trekker as marveling.

The silhouette of the distant mountains in the faint moonlight reminded me how difficult the journey from Gangtok had been by the light of day. It seemed suicidal to set off over the mountains before daybreak.

"Just one thing more," Ginkgo asked Norbu gently swinging the silk scarf and its contents by the knotted bow on top. "I need some tools: a knife, a file, and some sandpaper."

Again, I couldn't figure out what my companion had in mind. But he disappeared into the privacy of his room for the next hour, and I could hear the sounds of cutting, filing, and scraping mingled with the merry sounds of his flute.

At the appointed time, we set out with our things for the lower field. Small lights twinkled in the distance, growing in intensity as we neared our destination. The lights proved to be lanterns that had been laid out in a rectangle the size of a football field. As my eyes adjusted to the darkness, I saw small figures holding the lanterns at the four corners and midpoints.

"Norbu's eight children," Ginkgo whispered motioning for me to stop.

In the middle of the field stood a taller figure whom we soon identified as Norbu. He had on a miner or construction worker's hard hat with a soft yellow light on top, a heavy jacket with a woolly collar, and long white scarf. He held something in each hand.

Watching from the sidelines, we became conscious of a distant hum. Norbu, who had heard the sound several seconds before we did, was making semaphore patterns with the flashlights and tracing a large circle in the middle of the field.

"A plane," I marveled as the purpose of the lights and shape of the field became clear.

Ginkgo pointed wordlessly to a silver speck in the northeast.

In less than a minute, a small piper cub descended and taxied to a halt in the middle of the field. Norbu waved us forward with the flashlight.

"Allow me to introduce Potala," the little sweeper said, saluting the fierce-looking pilot at the controls. "He will take you across the snow mountains.

"We will be forever in your debt," Ginkgo said as we climbed aboard.

"Chinkgo, the Regent assured me that you are on a sacred mission to protect the *dharma*," the sweeper replied. "That is thanks enough."

"But for my poor wife and long-suffering children," he added turning back with a grin, "there is one small favor."

"Name it," Ginkgo said fastening his seat belt.

"Could my wife and wee ones take care of Thunderclap until you come back?"

"The yak?" Ginkgo chuckled. "I'm afraid you'll have to ask our Sherpa guide."

"He left this afternoon with the young lady and mountain climber," Norbu revealed. "He said that the yak was now rightly yours because you had trained it to cross the swaying bridge."

"Well, then, by all means, we are happy to present Thunderclap to you and your noble family as a small token of our appreciation," Ginkgo thanked him with a thumbs up salute as the pilot revved up the engines.

In this improbable way, we made our departure from Pleasant Valley. Air Tibet, our carrier, of course, was an unscheduled airline, part of the clandestine fleet operated by Five Valleys and Six Peaks, the underground network of Tibetan freedom fighters in the Himalayas. Potala, the scar-marked pilot with a bandoleer of rice slung around his broad shoulders, confided that all the money Norbu and his family earned from whiskey, cigarettes, cassettes, videos, watches, cameras, and other concessions at the monastery found its way into the Tibetan independence movement. My admiration for Norbu and his large family knew no boundaries. The spirit of the Baker Street Irregulars continued to live on in this remote corner of the world.

From Sikkim, we flew southeast to Thailand and reached Maxwell Air Force Base by morning. After Ginkgo made a few international telephone calls, we were escorted to a maximum security area where an F-16 U.S. Air-Force fighter jet was waiting. Ginkgo explained that he had called Christopher Loring at the State Department and convinced him to put another plane at our disposal. Evidently he hadn't heard yet from Lance. I wasn't sure whether that was a good or bad sign. Maybe he and Kalavinka had taken a romantic detour after all.

But that was all water under the bridge of the River of Sorrows. Soon we were over the Pacific in one of the world's swiftest aircraft in a race against time and a seven-hundred-year-old prophecy. Less than a day to go until the Black Hat Ceremony in the Arizona desert and only two days until the ritual in Boston.

16

THE DRAGON DANCE

Less than twenty hours after leaving Thailand, we touched down at Windridge Air Force Base in the Arizona desert north of Flagstaff. Ginkgo spent most of the flight fiddling with his flute. If Vajra's telepathic message had succeeded in gaining us an extra day, we would be just in time for the ceremony at the Hopi Mesa.

Waiting for us on the red clay embankment at the end of the tarmac was an old Dodge Charger. Against the dazzling hues of the midday sun, the large white convertible looked like a parched skull in a Georgia O'Keeffe canvass. Wing, the jaunty curator from the Museum of Fine Arts in Boston, sat cross-legged on the front fender with a teacup and saucer balanced on one knee. He waved and tipped his Red Sox cap to us in greeting as we alighted.

"I trust the ceremony is rescheduled for today," Ginkgo stated raising his walking stick and returning the Japanese's welcome.

"Just as you predicted in your call from Bangkok, the ceremony with the Indians was rained out, so to speak," Keiji Aso replied in awe, ushering us into his cavernous vehicle. "The Dharmapa's astrologer had an unusually powerful and symbolic dream during the night in which he saw a lotus blossom with twenty-nine petals. The first eight petals were white, the ninth was black, the tenth and the eleventh were gold, and the rest were white."

"What kind of lotus has twenty-nine petals?" I asked.

"The twenty-nine petals symbolize the days of the lunar month," Ginkgo explained. "The astrologer saw the dream as an omen warning that the ninth day, colored black, was inauspicious, but that the tenth and eleventh—colored gold—were auspicious for enacting the Black Hat Ceremony."

"Correct you are, Inspector," the little Japanese acknowledged. "After consulting with the Dharmapa, it was agreed to postpone events for twenty-four hours. The lama saw the dream as a direct communication from Avalokiteshvara, the Bodhisattva of Mercy who is often symbolized by the lotus. What puzzles me is how you knew this would happen in advance."

"I had the same dream—only I had it the night before," Ginkgo chuckled.

"You might say we were on the other side of the international dream line and gained a day like the travelers in *Around the World in Eighty Days*," I chimed in.

Wing eyed us skeptically but didn't press the point.

"I would have thought you'd be driving a Toyota or Honda," I observed changing the topic as we peeled out from the airfield.

"There's nothing like the torque of a V-8 and 400 horses," the little Japanese replied gunning the engine. "The imports don't hold a candle to the raw power of these Motown babies."

He motioned for us to help ourselves to a thermos of bancha tea on the seat. To my relief, the teacups were the K-Mart variety, not Ming heirlooms, and I needn't fear breaking them. The tea felt good. The desert heat and roadside dust were oppressive, and I wiped away perspiration that had already formed on my brow.

"Did you have any trouble borrowing this?" Ginkgo grinned, pointing to a large article of clothing hanging by the window on the clothes knob.

"No, everything went smoothly. I snuck it out in a dry cleaning bag," Wing laughed, as he slowed down and passed through the security checkpoint with a brisk salute to the crewcut young guard on duty.

"But if my boss or some school kid notices that it's missing," he continued with an expressive gesture with a finger drawn across his neck, "heads will roll."

I couldn't tell what they were talking about because whatever he had smuggled out of the museum was covered in a large white garment bag with "Prudential Cleaners" stenciled across the front.

Ginkgo had not filled me in on his plan, though in his telephone call from Bangkok he had obviously asked Wing to bring something that would figure in the ceremony.

"It's too bad that Lance and Kalavinka took the German imitation hat," I had remarked earlier on the plane. "We could use it in Arizona and Boston."

"On the contrary, Milton," Ginkgo had replied. "Fooling Starov, Lance, and Kalavinka with a clever duplicate is one thing, fooling the Dharmapa is another. He would immediately see through the charade."

"But if the real Black Hat doesn't turn up, how can the ceremony proceed?" I continued puzzled.

"Perhaps there is a way we can proceed without it," he had replied enigmatically tapping the large white conch shell. "Our little talk last night with Vajra gave me an idea."

But to all my further inquiries, he just smiled and kept his plan to himself. Now the large coat or suit jacket that Wing had taken from the Museum only heightened the mystery. There was nothing for me to do but buckle my seat belt and wait for the ceremony to unfold.

"How far are we from the mesa?" Ginkgo inquired as we pulled onto the main highway.

"About 90 miles as the heron flies," the little Japanese curator answered. "The ceremonies have already started. But don't worry. We have an insurance run. The Hopis are doing a welcoming ritual. The Tibetan performance won't start for at least an hour, and I've coached Bardo so he knows his part."

I glanced at the speedometer. The red line extended the full length of the dash. We must have been exceeding 120 mph. Despite Wing's handicap, I felt strangely confident hurtling across the desert with a one-armed former Kamikaze pilot at the wheel.

The turquoise sky was streaked with tan and rose when we arrived at the pueblos. I had never seen the Southwest before and was amazed at the sandstone cliffs arising out of the desert plain. We left the Charger by a field of parched corn and ascended a steep trail which wound around the clifftop dwellings to a horseshoe-shaped clearing on the flat top of a rocky mesa. Flickering lights and the low drone of chanting alerted us to human activity ahead. At the end of the sagebrush trail, a group of about seventy-five people sat in a circle around a campfire.

Wing motioned for me to be seated, and several Hopi ushered us to the front of the group. Ginkgo disappeared in the outcropping of a rocky ledge, the long garment bag and some yarrow stalks he had picked under his arm. I thought I glimpsed Bardo's plain round face but couldn't be sure. There most have been at least a half dozen Tibetan Buddhist monks scattered in the midst of the gathering. The rest consisted of Hopi men, women, and children. I was surprised at how dark the Indians were in complexion. The children's bright countenances and wide-eyed looks bore an uncanny resemblance to Norbu's children.

At the top of the circle, I recognized the Dharmapa, attired in deep maroon robes with a gold fringe and an Indian headdress, nodding earnestly to a Hopi elder on his left. Wing whispered that the old man's name was Jonathan Corn Silk. With his wrinkles and bony frame, he looked as ancient as Vajra. His long white hair was braided, and he shook a rattle intermittently to the accompaniment of the chanting by the young men dancing in the center of the circle.

Wing explained that the dancers were reenacting the Hopi creation story. According to their myths, the world had been created four times. Each time, the Hopis had emerged from the Four Corners region and migrated over the continent. Now the end of the fourth world through nuclear war and environmental destruction was believed to be imminent. Only true Hopis would survive and emerge into the new Fifth World.

Though all the Hopi dancers were men, off to one side I noticed a young Indian woman in ceremonial robes. Her freshly washed black hair fell softly around her shoulders. She was squatting on a woven plaque filled with corn, beans, and squash seeds and prayer arrows. Wing explained that she was the Hawk Maiden, nurturing the community's seeds for planting. However, this year's harvest was threatened by a continuation of the drought in the Southwest, and the male performers were singing and dancing for rain.

Catching sight of the deerstalker which I had taken from my back pocket and placed on the ground in front of me, Jonathan Corn Silk's eyes widened at this strange-looking headpiece. The Dharmapa grinned and motioned for me to pass it over. The portly lama nonchalantly put it on the old man as the dancers twirled about. It was all I could do to refrain from laughing at this incongruous gesture, but as I should have known by now, the Tibetan was an inveterate connoisseur of hats and liked to pass them around.

A layer of high, thin cirrus clouds formed overhead as the dance progressed, but no rain fell, and the ceremony ended with the discouraged young men resuming their seats. It was now time for the Tibetans to gather, and the monks assembled in the center of the circle to perform excerpts from the Great Prayer Festival that used to be held annually each spring in Lhasa and reached a peak at the full moon. The ritual commenced with the Dance of the Cemetery Lords, featuring a pair of masked dancers attired as red-and-white skeletons. To the fanfare of long brass horns, the clang of cymbals, and a trilling oboe, the two dancers skipped, hopped, and swung their arms.

The deep chanting of the accompanying monks had a ghostly quality to it, and as the chanting reached a crescendo, a third dancer entered the circle. Attired in an elegant yellow robe and a small round black cap, I recognized the vigorous dancer as Ginkgo. From the embroidered round designs of clouds and red, green, and blue dragons on the robe, I recognized his dress as the ceremonial robe of the Chinese Emperor that hung on display at the Museum of Fine Arts in Boston. So that was the mysterious article of apparel that Wing had smuggled out of the museum! With its six pairs of coiled dragons on the shoulders, front and back, and lower front and back and six pairs of designs, including sun, moon, star, mountain, dragon, flower, insect, bronze vessel, seaweed, fire, rice, ax, and a square spiral, the great robe was an embroidered *I Ching*.

From one of the long, wide sleeves, Ginkgo took out his Chinese flute and proceeded to play a simple melody. It had an extraordinary effect on everyone listening. Even I, who prefer rock 'n roll to classical or Far Eastern music, found it enchanting. I didn't know my friend could play so well. It seemed like some Oriental Apollo or Orpheus was playing through his bamboo pipe. The other musicians were awed, and I noticed the faintest of smiles cross the face of the Tibetan lama.

After bowing before the Dharmapa and the Hopi elder, Ginkgo put the flute back in his long flowing sleeve and launched into a highly stylized rendition of *Chi Kung*. Chi Kung is a set of warm up exercises based on the movements of animals and birds. Some consider it to be the origin of Tai Ch'i and other martial arts. Imitating the movements of a fish, an alligator, a crane, a tiger, and a monkey, Ginkgo expressively recapitulated the course of biological evolution. Woven into his choreography was the interrelationship between the vegetable and animal world. He mimicked, for example, the eating habits of a fish dining on smaller invertebrate life, the liking of the crane for fish, and the preference of the monkey for fruit and nuts.

Finally, accepting a sheath of grain from Bardo, who served as stage manager, Ginkgo assumed an upright posture, symbolizing the emergence of human beings. In this role, he performed a Tai Ch'i sword dance, using a stalk of corn and a sheath of rice in place of the sword. Gently blessing the Hawk Maiden with the grain stalks, he handed out small white squares of *mochi*—pounded sweet rice—to everyone present. Coming to a nimble stop before the Dharmapa and Jonathan Corn Silk, Ginkgo held the white conch up to heaven and blew a deep powerful Aum-like sound that transported all who heard it into a timeless dimension. At the snap of Ginkgo's fingers, Bardo appeared like some celestial messenger carrying the large ceremonial hatbox on a small ochre cushion. I recognized it as the same silver container that had been found empty in Bardo's room at the Snow Lion Meditation Center in Cambridge.

Delicately opening the lid of the box, Ginkgo went through the motions of lifting something out, unwrapping the silk cloth, and placing it on top of the Dharmapa's head. Could it be the Black Hat, I wondered leaning forward? At another wave of the hand, Ginkgo signaled for Bardo to hand the Dharmapa a large mirror inlaid with gold and turquoise. The Dharmapa, who had watched the ceremonies impassively until now, broke into a broad grin when he looked into the glass.

Jonathan Corn Silk, next to him, also registered an astonished look and pointed to the Dharmapa's head.

For the life of me, I couldn't understand what was happening, because there was nothing there! The Dharmapa's head was empty. There was no hat. Yet he, the Hopi elder, Ginkgo, and Bardo were all nodding admiringly as if there were.

Then I remembered that the Dharmapa was said to have a spiritual hat above his head that only the most advanced meditators could perceive. Now Ginkgo's stratagem became clear to me. He had disguised himself as the spirit of the Chinese Emperor who had originally given the Dharmapa the Black Hat and the white conch shell. He was making the Dharmapa believe that he had come from the spirit world to crown him again in symbolic reenactment of the original Black Hat ceremony five hundred years before. The ghostly chanting of the monks, the skeleton-like dancers, the authenticity of the ceremonial robe, the haunting beauty of the flute, and the sacred site of the performance all conspired to transport the Head Lama into the next world. By having the Dharmapa look in the mirror,

Ginkgo contrived for him to glimpse the spiritual Black Hat and take it for the physical one. Not only had Ginkgo's stratagem worked, but also the Hopi elder was so spiritually refined that he too could see the subtle Black Hat and comment on it to the Dharmapa. My companion couldn't have asked for more complete verification.

Gently removing the headdress from his head, throwing the end of his maroon robe over his shoulder, and arising from a sitting position, the Dharmapa proceeded to perform a dance of his own. I observed Ginkgo, alias the Chinese Emperor, watching breathlessly lest the Dharmapa try to take his ceremonial crown off and discover that it wasn't there. Hunched over in the billowing yellow robes, Ginkgo looked like a gigantic caterpillar with his antennae poised for the slightest tremor of imbalance. Accepting a large eagle feather from Jonathan Corn Silk and a jug of water from the Hawk Maiden, the Dharmapa proceeded to perform a purification ritual. Dripping the water from the eagle feather onto the mirror and chanting *The Song of Inconceivable Wisdom*, he symbolically cleansed the world. With arms outstretched to the setting sun, the Head Lama invoked the blessings of Avalokiteshvara, the Bodhisattva of Mercy. Within seconds, the sky darkened, lightning flashed, and thunder rolled. From seemingly out of nowhere, huge storm clouds condensed, and raindrops started to fall.

Everyone looked on with awe at the trance-like beauty of the proceedings. The adult Hopis wept joyfully, and the children laughed and cupped their little hands to catch the falling water. The Tibetan monks, including Bardo, glowed with a mixture of fear and pride. Even the intricate dragons on Ginkgo's robe seemed to be breaking through the embroidered clouds encircling them and laughing at the downpour. During the lama's dance, Ginkgo remained in the background, enveloped in the folds of the large yellow garment, slowly moving his outstretched hands in ever narrowing spirals and then clasping his fingers together tightly. Breaking his concentration as the rain fell, he prodded Bardo into holding a ceremonial umbrella over the Dharmapa's head while he pirouetted over and went through the motions of putting the Black Hat back into its ceremonial box.

The rejoicing went on for another half hour while the storm clouds unleashed torrents of precious rain, nourishing the crops and uplifting everyone's spirits.

After the downpour had stopped, an eagle flew over the assembly and dropped grains of blue Hopi corn from its beak. After three circuits, the majestic bird tipped its wing and flew off in an auspicious southwesterly direction. As the sun set, sending long shadows of the mesas and buttes across the valley, Jonathan Corn Silk spoke for the community. Tying back the earflaps to the Sherlock Holmes cap which he had pulled down during the rainspell, he said that in talking with the Dharmapa he discovered that the Hopi word for *moon* is the Tibetan word for *sun*, and the Hopi word for *sun* is the Tibetan word for *moon*. Explaining that the arrival of the Tibetans confirmed their ancient prophecy about the return of a long lost clan brother from the East, the white-haired venerable proposed that renewed ties between the two cultures be celebrated with a betrothal.

Asked to select one of his party to marry the Hawk Maiden, the lovely granddaughter of the Hopi elder, the Dharmapa surveyed his associates and at last settled his compassionate eyes on the hapless Bardo. Over the objections of the plain little monk who protested that he was unworthy of such an honor, the Dharmapa prevailed upon him to accept. He promised Bardo that he would be reborn ten thousand times in the highest heaven for sacrificing his ascetic vows on behalf of East-West friendship and fulfillment of the ancient prophecy that "when the iron bird flies and horses run on wheels, the Dharma will come to the land of the Red Man."

17

CURE BY MISCHIEF

Soft futon-like clouds drifted lazily across the sky, and the fragrance of dogwoods filled the air. Ginkgo and I sat on the light green carpet of the Cambridge Common watching the spring crowd pass by and contemplating our next move. We had flown home from Arizona late the previous night and had until this afternoon to locate the real Black Hat.

"Your performance last night was flawless," I congratulated my companion. "What inspired you to dress up as the Chinese Emperor and present the Dharmapa with his own subtle Black Hat?"

"At the monastery, Vajra mentioned that during meditation the Dharmapa once was able to be in both Lhasa and Beijing at the same time," Ginkgo replied chewing on a long blade of grass.

"That led me to recall that a highly spiritually developed person could see both the visible and invisible Black Hats over the Head Lama's head at the same time. Now who better to set the stage for the ceremony in the desert than the wandering spirit of the Chinese Emperor, the student who originally fashioned the Black Hat after seeing the Platonic original? As for convincing the Dharmapa to look in the mirror, I took my cue from our motley friend here."

He waved the grassy stalk at a group of strolling players performing on the green. I recognized Annemarie, the lithe young woman in leotards who played the part of The Fool in the pantomime which we had seen the afternoon our adventure began. She was now attired in a white smock and black tights and surrounded by jugglers, musicians, and other dancers acting out some rites of spring.

"The Jester?" I asked.

"Don't you remember 'The Education of a Basilisk?'" Ginkgo grinned, watching a knot of professors weighed down with large briefcases trudge up Mass Ave and cut across toward the Kennedy School of Government.

"The mirror!" I exclaimed. "The Fool tricked the monster into looking in the mirror and turning it to stone. So that's where you got the idea for the Dharmapa to look into the mirror?"

"Very good, Milton," Ginkgo went on tapping his head with his forefinger. "Fortunately, a mirror is one of the eight sacred objects in Tibetan Buddhism and figures prominently in their rituals. Bardo's oversize trunk of religious paraphernalia contained the large turquoise and gold inlaid mirror which we used in last night's ceremony."

"I hope you don't mean to compare the Dharmapa to a Basilisk?" I laughed tying the laces to my high-top Larry Bird sneakers.

"To a dragon perhaps," Ginkgo chuckled. "Last night's thunderstorm revealed a sublime mind beneath the Black Hat.

"If that's the case, then the prophecies were fulfilled with last night's performance," I hazarded. "As the Dharmapa indicated, the union of the Hopi maiden and the Tibetan monk marked the start of a new era. Tonight's ceremony is anticlimatic."

"On the contrary, the ceremony in the desert was a private affair, a dress rehearsal to today's public performance," Ginkgo observed, contracting his shaggy brow. "If the Black Hat ritual doesn't proceed flawlessly tonight, the opportunity for the country to develop the universal awareness symbolized by the Buddha's teachings may be lost. Needless to say, the engagement between Bardo and the Hawk Maiden would be broken."

"It won't be easy to materialize the Black Hat at tonight's shindig," I despaired, as pity welled up in my breast for the hapless Tibetan monk who stood to get the better half of the bargain. "The thousand or more people who are expected to attend, not to mention assorted spies and journalists, will not be mystified so easily as a small group of Hopis and Tibetans. The spirit of the Chinese Emperor—or Houdini's ghost for that matter—won't be of much help tonight."

"Alas, I am stumped, Milton," Ginkgo admitted scratching his craggy head. "The astrology card brought us an extra day and the Emperor's robe enabled us to carry out the mock Black Hat ceremony in the desert. But unless we can find the real Black Hat before to-

Cure by Mischief: 215

night's performance, all of our efforts have been in vain."

"Well, maybe this will help," I said pulling out the Sherlock Holmes hat from a velcro pocket in my windbreaker.

Ginkgo good-naturedly put it on and drew himself into the lotus position. As I left him to meditate on a solution to our dilemma, I noticed the agile pantomime come up and curtsey before him. With a flourish, she presented her large plumed troubador's hat in expectation of a contribution for her skit. Ginkgo opened his half-closed eyes and offered her a small bag of foxtail millet he had brought back from Sikkim.

"Ah, the jewel in the lotus," she said cheerfully holding it up to the light and pressing it to her heart.

"May it nourish the awakened intelligence of the Buddha mind," Ginkgo smiled in reply, adjusting the back of the checkered cap on his head.

I left them there bantering and headed up Mass Ave for Erewhon Natural Foods Store in hope of scoring a piece of organic apple pie. I was getting too yang and beginning to feel like a Basilisk from all the travel and stress.

The Vajra Crown Ceremony was scheduled to take place early that evening at Trinity Church in Copley Square, a stately Episcopalian cathedral opposite the Boston Public Library. The rest of the afternoon is a complete blank. The last thing I remember is polishing off a couple of blueberry muffins after my last piece of squash pie a la mode (they were out of apple). Probably I returned to the Common or Holyoke Plaza to practice my visual diagnosis on the Cliffies strolling by. But in all truthfulness I can't recall a thing.

In any event, I pulled myself together and took the T from Harvard Square downtown, switched to the Green Line at Park Street Station, and arrived at Copley Square by 6:30 p.m. It was a warm and balmy evening. Against the crimson rays of the setting sun, the high dome and lofty arches of the church shone with a splendor suitable for the occasion.

The large crowd milling around outside reminded me of Fenway Park before a big Red Sox game. As I crossed Dartmouth Street, it became clear that many people were standing in a long waiting line. The Black Hat ceremony was sold out and only a few "bleacher" seats in the back pews were available. I momentarily panicked at the thought I hadn't brought my ticket for the ceremony which Wing had given us. But a hasty check in my wallet showed that it was there, sandwiched between my press card and Mass Ave Video Rental card. (I had rented a video of Kukla, Fran, and Ollie for Ginkgo. Ollie, the whimsical dragon with one big tooth, was Ginkgo's favorite TV star.)

As I approached, a young woman pushing a stroller offered to part with her ticket for $100 because she "couldn't find a baby sitter." I told her I'd be happy to watch the baby while she got enlightened. "What are you, a cop or something?" she retorted, turning on her heel. It was comforting to realize even among the spiritual crowd there was nothing so mystical as money. The thought occurred to scalp my own ticket, especially since I knew tonight's performance, so to speak, would be rained out. But Ginkgo was expecting me, and I was curious what he would do. Apart from jinxing the prophecy, the failure to produce the genuine article could trigger the crowd to demand a refund. I smiled at the thought of Tyler Chase and the other smug senior disciples in the three-piece suits having to cough up all the cold cash they had collected. At $25 a head for front row "box seats" and $11 a head for "the grandstand," plus sales of incense, beads, and other concessions, the gate amounted to a pretty penny.

Inside, every seat appeared to be taken, and I doubted the church had been this full since the days of Phillips Brooks, its famous nineteenth century revivalist preacher. A large gold cross flanked by six white candles remained in its honored place on the large front altar. Clearly, the church fathers drew the line at removing their sacred props from display even for this ecumenical occasion. But swaths of saffron and red brocade material draped the railings around the altar and the balconies, transforming the elegant house of worship into an Oriental temple. The congregation too was not your ordinary Sunday go-to-meeting crowd. Sprinkled among those assembled were a disproportionate number of men with beards and long hair and women with bangles and beads. In this throng, I caught sight of a familiar maroon shirt and located Ginkgo near a stained glass window on the far right hand side conversing in long tones with Wing. He was not standing so much as rooted—a world tree holding up and embracing the rest of creation.

Ginkgo hailed me as I approached, radiating supreme confidence. Of all things, I overheard him talking about baseball to his Japanese listener. He described the team on the field as a nine-petaled flower, opening and closing, expanding and contracting, with every pitch. Wing marveled in agreement at the image of fielders doubling over with their gloves at the ready for the pitch and then straightening up after every ball and strike. "I never looked at it like that," he admitted flashing a row of bad teeth.

"Even the national pastime follows the Order of the Universe," Ginkgo chuckled.

After tipping his Red Sox cap to me in greeting and mumbling something about how he hoped our team this evening would have "the home-field advantage," Wing excused himself with the wave of his hand to greet someone across the aisle.

"Elsa Klein," Ginkgo observed, also waving to the attractive German broadcaster. I hadn't recognized her at first. Attired in a light green evening dress, felt riding hat, beige scarf with an orange pattern, and white pearl earrings, she looked much fresher and more dignified than the bleary-eyed house frau we had met in Zurich. Next to her was a little girl with the same high cheekbones and upturned nose.

"Her daughter, Ingrid," I exclaimed.

"The color is returning to her face," Ginkgo noted approvingly, waving to the shy, wide-eyed little girl as her mother took her hand and waved back. I noticed that she was holding a sheet of nori in her tiny hand.

"She has already started to eat better. I think she'll make it," Ginkgo explained.

"Isn't that Descartes?" I exclaimed, noting the familiar black and white cat rubbing up against the little girl's legs.

"I brought him to the ceremony in case she came," Ginkgo acknowledged. "He will make her feel more relaxed, and his strong ki will help her condition."

More likely Ginkgo brought Descartes in hope that he would be enlightened by the sight of the Black Hat and mend his ways. The unruly cat jumped in the little girl's arms and beamed like an angel. She was clearly delighted in his company, even when he reached up and snatched a bite of her seaweed.

Next to Elsa was a distinguished looking man with silver hair and a cherubic smile whom I recognized as Senator Matthew Fairway, Republican Chairman of the Senate Foreign Relations Committee. He was not here in his official capacity—though military secrets, in a way, came under his hat—but to accompany his wife, Mildred, a doyen of Oriental art and a closet Tibetan Buddhist.

Done up in a red dress with a turquoise brooch, she held court for a number of reporters and broadcasters who jotted down her every word while her husband looked benignly on.

Other dignitaries included the vice presidents of Harvard and MIT, the provosts of other universities and colleges, the Deputy Mayor of Boston, and a host of other stand-ins and lesser officials who, out of courtesy, had been assigned to represent their institutions at this cultural function. Evidently the head men were too preoccupied with weightier things to attend the age-old ceremony that was said to confer enlightenment on sight, and these underlings had drawn the short straw in the office pool to see who would attend.

The line from the Bible, "Many are called but few are chosen," came to mind, and I felt ashamed at my own doubts. Just a few minutes before, I had been ready to barter away my own immortal salvation for thirty pieces of silver. Already the loftiness of this imposing gilded structure and the stern gaze of the patriarchs in the stained glass windows around the domed nave impressed me with a feeling of my own insignificance. It would have been a good time to pass the collection plate. Like young Ben Franklin who went to his first tent revival to scoff, I experienced the fear of the Lord and would have given everything I had.

To the other side of the Senator and his wife, I glimpsed a nautical figure with gold-epauletted jacket and white cap whom I took to be the Admiral. This legendary personage, I recalled from our trip to the British Hat Museum, boasted one of the largest collection of hats in the United States—and its offshore territorial waters. I figured that if he couldn't possess the Vajra Crown, at least in the manner of a bird-watcher tallying his sightings, he could observe it firsthand. Craning his thick neck with a hand shielding his brow as if looking for dry land, I traced his line of vision to a lithe young woman in the balcony wearing tight-fitting brown corduroys, a green cotton jersey, and a patchwork denim cap with a round rim. The article of apparel I saw first, he saw last and vice versa.

Aside from the dignitaries and a scattering of older people, the overwhelming majority of observers was composed of young adults, including many couples with children. By now, every seat was taken, and the overflow was allowed to sit cross-legged in the aisles. Again the baseball metaphor came to mind—"a sitting-room only" crowd.

Seven o'clock came and went. Many in the audience were used to the relaxed Far Eastern pace of time, but by 7:45, a growing number of people were fidgeting. I noticed a number thumbing through the hymnals. The hymns from Sunday's sermon were still posted behind the pulpit. Ginkgo had disappeared behind the dais, stage right, and I glimpsed Bardo's bald pate poking out from an exit. I concluded that Ginkgo must be playing for more time to come up with a solution. Unless the ceremony started soon, the crowd might be moved to stamp their feet, whistle, and jeer. In any event, this would be Bardo's last at bat. Too bad he would have to come up empty in the clutch. I looked over at the demur Indian maiden who sat in a front pew stoically contemplating her destiny. Catching sight of Ginkgo and me, her face momentarily brightened, and she tugged gently at her ear and pointed to my companion. Among the Hopi on the Mesa, he had earned the nickname Big Earlobes.

Finally, a trill on the church's gigantic organ signaled the beginning of pregame festivities. Tyler Chase, decked out in a three-piece suit with flared pants, took the microphone and instructed the assembled in the precepts of Buddhism. His lack of conviction and nasal droning grated on my nerves, and when someone in the row behind asked who was speaking I turned and whispered the head of the Snow Lion Medication Center. He reminded the audience that at the conclusion of the ceremony they could come up to receive blessings from the Dharmapa and "leave any offering at His Holiness' feet." Like his counterparts at Fenway Park, he was scanning the crowd and already counting the gate. Too bad, I thought, there was no beer concession or seventh inning stretch.

The next speaker was a young Tibetan in starched white shirt, suit and tie, and penny loafers who discoursed on the need to preserve "the Tibetan culture and way of life." His dress and pronounced British accent also did little to inspire confidence in this worthy end. Fortunately, a little Tibetan boy in robes—probably a *tulku*, or child lama—ventured out from behind the curtain and captivated the crowd with his Instamatic and puckish smile.

Professor Wilkins, the Dharmapa's pipe-smoking translator from Brandeis, appeared next. In a relaxed, professorial manner, he related the origin and development of Buddhism in Tibet, described the different lineages, and presented a capsule biography of the current Head Lama and his flight to freedom in Sikkim. He stressed that "his holiness was interested in spiritual aspects not in politics."

He recounted the history of the Vajra Crown, mentioned Padmasambhava's ancient prophecy, and noted that tonight marked the first public performance of the Black Hat Ceremony in the West and was unusually auspicious.

To the drone of long Tibetan horns, the Dharmapa himself finally appeared and mounted a brocade-covered throne that had been erected by the podium. He seemed heavier than the night before in the Arizona desert, but he was beaming and clearly in a gay mood. As he flickered his eyes over the hushed crowd, he regally adjusted the red robe under his right shoulder and the yellow robe on his right.

By this time, Ginkgo had quietly slipped back into his seat next to me. He gazed intently at the portly figure on stage, but I couldn't tell what was going through his mind.

Accompanied by much ritual fanfare and suspense, the age-old Tibetan ritual began to unfold. Nine monks with Tibetan horns began playing and chanting in low, guttural tones which the wise guy in the pew behind me compared to "an automobile anti-theft siren stuck on one note." The opening set was hypnotic and impressive, with the monks scurrying about the stage, settling themselves into position to chant, and smoothing out their long robes.

Like a queen bee in her hive, the Dharmapa then put on a small white ceremonial meditation hat, while the monks at his feet performed grand prostrations and requested him to assume the transcendental form of Avalokiteshvara, the Bodhisattva of Mercy. Many in the audience mistook the small yarmulke for the Vajra Crown. How anyone could mistake the white beanie for the big black enchilada escaped me. But comparing the monks' graceful prostrations with the awkwardness of my own reminded me how innocent I had been. Who was I to judge their naive, open, beginner's mind?

Next the monks offered the Dharmapa rice on a large circular metal disk.

"A mandala symbolizing the infinite universe," Ginkgo observed joyfully elbowing me in the ribs.

The monks continued chanting, performing prostrations, and praying for "the merit of all sentient beings." In that category, I mentally included Tyler Chase, Sergei Starov (but not LDL or VLDL), Lance Andrews, Christopher Loring, the President, Joint Chiefs of Staff, Willy Cartwright, who beat me up in second grade, my high school math teacher, jilting sweethearts, and all others in need of sudden enlightenment. It was still too painful to include Kalavinka in this list. If only Lance hadn't survived his heroic dive from the bridge in Benares and picked up the scent, she probably would be here tonight next to me.

At last the Dharmapa, who had remained impassive to this spectacle, responded to the drones of the monks, removed the small white hat he was wearing, and entered into deep meditation. A trembling Bardo, who until now had not appeared on stage, materialized from behind the mushroom-shaped podium and held out the large ceremonial hatbox.

A hushed silence swept the auditorium. Time seemed to stop as in a close play at home plate when the whole ballpark beats with one heart before the umpire makes his call. Leaning forward in my pew, to my astonishment I found myself on bended knee on the green felt-covered prayer stool praying fervently for the Black Hat to materialize. Ginkgo also watched with keen anticipation and reached over and gently massaged my tense shoulders. The Dharmapa carefully unwrapped the silk cloth and with horns resounding removed what looked like the Vajra Crown. Taking a deep breath that seemed to take him into another dimension, he slowly placed the splendid headpiece on his head. Holding it lightly with one hand akimbo, he recited *"Om mani padme hum,"* the mantra of Avalokiteshvara, 108 times, as the light reflected in its jewels diffused through the sanctuary.

Transformed into the Bodhisattva of Mercy, the Dharmapa radiated energy, serenity, and peace. I felt a slight warmth in my heart chakra and wondered if this was the awakened intelligence of the Buddha dharma that sight of the Vajra Crown was said to confer. In general, a deep calm spread through the audience, though some people were still waiting for something to happen. They wore the puzzled expression of Fenway Park "Bleacher Creatures" whose faces had been buried in a hotdog and mustard when the game-winning home run had been hit over the left-field wall.

With extraordinary simplicity, the Tibetan lama removed the regal crown, wrapped it in its silk covering, and replaced it in the felt box. The ceremony was over. It had proceeded flawlessly as it had each time since the Fifth Dharmapa received the Black Hat from the Chinese Emperor in the early fifteenth century. Now there was a batting streak that outshone even Joe Dimaggio's.

The only disturbance, and a minor one at that, came at the end. I heard a gasp in the back of the sanctuary and turned to recognize Annemarie, the Cambridge pantomime. After the Dharmapa put the Black Hat back in its box, she appeared to have gone into a swoon and fainted. Those on either side loosened the collar of her multicolored jerkin and fanned her with their programs. As he so often does when someone is in distress, Ginkgo left his seat and bounded up the back stairs to assist her, returning a few minutes later and reporting that she would be all right.

With the conclusion of the ritual, people exited from the pews and formed a long line to the left of the stage. One by one, they filed forward to be blessed by the Head Lama. Sometimes he would simply touch them on the head with his hand. Other times he would use a small wooden reliquary or a stick with ribbons. As they left the altar area, the monks handed each one a small maroon protection cord to be worn about the neck. Donations were accepted in what appeared to be the church's collection plate, and nearly everyone contributed. No credit card machines were visible. I was impressed.

While we stood and watched this procession, Christopher Loring from the State Department came by. He looked more relaxed and trimmer than the night he came to our apartment, and the bags under his eyes were considerably diminished.

"Congratulations on outwitting the intelligence agencies of three nations," he greeted Ginkgo with an expansive gesture of his hands. "I don't suppose there would be any point searching the Black Hat now that it has reappeared?"

"For maps to hidden levels of awareness perhaps," my companion answered good naturedly, "but not for the latitudes of ordinary reality you have in mind."

"I feared as much," he sighed adjusting his slender green tie.

"By the way, whatever happened to Lance Andrews?" I inquired, curious at the fate of my nemesis.

"You will be happy to hear that he has been reassigned to the Ellsworth Mountains," he replied producing a pocketful of bancha tea bags and showing them to Ginkgo who nodded approvingly.

"Ellsworth Mountains, never heard of them," I said.

"Nor have most people. They're in Antarctica," he laughed turning on his heel in the direction of the Senator and his wife. "There Lance will be able to pursue his love of solitude for the next three years uninterrupted. There's not a woman within a thousand miles."

"Holy shit!" I proclaimed at these welcome tidings.

As we crossed to the other side of the nave, I suddenly recognized Kalavinka in a side pew. She was wearing faded jeans and a loose-fitting white shirt. Her concentration was fixed on Bardo who still held the big hatbox like a statue. I can't begin to describe the conflicting emotions that surfaced in that instant, but they were predominantly wrathful. As I started toward her like an angry *raksha* bent on giving her a good larruping, I felt Ginkgo's powerful hand lift me by the scruff of the neck and firmly lead me to the exit. On the way out, we spotted Phil Lord, the deprogrammer, in a back pew with several of his pony-tailed disciples. Ginkgo whispered something into his ear as we emerged into the dusk.

18

THE WAY TO SHAMBHALLA

Walking along the Charles River, Ginkgo explained to me that Annemarie, the pantomime, originally took the Black Hat at the reception when Bardo stepped out of the room.

She gained entry to the Snow Lion Meditation Center by shinnying up the oak tree outside his window, a formidable feat but not an impossible one for a seasoned acrobat and performer. I faintly recalled her scaling the tree on the Cambridge Common during the skit about the education of a Basilisk.

As a wandering minstrel who performed outdoors free for everyone, she resisted the pomp, circumstance, and stiff admission price of the Tibetan ritual. She hoped the theft would go unnoticed and that the hatbox would be opened empty during the Vajra Crown Ceremony to show that the emperor had no clothes—or in this case—no hat. In this way, she wanted to teach that everyone is responsibile for his or her own inner growth and spiritual development.

Acting upon a sudden inspiration, Ginkgo revealed how he surreptitiously retrieved the Black Hat earlier that afternoon from her studio in Central Square and with Bardo's assistance returned it to the box just before the ceremony.

I remarked that the shock of seeing the hat back in its container must have been the reason Annemarie fainted in the back of the church.

Shaking his dragonlike mane, Ginkgo replied to the contrary that she didn't faint but went into *satori* or experienced sudden illumination. And she did so, he reminded me, not when the hat was taken out of the box but when it was put back in. He took this as evidence that the perceptive pantomime was able to see the subtle Black Hat over the lama's head after he took off the physical hat. Ginkgo surmised that Annemarie would now become a student of the Dharmapa's and possibly one day even succeed him.

I asked Ginkgo about the map in the hat. He shrugged and said that he looked in the hat's inner lining and searched Annemarie's room but could find none. He said that after the ceremony in the church, he went up to the balcony where she was resting, massaged her pancreas which had become too tight, and queried her on the hat's whereabouts, but she disclaimed knowledge of any letter or map hidden inside.

"At least it didn't fall into Kalavinka's treacherous hands," I remarked.

"Now don't be dualistic," Ginkgo chided me looking back at Descartes, his plucky cat who followed at a measured distance. "If it weren't for her, you never would have taken the Bodhisattva vow to help all beings live according to the Order of the Universe. You'd still be chasing girls with bad ears."

"Before I become involved with womankind again, I'll put my thinking cap on," I resolved.

"That's it, Milton," Ginkgo declared, breaking into a big smile.

"That's what?" I responded, wondering what earth-shaking insight into the battle of the sexes I had achieved.

Fishing through his rucksack, Ginkgo pulled out the faded deerstalker that he got in London and which the Dharmapa, Kalavinka, and he and I had worn on various occasions. Untying the laced up earflaps, we found that one of them had been delicately slit in the middle.

Extracting a thin piece of rice paper that had been inserted inside, Ginkgo held it up to the faint light and read as follows:

To His Holiness, the Head Lama,

Esteemed friend and teacher, I have journeyed from Shambhala, the source of happiness, where I have spent the last several decades perfecting my understanding of the Law and cultivating the secrets of immortality as you once advised me. I left to bring the good news of this hidden paradise to the world I left behind. But on my journey to your present domicile, I discovered how much the globe has changed. Men and women are more divided than ever, civilization is in decline, the nations of the world have weapons that can destroy all life on earth. Crossing the Himalayas, which I explored in my younger days, I learned that a modern listening device that emits lethal rays has disappeared in an avalanche and threatens to pollute the headwaters of the Ganges.

From certain markings in the snow and ice, bird and animal tracks, and geological formations, I have pinpointed the location of this infernal engine and plotted its coordinates on the back of this paper. On my journey, I have also observed and recorded the secret sites of other mass death-dealing weapons the Great Powers have established in Central Asia.

I hasten to finish this missive before my strength ebbs entirely, for if I am not mistaken, the sound of heavenly violins beckons. Might I trouble you to use this intelligence to unmask these scourges and help turn mankind from its present course of self-destruction. Until a fresh breeze blows and human reason returns to its rightful orbit, I perceive it is wiser not to disclose the whereabouts of Shambhala.

I remain, as ever, your faithful friend and companion,

Olé Sigerson

"Of course, Sigerson was Sherlock Holmes's alias on his original Tibetan journey and the one by which he would be known by the Head Lama," I noted reverently. "It never occurred to me that he was the tall, gaunt refugee who had arrived at the Dharmapa's monastery from Central Asia."

"Holmes was a master at disguise and his name, Tra Tsil, or Beeswax, should have been a clue," Ginkgo murmured gazing at the soft golden cones of the headlights on Memorial Drive across the river.

At his feet, Descartes rubbed up against him with the same beatific look I had seen on the face of many disciples in the church.

"Evidently early in the century, the great detective had grown restless of beekeeping in the English countryside and journeyed to Central Asia where he hoped to find an eternal game afoot," he went on. "According to Nine Star Ki, he was a #3 Tree—by nature a traveler and very romantic, poetic, and musical—very different from the cold, calculating machine that he is portrayed in Dr. Watson's account.

"No doubt, in retirement—a retirement hastened by Britain's intervention in Tibet—Holmes's thoughts turned increasingly from matters of state to matters of the spirit. But there would appear to be biological reasons as well for his last odyssey to the East. From ingesting so much honey and royal jelly on the Sussex Downs, Holmes virtually turned into a bee. Like the little insects he loved, he floated off in quest of the nectar of immortality. His remarkably long life can be attributed to working with these little insects and to advanced spiritual practices he learned in Shambhala. Returning to visit his old friend and teacher, the Dharmapa, he happened upon the location of Russian and Chinese nuclear test sites in Central Asia and the place where the United States's nuclear-powered spy station was lost. His mission to the Tibetan's monastery took on a special urgency."

"I'm still puzzled by several things," I admitted as we strolled past a small lagoon. "The mention of 'heavenly music' sounds like Holmes knew he was about to die. But why wasn't there any trace of his body at the open-air burial site?"

"As Holmes himself would say, Milton," Ginkgo replied raising his walking stick and pointing to a remote star twinkling faintly in the distance, "when you have ruled out the impossible, whatever remains, however improbable, must be the truth.

"The simplest explanation is that Sherlock Holmes didn't die. Don't you think there is a connection between the heavenly violins and the lingering presence of the celestial music heard by the Dharmapa, Vajra, and countless pilgrims?"

"And what might that be?" I asked, unable to see any connection.

"You as well as anyone should know the answer," Ginkgo teased me, poking the little carved bird that Kalavinka left me which was in the front pocket of my windbreaker.

"The wondrous song of a Kalavinka bird appears to have revived our traveler in the grove and brought him back to life," he enlightened me. "My hunch is that Sherlock Holmes resumed his journey back to the hidden land of perfect peace. But he left behind the hastily scribbled letter and map in his deerstalker for his old teacher to find. When the Head Lama came along the next day, he recognized the checkered cap and was inspired to press forward on his sacred mission to the West. But he did not think to look inside the distinctive earflaps, as Holmes intended, in the manner of the mystic inscription hidden in the Enchanted Shoes. Fortunately, the lama took the deerstalker with him on his journey West and left it at the British Hat Museum, where it passed providentially into our hands. The Order of the Universe works in mysterious ways!"

"Aha, now I understand," I exclaimed as the clouds in my imagination parted. "Tra Tsil didn't write the letter in the monastery at all, as we presumed. He wrote it after being revived in the burial grove. And he didn't put it in the Black Hat for safekeeping, as we thought, but in his own deerstalker. That was the source of the confusion from the beginning! Probably one of Norbu's children accompanied the Dharmapa to the burial site and gave a garbled account of what happened to his or her father."

"Not only that, Milton," Ginkgo affirmed as we followed the curving footpath toward the Mass Ave Bridge. "Holmes's spirit has also been guiding us all along the way. Whenever the Dharmapa, Kalavinka, or you and I put on the deerstalker, our logical faculties were stimulated. We intuitively knew what to do to avert danger and resolve the mysteries at hand. At the Reichenbach, just after you put the hat on, you solved the mystery of St. Francis's skullcap and saved Kalavinka from the avalanche. In Benares, Kalavinka was wearing the cloth cap and solved the Case of the Truculent Trident and averted danger when Starov and his wrathful Bodhisattvas surfaced. In Sikkim, you put the deerstalker on and deduced the identity of the mysterious Travelers who sacrificed their lives to save a small Tibetan village. While wearing it, its strong ki—or soul as James Ryder at the British Hat Museum would say—also inspired you to think of contacting the official Tibetan astrologer and adding an extra day to our quest."

"And when you put on the hat," I marveled, "you identified Vajra as the little boy who set the fire and later become a monk. Later, donning the deerstalker, you were inspired to dress up as the Chinese Emperor at the ceremony in the desert. And this afternoon, on the Cambridge Common, I left you wearing the checkered hat, and you had the sudden intuition to suspect Annemarie, the pantomime, and recover the Vajra Crown."

"Thanks to this remarkable hat," Ginkgo mused gently retying the earflaps, "the ancient prophecy heralding a peaceful union of East and West is fulfilled, leading to the coming of an era in which a new spiritual human being will evolve."

"When you tipped the invisible hat to Avalokiteshvara on the Hopi mesa, you were unknowingly showing your gratitude to Sherlock Holmes," I observed.

"He came back one last time," Ginkgo noted thoughtfully, "to help suffering humanity, a Bodhisattva in the end."

Returning the letter to his pocket, Ginkgo promised that he would ensure that the portable nuclear-powered spy station lost at the headwaters of the Ganges was retrieved and that the other atomic sites in Central Asia were publicly acknowledged. The reader may recall not long thereafter an announcement by Xinhua, the Chinese news agency, of the establishment of the world's largest animal reserve in the Qangtang grassland area in northern Tibet. Home to eighty species of rare animals, including yaks, antelopes, snow leopards, blue sheep, bears, donkeys, and argali—a species of wild sheep—the area would be closed to hunters and open to ecologists for the study of animal and plant life at high altitudes. The wildlife preserve, launched with unheralded financial contributions by the United States and India, helped ease further embarrassment the nuclear nations suffered after disclosure of atomic incursions in the region and signalled their intention, however nominal, to respect the natural beauty and wildlife of Central Asia in the future.

In most other respects, our adventure had a happy outcome. Bardo and the Hopi maiden tied the knot, settled down in Phoenix to open a gift store for Tibetan and Native American handcrafts, and became the proud parents of twins. Wedding bells also rang for James Ryder, Jr. and Rani Ras. At Ginkgo's suggestion, the English widower and Indian widow exchanged correspondence. The old curator of the British Hat Museum shelved plans to retire in Montecristi and promote panamas and now lives with his bride in a houseboat in Kashmir. He reports that the weather is more congenial to his arthritis, and he now enjoys making turbans and handling the books for The Lotus Root, Mataji's floating macrobiotic restaurant and discotheque. Elsa Klein and her daughter stayed at the Kushi Institute in Becket for four months perfecting their way of eating. To the amazement of her doctors in Germany, Ingrid's leukemia went into remission. Mother and daughter are now back in Zurich, giving performances on weekends at hospitals and schools for the Sourdough Bread and Puppet Theatre which they organized.

Fate also smiled on Sergei Starov and his high-cholesterol comrades. Several days after we left Sikkim, they arrived cold on the trail of the Black Hat at the monastery of the Dharmapa and were caught breaking into and entering the monastery. They were not so much apprehended as caught in an avalanche when they broke into the main sanctuary in the middle of the night and ran into the twenty-foot-high sculpture of a greedy *raksha*. Hundreds of pounds of butter, sugar, and pastry flour fell on top of them. Except for the timely rescue by Norbu and his children, and Thunderclap the yak who pulled them to safety with a rope, they would be remembered as footnotes, or finger pastries, in our little adventure. At last report, Starov and his butcherblock compatriots are undergoing voluntary instruction in the precepts of Buddhism, experimenting with a vegetarian diet, and ignoring faxes from the home office. Hard to believe, but LDL and VLDL are well on their way to becoming HDLs, or good cholesterols.

Closer to home, there was a shake up in the American Tibetan Buddhist community. Tyler Smith resigned as director of the Snow Lion Meditation Center and signed up for a three-year silent retreat. He was succeeded by Sunyata, the nettle-eating ascetic who had a vision while meditating in the cemetery that he should return to civilization and don a tweed jacket, if not a three-piece suit. The Dharmapa returned to Sikkim with his illustrious hat, the white conch shell, and a Ms. Pac-Man game for Vajra which Ginkgo sent along as a small token of our appreciation. Annemarie, the pantomime, left for the Himalayas to study Tibetan Buddhism.

"The Black Hat lived up to its enlightening reputation," my companion mused one evening over saké at Potter Park.

"As our little adventure shows, it had the power to reflect people's deepest level of consciousness," he continued pouring tiny cups of rice wine for Descartes and Kombu, the recuperating northern spotted owl, who had become fast friends. Ginkgo had named the little owl after a sweet seaweed found native to the Pacific coast which he used to nurse it back to health.

"In some cases this was envy, greed, fear, and pride; in others cooperation, self-sacrifice, and compassion. The Black Hat held up a mirror to daily life and human strength and weakness. It led people who were sick, imbalanced, and without hope to change their lives and take responsibility for their destiny. For those who were already in harmony with their environment, it awakened within them an even greater appreciation of natural order. It is truly a Bodhisattva's crown, a hat full of mercy."

As for "the woman" in our story, her karma also quickly caught up with her. On the parkway along the Esplanade that evening as we returned from the Ceremony, a long white Cadillac passed by and slowed down. The driver, Phil Lord, the deprogrammer, honked and pointed to Kalavinka in the back seat, wedged between two burly ex-devotees, the turquoise scarf securely fastened around her mouth.

"She won't get away again," Lord promised, as he headed back home to a remote desert region in southern California noted for its fundamentalist Bible camps. The Earth Fire Bird cast a forlorn look as the car swept past, but it would be a long time before the Male Iron Mouse rescued her again.

Another young woman—a Gemini with terrific kidneys—came up to me along the riverbank and asked if I were interested in buying a home-made candle. Ginkgo slipped me some money to buy the whole lot, and we went off together. Crossing a bridge over the serene river, to the Cambridge side of the land once known as Living Waters, Ginkgo put on the faded deerstalker. Playing *The Song of Ephemerality* on his bamboo flute and followed worshipfully by Descartes, his suddenly enlightened cat, he strolled into the moonlit night.

> . . . U - i No Oku Ya Ma
> Kyo - ko E Te
> A - sa Ki
> Yu Me Mi Sti
> E Hi Mo Se Su . . .

The lineage of great detectives continues.

Resources

One Peaceful World

One Peaceful World is an international information network and friendship society founded by Michio and Aveline Kushi. Its members include individuals, families, educational centers, organic farmers, teachers, parents and children, authors and artists, homemakers and business people, and others devoted to the realization of one healthy, peaceful world.

Activities include educational and spiritual tours, assemblies and forums, international food aid and environmental awareness, One Peaceful World Press, and other activities to help humanity pass safely into a new world of planetary health and peace.

Annual membership is $30 for individuals, $50 for families, and $100 for supporting members. Benefits include the quarterly *One Peaceful World Newsletter* edited by Alex Jack, discounts on selected books, cassettes, and videos, and special mailings and communications.

To enroll or for further information, please contact:

One Peaceful World
Box 10
Becket, MA 01223
(413) 623-2322
Fax (413) 623-8827

Kushi Institute

A center for macrobiotic and holistic studies located in the Berkshire mountains in western Massachusetts offering year-round programs and seminars in macrobiotic cooking, Far Eastern philosophy and medicine, natural foods processing, spiritual development training, and other disciplines. For further information, please contact:

Kushi Institute
Box 7
Becket, MA 01223
(413) 623-5741
Fax (413) 623-8827

Further Reading

Books by Alex Jack

THE ADVENTURE OF THE FADING FIANCE
By Alex Jack
Kanthaka Press, $4.95

The original Ginkgo short story about two star-crossed lovers and an armored car robbery.

THE ADAMANTINE SHERLOCK HOLMES
The Adventures in Tibet and India
By Alex Jack
Kanthaka Press, $8.95

"Important adventure . . . Holmes visits Tibet where he meets two old foes, Moriarty and Irene Adler."
— *Los Angeles Times*

"A hilarious scrutiny of every step of Holmes' career . . . In the hands of a kindred soul . . . the adventures of Sherlock Holmes become again what Doyle meant them to be: parables and metaphysical mirrors of life, cases histories of the laws of Providence and karma." — *High Times*

"Series of hilarious misadventures suitably presented in a serpentine, adamantine (Buddhist, Diamond-wisdom Sutra) manner. Highly recommended to anyone who can enjoy and profit from one, two, even three or four nights spirited reading." — *C. Stark & Co.*

DRAGON BROOD
By Alex Jack
Kanthaka Press, $7.95

"The characters in this colorful, precise, and tragic epic poem of Vietnam and America include the warmakers on both sides, plus those who (like the author) covered the war .... Of the many books, fiction and nonfiction, available on the Vietnam entanglement, this is surely the most artistic and perhaps the truest in terms of the recollection of extreme human experience." — *New Age Journal*

THE NEW AGE DICTIONARY
Edited by Alex Jack
Japan Publications, $14.95

Major terms, teachings, and concepts of Sri Aurobindo, Alice Bailey, Wendell Berry, Robert Bly, Edgar Cayce, Joseph Campbell, Riane Eisler, Mahatma Gandhi, Buckminster Fuller, Michio and Aveline Kushi, don Juan, Carl Jung, James Lovelock, Gary Snyder, Teilhard de Chardin, and other visionary pioneers.

"I think it is likely to become the first dictionary I will have read from cover to cover, like a novel. It is a magnificent (and needed!) work." — *Fritz Blackwell, Professor of Language and Literature, Washington State University*

"It touches on occultism, nuclear physics, pop culture, the peace movement, cult movies, ESP, UFO's.... There is material here not readily found elsewhere." — *Choice*

"A fascinating collection reflecting new (since paleolithic times) streams and eddies in U.S. culture." — *Professional Translator*

OUT OF THIN AIR
A Satire on Owls & Ozone,
Beef & Biodiversity,
Grains & Global Warming
By Alex Jack
One Peaceful World Press, $7.95

"A satirical play about an advertising exectutive who is catapulted into the 21st century and arrested for refusing to pay $15,000 for a hamburger (the *real* price, when environmental and health costs are taken into account). With a wide array of bioregional witnesses and a jury of endangered species, the modern diet is put on trial. Funny and affecting." — *Vegetarian Times*

"A modern Utopia—the *Erewhon* of the 21st Century." — *Edward Esko*

Books from One Peaceful World Press

Fire, Water, Wind: Revelations on the Fate of the Earth. Hanai Sudo, 1992, $8.95.
Forgotten Worlds. Michio Kushi with Edward Esko, 1992, $10.95.
Healing Planet Earth. Edward Esko, 1992, $5.95.
Let Food Be Thy Medicine: 185 Scientific Studies Showing the Physical, Mental, & Environmental Benefits of Whole Foods. Alex Jack, 1991, $10.95.
Medicine Men. Jack Harris-Bonham, 1993, $7.95.
Nine Star Ki. Michio Kushi, with Edward Esko and special contribution by Gale Jack, 1991, $12.95.
Notes from the Boundless Frontier. Edward Esko, 1992, $7.95.
One Peaceful World. Michio Kushi with Alex Jack, 1986, $17.95.
Physician, Heal Thyself: A Doctor's Dietary Recovery from Incurable Cancer. Dr. Hugh Faulkner, 1992, $7.95.
Standard Macrobiotic Diet. Michio Kushi, 1991, $5.95.
The Teachings of Michio Kushi. Michio Kushi, edited by Edward Esko, 1993, $12.95.
Macrobiotic Home Food Processing. Guy Lalumiere, 1993, $8.95.

Publications

One Peaceful World, Becket, Massachusetts
MacroNews, Philadelphia, Pennsylvania
Macrobiotics Today, Oroville, California

Books by Mail Order

The books listed above, as well as additional copies of *Inspector Ginkgo Tips His Hat to Sherlock Holmes*, are available by mail order from One Peaceful World Press.

Please send check or money order payable to One Peaceful World Press and include $2.00 postage for the first book and $1.00 for each additional book.

Outside of the U.S., please pay in U.S. funds drawn on a U.S. bank or by International Postal Money Order. Add 20% of total cost for surface postage and 40% for airmail postage.

Visa/Master Card also accepted. Please include card number, expiration date, and authorized signature.

>One Peaceful World Press
>Leland Road, Box 10
>Becket, MA 01223

About the Author

Alex Jack is an author, journalist, and teacher. He served as a reporter in Vietnam, editor-in-chief of the *East West Journal*, and director of the Kushi Institute of the Berkshires. He is the author or co-author of many books including *The Cancer Prevention Diet* (with Michio Kushi, St. Martin's Press, 1983; revised edition 1993), *Diet for a Strong Heart* (with Michio Kushi, St. Martin's Press, 1985), *Aveline Kushi's Complete Guide to Macrobiotic Cooking* (with Aveline Kushi, Warner Books, 1985), and *Amber Waves of Grain* (with Gale Jack, Japan Publications, 1992).

Alex teaches philosophy and healthcare at the Kushi Institute and has taught and traveled extensively in Russia, China, and other countries. He is director of the One Peaceful World society and lives in the Berkshires with his wife, Gale, a macrobiotic cooking teacher, and their two children, Jon and Masha.

Author's Note

Since the original Inspector Ginkgo short story appeared in the *East West Journal* fifteen years ago, I have periodically worked on this novel in between more substantive books and projects. There have been several drafts as my understanding has deepened and as events—such as the ending of the Cold War—necessitated major revisions. However, the essential features and characterizations are the same. In undertaking this work, the author is grateful to Michio and Aveline Kushi for their wonderful teachings and support and encouragement; to David Rome, his childhood friend with whom he visited the Samaye Ling Monastery in Scotland and who later became secretary to the Venerable Chogyam Trungpa, for his hospitality at the Naropa Institute in Boulder; to Ann Fawcett, Sherman Goldman and colleagues at the *East West Journal* for their comments; to Herb Wright for the suggestion to write a screenplay or novel-length Ginkgo adventure; to Barbara Anderson and her colleagues at St. Martin's Press for advice on character and plot development; to his wife, Gale, and mother, Esther, for copyediting and proofreading; and to his associates in Becket.

The Tibetan motifs in the novel have an historical foundation. There is a real Black Hat, as described in the story, that figures in a ceremony performed by the Karmapa, the leader of the Kargyudpa sect of Tibetan Buddhism. The sixteenth and most recent Karmapa was Rangjung Ringje Dorje. He was born in 1924, fled to exile in Sikkim, performed the Black Hat Ceremony in Boston in 1974 (which I had the good fortune to attend), and died in 1981. Though based on his title and office, the Dharmapa in this novel is completely fictional. In 1992, the *tulku*, or child incarnation, of the seventeenth Karmapa, Ugyen Tinley, was enthroned at Tsurphu Monastery near Lhasa, Tibet. Finally, the U.S. CIA really did build, install, and lose a portable nuclear-powered spy system in the Himalayas in an OPERATION H.A.T. as described in the novel.